THE FALLEN APPRENTICE

C.K. RIEKE

Books by C.K. Rieke

Song of the Ellydian I: The Scarred
Song of the Ellydian II: The Last Whistlewillow
Song of the Ellydian III: The Fallen Apprentice

Riders of Dark Dragons I: Mystics on the Mountain
Riders of Dark Dragons II: The Majestic Wilds
Riders of Dark Dragons III: Mages of the Arcane
Riders of Dark Dragons IV: The Fallen and the Flames
Riders of Dark Dragons V: War of the Mystics

The Dragon Sands I: Assassin Born
The Dragon Sands II: Revenge Song
The Dragon Sands III: Serpentine Risen
The Dragon Sands IV: War Dragons
The Dragon Sands V: War's End

The Path of Zaan I: The Road to Light
The Path of Zaan II: The Crooked Knight
The Path of Zaan III: The Devil King

Copyright

This novel was published by Crimson Cro Publishing
Copyright © 2024 Hierarchy LLC

All Rights Reserved.

Edited by Tiffany Shand
And Zach Ritz.

All characters and events in this book are fictitious.
Printed in the United States of America. No part of this book may be used or reproduced in any manner whatsoever without written permission except in the case of brief quotations embodied in critical articles or reviews.
This book is a work of fiction. Names, characters, businesses, organizations, places, events and incidents either are the product of the author's imagination or are used fictitiously. Any resemblance to actual persons, living or dead, events, or locales is entirely coincidental.

Please don't pirate this book.

Sign up to join the Reader's Group
CKRieke.com

Beginning Pronuciations

Ellydian is pronounced Ell-i-dee-en

C.K. Rieke is pronounced C.K. Ricky

ALADRAN
and its
Six Kingdoms
Arkakus
Ikarus
Celestra
Silvergale Lake
Lynthyn
The Larghos Sea
The Driftmore
Zatan
Cascadia
Guillead
The Dyadric Desert
The Lyones
The Dirkwood
Myngorn
Golbizarath
Faulker
The Ashgrove
Arnor
Herne Forest
Socrun Ür
Londindam
Erhil
Katamon
Fae Veil Lake
Skylark
Taverras
The Ambler
The Rine
Belltop
The Borderlands
N
W
E
S
100 Miles
Grayhaven
The Tibers
The Sapphire Sea

PART I
THE ESCAPE

Chapter One

❦

P *ain of the body.*

U̲N̲L̲I̲K̲E̲ G̲R̲I̲E̲F̲ O̲F̲ T̲H̲E̲ S̲O̲U̲L̲, and distinct from the unwavering sickness of the mind, pain in the skin, the muscles, the bones is all-encompassing. For we are but walking temples, meandering shrines erected to serve the gods. But when that body breaks, that temple crumbles, it oft is the beginning of the end.

For without the temple, there seems no god left to worship. The god seems distant, forgotten, dead.

Sometimes the pain is temporary—it burns with the intensity of the fires of the Nine Hells. It scorches up through the skin like dragon fire. There aren't words to describe the feeling of unrelenting, crippling pain.

But there is a scripture from the old language of the first men that wasn't lost with the floods. In the common tongue, it says—'what doesn't kill you, will only make you stronger.'

Heed those words when the pain pulls you toward death's cold *embrace. For if it isn't the end, then life will go on. It must, for in the end, life is full of the full spectrum of every emotion created by the gods.*

-TRANSLATED *from the language of the Sundar. The Scriptures of the Ancients, Book IV, Chapter V.*

DECIMBRE 18, 1292

SOREN FELT the wet walls as his bloody hand slid along them, reaching out for something to grab to help him back up. His legs wobbled, and he struggled to get his boots under him as he trudged through the underparts of Grayhaven. He'd fallen to one knee, grimacing from the pain that wreaked havoc on his body.

The hundreds of cuts on his body were everywhere. From the battle with the ferocious, towering Black Fog, its tendrils had not only attacked his exposed skin, but managed to get under every piece of armor he wore. The adrenaline from the fight, and his tenacity to survive, had pushed him further into the monster, exposing what seemed like a vulnerability, like the soft flesh of the fruit beneath the hard, prickly exterior. He hadn't noticed the pain the tendrils had wrought in his body until after, when he collapsed from the pain, and the fog escaped back out into the plains. But now—it was all-consuming.

"Soren!" Kaile said, the tall boy in black exclaimed as he turned, trudging through the ankle-deep water of the under tunnels of the capital city of Londindam. He grabbed Soren under his arms, heaving him back up to his feet.

"I'm all right," Soren said. "I'm all right."

Each of them had paused to look back at Kaile helping

Soren. Davin, the marauding dwarf, possibly in as much pain as Soren after being burned by the wicked magical flames in the fight with the Synth Edward Glasse, who in a failed attempt to ascend to the highest level of the Ellydian—to become a Lyre—had exploded. Davin had a bloody cloth covering half his face, and was holding his burned arm with the other. The dwarf, although Soren hadn't known him long, was one of the toughest men he'd thought he'd encountered in his life. But these burns were magical, and severe. He'd need to be treated, and soon, Soren knew.

Beside him was Einrick, the spy from Skylark, and their attaché to Lady Drake's plan to kill Glasse in his own kingdom. Soren only trusted him as much as his intel turned out to be accurate. Which so far—it had. The tall, balding man with the graying beard and thin arms held the torch at their lead. Its warm light shimmered off the wet walls of the arching, low ceiling above. "C'mon, we've got to move. The hounds will be after us!"

Beside him, with her hand covering her mouth as she watched Soren struggle to get to his feet, covered in the red welts that blemished his skin all over his body—was his niece, Seph. With her black cat perched upon her shoulders, the small, young woman with the wild black hair and lime-colored eyes walked back through the stale water to put Soren's other arm around her back. The cat leaped onto a dry ledge that ran along the length of the tunnel.

"Leave me here." Soren groaned through clenched teeth. "I'll catch up with you later. I've just got to rest here a moment."

"We are *not* leaving you," Seph said. "Don't make me smack you again."

He groaned as Seph and Kaile hefted him back up.

"On your feet, soldier," Kaile said, wrapping Soren's arm around the back of the neck as he lifted him. Soren had never

C.K. RIEKE

thought of the boy as strong, but after the way the young Syncron performed against the seasoned Synth Glasse in the battle back on the streets of Grayhaven, Soren did now.

Soren's entire body felt as if it had red-hot wire wrapped tightly around every inch of his skin. And the pain was only getting worse. His stomach squeezed, and the vomit crept up his esophagus. He fought for breaths as his throat tightened. His eyelids were as heavy as rocks, and even the follicles of hair on his head felt like sharp pins being driven into his scalp.

"We have to hurry," Einrick said, loud enough that only Davin heard him.

"I know, I know," Davin said, irked. "Come on, drag him if ya have to!"

"We aren't going to be able to escape the city at this pace," Einrick said. "They're going to find us. Soren left Garland alive. He's going to tell the soldiers where we are."

"I know! I know!" Davin shouted. "Hurry now! Get his legs movin'."

Seph and Kaile helped Soren forward, with his legs splashing through the murky water.

Einrick whispered to Davin, "I won't be able to stay with you. I'm not getting caught in this city after that attack. I'm not getting strung up for no woman, or no rebellion."

Davin glowered up at the tall man. The dwarf only had one eye visible, but it was a mean glare. "What are ya willing to die for, spy?"

"Not this," Einrick said. "No amount of torrens can you take to the grave, let alone with my head cut from my body."

"Then go," Davin said. "Leave me the torch."

Einrick looked all around, unsure of what to do. He glanced back at Kaile and Seph, who both seemed only half in tune as to the conversation they were having up at the lead.

"May the goddess watch over you," Einrick said, clearing his throat, and handing the torch to Davin. "These tunnels head west. If you're truly heading to the desert of Zatan, and not back to Lady Drake, then keep going that way, and don't stop until you're safely to the mountains."

Davin took the torch, nodding with a gruff disdain—the wrinkles on his brow deepened. "Fine soldier, you are."

"Better to be a living spy, than a dead one. Shirava, watch over you."

Einrick ran off ahead, until he was gone from the torchlight, and his splashing faded away.

"We've got to get Soren moving." Davin spun back to them. He went nose to nose with Soren. He clapped his thick mitts onto Soren's cheeks. "Listen to me, you insane bastard! You're going to work through whatever you've got going on in that dull mind of yours, and move your feet!"

"I'm all right, I'm all right..." Soren muttered.

"I'm not asking that," Davin said, holding Soren by the chin to look into his eyes. "You see that girl next to you? Well, they're coming after her, and she's gonna get caught, taken away, and tortured... because of your lazy, whiny ass! Now get one godforsaken foot in front of the other and let's get the blazes out of this damned city."

Seph. The word sparked alive in his mind. *I've got to do it for her. She won't leave me. She's too stubborn.*

Whatever the tendrils of the Black Fog had done to him, whatever dark magic venom it had unleashed upon his body was wreaking havoc. His legs felt like iron had been cast to his ankles, and he felt his bones and joints were seizing together.

Push through it. You've done it before. This isn't the end. Need to get out of Grayhaven, then I can rest. Then I can rest...

"Get up, Soren," Kaile said. "You're a lot heavier than you look."

Soren forced steps forward, splashing at his knees as his hand found the side wall, and the cat meowed beside it.

"Let's go," Soren said. "We've stayed here too long." His

words were forced, but he'd fooled his own body before. The pain was only temporary, at least. He hoped it was.

Soren made his way forward, keeping his eyes on the light of the crackling torch Davin carried. Seph looked back repeatedly to check on him.

Within the tunnel under the city, the walls echoed with the stirring and splashing of the murky water below. The burning sound of the torch filled his head as Soren followed his comrades. Above, the city was alive with rushing footsteps, shouting, and a mad sense of confusion. Most of the footsteps were running behind them. They were heading to where Soren was leaving. In the early evening, all wanted to get a gander at the spectacle that was the aftermath of a battle with a Synth wizard, and the first Black Fog to enter a city.

Soren wanted nothing more than to leave that place, far, far behind.

Suddenly, though, the commotion changed overhead. Soren knew what it was immediately, but Seph and Kaile seemed confused by the shift in tone above. It had gone from a general feeling of confusion and curiosity to... anger.

"What's happening?" Seph asked, her eyes wide and her eyebrows cocked.

The harsh shouts grew above, and many ran the other way back, away from the wreckage of the battle.

Ahead, the water rocked into the walls. Soren drew Firelight, grabbing Seph by the wrist and pulling her behind him, which she did. Kaile held his staff out and Davin handed the torch back to Kaile, who took it. Davin took up his ax in his good hand, the one left with the strength to wield it.

In the torch's light, someone was approaching, and Kaile stepped in front of them all, striking a note on the staff. The hum of the tune rang brightly down the tunnel.

"Hold," the man said as he approached.

Soren recognized the man's voice.

"Einrick," Davin said in a gruff, perturbed voice. "What're you doin' back here?"

Einrick heaved breaths as he came back into their fold.

"The people..." he said between breaths. "They're... they're revolting."

"They're what?" Davin said, irritation thick in his voice. "Fools."

"No, this is good," Einrick said, hunching slightly in the tunnel, beads of sweat streaming down his balding head.

"They're going to get slaughtered," Davin said.

"It's good for, us!" Einrick said.

Seph and Kaile looked up, scratching their necks and touching their faces.

"They know Glasse wasn't what they'd been told," Kaile said. "They must've seen that he was the one who summoned the Black Fog. Who knows how many were killed by that thing rampaging through the city like it did. They're angry that someone they told was good would do something like that."

"I still can't believe it," Seph said. "How was he able to do that? Was that the Ellydian?"

"I—I don't know," Kaile said. "He used a B Minor, so it was based on the same principles as the Ellydian. We've got to get word to Mihelik about this."

"Tell me what needs to be relayed to him and Lady Drake," Einrick said. "I'll make sure it gets to them. But right now, we may have this blessing, but we have far to go before we are safe. Follow me. Soren, can you keep up?"

"Just lead the way," Soren growled, staggering in excruciating pain. "I've been in worse shape than this."

Chapter Two

Every step felt as though a vice was squeezing his legs. The blood in them was thick and burned like embers flowing through his veins. His heart raced so quickly he thought the arteries in his neck might rupture. But he trudged through the tunnel beneath the city. His fingers still found notches along the wall to cling to as he made his way forward—following the others.

Soren eyed Seph. She was carrying the cat then, cradled in both arms as its predatory eyes glared out into the darkness before them, beyond the light of the torch Einrick led with. Seph was completely distraught. Not by the fight with Glasse. Not by him exploding in what would traumatize almost anyone, and not even distraught by the Black Fog that nearly devoured them all. It was the people above—she was worried about *them*.

Soren wanted to say something to alleviate her worry. He wanted to be her protector—to shelter her from all the terrible things he'd seen in his life. But he knew the truth: there was no protecting her from the world anymore. He could fight by her side, save her as best he could from those that attempted to harm her. But she'd already seen the true Aladran.

She saw it when her family was murdered by the king in Tourmielle. She'd grown up a hard life, albeit it was hidden from those that would seek to use her for her power. Now, after all this, Soren knew what was coming. Perhaps not the complete extent of it in his current state—but he knew—war was coming.

If that bounty that already existed on his head wasn't enough before, the whole world was going to be after him, disguise or not. And it wasn't just going to be him. There were witnesses to her fighting Glasse, and whether every citizen of Grayhaven now knew Glasse was the true villain or not—the world now knew the heir of the legendary Whistlewillow line was alive, and not only that, but defeated one of the great Synths of Londindam.

Things weren't going to get any easier from here, in fact, it would be the stark opposite. It warmed his heart to watch Seph glare upward, biting her lips, wide-eyed and bumping into Kaile, who walked in front of her. As upset as she was at the thought of those innocent people being hurt up there, the fact that she cared that much sparked something alive in Soren— something that perhaps was dormant inside of him. It gave strength to his legs and caused the blood to pump freely around once again. Perhaps it was pride, or *hope* for her, and a future that wasn't all death and destruction.

She was worried about the carnage above, and all those that chose to stand their ground against trained, armored soldiers. They were mothers, fathers, brothers, sisters, sons, and daughters. And they were fighting against their own people.

The cat leaped from her arms with a meow, jumping down onto the ledge at the right, avoiding the splashing from Seph's steps. Seph itched her scalp, looking up still.

Soren walked up beside her. She was so lost in her

thoughts; she was startled back to the moment when Soren grabbed her gently by the wrist.

"You didn't do any of this. It's not because of you," he said.

"But…" she breathed.

"We came to kill Glasse, and we did it." His words were firm, but he tried to force a sense of calm into them, too. "The world will react how it will. But he needed to die. He *deserved* death. We did what we came to do. The world will react how it must. We have no control over that."

"But…" she muttered. "They're going to die up there."

"Couldn't have done anything differently, lass," Davin said, only turning his head to the side.

"And now we're just leaving…" she said, her hand covering her mouth.

"Yes," Soren said, squeezing her wrist gently. "We're leaving. We can't do anything for them up there. They've made their choice. They have their own battles, and their own war to wage."

"So, we're just going to run away?" Seph asked.

"We're not running away," Davin said, clearing his throat. "We're fleeing. There's a difference."

She shook her head in frustration at his failed attempt at a joke.

Soren pulled her toward him as they paused in the tunnel. She avoided his gaze.

"Look at me, Persephone."

Her chin rose, and she looked at him finally.

"Those soldiers up there aren't the ones who killed your parents. They aren't the ones who took Cirella from us. It was the king. It was the Knight Wolf. It was Alcarond. It was Synths like Glasse and Zertaan. Those are the ones who need to pay. If we linger, we'll be captured or killed. We need to fight our battle, so we need to let them fight theirs."

She nodded as her lips quivered.

"Now, c'mon," Soren said, putting his arm over her as they continued down the tunnel, letting the sounds of the battle overhead fade behind.

For hours, they made their way into the darkness. Further and further, they went deeper into the underbelly of the great, ancient city. Rats scurried along ledges beside them, fearless of the strangers that had entered their world. Beady eyes lit from the light of the torch Einrick carried, tiny little eyes that watched from all the hidden nooks and crannies underground.

If not for the constant pain that racked his mind and body, Soren would've been more concerned they were going *too* deep, *too* far into the depths beneath the surface. The Under Realm wasn't a place for humans. At least not since the Demons of Dusk had arrived in their world. It was enough to evade the reach of Lord Garriss of Londindam above, but to enter such lands where sunlight cannot reach… Soren only trusted that his companions had their faculties enough to evade such places.

Eventually, though, as each step seemed as if it may be Soren's last, before he'd be forced to collapse to the ground, a light appeared. It was distant, soft, and pale. No more than a hazy hue far down the passageway; it gave him a renowned vigor.

"A light," Seph said, her voice cracked. No one had spoken for the last hour, only pushing through in the depths.

"We are at the outskirts of the city," Einrick said. "This will be where we exit."

"Shouldn't be sunlight yet," Davin said. His voice was harsh and forced. Soren could tell the dwarf was also in a great deal of pain. Davin needed more than just rest, like Soren did. He'd lost skin, and even in the scant torchlight, Soren could see the blistered and missing skin on Davin's arms and the side of his face.

"No, that isn't sunlight," Einrick said, with a curious, excited tone in his voice he was trying to conceal. Soren was amused at the thought of the spy enjoying the figurative underbelly of a city, more than the actual one...

As they got closer, Soren saw the light was beaming through two holes above, both no larger than what you'd fit a quill through, but it was enough to glow onto the dust that wafted through the stagnant air.

Einrick tapped three times with his knuckles onto the square wooden plank above, and Soren quickly realized it was mounted with hinges on one side. He elbowed Kaile in the side, as Kaile looked down to see Soren slide Firelight free of her scabbard.

Kaile nodded and struck a C on his staff. Its crystalline harmony rolled down the tunnel sharply. Seph struck an A, and the two notes intertwined beautifully.

Einrick, without looking down, said, "You won't be needing those." He knocked one more time, a fourth. "But I do suppose, better to be cautious and not needed, and the opposite." With the last knock, Soren heard footsteps above. At least three pairs.

"Cast the spell," Soren said to Davin, who looked in a daze at first. The pain and fatigue of the battle were worn deep into the hardened dwarf. Davin sparked back to life with a couple of harsh blinks.

"Won't be needed," Einrick said flatly. "They know who you are. And we won't be out in the open." The door above cracked at the side opposite the hinges, and torchlight flooded down. "But you'll need that spell soon enough." A hand reached down from the blinding light above, and Einrick took it, as the man's arm heaved him up.

Seph put an arm up, but Soren pulled her back and shook his head. She stepped back to his side.

Davin was the next to be pulled up by the two men, whose

faces were becoming clearer as Soren's eyes adjusted. He didn't recognize their serious faces, which meant he'd never met them before. But as one by one they were pulled up; Soren became less concerned about the side these two men were on. He sheathed Firelight before the two men grabbed his hands last and pulled him up.

Soren was in the room above the tunnel, and finally above ground. He instinctually drove Seph behind him, though he kept Firelight cradled on his hip. Normally, his eyes would adjust quickly, and he'd gain great insight into the room, those in it, and any danger that lurked. But his body was at the brink of collapsing, his mind struggled to keep the creeping fingers of sleep at bay, and his vision fogged from both.

Before him, though, were three figures, two men—or boys rather—both in their teens, and a young girl, ten years perhaps, standing at the far corner of the room.

It was a rectangular room with candles burning on a table at the far end. One boy held a torch, which lit both their faces brightly. The girl's face was dimly lit by the candles.

Soren didn't recognize the three of them, but there was something there—some visage of familiarity. He hadn't met *them*, but he'd met someone that reminded him of them.

There were no windows in the room, only two doors, and not a hint of sunlight anywhere from behind the walls of the room.

Soren saw Kaile and Seph weren't disguised, and Davin was still in his male, dwarf-state.

"So," Soren said, rubbing his fingers at his side. "You obviously know who we are, but we don't have the same luxury."

"They're friends of the lady," Einrick said, walking over and shaking both the boy's hands. "Thank you." His voice was full of sincere relief. "Thank you for being here! Thank the goddess!"

"Who are you?" Davin asked with his brow furrowed. "Didn't answer Soren's question."

"They're the Silver Sparrows," Kaile said, folding his arms and leaning against the corner behind him. "That much is obvious."

Soren heard those words, and a moment from his past clicked into him. Although he didn't say anything, the three before him reminded him vaguely of the time Bael had dragged him and Alicen to meet with the Silver Sparrows in Erhil for the first time. He remembered meeting Amarra, with dark skin and silver hair. Also Helena, with blond hair, fair skin, and green eyes. And Gregor, stout and strong, with a flat mouth and dark eyes. That memory led to the other—their last moments—out on the plains outside the city as it burned asunder.

He remembered King Amón upon his grand steed. The king was in his armor crafted in Vellice, Storm Dragon, the grandest sword in existence, hanging at his hip. The king's piercing, unworldly iceberg-blue eyes beamed coldly at the three Silver Sparrows as they were murdered in cold blood. A smile crept from under the king's black beard. Soren's teeth clenched at the thought.

As they died, Archpriest Solemn Roane VII sat at the king's side. Younger than he out to be, the highest ranking member of the church of the goddess from the northern continent of Eldra. He was of fair skin with chiseled, lean features with long, wavy auburn hair and grace that exuded from him as he watched a town of innocents burn.

Alcarond Riberia, the archmage himself, was there too, with all the other Synths, including Glasse, who was currently splattered all over the road in the Broadmoor district of Grayhaven.

"We are," one man said, with blond hair that dropped to

his shoulders and green eyes glimmering from the light of the torch in his hand.

"Are you Syncrons?" Kaile asked forcefully, slowly pulling his staff before him, nearer to his tuning forks.

The three didn't respond, but the girl in the back finally spoke. "No, we are not Syncrons, but we're devoting our life to protecting them, so that they may help save this realm, and everyone in it."

Chapter Three

※※※

Soren's face twisted. He groaned in agony, finally feeling that Seph was somewhat safe. The strangers weren't Syncrons—or worse, Synths—and the Silver Sparrows at least thought they were on the side of good, and were surely there to aid Soren and his comrades. Soren staggered back to the wall behind him, sliding down until he sat on the floor. He clutched his side and gasped in shrill agony.

Davin, knowingly or not, caught that cue and pulled a chair to him and collapsed into it. He hid his face on the backrest as he let out a single roar from the unrelenting pain. It was so loud it echoed off the walls. It was guttural, barbaric, and full of raw pain.

The three in the room sparked alive then, with the girl running over and rummaging through a pack on the floor. The two boys scrambled, one running to Soren and the other to Davin. Seph, who clung to Soren, stepped back as the boy helped Soren to his feet.

"We need to get these clothes off," the boy said.

Soren's head fogged, and delirium was running rampant in his mind.

"Who... where... are you..." Soren muttered.

"Just come with me," the boy said. "One leg in front of the other. Hey, give me a hand, Kaile."

"Put me down," Soren said, but felt the strong arms pulling him to the far end of the room, through a door, and onto a soft, clean bed.

"Help me get these clothes off him," the boy with the green eyes said. He and Kaile pulled his shirts and pants off.

The young girl was suddenly hunched over Soren, with her dark gray eyes scanning his face and body. "He's absolutely covered," she said, as Soren's skin felt the chill of the air in the room on his chest and legs.

Davin screamed in the other room. Soren shot up, sitting up with his arms holding him up from behind. Davin was led into the room by the other boy and Einrick. Seph walked in behind with her hands covering her mouth.

They laid Davin into the other bed in the same room as Soren.

"Lay down." The girl had both her hands on Soren's shoulders, pressing him down futilely.

"Lay back, uncle," Seph said, running to his side, pressing him to lie back with her hand on his chest. He laid back. She grabbed him by the hand as the girl pulled out vials from the pack on the floor beside her. "They're here to help, and we need it. You're injured. Davin too. Just rest. You're safe now. You need to heal."

"No." Soren moaned as he thrashed his head from side to side on the pillow—fighting off that overwhelming fatigue from the constant roaring of pain in his body, and the soft sheets beneath it. "I don't trust them... I don't trust anyone... I only trust you, Persephone... I only trust you..."

Then everything went black, and sleep took him.

When he awoke, the first thing he noticed was the splitting pain that throbbed thickly in his head. His eyes ached as he opened them, with the glow of soft candlelight glowing at the far end of the room. He heard snoring then, rumbling in the bed next to him.

Soren sat up with his elbows under him, seeing it was only he and Davin in the room. Davin was sound asleep, but Soren's first thought was that he wanted to wake him—to stop the snoring—that Soren could feel in his head. It was like a sharp rock growing in size in his brain with every breath the dwarf drew.

Soren sat up completely, and his eyes shot open wide, increasing the growing migraine pain, but his heart pounded as he searched for it.

Where is Firelight?

He found it on the table beside him, still in her sheath. His fingers eagerly wrapped around it, pulling it up to his chest, slowing his racing heart.

She's the only reason I'm still alive. Thank you, Firelight... Thank you, girl...

He threw the covers off him, letting them fold at his feet. His body, from head to toe, was littered with bandages. Hundreds of them. Some white, some pink with soaked through blood. Setting down Firelight on the bed, he reached up and felt the bandages, mostly four inches long, along his neck and on his face.

That Black Fog did a number on me. I shouldn't be here. I should be dead like all the rest who've stood before those monsters. But I'm not. I've killed Shades and injured the biggest fog I've ever seen. If Shirava is real, then I really should be thanking her...

Another worry entered him then—*We shouldn't be here. We need to get moving! They'll surely be looking for us. We only walked for a few hours... slowly. We might still be in the city!*

"Davin," Soren said, raspy and weak. He cleared his dry throat harshly. "Davin, wake up."

"Let him rest," Kaile suddenly said, hushed.

Soren spun to see Kaile sitting on the other side of him, leaning back in a rocking chair. Kaile didn't seem like the same boy who escaped through a portal with him, Seph, and Mihelik. He sat calmly in the chair, delicately rocking back and forth, but only a few inches worth. His charcoal eyes stared at the floor to the side. His reddish-auburn hair covered half his face, and he had a few bandages of his own. One big one especially stood out on his chin. The way Kaile sat, he had the aura of a powerful Syncron, not the awkward, bumbling teenager who Soren had first met.

"We..." Soren said, his voice still cracking and dry. Kaile handed him a glass of water from another small round table in the corner behind them. Soren sipped it and sighed in relief as the cool water slid down his harsh throat. "We need to be going..."

"We're all right here, for the time being," Kaile said. "I doubt anyone will find us here."

"Why?" Soren asked.

Kaile's chin rose as he looked up at the ceiling of the room. His chin length hair fell back, showing the tan skin on his face as it radiated in the candlelight. Soren looked up as well, quickly noting what Kaile was alluding to, but hadn't said.

The back corners of the high ceiling weren't corners at all, but exposed rock, making that side of the room behind them looking more like the backside of an underground cave. Soren saw no windows in this room, either.

"Are we underground?"

"Not entirely," Kaile said, sitting back and rocking.

The squeaking of the chair made Soren wince.

Kaile halted in place. "Sorry... Here, take this. Eve asked

me to give this to you when you woke." He reached down to the floor and handed a vial to Soren, uncorking it before Soren grasped it. "Don't drink it all. Just half, she said."

"Eve? The young woman?"

Kaile nodded.

"Seph... where's...?"

"She's in the other room," Kaile whispered. "We've been taking turns in here. You can go back to sleep if you need."

"I've slept enough," Soren said, swinging his legs to the side of the bed, causing Kaile to shift nervously, tapping the arm of the rocking chair. "How long have I been out?"

"Ten hours?" Kaile said. "Roughly."

"Ten hours?" Soren asked, with both brows raised.

"Luckily for the others, you passed out so they could work on getting you bandaged without you fighting and squirming like you were. You really can be stubborn. Anybody ever told you that?"

"Shut up. Don't get cute with me," Soren sneered.

Kaile gulped. "Sorry."

Soren sighed, scratching his scalp, brushing his long hair back. "Listen, Kaile..." He cleared his throat again. "What you did back there. That was... impressive. What I mean to say is... um..."

Kaile stopped rocking entirely, not moving an inch, as if deeply anticipating something. Tiny beads of sweat dabbed his brow.

"Good job," Soren said. "You did a good job."

Kaile couldn't contain his smile as hard as he fought it. His teeth even showed a bit between his lips. He nodded eagerly, fighting that too.

"You too," Kaile said. "You drove that Black Fog away. I guess there's a reason the Silver Sparrows are after you like they are. They see something in you." He paused. "We all do."

Soren clapped his hand onto Kaile's knee and stood with a groan. "All right, enough of the sappy stuff. I need to speak with this... Eve."

"You sure you two don't want to hug and cry it out?" Davin asked, and what irked Soren even more than the dwarf's stubbornly annoying sense of humor was that Soren hadn't noticed the snoring had stopped and he was listening in.

Kaile laughed, but forced it back into his throat.

"Next time you snore like that while I'm actually getting good sleep, I'm gonna cut your huge head off your tiny body." Soren was staring at Davin as he said that. He was standing beside Kaile, looking over at the dwarf who still lay in bed on his side, half-covered in bandages.

"Huge head?" Davin was barely able to get out before he and Soren both erupted into laughter. Soren laughed so hard he laid his hand on his stomach, closed his eyes, and the pain roared all around his body. "It's not huge! It's perfectly proportionated to my body! And it's quite the insult in my culture, calling a dwarf's head huge!"

Seph burst into the room, letting the door swing wide open and bang onto the wall. "Uncle!" She ran into him and squeezed.

"I'm fine," he said, wiping the tears away and regaining his composure. He watched intently as the other three stood on the other side of the doorway. As the laughter quickly died, Soren released Seph. "We've got some things to talk about, don't we?"

Eve, standing in front of the two boys, nodded. "That, we do."

They all moved into the first room, with Kaile helping Davin up out of bed, and leading him by the arm. The room was arranged with chairs around two tables, with Seph, Soren, Kaile, and finally Davin sitting at the first. The others sat at the second, except Einrick. He stood at the corner by a cupboard, jostling glasses within.

Soren looked hard at the three at the other round table. There was still something about them—something unmistakably familiar about them. But he couldn't quite put his finger on it.

"Thanks for the work," Davin said, scratching the bandages on the side of the face. "Sure to leave some nasty scars, but I'm grateful just to be here still."

"We did what we could," Eve said with a slight somber glossiness in her eyes. "Your burns were extensive, and Soren's injuries were of some sort I'm not familiar with. Perhaps none are. You've been given a sedative to ease your pain while you heal."

Soren nodded. "Who are you three? I feel as if we've met, but I know we haven't."

"You haven't met us," the boy with the green eyes said. "But you've met our parents."

The revelation clicked in Soren's head as soon as the boy said that.

"You're the offspring of the Syncrons in Erhil."

The three nodded.

"You're Gregor's daughter," Soren said. "Same eyes."

She nodded.

"You're the son of Helena."

The boy with the blond hair and green eyes nodded. "Charles," the boy said.

"And I'm Roth, and yes, Amarra was my mother," the dark-skinned boy said last. He had curly, shining black hair that was brow length, stopping just short of his hazel eyes.

"I'm so sorry for your losses," Seph said, elbows on the table.

Einrick laid carafes of red wine on both tables, returning to the cupboard and setting down glasses for all, pouring them after.

"Thanks," Roth said. "They are missed."

There was a long pause as they all sipped their wine, and Einrick sat in a chair between the table, bridging the two. Soren heard the winds gust outside from the front.

"We're safe here," Einrick said, stroking his bushy, graying blond beard. He pulled a pipe off the table, with a candle to light it. He puffed off it, smiling with his yellow teeth showing. Putting the candle back on the table, he leaned back on the back two legs of the chair. "Nobody will find us here, because no one knows this place exists."

"Are we still in the city?" Kaile asked.

"Yes, and no," Einrick said. "More yes than no, though."

"Enough riddles," Davin growled. "This isn't a game, spy."

"This place was built into the cliffs as a safe house," Einrick said. "The backup, backup plan was to get us here. Let things blow over, then head back underground to get you all out of the city, back to Skylark. But that was not in the cards."

"No, no it wasn't," Davin grumbled.

"I didn't ask you to come," Soren said, taking a gulp of wine and setting the glass back down, folding his arms over his chest. "But I have to do this. I have to know who sent this Vellice dagger to me, through Garland."

"Garland," Davin said with a grave tone. "Shoulda killed that backstabbing bastard."

"Perhaps," Soren said, glancing at Kaile, who'd given the speech to perhaps let Lord Garland go, because he wasn't the evil they were out to hunt. "He's a weasel, yes, but now I know he's a weasel, I can get to squeal. I may need him later."

"That's a big *maybe*," Davin said. "He'll go squeal to the king now, surely."

"Good," Soren smirked, taking the glass and another gulp. "I want Amón to know what happened in Grayhaven. I want him to know he should be scared. I'm coming for him. Firelight already proved he's not invincible. I hope he looks at that scar every morning and thinks about how close I was to killing him in Erhil."

"But you didn't kill him," Charles said. "Our parents died there, and so did thousands of innocent children, women, and elderly."

"No. No, I did not."

Another failure. One I'm going to live with forever.

"None of us blame you for that," Charles said. "That's why we're here, actually."

"Yes, why is it that you are here?" Soren asked, putting both elbows on the table, steepling his fingers and leaning in. "Who knows where you all traveled from to get here for this. There's no way you all live in Grayhaven."

"We're here for the same reason our parents came to you," Roth said. "The Silver Sparrows need you, even more than before. Everything has changed now. The tides of war are approaching. It's more than you now, though. It's everything."

"What do you mean?" Seph asked.

Roth looked at Einrick, who puffed from his pipe, blowing a huge swirling plume up to the rafters. "The world is changing," he said, holding the pipe by his chest. "Regular folk are beginning to see with fresh, clear vision. They're revolting, they're muttering, and they're planning. And what you did up there, Soren… that was nothing short of legendary."

"It was Firelight," Soren said. "The Demons of Dusk are vulnerable to Vellice forged steel."

"It doesn't matter," Einrick said. "You could've had dragon fire blowing from your mouth. It was you. That's what the people care about. You're the Scarred, you're supposed to be the villain, and you saved that city from absolute carnage."

Soren's mouth twisted. He wanted to say it was luck. He wanted to say anyone would've done the same. But, instead, he thought about clawing his way deeper and deeper into the Black Fog. He thought he was dead; he thought there was no escape, but he found a way lay within the black demon. It wasn't luck that drove him that deep. It was rage. Pure, unbridled rage at everything that burned in him. It was rage stewed from all the hurt in his life, all the injustice, and all the loss.

"You killed Shades, too," Roth said. "Those bodies you left were found. Word is starting to spread. Word that you're a hero. They're saying that you're the one. You're the one who's going to rid the world of the Demons of Dusk."

Soren fell back into his chair with his arms folded, sighing. "I'm no hero."

"Yes you are," Seph said. "Even if you don't believe it. You're a hero to them, and you're a hero to me."

"You don't know what you're saying," Soren said. "I'm just going after my revenge. Whether or not that makes me a Sparrow is up to you. You give me the tools to complete my missions, and I'll see them done. All the way."

"You don't understand," Eve said. Her words were firm, yet gentle. She sat up straight. "The Black Fog invaded a capital city. That is the first time in history that's happened. And it was a Syncron of the king that called it. People are frightened. You've lost loved ones, Soren. You know that fear they feel. And you know what? You're their one fucking hope."

Soren didn't have the strength to fight her, and the two that sat beside her, so he didn't respond.

"You're becoming a symbol," Eve said. "And symbols, more than men, can live long past their day."

"What are you saying?" Seph asked, her eyebrow raised.

"We want you, Soren Stormrose, to lead the Silver Sparrows," Eve said. "We want you to lead us to victory against the king. That's what our parents came to you for. That's what we need from you now. Right now we're in the shadows. But the light of the salvation sun is rising. But before we arise, we need a leader, a guiding light in the darkness. If the people see you, then they'll know that we are here for good. We are here to save this world. We're the good ones. We are the Syncrons, not the Synths like they call us."

"How do you know?" Kaile asked, jarring all in the room.

"What?" Eve asked, pulling her hands down into her lap.

"How do you *know* we're the good ones?"

Chapter Four

"What do you mean?" Eve asked, her hands back out wide and irritation thick in her words. "Of course we are good."

"What are you asking?" Seph asked Kaile.

Kaile took a deep breath, playing with the stem of the glass on the table. His hair flapped down in front of a side of his face.

"Are we all sure what we're doing is right?"

Soren listened intently, as many grew agitated in the room.

"Just because you came from their side," Roth spat, "doesn't give you the right to challenge our beliefs. You were in with the enemy, and Mihelik chose to save you, because he sees something in you. But make no mistake, we are on the right side of this war. Amón is evil, and we're going to make the world right again when he is dead."

"How?" Kaile asked.

Roth slammed both fists onto the table, rising from his seat with his face twisted in anger. Charles stood and put a hand on his friend's arm.

"I understand killing the king," Kaile said. "Perhaps more

than any here, because I know him. I've sat at his table at dinner. I've seen the man for what he is. But what then? What will you do to right the world when he's dead? Are you certain you won't put someone on the throne who will do just as much damage?"

Kaile stood, meeting the angry boy's gaze, while Kaile towered over. Seph grabbed Kaile's wrist, still sitting.

"Of course they will be better, you traitor!" Roth said. "A fucking slug would be better!"

"I agree," Kaile said through clenched teeth. "And don't call me a traitor."

Soren watched with piqued curiosity at Kaile. It was almost as if he was watching the transformation from a caterpillar, struggling to free itself from its cocoon to become the soaring moth it was meant to be.

"Sit down, you two," Davin said. "Don't need a damned fistfight right now."

Kaile didn't take his gaze off Roth, as Roth was the first to sit. Kaile slowly sat after, with Seph turning her back to him and showing a visible gulp to Soren.

"So, you want Soren to lead your rebellion?" Davin asked. "Makes sense from the perspective of recruiting. So he'd be the face, and Lady Drake would be the real woman in charge?"

The three shifted in their seats, uncertain how to answer.

"It's not like that," Eve finally said. "We're all going to be in the fight together. But we need you to lead us."

"No," Soren said. "I have my own war, and my own way. I don't need to lead anyone. I'm better on my own."

Seph tilted her head to the side, looking down at the ground.

"The Shades and Black Fog are going to enter the cities," Charles said. "Goddess knows when, but Shirava help us all when that happens, because there won't be anywhere to hide. They're going to multiply and overrun everything. Then this war won't matter. We need you to help with this, too. You've killed Shades. You've fought the fog. Help us, Soren."

"There's something inside the Black Fog," he said. "You need to get word to Mihelik about it. Deep within, there's a light inside them. It's buried deep, but it's like a molten liquid, shining from within. It's vulnerable there. Beyond its fog, there's like a certain, contained pool inside. That's where it can be harmed. We just need to figure out a way to break through the black skin."

"And we need Vellice weapons," Seph said.

"That's a problem," Davin said. "There aren't any. Except the ones we know about. And those are owned by the king, the Knight Wolf, and Soren."

"Doesn't mean there's not more of them," Seph said.

"So what do you say, then?" Einrick asked Soren.

"Bael told me before he died that the Silver Sparrows had found something. It was something your parents wanted to bring up to me when they were trying to get me on their side. What was it?"

Soren waited for the three to answer.

"We need your word to fight with us," Roth said after a long, breathless moment.

"Why are you here?" Soren asked. "How is it that all of you are in Grayhaven at this time? This can't be chance."

"Lady Drake knew that killing Edward Glasse would spark something here," Eve said, crossing her legs under the table and tapping it with her fingers. "She'd hoped it would be hope."

"Hope?" Seph asked. "For what? Killing Synths? But the people didn't know he was evil…"

"She hoped it would bring more to our cause," Eve said, with a proud, playful raise of an eyebrow, and a smirk creeping on the corner of her mouth. "Those that wield the Ellydian may be facing a turning point. If they all knew what happened in Erhil, and in Tourmielle... if they knew the truth, they may join us."

"So, you're here for recruitment?" Soren asked. "Good plan."

"What do you say?" Eve asked. "We ask you again. Will you help us?"

Soren thought about it—genuinely. He'd had military training, he knew war, and he knew everything that came with it. But what was more important to him?

I can help them save this world that they are so passionate about saving, or I could get my revenge on those that took everything from me... Both may have the same end goals, but in the end, I have to do what is surest to succeed, because killing that bastard king is too fucking important.

Soren uncrossed his arms, sat up straight in his chair, and said, "I will kill the king, but I will lead no army or rebellion. I will do it alone."

Eve sat back and nodded to herself, thinking. Roth exhaled harshly through his nostrils and Charles' shoulders slumped.

"You sure?" Enrich asked with both hands up. "I can appreciate working in the shadows just about as much as anyone, but there's going to be a lot more advantages to working with Lady Drake. Not to mention glory. If you win, you could be king for all we know..."

Soren laughed, clapping his hands. "That's rich. We just killed their Doren lord, and you think there's going to be a 'happily ever after' after this? You don't know them very well then. Have you seen the evil in William Wolf? Those men you talk about killing as if they are mere lords in small castles, you think you're going to just 'win' a war with an 'army'? What army? A handful of Syncrons, and what? A few thousand brave as fuck, but surely with one foot in the grave, men and women from Grayhaven? No, you need me to go out into the wilds and shadows and cut away their legs from under them, one by one, until you're staring straight into the eyes of the beast. And first, I'm going to start with this Lord Belzaar in the desert."

"You should be going back east, not further west," Roth said, gripping the side of the table as the candles flickered.

"And who are you to tell me where I should and shouldn't go?" Soren said with squared shoulders, gazing at the young man with an icy gaze. "You? How old are you? Sixteen? What do you know about war?"

"I know that my mother believed enough in saving this world that she left us to fight for a better one, and never came home again," Roth said. "She gave her life for the cause we speak of. She refused to bend the knee to the king and serve him like everyone else did. She could have been a part of burning that town, but by not bowing, she died there instead. So yeah, I know a bit about war."

"Again," Soren said. "I'm sorry for your loss. She was a good woman."

Roth calmed, taking a sip of wine with a slight shaking of his hand and fingers.

"Soren," Davin chimed in. He bit his lip, but had a firm tone in his voice. "I'm only gonna ask this one time." He cleared his throat, hunching over, putting an elbow on his thigh. "We've traveled a bit together now, and fought side by side. We've become sort of comrades, yes?"

Soren nodded.

"So I ask this, and again, only once. Why go to the desert? Why not go back to Skylark and let Seph train with Mihelik? Why not go back to the lady and formulate a plan? Regroup and heal? Neither of us is in the shape to keep pressing forward into the unknown. We don't have camels; we are maybe half our fighting strength. Instead, you want us to head out into the desert, in the middle of what will be the biggest hunt in years for Aladran. It's not going to be just soldiers coming after us now. That bounty on your head? You can damn well expect that to multiply like the Shades themselves. This will be a hard, grueling road ahead, and not just for you, but for them too."

Soren looked at Seph and Kaile, sitting side by side, who glanced at one another, as if speaking without words.

"You know where I'm going," Seph said, and none gave rebuttals.

"Me too," Kaile said. "Where they go, I go. I believe that fate has brought us together for a reason. I jumped in that portal for a reason, whether I fully understand where I path takes us, or not."

Davin sighed. "I'm in."

"Lady Drake won't be pleased to hear this," Einrick said. "Although she can also be a surprising woman."

"This may put a kink in her plans," Seph said. "But we're off to fight this battle for her. She should understand that, right?"

Eve, Roth, and Charles looked at one another, without words, but with an unspoken agreement to speak in private. They rose together and went back into the other room, closing the door behind them.

"Should we listen?" Kaile asked.

"You can," Soren said, leaning back in his chair, extending his hand in Davin's direction. Flicking his fingers, Soren pointed to the pipe on the table, and Davin handed it to him, as well as the pouch of tobacco. Soren stuffed it into the pipe, but before lighting it with the candle, looked over at Kaile, who was curiously staring at Soren. "Let them make their plans, on second thought. We're all on the same team, with the same enemies. As long as we have pendants with the disguising spell, we should be safe enough. They'll be looking for us, surely, and you're right, Davin. I expect the price on my head to be quite the lucrative one. If I was still in that business, even I'd be tempted to go after me. Although, I would know that I'm not what they say I am. I only go after the ones who deserve justice, not the victims of the King's spite."

"Makes you wonder what lies they'll be spinnin' about you," Einrick said. "I can only imagine they're good ones." He laughed.

"I'm sure they are," Soren said.

For half an hour, the five of them sat in the room together, talking in half-serious matters and drinking wine after a hard-earned victory. While Soren enjoyed the banter and the indulgence, he knew the journey needed to continue. Waiting in Grayhaven wasn't going to lead to his vengeance, and he still wondered why they were "so" safe in their current safe house. He didn't trust anyone as much as he trusted himself, although his current party was the most he'd trusted anyone in a long, long time.

The last people he trusted, Bael and Alicen, turned out to be a fucking disaster, and his heart still ached from that fresh wound.

As the door swung open again, and Eve, Charles, and Roth walked back into the room, sitting down in their chairs with serious looks on their faces, Soren couldn't help but be entertained by the youth of the three. If it wasn't for their last names and their parents, Soren wouldn't take advice on how to stomp on ants from these children.

He'd gone from speaking directly with the Lady of Cascadia and the former archmage himself, to waiting to hear what these three teenagers had come up with in the other room between themselves.

"We will aid you in your journey," Eve said. "Although we wish your choice was different, your reputation doesn't disappoint, Soren Dakard Stormrose of the Knights of Tourmielle. Stubborn, ruthless, and valiant, you choose to fight the war from within, and we can respect that."

"We sincerely hope you'll change your mind later, though," Charles said, scratching his neck.

"We have a way for you to escape the city," Eve said. "Lady Drake had it as another backup plan, but instead of taking it back to her, you'll take it west. If you like, we'll leave at dusk."

"Dusk?" Seph scratched her temple. "What time is it now?"

"The first light is approaching," Eve said. "So, you'll have the day to rest."

"Are we going back underground?" Einrick rubbed his brow.

Soren was surprised he didn't know about this part of the plan, but he also understood the importance of secrecy in some things. Lady Drake had brought three children of former Syncrons of the Silver Sparrows to Grayhaven, just as a sort of backup plan. It made Soren wonder about the myriad of other schemes Lady Drake spun in her time under Skylark.

"Yes, we'll go underground again." Roth stomped the ground with his boot's heel. "That'll lead to the outskirts of the city, where the wagon awaits."

"Wagon, eh?" Davin swiped his broad nose. "Wouldn't mind laying in a wagon, and not straddling a horse.

"Well," Soren said, "horses are only so good in the desert. Once we get to the Dyadric Desert, we'll need to get camels. It's still winter, and the desert doesn't offer much reprieve from cold nights."

"Are…" Seph rubbed her hands nervously, fidgeting with her fingers. "Are there Shades in the desert? Are there woods to hide in?"

Soren remembered Seph had never really been anywhere except for Guillead.

"We'll find ways to avoid them," Soren said. He turned to the three Sparrows. "I need to know where this Lord Belzaar is. Can you find that information out for me?"

"We've never heard the name," Eve said. "But we will find out. If this man truly exists and Garland didn't make him up, to save his own skin."

"He was telling the truth," Soren said. "As much as I can tell, I believe he was true in his words." He paused. "I need to find out how this Vellice dagger came into my possession, intentionally. It's far too much of a coincidence that the one weapon that can defeat the Demons of Dusk was meant to come to me. I have a feeling this question will lead to important answers."

"And perhaps bigger questions," Kaile said.

"Either way," Soren said. "I need to know, because whoever orchestrated this—I think—knew this weapon could kill Shades, and delivered it to me. It's safe to say, the only reason the five of us are still alive is because someone had Garland deliver Firelight to me."

"And perhaps a mountain of luck," Davin said.

"There's no luck in my life, not anymore," Soren said. "Only this curse I carry."

Davin winked, or perhaps just blinked, with his one eye showing. "That's the dark, depressing Soren I know. I was worried you were getting soft on me."

Chapter Five

※

The winds whistled and howled beyond the walls of their room. They were in the depths of winter, and its icy reach lingered out there, waiting, wanting.

It was perhaps midday, with the candles still glowing their amber light into the room. No sunlight made its way in, but in the midday, Soren was the only of his companions left awake. Seph and Kaile slept in the other room on the beds, with Seph's cat surely snuggling in next to her. Davin slumped over onto the table, snoring out of one nostril. Einrick and Roth had gone out into the city, leaving through the front door, which was the only glimpse Soren had of the world for that brief moment.

Soren wasn't tired, or even content. He heard the winds; he felt the chill, and mostly—he wanted answers. He sat back in the rocking chair, with Eve and Charles sitting at a table beside him, glancing at him and around the room. On the table was tea, water, deep red wine, crackers, and butter. Soren sat puffing on the pipe, sipping down wine every few minutes to wet his lips and throat.

Eve, as young as she was, gazed out of the side of her eyes

at Soren often, and he assumed she had mountains of questions for him. But instead of telling her to ask, he sat with those mountains already floating around in his mind. His thoughts raced through the past, the present, and the very uncertain future.

He blew out a cloud of smoke above, reaching forward to ash the pipe, and take another swill of wine. Soren heard Eve and Charles whispering to each other, but he didn't listen in on what about. But he caught Charles nudge Eve with his elbow onto her arm.

"Ask," Soren heard Charles say.

Eve cleared her throat, and at that moment, she appeared like a child to him. Before, she was the young woman asking, even pressing for Soren's help. Now she resembled a young Persephone—an innocent young girl who was lost and in search of something.

"Yes," Soren finally said. "Out with it."

"I'm embarrassed to ask," Eve said, her hands curling around her middle.

She's in pain. Not the physical though... it's something deeper.

"I just had a question," she said, looking down. "How do you get past it?" Her voice was wrought with anguish, and Soren could see the tears welling in her eyes.

"Pain?" he said.

She nodded, not meeting his gaze. Charles averted his gaze as well, choking back tears.

"I remember when I lost my parents," Soren said, exhaling deeply. "Feels like the world is over. Your protectors are gone, the only ones who really, *really* loved you."

Eve folded over, her chest falling to her knees. Charles turned away, wiping tears from his face.

"It hurts so much," Eve cried. "I miss my dad. I think about him all the time. The way he died; it just feels like a piece of me died too that day. I'd give anything to have him back."

Soren reached over and put his hand on her back. She heaved heavy tears.

"Your father was brave," Soren said. "I didn't know Gregor well, but I admired that in him. He was a warrior, a great Syncron. It took a lot of courage to do what he did. Your mother, too, Charles. Helena was a brave woman. I'm sure she was an incredible mother."

"You lost your family," Eve said. "The same way we lost ours. Does it… does it get easier? Does the pain hurt less?"

Soren patted her back, then reached out for the carafe of wine and poured a glass for her and Charles.

"Not really," Soren said. "But the tears come less often, and the tightness in your stomach will relax."

"I want that king to die so badly," Charles said, taking the glass of wine and taking down half of it in one gulp. He put the glass back on the table with a dull clank and looked sharply over at Soren. "Please kill him. And please make it hurt. I want him to die in pain, like the way he killed our parents. I want it to hurt."

Soren flattened his mouth and tucked his chin to his chest.

Charles rubbed his neck, waiting for an answer.

"Killing the king won't bring your family back to you," Soren said. "Or right the wrongs he did. It will help seal the wound hopefully, but you've got to find your own new way forward. That may not be the answer you want, but I can't promise King Amón will suffer. I can't even promise he'll miss sleep. But I can promise you two this one thing—there are only two things that matter to me in this unfair, miserable world— killing those monsters, and that girl sleeping in that bed over there. If there's breath in these lungs, and strength in this hand enough to grip this dagger, then you better believe I'm gonna try to kill the king, and every last one that did this to us."

Eve and Charles were both staring deep into Soren's eyes as he said that. Their eyes held thick tears, but held a faint semblance of hope in them.

"I miss Cirella every day," he said. "I miss Persephone's mother and father every day as well. Everyone in Tourmielle, I can remember. I grew up there. They were all my family. They were all my home. And they took that from me, and that devil liked it. He felt happiness while that town burned and erased an entire history, generations even, because of what he did. Make no mistake, my whole life is dedicated to making sure that man feels no happiness, or anything for that matter, ever again."

"Please, Soren," Eve said, reaching over and grabbing his wrist. "Please, kill him. Kill him for us, and for everyone in Aladran. We think you're the only chance we've got at vengeance and justice. Their Synths are too powerful. They have all the old knowledge that the king gives them. We have Mihelik now, and he's showing the Sparrows things, but against Alcarond and the other Synths of the king, I fear we will lose."

Soren clapped the back of her hand.

"Mihelik is powerful, but old," Soren said. "This war will be long, most likely. Waging a war against the king like this, with the fortress and strength he's amassed, will be a mountain to climb. But I see the strength in you two. I feel the fight in your voice. You're the next generation of warriors that can change the world. And... you have perhaps the greatest weapon in this war... whether you realize it or not..."

Both of them raised their eyebrows, and Eve drew her hand back, itching her pant leg.

Soren cocked his head toward the other room.

Eve and Charles both looked over at the closed door and thought about what lay on the other side.

"You ask me to be your soldier, to lead your army. But on the other side of that wall, you have perhaps the most coveted

Syncron in all of Aladran. He was handpicked by the archmage himself to take up his position as the most powerful being in all of Aladran. And beside him is the heir to the Whistlewillow blood, the only bloodline that produces wielders of the Ellydian through each generation. You want me? If you were wise, you'd be after them."

"But they follow you," Eve said quickly in rebuttal.

Soren wasn't ready for that response, and looked to his side, away from them, and at the wall.

"Lady Drake and Mihelik know Seph will follow you into whatever darkness, because you are all she has," Eve said. "And Kaile, well, he seems bound to you, or her, for some reason. He admires you and has some sort of attraction to your niece."

"Easy," Soren growled.

"I don't mean sexually, necessarily," Eve said, softening her words. "But you three are steadfast on your journey. Three of the most powerful—and dangerous—people out there. Yes, the Silver Sparrows want Seph and Kaile on their side, but you're the key, Soren, whether you acknowledge it or not. So much in this world sways upon you, it teeters on your decisions and your ferocity."

"But then I better not fuck it up, eh?"

"Soren," Eve said. "To half the world, you're going to be a hero and savior, and to the other half, you'll be what the king makes you out to be. But I believe you'll show them what you are. You're more than the lost man who had those scars cut into his face. You're becoming more. You're becoming a symbol."

Soren laughed. "A symbol. I'm an arm with a dagger attached to it. A highly trained soldier. That's all I am, and that's all I need to be. That pain you feel now. You said it took part of you away? I know *exactly* what you're referring to. Part of me died back there in Tourmielle. I don't care about my life. I don't care about being a symbol. I don't want to be a hero. I just want to kill those monsters, and then, I just want to be left alone."

"You can't do that." Eve stood suddenly, sending her chair scooting back. "Just because you don't want to be our savior, doesn't mean you don't *have* to be it. You've inspired people that there is a better way to live. You fought off that fucking Black Fog by *yourself*! You don't think that's going to give people hope? They have every right to feel hope after that. They want to believe in something. They *need* to believe in something, in *someone*... and that someone is you, Soren Stormrose. Whether you want to admit that to yourself or not."

Soren sat, watching the young woman with her arms out, nearly yelling into his face. He listened, although he didn't enjoy the words. The world should look up to Lady Ellaina Drake, Mihelik Starshadow, even the young woman standing over him then. Soren had made too many awful mistakes in his life to repent for.

I'm nobody's hero.

A key slid into the lock from the outside of the door.

Soren wasn't alarmed, for a key was far different than a battering ram he would expect if it was soldiers.

Eve returned to her seat, with cheeks flushed and rubbing the back of her neck.

The door opened inward, and the pure white light of snow flooded the inside of the room. Davin was startled awake, clutching his ax at his side as it rested on the floor, tilted up on the wall. Einrick stomped in with heavy, snow-covered boots, and Roth entered behind. They shut the door quickly behind them, locking it soundly.

Soren tried to get a look at where they were, but all he saw was the falling snow, no buildings or trees, even.

"It's a full-on damned blizzard out there," Einrick said, running over to the wood oven in the far corner of the room.

"Take yer boots off," Eve said, groaning.

Einrick took off his boots, and threw his gloves to the ground, to warm them by the stove. Roth did the same.

"What did ya learn?" Davin asked, wiping the sleep out of his eye. Blood had soaked through the bandages on the other side of his face he'd been sleeping on.

"Well," Einrick said. "Glad I wore this thick coat and hood, because they're on to me now."

"What?" Seph asked, both her and Kaile standing in the doorway to the other room.

"You let that fool Garland live," Einrick said in a harsh voice, rubbing his shivering hands to calm them. "He and a couple of others saw us."

"Did they say if they saw us head underground?" Soren asked.

"Didn't hear anything about that," Einrick said. "But this snowstorm might be a blessing. Those soldiers sure do move a lot slower in a foot of snow and heavy armor. Although there are a *lot* of them out there."

"How's the storm help?" Kaile asked. "We can't travel much faster."

"Once we get out of the city," said Einrick, "the roads should be wide open."

"If we can see them," Davin said.

"We wait until dusk, then we head back under, and then out of the city," Einrick said. "And it looks like I'll be going with you, at least until we are out on the roads again."

"And I sent word to the lady and Mihelik," Roth said. "The raven is on its way."

"Good," Davin said, clearing his throat and picking up his pipe from the table. "Mind putting some water on while you're standing there, Einrick? Tea before wine, wine before sleep, sleep before coffee." He hummed the words to himself.

"What was that?" Seph asked him.

Davin gave a, "Hmm? Oh, that's just a little tune my ma used to sing to me when I was a boy."

"It is catchy," she said with a smirk, humming to herself.

Soren enjoyed the playfulness in Seph, with even Kaile yawning before giving a smile as she bobbed her head, singing the simple tune. She carried a pitch beautifully, Soren realized. He puffed his pipe, as Davin did while she sang the tune.

Enjoy this, for the winter roads and icy, howling winds call. Soon, it'll be nothing but freezing toes, struggling to make fires, and wrapping ourselves up in as much as possible.

And that's not mentioning the things that lurk in the night...

Chapter Six

The underbelly of the city was a different world. Unseen, forgotten, and rarely shown the light of day—it was dark, and miserable.

Their torches roared, pouring amber light before and behind them in the darkness, sending most of the rats scurrying away; but most of many still leaves many.

Seph screeched as a rat ran over her boot, and the cat hissed down at it from her shoulder.

"Was that a rat?" Kaile asked beside her, holding a torch, angling it down at the rat that ran behind and through Soren's legs. "That was as big as a dog!"

"I *hate* it down here," Seph said, scratching her forearms.

"At least it's warmer than up there," Kaile said.

"Aye," Davin said. "At least there's that."

"How far is it to the exit?" Soren asked, as they'd only been in the tunnel for ten minutes. His body ached, but it was slowly repairing itself. Whatever Eve had treated him with was soaking in—doing its work. His legs didn't feel as heavy, his hands had regained their strength, and his senses were alert. He was far from healed, but it was enough to work with.

"A few hours," Einrick said at the lead, turning back to look at Soren as he said that. Eve, Charles, and Roth were all in a pack with Einrick, with Seph and Kaile in the middle, and Soren and Davin walking side by side in the back. "There are a few spots we could exit safely, but the one we've chosen will have gear and horses ready."

Soren thought of Ursa, the horse that had been his companion most of the ten years he'd been alone, and he missed her. She was there with him over many a campfire. She was his friend, and they'd been through it all together. But she was left back at the burning of Erhil, and Soren wondered if she was even still alive out there, running through plains, meandering through forests, and drinking out of long-forgotten streams.

"Then how long will it be to Zatan?" Seph asked, pulling Kaile in tight by the arm as the rats watched her walk by with their hungry, black eyes.

"It's a hundred miles, maybe more to the Lyones Mountains," Soren said. "And depending if we take the mountains, or go to the south, around, will dictate that."

"I'm guessing the way around is easier," Seph said. "But has more eyes?"

"Yes," Soren said. "In our current situation, I'm guessing everyone here would say to take the mountain pass, even with Davin's spell."

"That would be true," Charles said. "Unless you had a good alibi."

Davin laughed, "And I assume we have one now."

"Yes," Charles said. "You won't be alone in the wagons."

"What?" Soren said in a harsh tone. "Your plan is to put others with us?"

"You're going to be merchants," Charles said. "Or at least, partly. You're going to be moving a sort of caravan."

"Might be better than four on horses," Kaile said, irking Soren. "They'll be looking for that."

"Of course they will," Soren said. He gritted his teeth. More than anything, he wanted to be alone, and to be with Ursa to find this Lord Belzaar, but Seph's insistence and persistence marked her as a true Whistlewillow. "So, tell me more about this plan…"

They walked through the dark tunnels, turning down passageways that Einrick and the other three decided on. The three of them laid out the plan for traveling as a merchant caravan—with actual merchants—to the south of the Lyones, where the end of the mountains touched the Sapphire Sea. Soren and the others would be able to rest, make camp with others, and be supplied with food and water. The road would take longer as a large group, but would be safer, and give Soren and Davin the rest to heal.

The more Soren heard, the more the plan grew on him. There was some merit to the thought of lying low after the battle with Glasse, and who in the Nine Hells would suspect Soren would head out into the barren desert, if what he truly wanted was revenge? He'd head north, toward Lynthyn, or back into Cascadia, his closest thing to home.

Then, sudden doubt rushed through him, deep into his core.

What if I'm wrong?

I try to be the man to take action, to follow my instincts, but for as much as they've led me true, they've also led me astray. And now I have Seph here with me. I can't let her down. I can't make any mistakes with her at my side.

Was he right about going into the desert? Was this mission the right one to take? Would the answer to this question be worth the risk?

Sadly, he knew there was only one way to find out. Whether he was wrong or not, he'd decided, and it appeared his comrades would travel into the abyss with him if that's what Soren had decided instead.

For hours they walked, with footsteps above scampering about, bell towers with huge bells ringing, and the sounds of hound dogs sniffing and barking. The one thing that shielded them underground from the dogs was the stream of murky water that flowed endlessly. It would hide their scent. But Soren's feet were completely soaked through the boots, and he assumed the others were as well. There's no way he'd let them go out into the frozen tundra with wet feet, but the way the young lads and lasses had laid out the escape plan for them, he assumed there was a plan for that.

They eventually reached a point where Einrick, Eve, Charles, and Roth stopped. It was a vast corridor with six converging tunnels. There was a ladder at its center, and gutter drains above. Through the rectangular drains that were laid into curbs above, harsh, whistling winds tore through. Soren saw the steam off all of their breaths, and from atop Seph's back, her cat shook the chill off.

Einrick and the others muttered between themselves, before deciding this would be the place to exit.

"Should be fine," Einrick said back to all of them. "Keep your weapons ready, but should be fine. Oh, and Kaile, if anyone comes down that ladder, that's not one of us... go ahead and kill them."

Kaile swallowed hard.

Roth was the first to climb the ladder, peering out through the drains first, then pushing the round, metal cover up and sliding it over. It skidded on the road above.

His head emerged out into the night air. A glow hit his face to the side, and Soren desperately wanted to know where they were, and what rested above. He didn't trust others to do the investigating for him, let alone these new ones that were so young. But they were Silver Sparrows, and Lady Drake and

Mihelik had proved to be right so far, at least with Kaile and Davin. So, Soren would trust them, at least, for now.

Roth looked all around above, twisting at the hip with both his feet still on the ladder. With a flick of his fingers at his hip, he waved for them to follow him up. He climbed all the way out, and Charles followed. Then Eve, then Einrick.

"I'm going first," Soren said. "Davin, you last." Davin nodded. "First, disguises though."

Each of them checked for their necklaces, touching them and the gemstones.

Davin held his pendant stone of eldrite through his shirt, it glowing a dark, deep shade of ocean blue, and then beamed a pale white under his thick, dwarfish hand. Soren felt the pixie-stone hum at the center of his chest.

As he watched the frazzled black hair on Seph's head lighten to an auburn, straighten and lengthen all the way to her rear, Soren was not only amazed at the spell of the dwarven stones, but irked by his lack of knowledge about it still.

Seph stood before him, completely transformed into a new woman. Kaile, too, stood three inches shorter, had short black hair and fair skin. Davin, at the rear of the pack, still muttering some enchanting words, had grown nearly twice his height to a stunning woman complete with all the right curves. Soren blinked, chuckling inside. He felt the scars on his face had vanished.

It was time to move.

Soren climbed the ladder, as Seph's cat leaped from her back to his, clawing its way up his back and onto his shoulder as he climbed.

He emerged above ground, quickly scanning the area.

The air still held the long chill of night, and the sky above was full of chalky white clouds. Thick snowflakes dwindled down from the heavens. Soren rose from the underground tunnels beneath Londindam to what appeared to be the outskirts of the city. They were filling an alleyway between two structures. The alleyway ran a couple hundred yards in length, and as Soren gazed east, he could see the lofty towers of the center of Londindam. Framed at the center of the mouth of the alley was the high-reaching Grandview Tower, from which Glasse had slithered down from before his explosive demise.

He reached down into the uncovered hole, grabbing Seph's arm and helping her up. The cat quickly leaped back to her proper human. Einrick was waiting beside the hole to the underground, while Eve, Charles, and Roth were at the other far end of the alley, standing out in the road, nonchalantly, hands in pockets.

"C'mon," Einrick said, waving for them to hurry up. "Got to get this lid back on and covered up."

Kaile and then Davin came back into the city, as Einrick slid the heavy iron cap back into place, shoving snow back over it.

"Are we following them?" Seph asked.

"Yes," Einrick said, "but first…" He reached into the inside coat pocket at his chest and pulled out a short stack of papers, all neatly folded, and still dry. "These are your papers. Kaile and Soren, you are laborers, helping to deliver cargo. Seph and Davin, since you're women, you're caregivers, and yes, you'll be expected to wash and cook during the journey."

"Cook?" Seph asked. "And they're expected to eat it? Well, that will blow my disguise right away."

"Just act the part," Einrick said. "It's only until you cross the border. Then you can do whatever you want. Until then, you're back to your cover names. Got it?"

"What kind of merchants are we with?" Kaile asked.

Einrick smirked. "Soren will like this. You're delivering a shipment of wine, ale, and barley. The caravan's main destination is a city called Taverras, but we tend to call it, the Brink."

"Last city before the Dyadric Desert," Soren said. "This caravan may be a good cover, after all."

At the far end of the alley, there was a commotion stirring in the direction of the three. Soren and the others snapped their attention that way, and Roth waved them over.

"Take these," Einrick said, inspecting each for the proper names before handing them out. "Take care of them, and for the sake of the goddess, don't lose them!"

Soren took his, and found his name, Victor LeSabre, there with a physical description of himself, and his role in the caravan. He tucked it snuggly away into his inner breast pocket. The others stashed theirs away too, rushing down the alley to meet the others.

"What is it?" Soren asked, hearing the shouting north.

"Don't know," Roth said. "But that's where the wagons are."

"How long do we have?" Soren asked.

"It's leaving soon," Roth said. "With or without you."

"Well, let's get going then," said Soren. "Don't want to be late for our ride outta this shithole of a city."

"Follow me," Roth said. "And act normal. There's more watching eyes than normal, and you've got the biggest bounty on your head these lands have ever seen."

Chapter Seven

The caravan was as welcoming a sight as Soren could've seen. Beneath the falling flurries of dancing snow were the three covered wagons, insulated with thick furs, already hooked up to the bridled horses, ready to plow through the thick snow. The horses that were set to pull the wagons were huge, far larger and stronger than steeds Soren would expect to see for traveling merchants.

The Silver Sparrows do have quite the reach, and fortitude, Soren thought. *This must have been the backup plan to the backup plan, and here it is—ready to roll out of the city.*

The shouting, however, was surely not in the plans.

Four soldiers were at the head of the caravan, by a middle-aged man, waving his hands at his sides as he defended himself against the barrage of commands by the angriest of the soldiers.

"Don't talk," Einrick said to Soren and the others. "Just get up into the last wagon like you've gotten in already a hundred times before. Don't speak unless spoken to, and don't talk back."

"And don't let them separate us," Seph said.

"Aye," Davin agreed.

The soldiers were dressed in silver armor, lined with furs of beavers and other rodents. Each fur was dotted with white snowflakes, and in the torchlight sparkling along the caravan, the snow looked serene, despite the nervousness Soren could feel in Kaile and Seph.

They walked toward the row of horses and wagons. There were the three wagons, each pulled by two horses, which stood a foot taller than the other six horses, all mounted by men. The wagons were covered with the thick furs, so Soren couldn't see on the inside, but they trudged through the snow to the last wagon in the row.

The shouting was loud enough that Soren didn't have to wonder what it was about. The loudest of soldiers yelled that they weren't allowed to leave the city under the current restrictions set by Lord Garriss of Greyhaven.

"No one is allowed to leave the city!" the soldier shouted, his gloved hands balled up into fists.

"But we have the documentation," the grizzly man of the caravan said back. "This ale will spoil if we don't get on the road today. We've planned for this for months, and all the documents were filed and approved through the clerk."

"I don't care if they were approved by the lord himself," the soldier barked back. "You're not leaving... not today!"

"C'mon," Einrick said, urging them to continue forward to the wagon. "Don't look at them, just act normal, like nothing's happening."

They walked with hoods up, nearing the wagon. Soren peered out of the corners of his eyes, just under the flaps of his hood. He usually did it to cover his scars, but this time to just make sure they didn't have any surprises.

Kaile was first to the wagon, drawing back the furs, putting a boot up onto the railing, grabbing the wooden frame, and pulling himself up.

"Hey," a soldier shouted.

Soren pressed Seph behind him gently, letting his finger swipe against Firelight's pommel, just to make sure she was ready if he needed her.

Eve, Roth, and Charles stood between the advancing pair of soldiers and Soren and the others. Kaile dropped back to the ground as the pair walked toward them. They walked past the other two wagons shortly and stood before Eve and the other two quickly.

"This wagon ain't goin' nowhere today," the soldier said, angry steam plumed past his dry lips.

"This caravan needs to be on its way," Roth said. "Ale's gonna go sour if it doesn't leave *today*."

"Not my problem," the soldier growled back.

"Not your problem?" Roth returned a growl. "Listen, I know you're doing your job, and the whole town is buzzing from the Black Fog, but we've still got our job to do."

The soldier's eyes softened at the mention of the Black Fog.

"By order of Lord Demetri Garriss, no one is to leave the city. Especially a fucking caravan!"

"This order is signed by Lady Sargoneth in Zatan," Roth said. "They already purchased all this load, and if it spoils or freezes, then it's gonna be a total waste of their money. How do you think she's gonna take that?"

"She'll have to understand," the soldier said. "Lord Garriss—"

"Lord Garriss is going to have to compensate her for this whole load," Roth said. "All the wasted merchandise, all the labor, time, horses, and all the rest. You think he'd rather get a bill from any angry lord in two weeks? Or we could just be on our way. It's already going to take us longer to get out of here in this storm. *And* it's already been signed and verified by Grayhaven. We are *expected* to leave, *right now!*"

The soldier looked to his partner, who gave him a raised eyebrow back.

"Let me see your papers…" the first soldier said.

Each of them brought out their papers and handed them to the soldier. Soren grabbed Seph's and handed it to the man, still keeping her behind him.

The soldier unfolded each and inspected them. The soldier and the man at the head of the caravan continued shouting. Inspecting the documents, the soldier looked back over his shoulder at the two shouting, grunted, and then inspected all of their faces.

The man stepped toward Soren, who struggled not to react. The soldier pulled Soren's hood down forcefully, eyeing his face. With a glower, the soldier shoved Soren back by the collar, holding their paperwork back out for them to take.

"Thanks," Einrick said.

The two soldiers stormed off to the front of the caravan. Eve, Charles, and Roth all followed.

"Up," Soren said, and Kaile rushed up into the wagon. Seph followed, and then Davin. Soren stayed out in the howling winds with Einrick, watching the argument.

"Just pay 'em," Einrick muttered.

"Agreed," Soren said.

They watched the argument unfold for another ten minutes, then something exchanged hands, and the soldiers slowly backed off. They backed up slowly, rumbling curses amongst themselves. The man at the lead mounted his horse, and Eve and the others stood between the soldiers and the caravan—as a sort of barrier, in case the soldiers had an unfortunate change of mind.

Soren turned to Einrick, and they shook hands. Soren trusted the man little, as a spy was possibly the least trustworthy you could have on your side—unless they were in your pocket.

But the man had led them that far, and was correct about his assertions and plans.

"Einrick," Soren simply said.

"Soren," he replied with a bow of his head.

Soren entered the wagon after. It was still brisk, and he saw his breath as the cover was open, but it was warm enough for him to sigh from the relief. With a wave of his hand, Kaile, who was sitting beside Seph, scooted away from her, and Soren sat in the tight spot Kaile had been. Soren quickly removed his boots and sopping wet socks.

In the wagon were the four of them all together, and two women who sat side by side next to Davin. They both averted their gazes and huddled together, both with a massive bear skin over their backs. The skin was so encompassing that it took Soren a moment to notice there was a child between one of the women and the back of the wagon. She was perhaps eight and glared up at Soren with inquisitive eyes.

Soren looked back at the girl. Her innocence and playful gaze reminded him of Seph all those years ago. He smirked and nodded. The girl smiled and shoved her face into the woman, who put her arm over her shoulder and pulled her in tight.

"Cute girl," Seph said to the two women.

The woman sitting directly before Seph opened her eyes to slits, just enough to see her, but then squeezed them tightly again.

Seph looked at Soren and Kaile. Soren said nothing, and Kaile just shrugged his shoulders. Suddenly, the wagon jolted, and the scraping of its wheels against the tall snow sounded beneath. Davin yawned and his head fell onto the front side of the wagon. He was snoring within a minute.

"Must be nice," Kaile said, removing his own boots and socks.

A candle burned between Davin and Kaile at the front. It

was a rocking light that gave the wagon a warmer feeling than it actually held. As the wagon rolled out of Grayhaven, the flickering light gave a relaxing feeling within. Seph yawned and rested her head against Soren. Kaile and Soren remained as the only two still awake.

Kaile shifted as if wanting to talk, but Soren kept his lips clamped tight.

"Did you mean what you said before?" Kaile finally asked, breaking past the crack in his voice.

"About what?" Soren asked, closing his eyes and tilting his head back.

Kaile cleared his throat and whispered. Whether it was from embarrassment or not wanting to wake the others, but by the tone in his voice, Soren guessed what Kaile was about to get confirmation of. "Are we really going to find him after all this?"

Soren knew he was talking about his brother Joseph, all the way on the other side of the continent—in Ikarus. They were so very far away from accomplishing their revenge, and saving what they could of the world, but Soren knew with absolute clarity his answer. "I promise you, we will."

Kaile relaxed in his seat quickly, didn't say another word, and was sound asleep within minutes.

Soren, again, was the one left awake. He wouldn't sleep. He knew that.

And again, he wondered if he was doing the right thing. But then again, what was the right thing? He only needed to do what was best to win their war. He thought there was no one right way. He just needed to stay alive and keep his friends safe.

But he also knew what was coming, or at least had an idea. King Amón was going to send out everything he had to kill Soren. It would be assassins, soldiers, lords, ladies, even the drakoons themselves. But Soren could handle all that. He could outfight and out-strategize any opponent. He knew what the real danger was. He knew, and the king knew, what Soren would be hardest pressed to withstand.

The Ellydian.

Soren feared that more than anything. And as he looked next to him, at the two Syncrons at both his sides, Soren grinned.

At least I've got them. At least we've got each other.

PART II
THE HUNTER BECOMES THE HUNTED

Chapter Eight

Hunters

The tiger, the lion, the bounty hunter.

All designed by nature to survive, and survival for the hunter means mastering the hunt.

Be wary where you swim and play, for the world has no shortage of means of death, but fate's cruelest irony is being hunted by your own. Assassins have plagued our world as long as the gods have been here to watch over us. And while their light shines upon us and guides us, so does the absence of light.

Where there is gold to be had, assassins and bounty hunters will always dwell. Those that master that calling are not easily evaded, for Aladran is a breeding ground for the merciless, the fearless, and the greedy.

-Translated *from the language of the Sundar. The Scriptures of the Ancients, Book III, Chapter X.*

. . .

It was as if they were cursed, and perhaps they were…

Throughout the ride in the wagon, not one word was spoken by the two women and the child to Soren and the others. Soon out onto the road, Soren had seen the glimpses of sunlight peeking through the cracks between the blankets of the wagon. They were thick enough as to not let it through, but when it did seep in, he relaxed, knowing the Demons of Dusk had retreated to their holes.

Soren was the only one who didn't sleep during that long ride. He dazed in and out, his head foggy, and his body rippling with sharp pain as the medicine's potency had waned. Seph slept soundly with the cat asleep half the time, the other half licking its paws or other, nether parts. Kaile slept too, accidentally resting his head on Soren's shoulder. Soren just rolled his eyes, trying not to think of the things that always went through his head when he couldn't sleep.

Once the wagon came to a halt, though, that's when the effects of the *curse* felt real. The two women and the child disembarked first out the back of the wagon, with two men holding the flaps open from the outside, letting the blinding sunlight pour in like pure gold filling the air.

The women didn't say a word, even hushing the child who breathed in Seph's direction while smiling at the cat on her lap. Soren was the first to follow the women out in the icy grasp of the winter winds. They gusted past as Soren pulled his hood back over his head. He was too used to hiding his scars, that he forgot, even as not a single soul in the caravan glanced his way, that the scars weren't there.

He helped Seph down next.

"Where are we?" she asked, shielding her eyes from the sunlight from directly above.

Soren saw the people of the caravan dismount and stretch

their legs and arms out, some yawning, and some getting to making two fires. They'd pulled just off the main road that led west of Grayhaven. Soren saw no other people along the long, snow-covered dirt road that was marked with piles of stones on both sides. They were in the middle of a vast tundra, one that bled white for as far as the eyes could see. To the very distant west, the tiniest caps of white mountaintops were blurred.

But not a single person talked to Soren, as Davin was the last to exit the wagon. Up at the head of the caravan, though, the bearded man who'd been yelling with the soldiers back in Grayhaven approached.

Soren and the others waited as he walked down the caravan, between the horses and the rocks stacked on the side of the road.

The crinkles at the corners of the man's eyes deepened as he stood before Soren, scanning him.

"They're not to speak to you, or you to them," he said. His voice was firm, but Soren could tell he was no fighter. Swords and training hadn't hardened this man. The world had. "We'll take ya to Taverras. Then we will split ways, and we'll most likely never see each other again."

Davin growled.

"It's all right," Soren said. "We understand. What would you like us to do?"

"Chop wood, make fires, don't speak to my people, and we'll be just fine with one another." The corner of the man's mouth quivered ever so slightly as he spoke.

Soren nodded. "What about food?"

"It'll be prepared by the women by the fires. You're welcome to your share, but…"

"…Don't talk to anyone," Seph said. "Got it."

"If you're any good at hunting, there's a few bows with good enough arrows," the man said.

"What about the Demons of Dusk?" Kaile asked. "Have you planned that out, where we'll stay, that is?"

The man nodded, glancing out at the tundra. "As long as they stay out here as they always have." He swallowed hard.

As long as… Soren thought. *That is quite a big hope now.*

"Get us to the Brink," Soren said. "And your end of whatever deal you made will be fulfilled."

The man nodded. "Good. The sooner we're rid of you, the better."

Soren reached out to shake the man's hand.

The man glanced down at it, unsure to take it or not. But he suddenly reached out, grabbed Soren's hand, shook it, and pulled Soren toward him. Soren let the man's mouth near his ear.

While bracing hands, the man whispered, "You may not have the scars now, but I know who you are. We are with you, but from the safety of secrecy. You're too dangerous a man to follow outright. But know that we, and many like us, are behind you. May the goddess watch over you."

The wrinkly eyed man pulled away, releasing his grip, and bowed his head subtly to each of them. He walked past them to his people, who were starting the fires and feeding the horses.

"What did he say?" Seph asked.

Soren smirked. "All the sudden, I don't think we're so alone in this fight."

And Soren felt just a little less cursed.

That day, they rested for a few hours before packing back up and being back on their way. After all, the tundra would be a terrible place to be when the veil of night wrapped herself around the lands.

Soren and the others ate and rested. Once the caravan was back on the path, though, they were in the same wagon as before, with the same two women and child. The cat couldn't hold back, and made its way onto the child's lap this time. The women didn't seem to mind, as long as the child paid attention to the cat, and not to Seph.

"You still need to name her," Kaile said. "If she's gonna stick around, we can't just be calling her cat all the time."

"I know," Seph said, her voice shaking from the bumpy ride. "I'm waiting for it to come to me, though. Nothing stands out, so it's nothing for now."

They didn't talk for quite some time, sitting in the darkness behind the thick animal furs. The candlelight that flickered within caused Soren to go to a dazed, dark place. Sleep's tendrils teased taking his mind, but sleep couldn't find him. His eyelids were nearly impossible to keep up, and he lay his head back, ready for it to take him. But it was the thoughts within that kept him awake.

The pain in his body—in the cuts behind his knees, in his armpits, and on the sides of his groin—were the worst. With his head back, eyes closed, he saw the warm glow of candlelight through his eyelids. As it flickered, it reminded him of fire —terrible fire.

Cirella. Oh, Cirella. How things could've been so different. If you were here, you'd know what to do. You always knew what was best. I'd give anything to see you again, to hear your laugh, to hold you once more...

Then his thoughts drifted to Alicen.

That wretch. That whore! She sold out everyone and everything in that town. Thousands are dead because of her, and for her to cry to me, asking for forgiveness. She needs to pray. She needs to ask those poor, butchered souls for forgiveness, not me.

Soren shook awake, startled at his thoughts, and realized he'd been dreaming. If only for a moment, it was enough for him to have to wipe the thin line of drool off his chin.

"Keep sleeping, uncle," Seph said. "It's my turn to keep watch."

He arched a brow at her, and then put his arm up and over her, behind her head. "I know you will."

He pressed the side of his head to hers.

Soren didn't catch a full sleep, but he got enough that his eyelids didn't weigh down like iron.

His knee bobbed as the day went on, and he knew night was approaching. Kaile's stomach rumbled beside him. An owl hooted far in the distance. The cat stretched its legs, walking over the two women toward Davin.

The caravan slowed, eventually coming to a halt. The horses neighed, and the sounds of lively footsteps pattered around. Seph folded one flap back, and Soren felt relaxed as he saw the trees. All around them—gorgeous, safe, trees.

But before Seph could get down from her seat, the leader of the caravan came up with another man. They carried two packs. The bearded leader with the crinkly eyes held up one pack for Seph to take, and then the other.

"What're these?" she asked.

"Supplies for the road ahead," he said. "From our acquaintance. Figured I'd give them to ya now. Warm clothes in there."

"Thanks." She nodded, and he began helping the child and the women down, quickly rushing back off.

They went through the packs, Seph through one, and Kaile through the other. Each of them was excited to see fresh boots for each of them, all wool lined on the inside, and made with sealed leather on the outside. As they all put them on, with fresh, new socks, they all let out pleased sighs. Soren wiggled his toes to find the boot fit perfectly.

"Fine tailors and cordwainers in Skylark," Kaile said.

"What else is in there?" Davin asked. "Tobacco? Wine?"

Kaile pulled out a pouch of tobacco and handed it to Davin, who sniffed it heartily, grinning widely.

"No weapons," Soren said. "And no notes. Smart, don't want to have any evidence of anything."

"New clothes is all," Kaile said, answering Davin's question. "No wine, and no food."

"Clothes will do!" Seph said. "I'm tired of stinking like a sewer."

Chapter Nine

The tree branches overhead scraped together as the winds blew by. The sound soothed Soren. A hawk flew high overhead in front of the moon as he gazed up at the star, interwoven past the myriad of rubbing branches. Even the bats that flew chaotically within the trees were a welcome sight.

They'd made it safely out of Grayhaven after finishing their mission. Glasse was dead. One down, many to go. And now they were safely out in the wilds, back to the safety of the trees and forests. The Black Fog and Shades were out there—multiplying even—but for the night, Soren felt as if they could rest easy.

Soren, Seph, Kaile, and Davin all sat at their own fire, away from the other two fire pits. They sat in their disguises, in more jovial moods than they'd had in days. The one problem with the caravan, Soren realized, was that it was an actual shipment of product to the Brink. None of the vast amount of wine and ale in the casks was to be consumed during the trip.

So Soren and Davin puffed their pipes of tobacco instead. Soren dearly missed wine to wet his throat.

They had lighthearted conversation about the road and their new clothes. The others brought them roasted potatoes and squash to eat, which was far more appetizing than they'd anticipated. The squash was finished with honey and the potatoes were slathered in butter and salt after being cooked.

"Not bad," Davin said. "Not bad at all."

They munched as the fire crackled and popped, Kaile stoking it with a branch. A child came over from one of the other fires, holding out a bag for them to take. Seph took it with a smile and a nod. The child only glanced at her, half weary-half curious, and then ran back.

"Is this what I think it is?" she asked herself, licking her lips.

Soren grinned as he watched her unfold the bag to reveal four chocolates in the palm of her hand. Her eyes widened as she glared at the four pearls of rich-smelling chocolate. She then closed her eyes and inhaled deeply, letting out a deep sigh from her core.

She held it out toward Soren and stood to deliver his to him, but he waved her away.

"You can have mine," he said.

"You sure?"

He nodded.

She continued standing to go to the other two.

"No. You go ahead, lass," Davin said. "It's all yours."

Kaile smiled, stoking the fire. "Have mine."

She stood in place, cocking her head.

"You sure?" Her voice revealed sincerity, but also the urge to eat all four, if they were offering. "You don't mind."

"They're all yours," Kaile said. "By the magical look in your eyes, I can tell they'd be wasted on us. You look you're about to fly off into the air, like a butterfly, or a dragon."

She gushed, nodding, and popped the first into her mouth. Her jaws squished down onto the first chocolate, and her whole body gave. It relaxed, and she sat back, moaning in ecstasy.

Soren glowered at Kaile as he watched her, with a far too pleasant a look on his face.

As Seph ate, Soren had a question for Kaile that he longed to know the answer to—the real answer.

Soren shifted on the log he sat upon. Pointing his knees toward Kaile, Davin noticed, watching with a keen eye as he puffed his pipe.

Kaile took far too long to notice, as he was entranced by the glee brimming in Seph. Davin cleared his throat, and Kaile looked at him, who flicked his chin toward Soren. Kaile finally saw Soren and gulped.

Soren was bent over with his elbows on his thighs, only a few feet from Kaile. The firelight radiated on both of them as Soren drew a long drag from the pipe, blowing it between the two of them.

Kaile fidgeted with his fingers in his lap.

"There's something I want to ask you," Soren said. "We're stuck in this whole mess together now, and you know quite a bit about our pasts, but I know little of yours."

Kaile tussled his hair, scratching his head nervously. "Oh."

"What happened in Ikarus?" Soren asked, and both Davin and Seph watched eagerly. "Why did Alcarond choose you as his apprentice? There must have been something in you that he knew could grow to rival the most powerful Syncrons in all of Aladran. How did he know that about you? I've never heard a whisper about it, and here you are—the apprentice to the archmage himself, at our fire."

"I don't want to talk about it," Kaile said. "Nothing happened. He just found me and took me away. That's it."

"Bullshit," Seph said, rolling her eyes. "Don't feed us that. We deserve to know. And we're here for you now. You're not alone anymore."

Kaile's demeanor grew dark as he retreated into himself.

His shoulder drew forward and his chest caved. His eyes softened as he glared at the fire. "I don't want to talk about it…"

"Kaile," Soren said, leaning over and putting his hand on the boy's knee. Kaile didn't even seem to notice the touch, though. "We've only known each other a short time now, but you need to tell us what happened. We're all about to get murdered together, or save the fucking world together. And Alcarond is the most powerful being alive. I need to know what he saw, sees, in you. Because if we're going to face him, as Glasse said, he'd surely be after you, then we need to know. It's important."

Kaile clamped down on his quivering jaw and cleared his throat.

"It's all right, Kaile," Seph said. "Whatever happened, you can tell us. We won't judge."

"You say that now," he said, giving her a somber glance.

"I mean it," she said. "I fear by the end of this, we'll all have done terrible things."

Soren scratched his thigh.

You have no idea, Seph…

"Tell us," she said. "It's all right…"

He breathed in deep and took a great, shaky exhale.

"I was ten." He reached over to Davin to hand him his pipe, which Davin quickly ashed, loaded with fresh tobacco, and handed to him. Kaile lit the leaves with a fiery twig, and with a deep inhale, his shaking nerves calmed. "I'm from a town called Krakoa."

"Never heard of it," Seph said.

"It's small," Kaile said. "All the families knew each other and were in each other's business, but it's a beautiful place. It really is. The water in summer is as clear as glass, and in the winter is as deep a blue as you could imagine. It's paradise in a way, but that beauty hides a darkness underneath."

The cat rose from Seph, stretching her legs, and with her tail curling, went over and sat in Kaile's lap.

"What kind of darkness?" Soren asked.

"My family has a sickness," Kaile said. "I don't know if it's born into us, or if my parents got it somehow else, but my parents… they aren't nice people, and they certainly aren't good parents. So I took to raising my brother the best I could, but I was only a boy still." He grabbed his hair, lowered his gaze, and shook his head. "He's still there. He's still there alone with them."

Seph and Soren looked at one another, unsure what to say or do for him.

"Go on," Davin said.

Kaile looked lost, deep in his thoughts.

"When did you know you had the Ellydian in you?" Soren asked.

Kaile stirred back to life at that word, petting the cat from head to tail with one hand and smoking the pipe with the other.

"Around six, I'd guess. Things started happening when I got upset. I thought I was cursed at first, or losing my mind. It was terrifying. It really was."

"That's common," Soren said. "Especially for someone as powerful as you."

"You know, Soren," Kaile said. "When I was a boy, I looked up to you."

Soren feigned a smile and nodded. He didn't like to think about those days anymore.

"Soren Stormrose of Tourmielle. The greatest soldier in all of Aladran," Kaile said. "Tales got all the way to Ikarus of your battles. I imagined you were seven feet tall, three hundred pounds of muscle, and had a cape of gold. I wanted to be just like you." He laughed. "I'd swing a piece of wood around like it was a training sword. I wanted to learn how to fight, but I was surrounded by fishermen. But I didn't want to grow up to be like them. I especially didn't want to be like my father. There might be a part of me that loved him, but I think I gave that up pretty early. There were too many beatings, and I couldn't take them all for everyone. I couldn't be there all the time…"

"I'm sorry, Kaile," Seph said.

"Eh, fuck him," Kaile said, dragging deeply off the pipe.

"So, what happened?" Soren asked. "What happened when you first started realizing you had the Ellydian in you?"

Kaile's eyes narrowed. "The first time I remember anything, was when there was a fat man playing a flute by the water. He was in a boat, waiting to head out into the sea, or maybe it was coming back, but my father came out swinging. He was drunk or on something, or both. He was on my mother so bad they spilled out of the house and into the street. She was praying to the goddess for mercy, and he was hitting her with his fists. I was so mad. I can't describe with words the feeling of watching something like that. I think I was crying, but I couldn't move. I wanted to run to her. My mother is far from perfect either, but I wanted to kill my father right then and there. And I don't remember what happened, but it was described to me later. They said there was a wooden mast that was laying nearby, and whether the goddess heard my mother's cries, or if a rogue wind picked it up—it launched through the air, crashing into my father's side as he was on top of my mother, beating her. It hit him so hard it broke ribs and sent him flying off her. I heard the fucker was knocked out so hard he snored loud enough that they heard him all the way a town over." Kaile laughed darkly.

"That's terrible," Seph said.

"Well, it got him to stop. And I'm pretty sure he didn't beat her out in the street ever again after that. It was all inside. Maybe he laid off her for a while after that too, but who knows, he probably blamed her for it. My mother withdrew at some point. I don't know if it was after that, or because of that, or whatever, but she wasn't a mother anymore. She laid in bed, she read her scriptures, and everything good or bad in the world was all because of good or evil. So when there was evil in us—she sure as anything made sure to purge that evil from us."

He coughed, shaking his head and ashing his pipe. "I don't really want to go into that, though. Let's just say when you think the actual devil is in your child, I guess that gives you permission to do whatever you think is necessary to get it out."

Seph covered her mouth with both hands, muttering to herself.

"This is all beside the point," Kaile said. "Sorry. It's hard for me to focus when I think about that stuff, and I hate talking about it more than anything. Worse—because they're still there. They're still alive, and Joseph is still with them. It's been seven or eight years now. I doubt he's the same brother I knew back then."

There was a long pause as the branches scraped over them, the harsh tundra winds blew hard, and there were the murmurs over at the other fires.

"So when does Alcarond come in?" Soren asked. "I can only imagine the sight of the archmage in your small town, when you have so much pain like that in your life."

"I still remember the first time I saw him," Kaile said. "I thought, if there were gods that walked among us, he must be one of them…"

Seph sat entranced, the firelight radiating off her face and glowing in her eyes. She didn't look as she normally did, still locked in Davin's disguise spell, but Soren watched her curiously. She was new to the world of the Ellydian, except for the words written in Cirella's journal.

There is so much to learn. She has no idea yet.

"What caused him to arrive in Ikarus?" Davin asked. "You? Or something else?"

Kaile sighed. "This is the part I really hate talking about. Yes, it was me, and what I did. The archmage arrived days later, maybe weeks even. But when he arrived on the largest, most incredible ship I'd ever seen, I knew everything changed."

"So, what happened, Kaile?" Seph asked, her eyes still beaming.

"I knew I had this power in me by then. I was ten. I'd seen it, and even tried to use and control it. Little things, lifting rocks, changing the direction the water swirled. Little stuff, nothing to anyone. That beam that broke my father's ribs was the only thing I'd ever done that had real power to it. And that ended up being blamed on sea winds. But the one time I actually tried to use it. The one time I tried to use it to help someone."

He exhaled, he rubbed his chin, then scratched his neck. He tried to light the pipe, but found it empty.

"Here, son," Davin said, holding his hand out as Kaile handed it to him.

"Go on," Soren said. "We've all done things we're not proud of."

"Aye," Davin said, stuffing the pipe with fresh tobacco and handing it back over.

"There... there was an accident," Kaile said, lighting the pipe, his fingers slightly trembling. "They were trying to go out, but a storm was coming in fast. Don't know why. They could've just gone out the next day, or they thought they'd get the big load since no one else was out. But for whatever reason, the three men on the ship set off into the choppy water. I sat there watching them from the dock. My parents were getting into it again, so Joseph and I watched the men paddle out."

The pipe slid between his lips, and he inhaled as the tobacco crackled and burned. He let out a slow exhale. He laughed, not of happiness, not of anything funny. It was that glint of remembrance. The tightly held memory that pops up once every few years, just enough to not forget. And when it returned, it swept you back to the past, enjoying a moment that could've been forgotten like so many other thousand moments, but this one stayed.

"I remember Joseph next to me. We were sitting on a box. I had a sealskin over us. We just sat there in the spring rain, listening to the thunder, watching the never-ending sea. And we watched the men go out onto the water. There were no parents, no one was fighting. It was just us, the rain, and the sea."

They waited for him as he paused, after enjoying the moment.

"All right. So, the men went out, or tried to, against the waves. But the goddess had other plans for them that day." His tone turned sour, and turned darker. "The waves got big, as big as I'd ever seen them, and they were in trouble. Eventually they tried coming back, but an enormous wave hit them starboard side, and they took on water. When a boat gets that heavy, it's impossible to paddle in waves like that. They panicked, yelling for help, but they were far out. Joseph and I were the only ones out to see it. I made Joseph run for help, and I decided to stay. I thought that if I tried really hard, then I might be able to help. They were so far out, I didn't think any other boats would risk the storm. But I was only ten. I was just a boy."

"Go on," Seph said. "It's all right. It's just us here."

"Joseph ran to get help, and I just remember standing there, at the edge of the dock. My hands were out, and the waves were enormous. I don't remember ever seeing waves like that. The storm was deafening. I've heard of storms like that far out at sea, but they never came in like that. A wave eventually crashed over the boat, flipping it over, while the three men panicked in the water."

"You used the Ellydian," Seph said.

"I'd used it before, and knew that music had to be around for it to work," he said. "So I hummed a note, any note, I didn't know the difference. I think in hindsight, it was a D Minor, maybe blued all over the place, though. I couldn't hum a clear note, and I was definitely panicking. But those are just excuses." He sighed. "I should've been better, or I should've waited for help, or... I don't know..."

"What happened, Kaile?" Soren asked.

"I hummed the note." He swallowed hard, years of deep sadness welling in his eyes. "And I tried to pull the men in, but it all went crazy. I don't know how it happened."

"What? What happened?" Soren pressed.

"Fire," Kaile said, pulling back the sleeve of his right arm to reveal the old scars from the wrist to elbow. On the underside, they were deep and cracked. "Fire... everywhere. It was so hot, and so instant, that I thought I'd died. I thought that if it wasn't a nightmare I was in, then it had to be it. I remember calling out to Joseph, telling him I'm sorry I wouldn't be there anymore." He shook his head, letting out a laugh into his hands. "Isn't that messed up? A ten-year-old boy who, with his last breath, apologizes that he can't protect his little brother from his parents anymore?"

They waited as his laughter turned dark, and then faded to an eerie calm.

"What was the fire?" Seph finally asked. "What did you do?"

"The fire?" Kaile said with hollow words, as if far off in a trance. "It burned so hot that the sea hissed like the goddess was gasping for breath. Steam poured up into the sky. The sea... the sea was on fire. It was everywhere. All I could see were the flames. They rose so high it filled my vision. And the men... they didn't die from drowning. Their bodies were pulled up later. Eyeballs burned out; hair burned off their heads. It wasn't the sea or the storm that killed them. It was me. I killed those men."

"You tried to save them," Seph said. "It wasn't your fault."

"No. It was my fault," Kaile said. "They might've lived. It was just a storm. They were just waves. They were strong swimmers. I knew those men my whole life. They could've made it, but I tried something completely foolish, and I murdered them."

"You set the sea on fire?" Soren asked, astonishment rife in his words.

Kaile nodded.

"That's what brought Alcarond to find you?" Soren asked.

Kaile nodded again. "Everyone heard about it. The boy who set the sea on fire. That was the story, instead of me murdering those men. Word spread so quickly to the capital that Alcarond appeared in Krakoa within a week."

"That week, I was treated like a monster," Kaile said. "Which I probably deserved. No one understood. They'd heard of Syncrons and Synths before, but never seen anything in their town like that. They thought the devil had awoken in me. My father and mother beat me so bad; I couldn't walk or eat real food. My jaw broke, my legs were bruised purple, and patches of my hair were yanked out. But when *he* came... he wore long, clean blue robes with gold that made him look like he floated down from the ship. I remember I was lying on the dock, half awake. I was thirsty. I remember that because my lips were cracked, and I had a bad sunburn on my forehead and nose. I guess I'd been left outside all those days, too."

"That's terrible," Seph said. "What kind of parents would do that to their own child?"

"I thought they all did," Kaile said.

"So, Alcarond came and took you with him? But not Joseph?" Soren asked.

"Yup," Kaile said. "Paid my parents something. I'm sure

my father was happy to be rid of me, and maybe get some torrens for it. And you know what's worse? I was happy to go. I wanted to leave. I hated my life. I hated where I lived. I hated who I was becoming. I was full of hate. Every hour I was awake, I tried to drown it out, but it was just a part of me. Too many beatings, too much torture. Humans just aren't meant to live through that kind of thing. I worried that if I continued to live there, then I'd just end up like them. I'd destroy the things I loved, resent them even."

"But Alcarond wouldn't take your brother?" Soren asked. "Why?"

"My parents wouldn't let him go."

"But he's the archmage," Soren said. "He could do whatever he wanted."

"I don't know," Kaile said. "I've spent many sleepless nights thinking that exact same thing. Maybe it was a head game for the archmage... a control tactic, or maybe it was as simple as he didn't need Joseph. He just needed the ten-year-old who could set the sea on fire. Maybe he wanted to train me to set the *world* on fire if the king wished it."

A shiver ran down Soren's neck, through his spine, and down to the tips of his toes.

Was it the king's wish? Of course it was...

"I'm so sorry, Kaile," Seph said.

"Aye," Davin said. "That's about as hard a hand dealt, I can remember, and quite ironic that it was you being so powerful that helped and hurt you so much."

"I just tried to be as good of an apprentice as I could after that. I wanted to be good enough that I would never do that again—not be in control of my power, and hurt innocent people. I want to help people who need it, not hurt."

"You're doing that now," Seph said. "I've seen it. You saved us. There's no way we would've killed Glasse without you."

Kaile didn't respond, only hunched over with his chin on

his hands, glaring into the fire. A deep look of remorse was thick in his eyes.

"That's one reason I ran after you into Mihelik's portal. I saw those people being slaughtered like that by the king, and I just couldn't handle it. I felt like I was that little boy again, and the fire was too much. I'd rather die than be a part of evil like that. I threw it all away, and I don't regret that, but I worry that Alcarond is going to have my brother hurt, just to hurt me."

"Would he do that?" Seph asked.

"You don't know him like I do." Kaile's voice was full of hurt. "Alcarond isn't an evil man, not like the king or the Knight Wolf, but he's the smartest, most cunning person I met in all my years in the capital, and that says a lot."

"We're going to have to deal with him, too," Soren said, as if speaking to himself. "They're all going to have to be dealt with if we're going to win this war."

"Well, you remember what Glasse said," Seph itched her cheek. "He's going to come for Kaile, sooner than we think."

"Well, if that's true," Soren said, looking at Kaile, waiting for Kaile to return the gaze. "Then you'd better be ready. Because you're the only one who's going to be able to stop him."

"Me?" Kaile asked with both eyebrows raised.

"Yes, Kaile, you," Soren said. "When and if the archmage comes, you will be our only chance of defeating him."

The revelation washed over Kaile like a thick fog. His skin flushed and his lips parted.

"You'd better get to training Seph, too," Soren said. "There's a lot to learn for her, and not a lot of time…"

Chapter Ten

A bluebird darted over playfully, chirping a sweet, melodic tune. Another followed. They flew around one another, chirping away as if they hadn't a care in the world. A warming sun melted the snow at their feet, as Soren and Seph walked out of the caravan toward a hill to the north.

The melting snow crunched under their boots, and Soren pulled down his hood to feel the warmth on his skin. Davin and Kaile were just behind them, and just close enough for Davin's disguise spell to keep hold. Soren and Seph both had quivers on their backs, with bows in their hands. The bows were not of quality design, but Soren hadn't expected them to have been made that way. Any weaponry in the caravan was cheap. He saw chipped blades, rusty knives, and these brittle bows.

For hunting men, they'd surely fail, but for game, they'd do.

The air was still, and the chirping above rang down like a heavenly tune. They climbed the short hill, descending into a thicket. It grew dense, far ahead, but was easy to traverse at first, through the sparse, thin trees and shrubs on its outskirts.

"Step easy," Soren said. "They'll hear the snow. Step on anything else if you can, and walk slowly."

"What're we hunting out here?" Seph asked, holding an arrow loosely on the bowstring.

"Whatever we can eat," Soren said. "Lady Drake may have paid for our tickets to Zatan, but we should pay our way, our own way, if we can."

"Shouldn't I be learning about my power?" Seph asked. "I could hunt with the Ellydian."

"Well, I don't know how to teach you about that," Soren said. "And besides, we don't need an exploded deer. We need one intact."

She laughed, looked back at their friends, and raised an eyebrow as she asked, "If he's so powerful, why hasn't he attempted the Black Sacrament? He could be a Lyre. He could create portals like Mihelik did, and only the goddess knows what else."

"Again…" Soren said grimly. "Explosion."

"But he wouldn't fail like Glasse," she said. "He'd succeed. I know he would!"

"But… what if he *didn't?*"

She didn't reply, frowning down at the ground.

"He would," she muttered to herself. "He'd do it."

"Ever killed anything before?" he asked, pulling the arrow back on his bowstring, testing it, and getting a feeling for it.

"A couple mice," she said with a twisted expression. "I hated it."

"Men are much different from mice," he said, not looking at her, as they both walked side by side through the thicket. The snow had melted enough, especially in the less shaded areas, that they moved quieter, over hard ground.

"I know," she said, forcing the words from her throat.

"You could've killed Glasse," Soren said. He made the words as delicate as he could.

She didn't answer, but he could feel her grow tense. Her hand tightened on the bow, and she drew it back ever so slightly.

He didn't press the issue.

"See anything?" he asked.

"Just birds."

As they made their way into the thicket, and as it grew denser, more branches tugged at their coats as they stalked in. Davin and Kaile were in quiet conversation as they followed behind. Soren and Seph both scanned the woods, with sunlight twinkling down, reflecting off the wet leaves and slick trunks.

Suddenly, a bush rustled ahead. They both froze, not speaking a word. The bush was ahead, twenty yards out. They watched and waited.

"Get a clear shot," Soren whispered, turning behind him, raising his hand, making them stay back—which they quickly gathered. "You'll only get one chance."

Out from under the bush, something moved. Against the white snow, the brown dead grass, and the mud—black feathers emerged.

"A grouse," Soren said. "Get a clear shot, aim true, and take your shot."

Seph took a slow step to her left, pulling the nock back in the bowstring. She closed one eye, aiming with the other down the shaft of the arrow. The grouse stayed at the edge of the bush, cocking its head.

"When you're ready," he said, "shoot."

Seph took a deep breath, held it in, and let the arrow fly with a *fwap* of the bowstring. The arrow whizzed through the air, hurtling at the bird. It landed in the bush with a rustling sound, and the grouse took off into the air, leaving the arrow behind.

"Fuck," she yelled.

Soren raised his bow, drew his arrow back, and less than a

second after aiming, let the arrow fly. It zipped through the cold air, flying up into the sky as the grouse flapped its wings, flying upward quickly. The arrow plunged through its chest, knocking it back out of the air, falling back to the ground. Seph looked at Soren with wide eyes and a slack mouth.

"You'll get the next one," Soren said.

"All right," Davin said, catching up with them. "Hot meat for dinner! Excellent shot, Soren."

Kaile and Seph exchanged glances.

"Did you know he was like that with a bow, too? Not just a dagger?" Kaile asked. Seph glowered in return. "Of course he is…" Kaile laughed.

They searched for another half an hour, but found nothing except a small bird flying high in the trees. They made their way back to the caravan, with Soren carrying the grouse, looking at his footing as he walked through the melting snow. And once he could see the end of the thicket appearing, and the hill which hid the caravan on its backside—something caught his eye. Something troubling.

He paused, inspecting the ground, and stepping back.

Seph was the first to notice. "What is it?"

Soren knelt, laying the grouse on the ground beside him.

Davin joined him at his side and knelt, looking with his one unbandaged eye at the ground as well.

"What do you think that means?" Davin asked, worry in his voice.

Soren was looking at a set of prints. He pointed down at them, analyzing them for the others to see.

"Three clawed toes in front, and one in back. This over here with the long drag is the tail." Soren looked up above, with the thin trees swaying above.

"Shades," Seph said, itching her elbow. "They're… they're in the trees?"

Soren groaned.

"Wait," Kaile said, with a gulp. "They're coming into the forest now? They've never done that before."

"Well, there was never a Black Fog in the middle of a city either," Seph said.

"I'm well aware," Kaile replied.

"Glasse did something," Soren said. "When he summoned that fog, however he did, it looks as if he changed the game. The Shades are testing the forests now, because, you can see— they came in this way, and left this way. Maybe three of them."

"But..." Kaile said. "That would mean we aren't safe in the forests anymore from them. Where will people hide?"

"Cities won't be safe forever either," Davin said.

"This is bad," Seph said.

Soren put his hand on Firelight's grip.

This is the only known weapon to fight against these monsters, and I can't fight them all. If the Shades begin killing in the forests, what would keep the fog from doing the same?

"This is bad," Seph repeated. "This is really fucking bad."

"We need to get the caravan moving," Soren said. "We've got to get to a town. I fear the forests won't protect us like they used to. Not for much longer. The Shades are testing now, but what's to keep them from getting braver when they're hungry?"

"We need to get this caravan moving," Davin said.

"Aye," Soren said, as he picked the grouse up and they all walked up over the hill and back down to the caravan.

The women were busy feeding the horses, playing with the children, while the men rested and ate.

Soren and the others walked toward the ring of men eating their lunch. Soren stopped beyond the group, staring at the bearded man who led the caravan. He caught Soren's glare and groaned, setting his food down. He walked past the men and to Soren. The man put his hand on Soren's back, to turn him away from the men.

"What is it?" the man asked.

Soren told him about the Shades, and his worry for not only the caravan, but for all of Aladran.

The bearded man's face flushed, rubbing his eyebrow.

"How will we travel?" he muttered. "How will we do business? How will anyone do business? There won't be anywhere to hide from those things." His eyes darted around at the ground.

Soren put his hand on the back of the man's neck, squeezing.

"I'll figure something out," Soren said.

The man looked up at Soren with his brow wrinkling and his eyes wide.

"You?"

"I'll figure something out. There has to be a way to stop them."

"Soren Stormrose," the man said in awe. "You truly are the hero they speak of. You're going to save us from the Demons of Dusk?" The man's eyes wetted. "Shirava sent you from the Halls of Everice to watch over us, didn't she?"

"No, she did not. I'm just me."

"I don't believe you," he said. "I think you were sent here for a reason. You're going to save us."

"I could die if this grouse gives me worms," Soren said, feigning a laugh.

The man grabbed Soren by both arms, his eyes piercing and his grip intense.

"Protect us," he said. "Protect my people. There are women and children here with us. If those... things... come... they won't stop until we're all dead. Please, Soren, protect us..."

Soren sighed. "I'll try."

"Then that has to be enough," the man said, clapping both of Soren's shoulders before walking off back to the men.

Seph, Kaile, and Davin all stood behind Soren, with the cat snaking between their legs.

They didn't know what to say, so they said nothing.

It was all too heavy. Everyone knew Soren couldn't protect the whole world from the Demons of Dusk, and the magic of the Ellydian was useless upon them.

They were entering a new world, Soren knew, one there was possibly no going back from. No walls could keep the monstrous, raw power of the Black Fog away, especially the size of the one in Greyhaven. And the real dread tore into Soren's core. If the fog multiplied the number of Shades by killing more people in the cities and in the forests, it wouldn't take long for the whole world to be overrun.

There had to be a solution. There had to be a way.

I wish Mihelik was here with us. I need to speak with him. He might know a way. He might help me think of a way through this.

But Mihelik wasn't. He was hundreds of miles away, back in Skylark. But Soren had three comrades with him, and whose trust was growing with each day.

This is enough. This has to be enough. We will find a way to fix this. Because we have to.

Chapter Eleven

Soren sat on the outskirts of the forest, watching the night plains under the sky of dark clouds that stretched out like charcoal-dusted cotton. The snow had melted over the three days and nights the caravan had traveled since the revelation about the Shades entering the forest. During that time, Soren had taken up the mantle of protector of the caravan during those nights.

He slept when he could during the day. An hour here, ten minutes there. But at night, the fatigue of weariness was rare. He had a job to do. If the Shades came, he'd be the only chance all those people would have. Firelight was the only thing that could stop them, so he kept her close, and his gaze vigilant.

Out in the distance, on the western rolling hills of Londindam—Black Fog were out there—scouring, hunting, hungry. Out on the rolling plains, he counted eight of them. They were spread out in the distance. The nearest one being a half mile out, and the furthest, perhaps ten.

They slunk like worms. Their black, smoky bodies hid their ferocious natures, and Soren was reminded of the monstrous one that Glasse called into Greyhaven. The thought made the cuts on his body sear in pain. Soren was barely able to survive the attack and send the fog back off out of the city. He wondered what he'd have to do to kill one. But Firelight was so very small, and the fog was the ultimate death-bringer of Aladran.

My only chance would be to pierce that soft, watery membrane beneath its black body.

But it was so deep. How would he get the chance to get in that close again? He wondered if the fog remembered him, and if it would tell the others, if they had brains that could communicate at all…

Soren thought he may have seen a pack of Shades to the northeast, scampering down a cliff into the grassy plains, but at that distance, he couldn't be sure. It could've been rocks falling or deer running.

The world Soren knew had changed so much over not only the last ten years, but twenty, thirty even. The Demons of Dusk had changed everything.

The night brought with it absolute terror now. The things that lurked in the dark were pure death. If anyone was unfortunate enough to be spotted by those things, they were devoured and cut to pieces by the Shades. Soren knew he was the sole person who'd defeated any of them, and it was all because of the Vellice dagger at his hip. And he desperately needed to know who made the order to deliver it to him.

He wondered if he'd recognize who it was, or if it was some random lord who thought he may be the one to fight the Demons of Dusk. Or was it all just a coincidence? He didn't think so. And if this person did know Firelight could hurt these monsters, what else did they know? That question bored deep into Soren. He had to know the answer. He absolutely had to know the answers.

Behind him suddenly, he felt something at his back. It slid

along his spine gently and casually let out a rumbling purr. Soren turned and picked the cat up and placed her on his lap.

"Snuck up on me, didn't ya?"

He pet her head and she moved back and forth between his legs, eventually settling into a ball, and dozing off.

"Came a long way up here from Seph to come see me," he said, slowly petting her soft fur. He welcomed the company as he watched the fog hunt.

Soren wondered what the future held. Was this it? Would there be only Demons of Dusk in a new world? Or would they somehow figure out a way to drive them from Aladran? Making the world safe again? Even the evil king would want them gone, Soren thought. But then that brought up the other, more pervasive question—how and why did Glasse summon the Black Fog? Was it just him who was able to do that, or all the Synths? Did it have to do with the dark magic Mihelik fought to conceal? Because Mihelik was sure that was buried with the burning of the ancient documents.

There were so many unanswered questions, and time was running out. Soren was now the hunted, and he knew they were coming…

~

HE FELT a jolt in his shoulder while he slept. Not at all a gentle nudge to wake. Soren heard her calling his name with alarm in her voice. He was irked he hadn't sensed her enter the wagon before, but perhaps he'd instinctually learned to drop his guard when he subconsciously sensed it was her.

"Soren, Soren, wake up."

He sat up quickly, seeing her still nudging him, while she looked out the backside of the wagon—sunlight pouring in.

"What is it?" His head fogged, but from the tone in her

voice, his instinct was kicking back alive. He didn't know for how long he'd been asleep, but he welcomed whatever he got.

"Men," she said. "They rode from the east." She leaned in close and whispered, "I think they're looking for us."

Soren exited the wagon quickly, Firelight tucked under his cloak. Davin and Kaile were just outside, and Soren could feel the tension in them. Their expressions were sour, and their posture stiff. Even in their disguises, they looked like outsiders to the caravan. The people that worked the caravan were overworked men with strong but bad backs—weathered faces and calloused hands. The women were sullen and withdrawn. The four of Soren and his comrades were all of fighting age, and all with the fire in their eyes of men and women on a mission. There was determination and spirit in them, a spirit the dwarven spell couldn't hide.

Soren saw the men get down from their horses at the rear of the caravan.

They must've ridden hard up the hill behind to catch up to the caravan with as little notice as Seph had given him.

Their horses panted as the three men glared around at the caravan, which had stopped in the middle of the day for lunch. Soren immediately recognized the danger in the three men as they spread out. The bearded leader of the caravan ran past Soren, giving him a quick glance over his shoulder.

The three men, one short—a little taller than Seph—was accompanied by two gigantic men, as tall as Kaile but built like oxen. The short man waited for the caravan leader to run up to him. Soren rested back against the wagon with his arms crossed, appearing relaxed, but analyzing every movement of the three. He paid attention to the clothing of the two large men, where other weapons were kept. He saw dimples on their clothes, under their arms, signaling other weapons beside the swords at their hips. They had daggers in their boots, clearly shown by the handles sticking out, not quite hidden under their pants.

"They're killers," Davin muttered in his feminine voice.

"I recognize them," Kaile said, drawing each of their gazes.

"You do?" Seph asked.

"I've seen them in the capital. They're killers all right," said Kaile, scratching his chin.

"Don't scratch," Soren said. "Do nothing, but stay calm and relaxed."

"I'm trying," Kaile said, forcing his hands into his pockets.

The people of the caravan slowly dispersed away from the foreign men, but Soren listened in.

"G'day, gentlemen," the bearded leader said. "I'm Dirk. How can I help you?"

The short man glowered, furrowing with deep wrinkles in his brow. He took off his maroon helmet and held it at his side. He wore a faded white cloak over the rest of his armor, decorated with the same maroon leather and black buckles.

"Dirk," the man said, licking his molars. "Don't meet many of those."

"And who do I have the pleasure..." Dirk began.

"It's no pleasure," the short man said. "The name is Gideon. These are my associates."

"Gideon," Soren said. "I know that name. Bounty hunters from the north."

"Gideon's one of the king's men," Kaile said. "He's one of the ones I see come into the capital, sometimes with captives, sometimes with just a head."

Seph gulped.

"Well, what can I do for you?" Dirk asked, not able to hide the shakiness in his voice.

The man Gideon licked his teeth and spat to the side, not looking at the leader, but past him. One of the brutes behind

Gideon glared at Soren for a moment. Soren averted his gaze, as if nervous.

"Looking for someone," Gideon said. His eye twitched, and his face caught the light just right that Soren noticed a long scar down the side of his face.

"Well, we're just making our way to Zatan," Dirk said. "Haven't run into anyone on these icy roads these three days. Who are you lookin' for?"

Gideon's demeanor darkened. Any inkling of warmth on his face disappeared. He cleared his throat and clenched his teeth, staring into the leader's eyes. Dirk shied away, stepping back subconsciously.

"What do you mean, who am I looking for?" Gideon was a full head shorter than Dirk, but Dirk was on the brink of trembling from terror. "Where the fuck did you just ride out of? Was it the town where a fucking Syncron for the king was just murdered? What the fuck do you mean, who am I looking for?"

"Apologies." Dirk fought to drive the words from his tight throat. "Yes, of course. The attack on Greyhaven. I'm aware."

Gideon grabbed Dirk by the cuff of the shirt with one hand. His hand was muscly, with thick veins on its back. Dirk's eyes grew wide, and Soren fought the urge to react. If he overreacted, he may reveal something unwanted to the men, but he also didn't want Dirk to die. He was a good man, and the caravan needed him.

If I act, I'm going to have to kill those men, and that would lead the king our way. Got to find another way out of this... if I can...

"Do you know where Soren Stormrose is?" Gideon yelled into Dirk's face, spit flinging from his dry lips and yellow teeth. "You were the only lot to leave the city. Tell me where he is. Tell me!"

Dirk sniveled and shook. "I don't know. I don't know where that man is, I swear it."

Convincing, Soren thought. He only hoped Gideon and his oafs agreed.

"I don't believe you," Gideon said, tossing Dirk away with a release of his hand. Dirk staggered back, trying to regain his composure. Gideon eyed the caravan as the women gathered the children, retreating behind the wagons and horses.

"Check the place," Gideon said, and with that, the two huge men lumbered forward.

There was something about the two men that Soren couldn't place. He didn't think they had enchantments on them, as Kaile said nothing about Gideon having the Ellydian. But they didn't seem natural. Even the Knight Wolf himself, a monster of a man, weighed a hundred pounds less than each of the towering men.

Both the men had lean, muscular arms hanging from their armor and gray and white wolf furs. Their skin was a tan complexion, and they almost looked like they could be twins. They had the same thin-lipped mouths, strong chins, and sunken eyes. But one had a completely bald, shiny head, and the other long black hair pulled back to a thick braid.

"Who are those men?" Davin asked Kaile, before Soren had a chance to.

"Mercenaries from Arkakus," Kaile said, with a dark tone lining his words.

"Of course they are." Davin cracked his knuckles.

The two men strode forward as the women behind hastily shuffled the children into the wagons. Soren and the others didn't move. They remained standing at the back of their wagon. He supposed he should act frightened like the others, but secretly, he wanted to kill the two monstrous men. He saw in their eyes what they were. They were killers, through and through. And they'd done more than bounty hunting. Soren would wager everything he had on that.

"Have everyone get their papers ready," Gideon said, turning back to Dirk. "And open some of that mead, now!"

"Yes, of course," Dirk said. He ran past the three men, glancing at Soren with a look of not knowing what to do.

Soren met his glance, but for only a moment, as Gideon and the two enormous men were heading toward him.

"Don't look at them," Davin muttered. "Act scared."

"You," Gideon said, holding up a finger pointed directly at Soren. "You don't look like a traveling merchant."

Soren didn't respond, and kept his gaze at his feet.

"Papers," Gideon said, walking up to Soren, scowling up at him, scrutinizing his face with narrowed eyes.

Soren took his papers from his inside breast pocket and handed them to the short man.

Gideon hardly inspected them. But he apparently saw enough for him to hand them back quickly.

"Answer me," Gideon said. "You're no merchant. You're a fighter. Why are you here?"

"Protection," Soren said, not meeting Gideon's inquisitive gaze, as the two gigantic men stood just behind Gideon, casting a shadow upon them.

"From what?" Gideon asked.

"Raiders," Soren said.

"What about you three?" Gideon asked. "Two kids and a woman looking to get pregnant."

"And you're looking to lose your tongue," Davin replied quickly, and with a nasty tone.

Gideon's demeanor darkened, and he gritted his teeth.

"They're with me," Soren said. "Pardon my wife. She's... spirited, forgive her words, but she's done getting pregnant, and if she was, it would only be by me. These are my children —Pricilla and Alfred."

"They don't look like your children," Gideon said with a raised eyebrow, still partly scowling at Davin.

"Adopted," Soren said. "Lost their parents when they were young, so I took them in. Good kids, and have been helpful around the caravan. Any other questions?"

Gideon seemed hateful and unpredictable to Soren, two traits that never went well together. Soren kept Firelight ready. It would only take him a split second to slit Gideon's throat should the need arise, but again, he needed these men to leave of their own accord. That would be best for everyone—especially the innocent people of the caravan.

"I don't like you," Gideon hissed, stepping into Soren's area. He was so close that Soren could smell the stale alcohol on his breath. "I don't like your look. I don't like that this caravan has hired protection, and I don't like that you're hiding something from me."

"I'm not hiding anything," Soren said, turning to face Gideon.

The two men behind shifted, moving their massive hands to the grips of their swords.

Soren put his palms up at shoulder level.

"You can inspect the caravan," Soren said. "We had planned to leave that day, so we could make good travel time on wintry roads. Can't let the cargo spoil. Lady Sargonenth of the Brink is expecting this on time."

Gideon glowered.

The cat purred as it walked through Soren's legs from behind. Gideon drew his boot back, sending it forward to knock into the cat's side, but Soren suddenly drove his leg in the way. Gideon's shin slammed into Soren's calf. The cat bounded off back to Seph, and Gideon was left wide-eyed at Soren, in disbelief about his speed.

The two men behind shifted to wide stances; their dark gazes fixed on Soren while they waited for Gideon's command.

"You're quick," Gideon said. "Maybe I should be offering you a job. Pays more than this poor lot here."

Soren looked away to Seph, who scooped the cat up in her arms. A look of detest crinkled on her face.

"I have a job," Soren said.

Gideon gave a *humph* and spat. "Fucking pathetic. Stay out of my way. What was your name again?" He leaned in close, grabbing Soren by the arm and spinning him to face him.

"Victor LeSabre."

"Well, Victor. Stay the fuck out of my way. I've got a menace to catch. The king wants his prize, and I'm itching for a good fight."

Soren nodded, looked down at Gideon's hand, still holding onto his arm. "You finished?"

Gideon scowled, taking his hand away slowly.

"C'mon, lads, check the wagons."

The three stormed off down the caravan. They moved as alpha predators would, without a care for something more fearsome than themselves. Soren greatly enjoyed the thought that even Seph alone would send them to early graves if given the chance, let alone all four of them.

"I hate that man," Seph said, stroking the purring cat's head and neck.

"They were bound to come out eventually," Davin said. "With the price the king put on your head, I fear this is just the beginning."

Chapter Twelve

Two days later.
The bounty hunters had gone off back on their own, riding ahead on the western road. Gideon had left an impression on Soren, not one of fear, but of foreshadowing. He was just the beginning, Soren thought. There was sure to be more.

The warmest breath of sunlight had kissed itself away. Twilight was approaching as the winds howled, flowing over the plains in endless swaths. Soren held his hood over his head as he walked beside the wagon, his cloak tails flapping to the side, and the foothills of the mountains were only ten minutes off. The sun was dipping fast, fading to a red hue like a fresh spring rose.

Wagons moved frustratingly sluggishly, but they provided all sorts of advantages. They'd make it into the foothills and tree line before the sun slid past the horizon, but that didn't stop Soren from checking behind them. The Demons of Dusk were soon to emerge, and he knew more than anyone—not only how dangerous they were, but how plentiful as well.

Night after night he'd watched the caravan, hoping dearly

the monsters of the dark would stay where they were meant to—on the plains, not in the trees. And night after night, he saw the Black Fog feed, and the Shades creep from shadow to shadow—hunting.

The flaps of the wagon opened outward, and Davin stepped out. He jumped down and walked at Soren's side. He looked as healthy as anyone else, but Soren knew under the visage of the beautiful woman, a dwarf lay, burned and scarred.

"How are you healing?" Soren asked, scratching his stubbly chin.

"Eh, not dead yet." He looked ahead, and not at Soren. "You?"

Soren nodded in agreement. "Same."

"We're almost there," Davin said, gazing out at the foothills turning to mountains beyond.

To their left, a mile down, was the sparkling Sapphire Sea. Glorious in her shimmering waves and endless splendor. To their right were the Lyones Mountains—deep gray, jagged, and snowcapped. The road had mostly dried over the five days after the blizzard, and after they left Grayhaven. Even as the frigid winds blew in, stinging his eyes, somewhere ahead, past the Lyones, was the vast desert land of Zatan. They'd be there in a day, Soren thought, and then a whole new set of challenges would emerge, even if the snowfall would be left back in Londindam and Cascadia.

The caravan made their way into the tree line just before dusk. The wagon wheels hit hard rock as they made their way uphill into the foothills. Thousand-year-old trails curved their way up, and horses pulled with great effort, before they found their spot to camp. It was a clearing in the woods of fir trees, where the winds didn't quite bite so hard.

The men went to making fires, and the women prepared

for making the meals and getting ready for the night. Soren and Davin were soon joined by Seph and Kaile.

"Last night before Zatan," Soren said, mostly to Seph. "And last night in a wagon. We should be sleeping in beds tomorrow, in Taverras."

"I'd kill for a bed," Seph said with a yawn, spreading her thin arms out wide.

"Could be worse, lass," Davin said. Soren was always amused at the sight of the tall woman with long hair calling anyone a lass. "Could be sleeping on the ground."

"This is far better than that," she replied. "But a warm room and soft bed trumps all."

"I agree," Soren said with a wink.

They made their way over to a circle of rocks, away from where the men of the caravan were getting their fire started. Soren and Kaile went and gathered wood beneath the trees, staying within range of Davin's spell. Moments later, Soren sparked the campfire alight. It was so much easier to get a fire going with dry wood than wet, Soren thought to himself.

Sitting around the fire, a chill blew in. They crept closer to the fire as the icy winds howled. There was no illusion to them that spring was long in coming. It was still deep into Decimbre, and it was sure to get colder before warmer.

A pair of women came over and brought them food—stale bread, butter, dried sausage, and potatoes. They took them eagerly, but said nothing, only bowing their heads in thanks.

As they ate, Seph scratched her knees and neck often.

"Out with it," Soren said. She snapped out of her long stare at the fire.

"Huh?"

"What's on your mind?" Soren asked. "Clearly it's something."

The black cat did figure eights between her shins, while she scratched her chin.

"I'm just excited is all," Seph said.

"Excited for what?" Kaile asked, chewing on bread and butter.

"Zatan," she said. "I've never been anywhere. I don't know if you were right in putting me in Guillead to protect me, but I'm so happy to be anywhere but there."

"The desert in winter is as harsh as it is during the summer," Soren said. "The sun and thirst won't kill you, but the cold and the Shades might. The Calica Clan too. Brutal as any other gang out there. I pray to the goddess we don't run into them."

"I don't care," Seph said. "For the first time since Tourmielle, I feel alive. And I couldn't have picked better companions if I tried."

Soren didn't smile at the notion. The desert would be far harsher than she might think. And to find one lord may take months. There would be more challenges than the safety of the caravan provided. They were heading back out into the wild.

"I'm ready, too," Kaile said. "This is the beginning of something important. I can feel it. We are all changing, as the world shifts in a new direction. The old, cruel world is crumbling, one bastard at a time. You're inspiring people, Soren. You're giving them hope, where there was none before. Just like when I was a boy, acting like you, acting like a stick was my sword, as I fought the bad guys."

Soren didn't reply, but stoked the fire as embers floated up into the trees.

"Nothing grim to say?" Davin asked with a grin.

"No," Soren said. "One day at a time."

"What's that mean?" Davin asked. "That's a strange answer. But then again, you're a strange man."

"Everything is going to get hard," Soren said, still prodding the fire. "They're going to be coming from everywhere now. It's not the king, or the Knight Wolf. Synths, hunters, shit... any farmer with the twinkle of gold in his eyes will try their grit against us. There are things in the desert that don't exist in the rest of Aladran as well. I've even heard rumors of Manans. No dragons though, thank the goddess."

"We'll be fine," Seph said in an uplifting tone. "We've got each other. We're stronger than you may think."

The cat suddenly jumped onto Seph's legs, putting her front paws on her shoulder, looking up at the sky. Each of them watched the cat stare off to the east. Seph turned to look behind her, and just as she did, a raven came and landed on Davin's shoulder, something attached to its leg.

Soren quickly spun, looking at the other fire. None of them appeared to care what was happening at Soren's fire.

"A note," Davin whispered, grabbing the raven gently, pulling it down, and untying the wrapped scroll from its leg. Once the scroll was free, the raven took back off into the air with a set of caws. Each of them waited eagerly for Davin to unroll it, which was eight inches long and only an inch wide. Davin had to squint to read the tiny lettering. "It's from… the Archmage Mihelik."

"What's it say?" Soren asked quickly.

Davin's eyes narrowed as he read the letters, just visible from the backside of the thin scroll.

Soren glanced around again, watching for prying eyes and perked ears, but found none.

Davin continued reading before clearing his throat and reading aloud.

"May this find you well. The need for vagueness and secrecy is at its utmost importance, but also there are things you must know. Your actions in Grayhaven have sent shockwaves throughout Aladran. Your mission was a success, and you are given great thanks for doing so. I wish you could enjoy your victory, but in this fight, one victory beckons another. I am shocked at the way Glasse passed. The Black Sacrament has ended the lives of many great Syncrons, but it took a dark Synth from this world, and that, I smile about at night."

Soren couldn't help but smirk at the visual of the old man smoking his pipe in his quarters, smiling at the thought of a Synth for the king splattering all over the city quarter.

Davin continued, "The fact remains, however, that Glasse summoned a Black Fog into the city. This deeply troubles me. The question not only remains of how he was able to do this, but also—who else has such abilities? I cannot imagine the Ellydian could do such a thing, as it has no effect on them. But we need to figure out the nature of that spell, and the magic behind it. As for the king, we have gotten word that the king has gone into a mad rage. Losing his Synth has spiraled him into beating his servants and screaming out from the top of his tower. This also causing a smile on this old man's face. However, the Knight Wolf is stirring. He's been summoned from his manor to the capital."

Soren grimaced and sighed.

Seph put her hand on his, squeezing it.

"That brings me to the archmage," Davin read. "The archmage is en route to Grayhaven. He left against the word of the king. It seems Glasse's actions in calling the fog have gotten Alcarond's attention more than any. I do not know if his curiosity is for how Glasse summoned the monster, or if he wishes to learn it himself. But the fact remains—the archmage is coming. Beware. His magic is far too powerful. He will not fall like Glasse. He will kill you if you see him. He wants his apprentice back, and he will wish to turn *her*. Do not let the archmage find you."

Kaile's face flushed, and he swallowed hard.

"Alcarond is coming, here?" Seph asked.

Davin nodded grimly.

"There's more," he said. "Although I and our mutual friend do not agree with your need to find the answers you seek, and where you seek them, we trust you and will guide you as best we can. Find your answers, but then return to the quest. The war has started, and there's no going back now. The lord you seek is currently in Golbizarath, far to the west. It's a fortress that few would dare adventure to. Be careful, be safe, and fight hard. The Sparrows are growing in number every minute. You've started the war. Now let's win it. -Mihelik Starshadow."

Soren scratched his cheek, glaring at Kaile and Seph, watching their demeanors turn dark.

I can't let him get to them. But how could I stop the archmage if he came? I'd be powerless against the most powerful Synth in the world. Even with Firelight...

"You all right, lass?" Davin asked.

She didn't answer, but glared into the fire, with its amber light reflecting in her wide, glassy eyes.

"Seph," Soren said. Still, she didn't stir or respond.

Kaile placed his hand on her upper arm. "Seph..."

"This was why you hid me," she finally said. "They would have come for me. I wanted to think I would've been fine anywhere else, or with you, but you were right, weren't you?"

Soren sat quietly, not enjoying hearing her words and her final self-realization.

"They want me for my power, and because of my name."

"You are the only family line whose offspring carry the Ellydian," Kaile said. "We teach and study your lineage. It's legendary. Don't know if you know how special you really are."

"I don't want it though," she muttered, not blinking.

"I know," Kaile said. "Neither did I at first, but eventually you learn to live with it, and accept the responsibility that comes with it. You will, someday."

"What about you?" Seph said, sudden spite on her tongue. "Did you accept it before or after you were taken from your home and forced to kneel to the king and his demands?"

Kaile withdrew his touch and retreated into himself. He folded his arms and let his hair fall before his face. "After..."

"That's what I thought!" Seph said, standing up suddenly, fists in balls. "He's coming to take us back to the capital. They want to kill Soren and Davin and kidnap me. And what will you do? Will you stop him? Can you protect me?"

"I—I don't know," Kaile said. "I know Alcarond, and he won't stop once he's decided something. He fixates. He obsesses."

"Will you fight for me, when the time comes?" Her words were forceful, biting deep into him.

"Yes... yes, of course I will."

"You better," she said. "You better fight for us, or you might as well just leave now..."

Chapter Thirteen

❧❧❧

That was the real first time Soren could sense that Seph had a level of mistrust for Kaile. She always seemed to be the one most accepting, trusting, and right in her intuition. Kaile had proved to be a worthy and powerful ally. But her sudden questioning of his loyalty aroused questions in Soren…

Had he been tempted by his power? Was he the victim he played out to be? Or was there something darker in there, after all?

I've seen the darkness, in glimpses, and fleeting moments. It's there. But how embedded is it? I truly hope the lust for power hasn't sunk in deep.

"I hope I don't need to tell you I'll do everything in my power to protect you," Kaile said. The words seemed true as they left his lips, but the shadow of doubt had been planted.

"I trust you," Seph breathed. "I do. But who's to say Alcarond doesn't have more power over you than you think?"

Kaile shrugged. "I'm me, and he's him. I'm not him. I'll never be like him. He's a puppet for the king."

"You don't envy his power?" Soren asked bluntly. "If you

said no, I wouldn't believe you. He's the most powerful being in the world possibly, and who knows how much more so, since he cast out Mihelik with the Wraithfire spell? He nearly killed the old archmage, and took his vision with that spell. Who knows what Alcarond is capable of now…"

"I know," Kaile said with slumped shoulders and a twitch in his eye. "And if he is coming, and finds us…" He lifted his head further and sighed up toward the sky. "I don't think there's a damned thing we could do to stop him from doing whatever he wanted with us. He knows all my spells. He taught them to me. He taught me my tricks, and he knows my weaknesses—which are *many*."

"Well then," Soren said, sitting up and dusting his backside off. "Better get to learning new spells and new tricks." He began to walk off down the hill, toward the edge of the forest.

"How do I do that?" Kaile asked with his arms out.

"Don't ask me," Soren said, only turning enough to see Kaile out of the corner of his eye. "You're the archmage's apprentice. Figure it out!"

Soren walked into the trees under the light of the moon, sliding between the thousands of branches, casting needle-like shadows on the winter ground.

"Wait up," Seph called as she jogged to catch up. The cat ran after.

Soren paused as she ran to his side.

"Might get cold out here," he said.

"I'll be fine."

They walked together through the scattered trees, eventually coming to the lowest part of the tree line in the foothills that rose behind the majestic Lyones.

Soren knelt and sat on a toppled tree from long ago. Perhaps a storm a decade ago or more. Seph sat next to him, and the cat quickly leaped to the slim spot between them, tucking herself in to both of their warmth, and they felt her purrs on their sides.

Soren stroked her back.

"Gotta name this thing," he said. "It's weird calling her cat, and she's finally starting to grow on me. Goddess knows she's never going to leave your side again."

"I've been thinking about that," she said with pursed lips and a scrunched nose. "How do you say cat in Dwarvish? Or should I ask Davin?"

"You won't like it," Soren said.

"You know it? What is it?"

"Forgloin." A smirk crossed Soren's face.

"Forgloin?" Both corners of Seph's mouth curved down and her brow furrowed.

"Yup, forgloin."

"That's hideous." She looked as if she'd just swallowed a big bite of sour fruit.

"I told you." He clapped his thigh.

"Ugh. Who would name a cat that?"

"Not us, I'm guessing." He laughed.

"Definitely not." She stuck her tongue out and squinted.

"So, what'll it be?" he asked. "Or is it going to be kitty forever? Or until it jumps off a cliff after you to save you?"

She thought long and hard. "I don't know. Nothing seems right."

"Guess it'll have to wait then," he said. "It'll build the suspense." He nudged her with his elbow. "But that means it's got to be extra special when it does come."

"It will be," she said, petting the cat. "I'm glad she followed us. I like the company." Her smile faded to a frown and a quivering lip. "Sorry I gave you so much grief for putting me in that place. As much as I hated it, and part of me is still furious at you for doing it, I should say thank you. I'd be dead or turned to what my family fought against their whole lives. So, sorry, I've been a bitchy brat. I'm still mad. But I'm getting better…"

He put his arm behind her and pulled her into him.

"We've got each other now. That's all that matters. I'll protect you."

There was a heavy silence as they glared down at the long plains, and saw the Black Fog begin to emerge from their hiding holes, ready to feed. Three of them, several times larger than the biggest horses.

"Can you though?" she asked shyly.

He groaned, staring down at the three shadowy monsters.

"I will," he said. "But I hate to say it, but I can't do it alone anymore. There's too many forces at work now. We need Kaile. And we need Davin. To be blunt—we need all the help we can get."

"You started something, uncle," Seph said. "The Silver Sparrows are growing. Mihelik said so. The tide is turning. There's hope again. We can kill the king, get revenge for our family, defeat the Chimaera that's killing us, and even rid the world of the Demons of Dusk. There's hope!"

He held her in his arm at his side, thinking of all the things that would have to happen to create the world that she spoke of, and knew there was no way he'd live long enough to see that happen. He was now the most wanted man in all of Aladran, and sooner or later he'd get what was his. Possibly what he deserved, he thought.

"You know, Soren, Cirella would be proud of you…"

"Ugh," Soren grunted. "She'd be disgusted."

"No, she wouldn't. Don't think that."

"Yes, she would."

"Why do you think that?"

"I just know. You don't know what I've done, Persephone. I love you, but you don't know. There's another side to me. Something happened to me in Tourmielle that night. Something snapped that can't be repaired. It's a sickness or a disease. I try to control it. I try to point it in the right direction when it pokes its ugly head out of my soul, and I hope you never see it. I'm not the person who Kaile looked up to when he was a boy." He pulled his arm away from her and felt a rage in him. Not at anything, but at himself. His body tensed. "I hate who I've become. So yes, she'd be disappointed in me, and that makes me angry. I hate it when people call me a hero. I can't stand when people say they look at me with hope. Hope…"

He picked up a stone from the ground and chucked it out past the trees.

"Hope," he muttered. "Hope." He laughed darkly.

Seph grabbed his wrist, but said nothing.

Moments passed as a bitter wind gusted in, and another Black Fog appeared from the gloom.

"You're still in there," she whispered, almost to herself and not to him. "I know you're the uncle who cared for me and made me feel safe when I was just a girl. You're still in there. I see it all the time. You just focus on the demon while I see the guiding angel. You're all I have."

"Me and this unnamed cat," he laughed.

"Angel," she breathed. "How do you say that in Dwarvish?"

"Celedor," he said.

"No, not that either," she said.

"How about the word of angel in the language of the Sundar?" he asked.

"You don't know Sundar," she said with a raised eyebrow.

"I don't?"

"You never told me that," she said.

"My mentor Landran taught me some. He was a very wise man, after all. Not only deadly with a sword, but sharp as anyone I've ever met."

"So what is it?"

"Sable."

"Sable," she said to herself. "Sable... So you know Dwarvish and Sundar?"

"A bit."

"Sable," she said with a wide smile.

They sat for ten minutes, watching the clouds drift lazily through the sky, and the Black Fog meander, searching for their next victims.

"So, we are going to Golbizarath?" Seph asked. "Do you know anything about that place?"

"No," Soren said. "I've never heard of it. But Mihelik said it was far west. I've never crossed the Dyadric Desert, even though I've been in it more times than I care. We are going somewhere I've never been."

"I wonder why he warned us about it?"

"I suppose we'll find out," he said.

"Are you going to kill him? Lord Belzaar?"

He sighed. "I don't know. Do you want me to, or not want me to?"

She laughed, picking up a stone from the ground and tossing it beyond the trees. "I'm beginning to see that it is kill or be killed in war. I'm still quite shocked you let Garland live."

"He's a worm," Soren spat. "We will cross paths with him again if the goddess has her way. I hope my instinct to spare him proves to be valid. I'm not on a great streak, though. My instinct used to be flawless."

She reached up and tried to touch his face, but he flinched away. But she pressed in, trailing her fingers down the scars on his face.

"Until these, huh?" she said.

He lifted his chin and looked up at the moon, dreading its pale light, reminding him of the night the Knight Wolf carved the three scars into his face with the magical blade, and the bitch Synth Zertaan cast the curse on him.

"You're still in there, you know," Seph said, getting to her feet, stirring Sable awake. "And you're wrong. Cirella *would* be proud. I remember her well enough to know that with all my heart. Goodnight uncle."

She was a dozen feet away by the time he breathed the words, "Goodnight."

As Seph left him to spend another lonely night watching over the caravan, one thought took over his mind, and clutched him by the core—his lost love, Cirella.

He remembered a similar chilly night, perhaps twenty years ago, sitting on a log with a view not so different from this night. She was beside him, and he reached over to where her hand would have been, but instead he found only scratchy bark with his fingernails. Soren sighed as his hand squeezed into a fist, as he closed his eyes tightly. He slammed his fist into the wood; the grief gripped him hard.

In his mind, he saw the golden hair flowing over his shoulder as she lay her head on him. Her head was angled up just enough so that her sky-blue eyes peered up lovingly at him. She held a warm smile on her perfect lips, and the moonlight made her tan skin glisten.

That moment in his mind made him feel old, broken.

They were maybe sixteen or seventeen when they sat there together, and it was the first time Soren had told her he loved her. Her response was as perfect as she was. He'd told her he thought he was falling in love with her, and her response was simply, "I know."

They'd made love in their tent before they went to sit under the stars, watching for shooting stars. He couldn't get close enough to her as she cuddled into him for warmth. Her hand glided up from his knee to his inner thigh, resting in the warmth there. He leaned over and kissed her, and he felt truly alive, then.

Now, he felt like half of him had been ripped from himself,

and was wandering half-empty, searching for something to fill the hole.

That thought reminded him of Alicen and the nights they'd spent together over the years. He always paid for those nights, just as every other bloke did, but he would fool himself into thinking there was something there that could help mend his broken heart. He couldn't have been more wrong.

Chapter Fourteen

He jolted awake. His boot skidded across the slick sheet of frost on the ground as he drew Firelight instinctively. Seph pulled her hand back as he squinted through heavy eyelids up at her. The golden glow of the rising sun washed over the side of her face.

Soren slid Firelight back into her scabbard with a sharp ring as it kissed the metal at the sides of the leather. Small snowflakes floated angelically down from the heavens, and Sable leaped up by his side and nuzzled his leg and made his way into his lap.

Rubbing his eyes of the brief sleep he'd gotten, he petted the cat with his hand that wore the Twilight Veil's bracelet and ring. Its blue gemstones and golden bands sparkled in the golden glow of the welcoming sunlight.

"Ready?" she asked. Behind her were Davin and Kaile, concealed in their spell. Soren knew he'd changed from the close proximity of Davin's pendant of eldrite stone. The Twilight Veil was enough to hide him in the shadows of night, but Soren welcomed the dwarf's spell in the sunlight.

Soren got to his feet, pushing away his fatigue with a yawn and a subtle shake of his muscles. He nodded.

They went back to the caravan, which was already packing up, ready to go back down the foothills, where the borderlands between Londindam and Zatan lay.

Less than an hour later, they were heading down the path, out of the trees and into the valley that nestled between the great Lyones range and the majestic Sapphire Sea. Soren didn't marvel at the thin, snow-blanketed landscape. Perhaps one of the most picturesque views in all the kingdom of Londindam—was quite breathtaking normally.

But instead—Soren had his sights set on the border towers. As he walked beside the wagon, he saw the two stone towers rise three stories high, with a single wall between the two of them. Not enough to keep any in or out of the kingdom, but enough to be a symbol of such a statement. It was the twenty or more soldiers who garnered Soren's attention. They were already stirring awake at first light. And there were surely more inside, he thought.

But beyond the towers—was Zatan, Lord Belzaar, and answers he desperately needed.

The caravan made its way down toward the towers, winding down the snaking trail, and the soldiers' attention was quickly upon them. They could've taken a mountain pass further to the north, but that would've taken extra days, a week even, and there would certainly be soldiers patrolling there too. They had their permits in place, and that should be enough, Soren thought.

Soren walked beside the wagon, but the others stayed within, to not draw unwanted attention to the four of them, who certainly stood out from the others. Dirk rode his horse ahead of the caravan, riding into the platoon. He talked for a few moments, still mounted, but the soldiers quickly ushered for him to dismount, which he did.

"How many?" Davin asked from inside the wagon, covered in thick furs.

"Twenty-three," Soren said. "Probably more inside."

Davin didn't reply, and the caravan continued forward.

They rode to the border station, which a pair of soldiers led them to directly ahead, moving to the gate between the two towers, left open, with its iron bars spread, and the first breath of the desert lands just beyond. The caravan paused, and the horses neighed as the soldiers began walking down both sides of the long line of horses, men, women, and wagons.

Soren immediately knew what kind of men he was dealing with. They were hardened, weathered by rough years. Some held their swords with good grips, but were sure to be slow by their posture, and others had folds of skin peeking out of where their armor had grown too tight, and as soon as they walked past Soren, he could smell the stench of strong, biting spirits on them. This had been a long, desolate winter, Soren thought—not enough action, and a lot of boredom in these two old towers.

The men hardly gave Soren a second glance as they walked by, but it was clear what they were searching for—they didn't care about the wine, or cargo loaded up on the wagons, or the nervous women and children hiding in the wagons—the soldiers were looking for the scars. They were only looking for Soren.

Dirk and a pair of soldiers argued up by the gate, with Dirk holding papers in his hands. The soldiers looked unimpressed, one with his arms crossed and the other waving his arms around, pointing at the first wagon and then past the gate.

A soldier approached the back of the wagon they were in, and Soren moved to the side of the back flaps, staying as calm as he could.

"Stay there," the soldier said directly to him. His eyes were reddened and his throat dry. Soren nodded and stayed where he was, putting his back to the wagon. He heard another soldier walk around the backside of the wagon, and stopped next to Soren, glaring at him as the first soldier peered up into the wagon's interior.

"Everyone out, papers ready," he said. "C'mon, quick now!"

"Papers," the gruff soldier standing beside Soren said.

Soren reached into his inner pocket casually and pulled his paperwork free, handing it to the man. He said nothing, trying to keep as cool as he could muster. Soren desperately wanted to move through the gate without incident. Any altercation here would quickly spread word back into Londindam and bring with it a new world of trouble.

The soldier examined his papers as Davin, Seph, Kaile, and the women and child came out of the wagon. They all kept their gazes down at their feet, holding their papers ready. Another soldier came over, and the two collected and thumbed through them.

It wasn't the soldiers that worried Soren then... it was something else, something Soren didn't expect that made his nerves rattle.

Riding down the path from the foothills, a quarter mile up, were three horses—one regular sized, and two huge steeds that carried two massive men.

Damn the Goddess. Not here. Not now. What is Gideon doing here? This is not what we need now...

The soldiers noticed him riding down, handing back the paperwork to Seph and the others. A group of soldiers were moving to the back of the caravan to meet the three riders approaching down the hill. A biting wind blew down from the mountains, and Soren glanced down at Dirk and the open gate beyond.

As the three soldiers that were with Soren and the others

left, Seph looked at Soren with a concerned gaze, pinching her chin.

He subtly shook his head. "Stay calm," he whispered.

Gideon rode to the soldiers, said something, and they let him pass, breaking the line of soldiers in half as the bounty hunter and the two giant men rode through.

Soren wasn't sure what he said to the soldiers, but he didn't like it. Gideon had a stern expression, with the wrinkles in his tan brow deepening. His thinning hair reflected the sunlight that shone through a break in the clouds above. A thin ponytail of slick black hair bounced behind him.

He rode down toward Soren and the others, stopping twenty paces away, and the two hulking men rode out wide. The three of them had Soren pinned with his back to the wagon.

Fuck. This isn't good. Not now... not this close...

Soren didn't speak. He told himself he'd act as if he didn't know what was going on, how to properly defend himself even. So he leaned back with his legs crossed and an eyebrow lifted.

"You know why I'm here?" Gideon asked in a low tone, and the two men behind sat expressionless upon their great steeds.

Soren shook his head. "I assume you're lost."

"One million torrens," Gideon said, his hand slid to the hilt of the sword at his hip. But as his cloak moved back, Soren saw it wasn't a sword sheath. No. Wasn't long enough, and there was a cord wound around his backside.

Soren glowered.

If he knows about the reward, then he knows it's me, even if Davin's spell has removed the scars.

The women rustled the children away, and much of the caravan moved away as well.

Davin, Seph, and Kaile didn't withdraw, though, drawing Gideon's spiteful gaze.

"You don't need to deny it. Saw the scars on your face. Whatever it is that is hiding the Knight Wolf's curse on you isn't going to hide who you really are. Not forever."

Soren thought of the night before when Seph touched the scars on his face, when he was outside of the shadow of the trees.

He must have been watching the whole time... waiting...

"So here's how this is going to work," Gideon said, his hand still on the grip of the weapon on his hip. "I assume these three are the ones who took down Edward Glasse. So, you're going to come with us, Soren Stormrose, and I'll let them live. You don't, and there's gonna be a damned bloody mess here, and I'll *still* get my reward."

Soren's hand moved to Firelight, gripping it tightly, and he heard the squeal of his palm on the leather.

"Why would you let us live?" Kaile asked through his disguise.

"Kaile Thorne," Gideon said with a snide smile. "You look far different from last we met in the capital, and you're in far different company."

Both the towering men with massive shoulders scowled at Kaile, their gazes menacing.

"To answer your question," Gideon said. "Because the bounty is for Soren... and you're not my targets. You're reserved for someone... with a little more... personal attachment, shall we say?"

Alcarond... he is coming...

"Leave us alone," Seph said. "You don't know what you're doing."

A soldier just beyond Gideon and the two men walked forward, scratching the stubble on the side of his face. It was the same one with the musty smell of old alcohol on his breath.

"If it's him," the soldier said. "We'll help bring him down. If you share the reward. Say... half?"

Gideon clamped his lips down hard, and a wicked scowl crossed his face as his nose crinkled at the top and the wrinkles in his face creased. He turned in his saddle, looking down at the soldier, who didn't seem wise enough to stay far away from such a man.

"Here's a better idea," Gideon spat. "Stay the fuck out of this, and I won't cut your balls off and feed them to the buzzards. Now stand the fuck back and let the adults talk."

He spun back in his saddle, facing Soren, who had Firelight ready to draw. He uncrossed his legs and took a wide stance— one boot forward, ready to pounce.

"You, you can't talk to soldiers of Londindam like that," the soldier behind said, shaking an angry finger, before pulling his sword free of his scabbard.

Fool. Absolute fool. But… this may be a blessing…

"By my authority, under the law of Lord Garriss, I order you to dismount and surrender your weapons."

"Boy," Gideon said, not turning to look at the soldier. "If you're thinking of taking him in for the reward yourself, you wouldn't live five seconds in a fight with this man. Your entire squadron would fall before you even had time to mess yourself."

"I said, off your horse and weapons on the ground!" the soldier shouted, and more soldiers approached.

That's when Soren noticed something different about the two enormous men with Gideon. He hadn't noticed it before, or perhaps he hadn't sensed it because it wasn't there until now… but there was an unnatural power stirring in the two. He felt it radiate like the sizzle of the air before a lightning strike, or the first breath of icy winds before a blizzard.

"The two," Soren mouthed the words to his friends, while Gideon was caught up with the soldiers. "Dangerous."

Seph and Kaile nodded, but Davin glared at the two quickly, with his head cocked slightly.

"You may not know me," Gideon said. "And you hail from Lord Garriss, well I work on the behalf of the king of Aladran. So stand down and let me do my job."

"I said, off your horse," the soldier pointed his sword at Gideon. "Now."

"Fucking peasants," Gideon muttered in anger. He turned and spoke to Soren again. "These things get messy sometimes. But my arrangement still stands. Surrender peacefully, and your friends live to fight another day. The king and archpriest want them alive, anyway. You, however, your bounty is dead or alive. But I have respect for you, Stormrose. In a different life, I think we might be comrades. Before you die by whatever the king plans, most likely incineration, I think I'd like to learn what you have to share. But if not, your head can come with us to Lynthyn, while your body rots here. Up to you."

"Go fuck yourself!" Seph spat.

"You must be the last Whistlewillow," Gideon said with a smirk. "Living up to your name, ain't ya?" He winked.

"Off your horse! Now!" the soldier yelled, irking Gideon as his eye twitched.

"What do we do?" Seph asked, as the soldier continued shouting at Gideon.

"I'm not going back there," Kaile said. A palpable fear gripped him, something deep, something fierce. "I'm never going back there. I'd rather die."

"We aren't going anywhere," Soren said, drawing Firelight slowly from her scabbard. The sunlight kissed the blade with a brilliant white glow, far different from its red hue from starlight.

Gideon's attention snapped back to Soren. "There it is. The Vellice blade that attacked the Black Fog. I don't know how that weapon came to you, Scarred, but I very much wish to possess that."

"Then come and take it," Soren growled.

Kaile and Seph walked to Soren's sides, both of them

pulling their staffs free, and striking them. Kaile with a C note, and Seph with an A. Their notes rang out in a shimmering ring that filled the air. There were gasps from all the way down the caravan.

All knew what those notes meant, and Dirk came running up from the head of the caravan, many soldiers running after him.

"There they are," Gideon said with his teeth showing. "Why not drop whatever spell it is that's hiding you? There's no need for that now. Let's all meet face to face."

"Don't do it," Soren said aloud, not directly to Davin. He wanted to keep the origin of the spell a secret.

Gideon glowered.

"Stop this!" Dirk panted as he ran between Soren and Gideon, with his hand pointed out at the soldier, still pointing his blade at Gideon. "Stop this at once."

"Out of the way," Gideon said, his hand still planted on the grip of the weapon on his hip. "The soldiers can deal with you, but I'm here for *him*."

"I'd try to talk you out of it," Soren said. "But that is a lot of money."

Gideon frowned. "It's not only about the money, but yes, it is a lot."

"What then?" Soren asked. "You just want the challenge?"

"You may have changed your name," Gideon said. "You wanted to conceal your past, but your reputation isn't so easily forgotten as that. Even your scars don't define you as much as your legacy. I'm going to be the one to take you down. You understand the thrill of the hunt, don't you, hunter?"

"I do."

"Good," Gideon said with a wide smirk. "Good."

"Don't!" Dirk said, waving his hands desperately. "There are women and children here."

"Get them out of here," Soren said. "Now!"

Dirk's eyes widened, and he wanted to make them stop, but at Soren's words, he was quickly off, yelling as loudly as he could for all to run to the towers and gate. The people of the caravan ran, flooding out of the wagons and jumping down off their horses.

"If what you want is legacy," Soren said, swaying the dagger from side to side, "then let's finish this, just you and me."

"I may be greedy," Gideon said. "But I'm no fool. I'm not going to get into a sword fight with you and wielders of the Ellydian." He paused and then glanced back at the two huge men behind him. "That's why I brought them."

"Get back!" Soren shouted instinctually.

The colossal man with the bald head lifted his monstrous fist into the air, and energy glowed from his forearm. It crackled and sizzled as streaks of golden-white power surged up his arm.

There was the sudden boom of thunder overhead, and as Soren and the others tried to run, a bolt of terrifying lightning crashed down into the giant man's arm, erupting in an enormous explosion of blinding white light.

The world disappeared, and all that was left was the pure white light, and the feeling of being blown back violently in searing heat.

Chapter Fifteen

※※※

Once Soren's vision cleared, and his eyesight returned, everything had changed. One of the towering men stood with his arms out wide, huge veins running down his muscular arms, and streams of golden lightning circled his forearms.

Elementals... damn! What are they doing with Gideon? In Aladran?

Soren got to his feet, and the battle began all around him at once. Seph and Kaile struck their staffs again. As the explosion had killed their last notes, Davin lifted the spell, and had his double-sided ax in his hands, and Gideon and the second gigantic man had revealed their weapons.

As the soldiers pulled back at the side of the man who appeared to control lightning, a god in his own right, Gideon pulled free the weapon he'd had on his hip. Upon his horse, he unleashed a menacing whip with a single tip of black metal. He cracked it toward Soren and the others, and it crashed into the wagon, shattering it into splinters with a thunderous explosion, sending the furs flying back, torn asunder.

Soren had his hands over his head as the splinters rained down.

As the lightning elemental coursed with energy, his eyes glowed that same golden hue, beaming with energy. The second man, with the thick black hair pulled into a rope of a braid, stood motionless, but there was something about him, something different, but something magical. Soren realized finally what the man was when his arms faded into the air, blowing into the wind.

He's an elemental also… Shit. I've got to kill them, and quickly.

"They're elementals!" Soren yelled to the others. "Kill them fast! Show them no mercy, for they'll show you none!"

To his side, Soren felt an intense heat as fire erupted from Kaile's staff, and he saw the blue light of the Skin of the Fae spell to protect Seph. Davin roared and ran forward, his ax thirsty for blood. Soren took his cue and ran forward, straight at Gideon.

A rush of wind caught them as Davin and Soren rushed forward. It was so immense, Soren dropped to a knee and shielded his face from the biting wind. There was a roar of thunder in the clouds above, as the two elementals stood side by side. The bald one coursing with searing lightning in the arms, the other with the black braid bursting fierce wind from his arms.

Soren sensed danger, and leaped to the side, the wind blowing him back eight feet in the air. Gideon's whip's tip shot into the spot Soren had been, sending the earth bursting up from the crack of the whip.

I've got to get to them. They're going to keep us at a distance. I've got to get close!

Kaile's flames poured from his staff forward, but were forced back from the intense, rushing winds.

Davin ran out wide, and Soren took his lead, running in the opposite direction. They couldn't fight on all sides, Soren thought, or hoped, rather.

Soren rushed for Gideon as Davin made his way to the two giant elementals.

"So this is how it has to be?" Gideon said with a wild grin on his face. He pulled the whip back and unleashed it at Soren, sending it from coiled back behind him, to streaking through the air straight at Soren. With a flick of Firelight, the dagger smacked the rushing black head of the whip away to the side.

It was hurtling to the ground, but Gideon drew it back quickly, coiling back above him.

Soren ran as fast as he could into the winds, and he was only twenty feet from Gideon, who snarled down Soren.

"Good," Gideon said. "I'm going to enjoy being the one to kill you. It's an accolade I'll wear with honor. And the king will pay handsomely for that dagger in your hand."

"Then take it from me," Soren said.

"I plan on it," Gideon said, sending his whip flying at Soren, straight toward his chest.

Soren twisted to the side, spinning in midair, slamming Firelight's edge at the black metal head of the whip, sending it tumbling away.

Gideon drew it back, this time not with glee, but with a dark expression on his face, clenching his teeth and tightening his brow.

As Soren ran at the bounty hunter, Davin made his way in a wide arc toward the two elementals, lightning pouring down into the bald one, as the glowing lightning grew at his forearms.

The elemental with the black braid continued gusting winds all around. The winds bit and stung, but mostly kept Soren and the others at bay, covering their eyes from the rushing winds. Kaile's flames couldn't penetrate the gale winds, and Seph remained in her spell of protection.

Davin, being so low to the ground, powered forward slowly,

his double-sided ax gripped tightly, ready to lop off the head of both the giants.

"Good company I keep, eh?" Gideon said, unleashing his whip at Soren, who knocked it away again, the whip cracking as it collided with the Vellice dagger. "Hired them especially for this. Not cheap, buying mercenaries from Eldra, but when you're dealing with Synths, can't be too careful now, can ya?"

Gideon cracked the whip again, this time not at Soren, but at his feet. Soren sensed the danger and leaped high, letting the wind carry him backward. The whip smashed into the ground, erupting in an explosion that sent dirt flying up, concealing Soren in the cloud of earth and dust.

I've got to get closer. His whip has missed so far, but I can't let it hit me. Every time it hits clean, it causes an explosion. That's no ordinary whip...

Davin powered forward, inching his way forward, growling. The wagon behind, crippled from the first explosion, toppled backward from the winds, tumbling end over end; cracking, splintering, and breaking.

The winds intensified as the black-braided elemental's eyes glowed an ivory white. The two elementals spoke to each other in a language Soren didn't understand, some thick dialect from the western lands of Eldra.

"Fire won't work," Soren yelled out in the hurricane winds to Kaile. "Think boy. Think!"

The fiery flames receded back into his staff, as Kaile thought for a moment.

Seph then said, "Lightning and wind... wind feeds fire, and lightning creates fire, but what stops the two?"

Kaile's note from his staff rang out, and he pointed its tip at the ground. The earth beneath their feet trembled and shook. Halfway between them and the elementals, the ground began to rise. A boulder buried deep within the ground rose, breaching the surface, rising six feet and stopping there. The thick boulder broke the winds enough that Kaile and Seph ran up to stand directly behind it, freeing themselves from the howling winds above.

Seph nodded to Kaile.

Soren and Davin were still at the mercy of the winds, straining to reach their enemies, when Davin suddenly shouted, "Lightning incoming, get down!"

Soren looked up at the sky. Above, a massive funnel of dark clouds had formed with the bald elemental at its epicenter. The funnel had streaks of golden lightning rushing through it, and the energy was building. Something was about to happen.

The thunder that had been booming before every few seconds had faded, and instead the twirling funnel shook with a vibrant electric static. Soren leaped back in the wind again, distancing himself from Gideon as the funnel glowed a brilliant, terrifying golden light, and the lightning came hurtling down.

Soren pressed his chest to the hard ground, watching just in time to see Kaile and Seph do the same.

The lightning exploded down in a blinding light. The explosion came from the side of the boulder opposite Kaile and Seph. It was so loud and violent Soren had to cover his ears, and felt the burst rush through him, causing his heart to skip a beat, and then thump wildly in his chest from the adrenaline pumping through his veins.

Seph and Kaile lay on the ground, covered in a layer of fresh dust. Soren was back on his feet, the dust from the explosion being blown back by the harsh winds. Gideon's whip was already streaming through the air, Soren knocking it away with a hard swipe to his right. He knew it would only take one successful hit of that whip's tip on him to cause the kind of explosion that could break the earth, and Soren knew he couldn't let it get close to him, or it may be the end.

Davin, however, full of rage, ran low in the winds. His short legs propelled him forward much faster than Soren could. He was quickly upon the two men, sending an immense arc of his ax at the elemental with the braid, and to his astonishment, the ax passed through it as it would through steam. Where it would have met with the immense man's knee, it found nothing but air.

He roared and spun around, sending his ax through the elemental's upper thigh, quite high for Davin to reach. Again, air. In frustration, and with a grin upon the elemental's face, Davin turned his attention to the bald elemental behind the other. He ran at the lightning elemental, but he lost his balance as he found his feet being lifted from the ground.

Soren's jaw slacked as he watched the air elemental squat powerfully, raising both powerful hands, rising with him as he stood. With him, a cyclone of air burst up from underneath Davin, carrying him up, high into the air as the dwarf fought, kicking and cursing. With a final burst of the wind, Davin was thrown twenty feet up into the air, flailing as he was thrown back, far over Seph and Kaile, hurtling back into the caravan.

Kaile and Seph were back on their feet, knocking the dust from their brows as they stood on the backside of the rock. They both struck their staffs and the crisp, clear notes rang out. Gideon's whip struck at Soren's outer thigh, and he knocked it away. Gideon reeled it back instantly, readying it for another strike.

Soren could hardly move. With Davin out of the battle, the wind elemental focused all of his power on Soren. The winds were so intense that Soren had to kneel, clinging to the ground. He wasn't nearly close enough for an attack, and Firelight may make it through the barrage of wind, but he wouldn't take the chance. He'd only throw her if it was his last chance.

But, while the air elemental turned his focus to Soren, the other elemental walked toward Seph and Kaile. They couldn't see it, as it was on the other side of the boulder Kaile had pulled up from deep in the earth, but the elemental that looked like a wicked god of thunder was summoning down enormous lightning from the dark funnel of clouds that circled above him. The roar was deafening.

Soren knocked another of the bounty hunter's strikes away, and Gideon's glee at the fight was turning to frustration. He scowled with his teeth gritting. "You defeated a Black Fog, Stormrose, but you can't beat us."

"Watch me," Soren said, gripping Firelight tightly. "Seph! He's coming!"

Seph quickly realized what Soren was saying as she looked up to the see the lightning streaks approaching, just on the other side of the boulder.

The whip cracked again, and this time, Soren was so caught up in the elemental that approached Seph, he didn't have the time he needed to react. The whip's tip dug into the ground before him, and he instantly felt the shockwave, even before the dirt flew up into his face. He was blown back by the explosion, and the fierce winds. Landing on his feet, he skidded back on the hard ground.

Soren was another twenty feet back then, watching the lightning build in the swirling funnel in the sky. With a light that filled the sky, the searing lighting careened downward, striking the boulder that separated the elemental from the two young Syncrons.

"Seph!" he yelled, but her name was silenced by the violent explosion that broke the enormous boulder.

In the bright light of the blast, Soren averted his eyes, but saw Kaile and Seph being thrown back by the explosion. When Soren could open his eyes and glare at the smoldering rock, he saw Seph laying on her back in a daze, with her staff feet from her. She moaned as she got her elbows under her to get up.

"Seph! Get up! Grab your staff!"

Soren was still caught in the winds, being pinned down. He

took hard strides in her direction, his hair and cloak whipping behind him. Kaile was up on his knee, still with his staff in his hand. He attempted to strike it, but was too late. The towering man was already upon him. He reached down with his enormous hand and wrapped his fingers around Kaile's neck, easily lifting him from the ground.

Kaile's feet dangled below him as Seph yelled out for him. She turned and crawled for her staff, but the second elemental noticed and sent his winds harshly in her direction. Her staff went skidding away.

Soren considered throwing his dagger, but he was far from Kaile's attacker, and the winds only complicated the throw. He'd need to land a kill shot on such a huge man, so it would have to be right between the eyes or nothing. Gideon was riding toward Soren to press his attack. The bounty hunter wasn't going to let Soren save Kaile. He readied his whip for another flurry of attacks.

What are you doing, Soren? Kaile's going to die unless you do something. We need him! You've got to save him... you've got to...

Suddenly, though, there was a flash of white by Kaile and the powerful elemental. It was a streak of glimmering steel in the light of the lightning storm above. The blade was in a woman's hand, as she flew in a huge arc of a flip, gliding through the air with the agility of a dancer, but the ferocity of a war-forged soldier. Her blade sliced through the air, and the familiar flash of crimson blood colored the final stroke of the flash of steel.

A figure emerged, seemingly from nowhere, and the figure of a woman Soren didn't recognize. She landed gracefully, but with a powerful posture at Kaile's side.

The elemental's head slid down the front side of his chest before its fingers even released themselves from Kaile's neck.

The ivory glow of the elemental's eyes dimmed as his head separated from his shoulders, tumbling down his chest, leaving blood gushing down his front. Kaile tore the fingers free from his neck and he fell, gasping for air. Seph ran to him, while the female figure rose from her kneeling position. She stood tall, her long, thick ropes of black hair whipping in the gusting winds. Her thin blade was at her side, dripping with fresh blood as the towering body of the mercenary from Eldra finally fell to the ground.

Seph wrapped her arms around Kaile as they stood behind the woman. Her glare was as mean as death, her skin the color of tree bark at midnight, and her stance earned Soren's respect immediately.

Whoever this woman is—she knows how to fight. She saved Kaile's life. And for now... she appears to be on our side...

Davin came up from behind Soren, finally rejoining the fight.

"Who is she?" Soren asked.

"Dunno, but I'm sure glad she's here."

Gideon and the wind elemental appeared to regroup, pulling together to analyze the new situation, but the elemental's face twisted. His eyes glowed brightly, and he roared with rage.

"The battle has shifted in our favor," Soren said. "We've got to take full advantage of it. Ready?"

"Always," Davin said with a wide smirk. "Let's show these bounty hunters why the price on your head is so high..."

Chapter Sixteen

With the elemental dead upon the ground, lying in a pool of blood, the storm above receded back whence it came. The twirling funnel cloud spun back into the heavens. Lifting with it their spirits, as the balance of battle had turned.

Kaile and Seph both struck the metal of their staffs, letting their tones ring out clear and wide. They had renewed energy as they pushed forward in the winds of the remaining elemental, who held a maddened look of utter rage on his face.

The wind elemental, with the winds rushing out from his forearms, strode forward, ready to enact his revenge upon them. But Gideon didn't ride forward with him. No, he remained upon his steed, his gaze darting around the scene, and especially upon the woman who had entered the fray. She stood unwavering in the winds, and many of the soldiers had returned to catch a glimpse of the woman who'd killed the man built like a mountain.

The soldiers watched from far outside the battle, and Soren could see them muttering to each other.

Seph and Kaile stood close, but with Kaile in between Seph and the newcomer with the bloodied blade.

"Thank you," Kaile said to the woman, who didn't respond. Her focus was entirely on the elemental and the bounty hunter before them.

Finally, Gideon seemed content with his analysis of the situation and turned back in his saddle.

"Fine," he shouted. "One hundred thousand torrens to help me capture the Scarred. Dead or alive."

The soldiers seemed surprised by the announcement from the bounty hunter. They raised eyebrows, shrugged shoulders and spoke between one another, but none of their swords left their sheaths.

After a few moments of deliberation, and Soren exchanging heated scowls with the remaining elemental, one soldier finally responded, "Nah. You go for it. We'd rather keep our heads."

Gideon spun back in his saddle; a dark glare on his face. His nose crinkled and his mouth flattened. The wrinkles in his brow tightened.

He's not used to losing. He hates it. But I can relate. I know the feeling all too well.

Suddenly, Gideon spoke in a language unfamiliar to Soren, and presumably to all. It was harsh, but song-like with rolled R's. The elemental calmed slightly, letting his massive, muscular shoulders relax.

The elemental with the thick black braid spoke in the same language back, his tone much lower and rocky than Gideon's. His words were spiteful, and full of anger.

Gideon replied, his words blunt but calming.

The elemental roared words back at him, but Gideon sat unaffected. The bounty hunter still held a dark glower on his face as he scowled at Soren. He cracked his whip at his side as it roared like thunder. He shouted one last thing at the monstrous man, with the wind still erupting from his arms. The elemental growled, letting out a huge grunt of anger as he lifted his arms to the sky.

The rushing winds ceased upon Soren and the others, but instead circled Gideon and him. They were so intense they rustled up enough dirt to nearly shield them completely. But beyond the dirt, Soren saw the bounty hunter. Their exchanged glares were a mix of resentment, adversity, but also respect strangely.

"We will meet again," the bounty hunter said inaudibly, but Soren understood every word.

The whirling winds shot up into the air like a tornado, lifting the two men and the horse high into the air, arcing back to the forest far behind, back in the foothills.

When the winds completely dissipated, leaving only a cool breeze, Soren and the others were left with the woman. She knelt next to the body of the elemental from Eldra she'd slain and wiped both sides of her shamshir blade on the back of his shirt.

While they all stood there in the battle's aftermath, crowding around the mountain of a man, left decapitated on the ground, Soren analyzed the woman who had appeared from nowhere. As she rose back to her feet, her frame was sturdy, with lean bare arms hanging from the loose tan linen shirt. Her grip was firm on the thin curved blade with a golden cross guard and pommel.

Her back was to Soren, but her head was turned to the side, glaring down at the fallen elemental. Her black dreadlocks of woven thick hair fell over her shoulders and down her back, nearly to her rear. She wore tightly fitted, narrow bracelets of copper and gold on both wrists, and had just barely visible tattoos down both arms.

The soldiers around approached cautiously, taking weary

steps forward, grouping together, unsure of what move to take next.

Seph stood with her mouth agape beside Kaile, both taking uncertain steps back, away from the woman. Davin held his ax in both hands as he pointed it in her direction. Soren held Firelight at his side, waiting to see what the woman did next.

The soldiers halted when they were thirty feet away, standing around the wreckage of the broken wagons with splintered wood, shredded canvas, and bearskin rugs strewn about. Mead, ale, and wine poured freely from the busted casks from the battle.

Dirk ran up, wrangling others to help stop the flow from the broken casks.

The soldiers muttered between themselves at the sight of the woman, who still stood silently, her gaze slowly moving from Seph to Kaile, to Davin, and eventually to Soren. Her turquoise eyes held an enchanting quality that sucked him in. They drew him in deep, swallowing him as he became entranced. They were like looking into the eyes of a wise predator—drawing its prey in with a false calm. *She is spectacular*, Soren thought. *Wild, fierce, ravishing.*

"It's the Desert Shadow," one soldier said, his croaking throat full of dread. They held their ground warily, looking at one another, with one soldier's weapon shaking from his trembling hands.

Desert Shadow? The Desert Shadow? She's so much younger than I'd imagine from the tales. She looks no older than thirty. The legendary blade of the Calica Clan. This is her?

"She's the Desert Shadow?" Davin asked beside Soren. His voice was tinged with apprehension.

The Calica Clan wasn't renowned for its valor, Soren knew. It was a ruthless, feared organization that ruled from the shadows of Zatan. It was the unwritten law of the desert. They carried out their own version of justice out on the sands. All in Zatan knew them, feared them, and abided by them.

"It appears so," Soren said, still keeping Firelight free of its sheath.

"So... she's on our side?" Davin asked, as much to himself as to Soren.

Seph and Kaile still seemed wary, walking slowly away from the woman, who still held her shamshir blade by her side. Its glimmering edge rippled sunlight off it like sea waves as its tip scraped the ground.

"Soren Stormrose." Her words broke the stiff silence.

He nodded. There were a dozen yards between them, each holding their weapons at the ready.

"I come to lead you into the desert." She glared at the soldiers, who gained a strange courage at the thought of the woman appearing to help Soren past their border, and into Zatan.

"Thank you for your help with our current situation," Soren said. "But why have you come to our aid?"

"That is a conversation for less ears," she said. Her voice was stern, direct, and her gaze scanned the many soldiers gathering around.

"This may be a good time to be taking our leave of the caravan," Davin said. "All of Londindam will know about all this mess, and us, soon enough."

"Agreed," Soren said, sheathing his dagger finally. He walked toward Seph and Kaile, who met him halfway. He grabbed Seph gently by the back of her shoulder, pulling her in. The Desert Shadow still held her ground firm, standing over the dead elemental who commanded the lighting and thunder itself before his demise.

"So, this is the last Whistlewillow," the woman said. "And the fallen apprentice of the archmage..."

"And you are?" Kaile responded quickly, not seeming to enjoy her description of him.

"She's Blaje Severaas," Soren said. "The Desert Shadow. First Blade of the Calica. I didn't expect them to send you."

"Them?" Seph asked.

"Roth and them," Kaile whispered.

"Oh," Seph said, realizing this was who the Silver Sparrows had sent as their guide.

"This is Davin Mosser of Mythren," Soren said, sensing their use of disguises and fake names was useless at the moment. "How do we know we can trust you?"

Blaje pointed the tip of her sword down at the elemental, whipping her dreads over her shoulder to her back. She cocked an eyebrow.

"Makes sense to me," Davin said.

"You're going nowhere," one brave soldier said, in the center of many.

"And who are you to stop us?" Davin growled. "You know who we are now. Are your lives worth trying to get a bounty outta that rotten king?"

The brave soldier suddenly didn't look so brave after looking around at his comrades, who gave him uncertain shrugs back.

"You're welcome to try," Davin said with a wide grin, and his mighty ax swaying before him. "But we are leaving. C'mon."

Soren followed Davin as he walked toward the gate to Zatan.

Each of them kept their weapons drawn as they walked down the caravan, Soren turning and nodding to Dirk, who nodded back. His men were hard at work trying to save the spilled merchandise.

Davin led the way, with Seph and Kaile behind—with Sable scampering along beside Seph. Soren and Blaje followed, standing within an arm's reach from one another, glancing at one another as they walked.

The soldiers on the way to the gate looked uneasy and nervous. It was the sort of nervous where any of them individually would have tried to stop them, for fear of punishment of the lord of Londindam, but since the entire platoon of soldiers were standing down, then they each followed suit. It was as if they'd been given orders to stand down, but none were given.

Soren knew they'd have their price to pay for letting Soren walk through the gate into Zatan, but they'd seen him fight, and they rightly feared the Desert Shadow. Even Soren had known to keep well away from such an infamous killer. Soren knew he was the best, or at least used to be, but if he ran into her ever—then one of them would surely die fighting the other if it came to it.

And here she was, walking beside him, ready to brave the storm with him. The Silver Sparrows and Lady Drake had sent him another gift to continue in his war. But it would take more than one beheading to assure him of her true intent. The Calica Clan wasn't renowned for their loyalty to outsiders. They had deep roots in the desert. They were there nearly as long as the longest lineages and strongest bloodlines of Zatan.

As they approached the gate, the soldiers remained in their positions, blocking the gate from those who attacked one of the Ayls of Londindam, and one of the king's Synths. But if these men were from Londindam, perhaps Soren fighting off the Black Fog had some sway over their minds, at least Soren hoped. There didn't need to be more bloodshed.

"Let us pass," Soren said.

The soldiers hefted their weapons. Some bit their lips, some had twitches in their eyes.

"We mean you or your people no harm," Soren said. "What happened back in your city was to help your people and your families. Let us continue on our way, or let us fight, but make your decision."

The bloodshot eyes of the soldiers scanned the five of them—the two young Syncrons, a mighty dwarf from the east, the Scarred, and now the Desert Shadow. Suddenly, being rich didn't seem to matter so much—or they just didn't want to lose their heads.

"Tell them we disappeared in the winds," Seph said. "Just as the bounty hunter did. We vanished, and you searched far and wide, but we escaped. The people of the caravan won't say otherwise. They don't want the trouble either. Just get out of our way, and we all live to fight and drink another day."

The gate behind the soldiers suddenly jolted. The sound of rattling chains from within the tower echoed. Large wheels spun, wrapping the chains around them as the gate rose.

They didn't need the gate, as Soren could just as easily go around the tower, but the opening gate became a welcome sight.

Not everything needs to be so difficult. We've got to get some small victories every once in a while. But Soren knew the truth—the soldiers were terrified of the woman at his side. Her legend rivaled that of perhaps only Soren and the Knight Wolf. They may have as well be standing before a pack of Shades, or one of the fog. The gate opened, and the soldiers parted, making way for Davin to begin their walk through.

As they walked through the gate, and into the kingdom of Zatan—the air smelled a little different. The earth cradled the sky in a somewhat new way, and Soren grinned.

Now, let's find this lord, and find out what the hell is really going on.

PART III
BLOODY KNUCKLES AND HEALING

Chapter Seventeen

The Old World

W̲H̲I̲S̲P̲E̲R̲S̲ *of the past harbor in cities of old.*

Weathered by floods, they still stand, monuments of the past. They remind us of what was and give us the inspiration for what can be.

The floods washed away much of our history—language, art, music, and even religion.

The Sundar and the Polonians were revered for their wondrous architecture, but bits and pieces remain from their once mighty civilizations.

They tell of old gods long lost to water and sand. They humble us, making us imagine generations long lost, strolling the same roads.

The old world was built by kings and queens whose names may have been forgotten, but some of their relics still stand. They stand as representations of the great, old world of Aladran, spectacular, grand, inspiring, and a reminder of the short breath that is life in the grander time span of our world.

The future is not promised. That is the one certainty above all else, for

even the names of the old gods who created our world are rarely spoken, and even less revered.
Remember the past, focus on the present, and build the future.

-TRANSLATED *from the language of the Sundar. The Scriptures of the Ancients, Book I, Chapter XVII.*

UPON EMERGING through the gate into Zatan, more symbolic than real, the world seemed to open up into a vast new horizon. The soldiers behind were left grumbling, scratching their cheeks, and pacing nervously.

Soren and the others entered the new kingdom with the fresh, exhilarating rush of anticipation for what was to come, but also a foreboding dread.

The five of them stood there, before the tundra that sprawled past the Lyones range, into a forever feeling sea that had dried up long ago. The winds howled up ahead, picking up dust and flinging it into the air, spiraling up toward the heavens. The Sapphire Sea, to their left, was a stark reminder of the feeling of utter thirst, while staring at the never-ending ocean of undrinkable water.

Soren had been to the Dyadric Desert, not feeling a fondness for the barren wasteland. But this time was different, he knew, whereas before his master Landran had taken him out—during the spring—to hunt. Now, he had a true master of the desert. Now, one of the most renowned in all of Zatan was at his side. He didn't doubt her aptitude for life in the desert. That would be foolish. He did, however, question her motives and allegiances.

The midday sun beamed down, warming their skin and drying their cloaks. The blue sky stretched out in all directions; the ominous clouds the elemental had conjured a thing of the past. Fluffy, pillowy white clouds dotted the sky instead. They floated lazily past the sun, casting down pleasant shadows onto the lands. If it were night, they may be mistaken for the Black Fog hunting in the desert.

That made Soren remember the mission, and the means to make it across the desert. They'd have to survive the night, and the Demons of Dusk long enough to make it to Golbizarath, where Mihelik had told them Lord Belzaar was. But first would be Taverras, the Brink.

"Follow me," Blaje said, beginning to walk down the bank from the border tower.

Soren and the others followed, but warily. They had to enter the desert, and distance themselves from the soldiers of Londindam, but there were still questions that needed answering.

"Who sent you?" Soren asked finally, breaking the silence that each of them wanted to break, but was unsure where to start. Soren thought that was one of the most pertinent questions.

"I will explain later, but first, we need to get you ready for the journey."

"No, you need to answer the question first," Soren said.

She halted and turned to look at him. Her brow slightly dipped, furrowing only a cinch. The corner of her mouth turned down, but only a whisper.

"The Calica Clan have answered the call of your Silver Sparrows," she said. "Now, let us make haste."

She turned and continued down the hill, away from the tower. Seph shrugged her shoulders at Soren, and they followed the Desert Shadow. Soren went last, looking behind them constantly for any sign of Gideon. He'd return, Soren knew. The wind elemental had the familiar signs of rage in him, from the murder of his companion. Soren knew they hadn't seen the last of either of the two bounty hunters.

The further they got from the tower, the more the soldiers pulled back from watching them, and turning to help put the pieces of the caravan back together.

"It's not far," Blaje said. "Just up ahead."

"You speak so well," Seph said.

Blaje didn't reply or even acknowledge her observation.

"Didn't mean to insult," Seph said. "Just assumed you'd speak Sarin, being from the west, and all…"

Again, no response.

"Did I say something?" Seph whispered to Kaile, but Soren heard it.

"Excuse me," Kaile said, hesitation thick in his throat. "Seph asked you a question…"

Blaje spun so quickly, Soren instinctively grabbed Firelight, pulling her halfway free.

"Let us get something clear," Blaje said. Her exotic eyes narrowed, and her teeth looked sharp as she put her face only inches from Kaile's. She was almost exactly the same height as him. His face paled as she glared at him. "This is my contract. You are my assignment. Where we are going, you're going to be more trouble than help. So, pay attention to me and what I do, but don't waste my time with silly questions. I'm not here to be your friend." She glared down at Seph with a flicker of resentment on her face. "You're contracts. And now you've got Gideon Shaw and the Yancor brothers after you."

"Yancor brothers?" Davin asked, stroking his beard. "Well, I suppose we can drop the 'S' on brothers now."

"We need to get deep into the desert," Blaje said.

"Hope we've got something other than feet to do that with," Davin said.

As they wound around the corner of the foothills, the answer revealed itself by a cave entrance in the rock. Soren breathed a sigh of relief at the sight.

Up the hill were a group of men up on their feet, looking

down the foothills, some with their arms crossed. Behind them was possibly the most wonderful sight they could behold—camels. There were only six of them, not enough for the men, Blaje, Soren, and the others. So, Soren wondered, were the men up there going to be traveling with them?

They walked up the hill, arriving at the area before the cave. The mouth of the cave was an open patch of rock, stained from old fires over the decades. Blaje nodded to the men, who stepped aside.

"Up," she said, walking straight to a camel, shoving her boot in the stirrup, climbing up into the saddle. "We have far to ride before nightfall."

Soren glared at the strange men around, uneasy.

"They were never here," Blaje said mysteriously. Then, the four men hefted the packs on their backs and walked into the cave, disappearing into the darkness, only the sounds of muffled footsteps were left behind. "Now, up!"

"Could you have picked a taller beast?" Davin asked. He was standing beside a camel with the bottom stirrup resting by his shoulder.

"Use the stone," Soren said.

"Ah," Davin said, seemingly forgetting about the eldrite stone around his neck. "I don't have another drixen stone for ya, my lady."

She nodded. Her focus was much more on the vast lands to the west than them, as they transformed appearances to the disguises they'd used to get this far. Davin easily mounted the camel, with Kaile helping Seph mount hers, and then getting atop his own.

Soren walked over to the last saddled camel, letting his palm glide over its scratchy coat of shimmering hues of the desert itself. The camel's head turned. It looked at Soren with its wise, knowing eye, peering deeply into him.

"Looks like we've got a long way to go together," Soren

said. "I gather you're probably more ready than any of us." He got up onto the camel's back, sitting in the saddle designed to cradle the two humps.

Blaje kicked her heels in, and her camel began leading them back down the foothills, straight toward the vast, auburn desert that filled the horizon. Behind her, the sixth extra camel towed with it heavy bags and rucksacks. Water sacks hung from its sides, sloshing as the camel followed the Desert Shadow.

The others followed her, and Soren trailed behind, scanning the foothills for any sign of Gideon. He found none, and nothing was left back by the cave except footprints, which the winds should cover with the grains of sands that rustled with them.

They rode down the hill and down into the valley, cascading with waves of dead grass that sprouted from frozen dirt. The Brink wasn't far off, and Soren assumed that was their destination before dark, and with the help of the camels, he hoped that would be.

Even with their disguises back, once word spread from the soldiers back to Lord Garriss of Londindam, the disguise spell would only take them so far. It was only a matter of time before they didn't work at all, and there'd be new bounties for not only the Scarred, but of all of them, with descriptions of both appearances. But for now, they were at least in the desert, which comforted him slightly. Few would venture out into the desert during the winter, or any season for that matter.

As they rode down the hill and the camels' hooves clapped into the flat valley, which turned from grassy plains to rocky sands over the next few miles, Kaile and Seph spoke to each other, riding side by side. Soren overheard they were talking about the Ellydian. She was asking about the spells Kaile had used during the fight, and he was explaining it to her in great detail.

"Quite the connection those two are building," Davin said.

He was back in his tall, female form, with long hair bouncing on his back as the camel carried him beside Soren.

Soren didn't respond. He was grateful Seph had someone so knowledgeable to teach her the ways of her family's gift. What he was unsure of, though, was how far their connection had gotten, and how much further it would get. He couldn't help but feel protective of his only remaining family. He didn't want her getting too wrapped up in a boy who was from a different world. Kaile had been deep in with the enemy for many years. Who knew what was deep in his heart. He'd been through so much already in his years, and working so closely with Alcarond must have been not only the most enlightening experience in the eyes of the Ellydian, but a massively warped one.

They needed to find a place to rest for the night, one preferably with baths and beds, Soren thought. They needed a safe place to rest and relax, because there was a mountain of questions he had for the legendary assassin. And he assumed she had her own for him.

After riding for the better part of an hour, Seph finally asked how far they had to ride for the day, and where their destination was.

"There's a place we will rest for the night. It's a suitable spot that will hide us from the cold. Then tomorrow we will ride for Taverras."

"Won't they expect us there?" Seph asked. "The caravan was heading to Taverras, so wouldn't they know we would go there?"

"You don't know Taverras," Blaje said. "We will blend in like a bluebird in the cloudless sky."

Chapter Eighteen

The winds gusted with a ferocity only the goddess could create, perhaps when she dreamed terrible dreams. All signs of life retreated as the last light of the sun touched the flat horizon. Its amber glow filled the air with a wonderful, breathtaking luster that glowed a bloody red hue on the thin clouds. Dusk approached.

The five of them rode to their destination for the night. It was a tower at the backside of a rocky outcrop that seemed as if Shirava had touched her finger to the middle of nowhere. The imprint raised huge boulders around the edges of her finger, and the tower was erected up from the ground itself as she pulled her hand back up to the heavens.

It was a round tower with few windows, except those arrow slits at its base and a few wide, thin openings at its top. Where Soren expected such an old, abandoned tower to be decrepit, with stones breaking down its sides, he was surprised when Blaje pulled a key from her pocket and placed it in the front steel door to the tower.

The key popped the lock, and she opened it inward as its hinges squealed. She entered the tower as the winds blew hard above, ramping up off the rocks that surrounded the tower on all sides. Soren went in directly behind her, putting up a hand for the others to wait. Sable ignored his signal and entered behind him, without permission.

Blaje walked to the right, and Soren followed, scanning the interior of the tower as he did so. There were open rooms at the tower's base, with a staircase that circled up to the next floor. In the center of the tower hay was strewn about, and buckets and brooms rested by the walls.

The desert assassin unlatched a hook on the wall and pulled a huge steel door to the side. Soren went and helped without her asking. She gave him a curious look, but together they swung the immense door open, exposing an entryway ten feet high and at least as wide. Blaje went out and led her camel in, and the others did the same.

Once all the animals were inside, Soren and Blaje swung the door closed. Just before it shut, he saw the last light of the sun fade from the rocks above.

"Get the saddles down," Blaje said.

Seph and Kaile, who were already beside the camels, unbuckled the saddles and began taking down saddlebags.

Soren stood beside Blaje and the door, as she took off her gloves, dusted them off. She removed her tan linen shawl and cloak, hanging them on a hook on the wall. Soren caught her smell as she rustled her hair. She smelled strongly of lavender as Soren crossed his arms, but she seemed not to notice.

Davin, who was standing back at the camels, lifted the spell of disguise, and walked over to her, standing so that the top of his head was only just at her chest.

"Yes, dwarf?" she said, brushing the sand from her clothes. Her sword was still on her hip.

"Now, we talk," Soren said firmly.

She stood back up tall and with her shoulders back. She

cracked her neck suddenly. "Now, we talk. Go on up to the next floor. I'll feed the camels and be up shortly."

"I'll wait," Soren said, staring at her sword. He'd seen her movement, and if she was to try anything, Soren knew he would need to be ready. If he didn't get his dagger up in time, she could cut his head from his shoulders with ease.

Seph and Kaile had just finished lightening the camels as they squatted down and lay on the hay.

Blaje went and pumped water from the room's corner into buckets and took them to the camels.

"Can I help?" Seph asked.

"No," she responded without even a glance Seph's way.

Davin cocked his head and looked at Soren.

She seems to have a strong distaste for Persephone. I need to find out why.

"I'm gonna go up and find a place to sit, or lay down," Seph said. Grains of sand littered her wild, frayed black hair after Davin's spell was removed. She headed up the stairs. Her boots made the floorboards creak as she turned the corner up into the dark room above.

Kaile remained downstairs, appearing to catch Blaje's coldness at Seph. His arms were folded, and he watched the assassin tend to the camels with a sort of riddling scorn on his face.

"There," Blaje said, going over and rinsing her hands from a pump of water. She splashed the water on her face, causing her skin to glisten. She wiped her face dry with the bottom of her shirt, exposing her stomach. It was lean, with muscular definition, but curvy—causing Soren's blood to stir.

She walked past, and walked up the stairs, with the three men exchanging curious glances at one another about the woman, but followed her up to the next room.

She seems so confident, so direct, and so deadly. I have a feeling she's going to be a difficult *addition to the group, but possibly a deadly, welcome one.*

"So," Soren said once they were up in the room above, and Seph had already lit candles on the tables, and a torch at the room's corner. "How much do you know?"

Blaje looked irritated by the question, scratching her eyebrow, and giving a brief groan. She went to the fireplace in the center of the long exterior wall and placed logs into it. There were no windows in the room, only dim old stones, a dusty carpet with two long tables upon it, and dozens of chairs scattered around the tables and walls of the room.

"How much do I know? Quite a lot, I'd wager. How much do you know?"

The question being redirected at Soren irked him. He put his knuckles on the table and pressed down on them, hunching his shoulders.

"You're of the Calica Clan," he said. "Why are they working with the Sparrows? What's in it for them?"

"Freedom," Blaje said, stacking logs, not looking at any of them. "The clan ultimately only wants what's best for Zatan, and even Aladran."

"The clan doesn't do anything that doesn't involve power and spreading its web," Soren said. He was pressing her on purpose. He wanted to see what a little antagonization would do. Blaje seemed so calm, but focused. He didn't have to wait long to find out.

She stood and spun. "Who doesn't do things for power in these lands? Look at you four, could the same not be said of you? Why are you here? Why are you here in my lands?" Her turquoise eyes reflected the amber candlelight, pulling Soren into them as if a spell had grabbed him by his core.

"The Synths have footholds all over Aladran," Kaile said. "There were two Aeols in Zatan last I heard, with over a dozen Dors. Is this still true?"

She nodded.

"What about at the Brink?" He folded his arms over his chest.

"Three Dorens." She folded her own arms and light gleamed off her lean muscles.

"Do you know them?" Kaile asked.

She again nodded, with a loose dread falling over one of her eyes.

Soren was listening, as it was pertinent information. He pulled his knuckles up from the tabletop and tapped his fingers instead.

"Why are we going to Taverras?" Davin asked. "Why risk going to where wielders of the Ellydian are? We don't need another fight. We need to get to Golbizarath."

"Ah, yes," Blaje said, grabbing the torch from its place on the wall, holding it up to watch its light, before guiding its flames into the logs in the hearth. The wood was so dry it caught almost immediately. A warm glow filled the room quickly. "Lord Belzaar. You wish to find him. That's why you're in my sands?"

Soren tapped his thumb hard. "Yes. I need information."

"I'll help you find Marcus Belzaar. But first we must reach Lady Sargonenth in Taverras. This was willed by the clan. We will help you, and we have aligned with the Silver Sparrows for this purpose. King Amón must fall. The time of his dark reign is nigh. A new law will arise when he falls, and we will guide in a just, new world."

Davin fidgeted with his fingers, taking a seat at the table. "I always get nervous when people start talking about new worlds." Sable leaped up onto the table, strolling before him.

Blaje didn't respond, but instead went over to a cupboard, opened it and pulled two bottles of what looked like red wine out, with glasses free of dust. She set them on the table, handing the key to Davin, who took it and began opening the bottles.

"Our paths are intertwined," she said. "So let us walk together while our goals are similar."

"Do we have a choice?" Soren asked.

Davin poured five glasses with the crisp, deep-colored wine.

"Not according to Lady Drake and Archmage Mihelik Starshadow," she said, taking up her glass and swishing it in the torchlight.

"So, what do you get out of this?" Soren asked. "Your new world? Does the clan want to expand out of Zatan?"

"The women of the Calica know the old world better than most. We know the cycles of this world. The floods seem like the catalyst for change—the purification of an old, corrupt world. But it isn't the floods that wash away the shit that stains these lands. It's people. People like us. Belzaar may not be one of the most powerful lords in Zatan, but to get to him, you'll need me. I don't care if that old man lives or dies, but if you need to get to him, I'm your only way into Golbizarath. Now, let me ask you, Soren Stormrose. What do you want with the lord?"

Soren touched his collar, rubbing it between his fingers.

He unbuckled Firelight from his hip and placed it on the table before him, still tucked into her scabbard. The infinite, deep, black pommel had an unnatural, magical aura to it. She leaned in, inspecting it, but not touching it. Soren kept his hands closer to the dagger than hers.

"Exquisite," she muttered.

"This came to me by way of Lord Garland Messemire. It was some sort of plot to get the dagger to me, without my knowledge. I was under the impression the dagger was Garland's, and he gave it to me freely, but after our fight with Glasse and the Black Fog in Greyhaven, Garland told me that wasn't true. He said Lord Belzaar gave him the blade with instructions to get it to me. I need to know why."

She stood up straight, scratching her chin with her fingernails. Grabbing her glass, she lifted it to her lips and took a delicate sip.

"Why would a desert lord make such an effort to give such a rare, priceless blade to a man all the way in Cascadia?" she asked the question, almost to herself.

"So he could kill Shades," Seph said quickly. "He could've killed that Black Fog with it, if he had to."

Sable walked across the tabletop from Seph toward Blaje, who leaned back.

The cat strolled past, not able to rub herself against the desert woman.

"But did they know that at the time?" Kaile asked. "Did Lord Belzaar know the dagger's capabilities against the Demons of Dusk? How could anyone know that without testing it? No one has ever killed—hell, even hurt a Shade until Soren saved you from them, Seph."

"Seems curious," Blaje said. "So that's what brought you into my desert realm?"

Soren nodded.

"We will speak with Lady Sargonenth in Taverras. But be warned, the people of our desert lands are not the same as the people of the rest of Aladran." Blaje had a cold, deep look in her eyes, as if staring off into another world. "Trust only those worthy of it. And any person out in the desert in the winter is a foe until proven otherwise."

Chapter Nineteen

※✦※

The desert was just as Soren had remembered it. Cold. Harsh. Unforgiving.

In the top of the tower, beaming with candlelight from its top windows—it was surely a beacon in the bleakness of the frigid, barren lands. They were hardly in the desert yet, but it was already a different world. And as Soren looked down at the moonlit sands, one thing remained the same—the Black Fog were hungry.

There was no escape from the Demons of Dusk, and without a single shelter of forest or mountains visible, Soren glared down at the dozens of them scouring the flat desert tundra.

"There's so many of them," Kaile said, his voice scratchy and dry. He smoked a pipe, as all of them did while looking out the rectangular windows. Seph was the only one not with them. She had rinsed her body and cuddled up into a bed on the third floor of the tower. Sable tucked herself up in between her legs.

Blaje scratched her forehead with the mouthpiece of her pipe. "Their numbers are growing."

"Is there anything left out there?" Davin asked. "Besides them?"

Blaje puffed her pipe, shaking her head. "Hardly. They've devoured nearly everything. And countless souls over the decades. A true curse."

"Where's home to you?" Davin asked her.

"This is my home," Blaje said. "These are my lands."

"You don't mean that literally?" Davin asked. "Ya don't have a place to call home? Just... this?"

"I swore myself a vow," she said, smoke bellowing from her mouth and nostrils like a dragon. "All the desert is my home, and I'll do whatever is necessary to see those that are born here, are protected from the evil that floods this world. Even if it means taking foreigners all the way across it, in the middle of winter."

"This is your home?" Kaile asked, leaning out the window on his elbows as the icy winds blew his reddish-brown hair all around his head. "It's so cold, so raw, so wild and free."

She nodded, a glimmer of a smile lit her face.

"Stark contrast from the capital city," Soren said. He and Kaile were at windows on either side of Blaje and Davin, who were in the center of their row. But Kaile heard and agreed with a deep inhale of crisp air and a nod.

"Do you miss it?" Blaje asked, causing Soren and Davin to raise eyebrows, curious about the boy's answer. "Do you regret running away? You forsook everything by jumping into that portal spell of the old archmage."

"No, well... yes... yes and no."

"Explain your answer," Blaje said.

"As fucked up as things are in Celestra, it was my new home. It was a school where I got to learn the secrets of the universe, and the Ellydian—the most powerful force in existence. Alcarond treated me with respect, something foreign to me my entire life. I was a somebody there. I even remember meeting the king for the first time, and the archpriest. It made all the bad stuff there easier. Sure, I miss the safety of living there. But when I saw what they did to those people in Erhil, it was all I needed to finally say I couldn't live in my delusion anymore. I couldn't help kill families and children in the name of saving the lands from the Chimaera. I couldn't help a cold-blooded murderer fulfill his dark urges, even if he was my king. So no, I don't regret it, but do I miss it, yes. I never had the constant feeling of sand between my toes up there."

"Aye," Davin said. "That's a real kick in the nuts feeling. I think we'll be finding sand for months if we make it out of this place alive."

Soren wanted to reassure the dwarf that they would, but that would be a lie. He didn't know that any of them would.

"Do you think they'll come for us, even here?" Kaile asked. "The bounty hunter, and more like him?"

"I don't know," Soren said. "Greed drives men more than anything, it seems."

"Greed and love," Blaje said. Her words made the swirling winds suddenly stop, and a heavy silence took the air.

"What?" Soren muttered.

"That's a saying in Zatan," she said. "Au gravenend ye amorndant lu istorian ses creaxi." The language was harsh, yet had a song-like quality as she said the words. "Greed and love are what drive man to do things worthy of writing history."

That saying hung in Soren's head as they watched the Black Fog sweep the forever sands of the desert.

Hours later, they had retreated to sleep. Rest was desperately needed, and they found comfort in their bunks with dry mattresses and sheets. Davin snored loudly as Soren remained on the upper floor, sleepless, scanning the darkness. Fatigue was heavy in his muscles and bones from the battle and the long travel, but his mind raced as if the next battle was just ahead—somewhere out in the darkness, watching, waiting.

He heard footsteps coming up the stairs from behind. They were light and delicate. It would be Blaje or Seph, he knew, and as Seph came up and put her elbows into the window beside him, she wiped the sleep from her eyes.

"What're you doing up?" he asked.

"I'd ask you the same question, but I already know the answer," she replied with a yawn. "I don't sleep, or, I'll sleep when I'm dead."

He huffed a laugh. "You got me. Do I really sound like that?" He nudged her with his elbow.

"I'm nervous, Soren."

"Why?" he asked, knowing there were so many things to be nervous about, but curious about which.

"I don't know about the Silver Sparrows working with this clan that Blaje is in. I mean, I trust Lady Drake, I think. I know I trust Mihelik, and he vouched for Davin, but this is all moving so fast. I'm worried about going to the Brink. I have this feeling that something bad is going to happen."

"I know I've said this before," he said. "But I want you to stick close to me here. Everywhere is danger." In the distance, there was a stir. Several of the Black Fog shot at incredible speeds toward something far off near the horizon. Soren couldn't tell what it was, but they surely consumed whatever it was quickly, possibly turning some unlucky wanderer into a cursed Shade. "At the Brink, we'll have Davin's spell hiding us, but stay with me."

She wrapped her arm around his, resting her head on his shoulder. "What do you think about her?"

Soren cocked his head and raised an eyebrow.

"Her. Blaje. Pretty isn't she?"

He forced a laugh. "She's more than pretty. She's deadly as sin."

"Play it off, but I saw the way you looked at her."

"I don't know what you're talking about."

"Sure, uncle. Sure…"

"Let's change the subject," he said. "Maybe to something relevant to anything else."

"All right," she said, pulling her arm back and tapping her fingers on the windowsill. He instantly saw she was playing something with a light, playful high end of treble notes, and it made him think of a butterfly flapping its wings in the spring. "Do you still play? You saw me, but when was the last time you pressed the keys?"

"Hmph. That's more of who I was. Not who I am."

"What a load of shit," she scoffed. "You could still play, if you cared to, or if we weren't in an all-out war with the rest of the world."

"I still dream about it sometimes," he said. "I remember the way the light hit the keys in our little cathedral in town. I remember the way the dust blew into the warm sunlight as the sounds filled the air. I remember you sitting beside me, just a little girl then, and look at you now. An Ayl wielder of the Ellydian. Tapped into the connection of all things. Hmph. Your parents would be proud of who you've become. I'm proud of who you are."

"You know… you wouldn't know me if I wouldn't have followed you out of Guillead, and have had you yell at me like you did."

"You were almost killed by Shades. Of course I was mad at you."

"But you killed them."

"I didn't know I could kill them. That's why we are here, in this wasteland. I didn't know the dagger could kill them, but we need to find who was behind this. Because we need to find a way to get more weapons to fight them. I hope we find a way. We need to find a way."

"Don't change the subject," she said with a playful glare.

"I'm glad you're here," he said. "Sort of not, but mostly glad."

"Sort of not?"

"Well, if you were still in Guillead, the whole capital wouldn't know you're alive. They would think you died back in Tourmielle. That's not good. The only way we survive this now is to win this war or flee. There's no other way."

"And the only way to do that is through the Brink," she said.

"That's the way," Soren said. "Lady Drake made the alliance. However, we want to move forward. We are the sword, and she is the armor."

"But you are the hand," Seph said, as Sable came up from behind and leaped onto the ledge, purring as she rubbed on Soren's forearm. "You chose our destination. If not for that, we would be on our way back to Skylark. I doubt we could've hidden there for long."

"Perhaps you're right," he said. "Even the old man hiding down in the depths beneath the castle is treason enough."

She sighed. "I had a nightmare. That's why I woke and came up here."

"What was it?"

Her lip quivered as she looked out at the horizon, as the clouds crept slowly across the dark sky. "We got separated. I got lost. I didn't know where I was, and I kept calling your name. It was dark where I was. But there were lots of people. I couldn't see their faces, and I was walking through them, like a mob bumping into me, and the more I yelled out for you, the louder their voices got."

He put his hand on hers.

"It was just a dream," he said.

"It felt so real."

"It'll be fine," said Soren. "We'll get to the Brink, and then we'll be on our way to get answers. I don't know Blaje, but I know her reputation, and she's a good ally to have on this path. She knows the desert better than perhaps anyone, and she's still young enough to fight."

"I want to trust her, but it's just hard for me. I don't think she likes me."

He squeezed her hand and pulled his away. "She'll turn around.

"I'm not so sure about that."

"She will. Give it time. I'll talk to her."

"I'm glad we're together," she said.

"Me too. Now go back to sleep. You'll need the rest."

She smiled and walked off, back to the stairs behind. Sable followed.

I should rest too. But there's too much noise to sleep.

Thoughts of the roaring, incinerating fires burned in his memories. He saw Cirella's face in the flames, and Bael's too. There was too much at stake. Everything was different now. It wasn't him wandering the lands as a Scarred vagabond. It was him against the world. And the world was so much more powerful than him. But he had Firelight, and his new friends. That was enough. That had to be enough…

Chapter Twenty

❦

The Brink was unlike any place Soren had seen in his travels of the rest of Aladran. As they crossed the last stretch of desert tundra upon the camels' backs, the sunlight bit hard at his vision. The distant city swayed in waves like rippling in a pond. He lowered his cowl to just below his brow. Sands rustled upon the desert floor at the camels' feet as the winds rushed by, with nothing to break them.

They'd ridden since daybreak, locking up the tower behind them with Blaje's key, making their way across the protection of the early morning rays. A half mile out, the city of Taverras stood seemingly as old as time, but as unusual as a fabled city that was more like to rest at the bottom of the sea than on the crust of their world.

Towers like jutting stalagmites from deep within a water-worn cave, windows seemingly cut from giant swords the size of dragons, and banners that blew fiercely in the biting winds. The colors grew from bland tans worn from long exposure to the sun to vibrant, exotic colors that hung from the tallest towers to the lines that held a family's laundry to dry.

Taverras, from that distance, wound in a giant spiral in its construction. Whether by man's hand or the powerful touch of Shirava's finger from heaven, the city seemed to twirl up from small dwellings in its outskirts to the massive towers at its center.

That's where Lady Sargonenth would be, Soren thought.

Get in. Do what needs to be done with the lady of the city and get out. Back on the sands, and toward our real destination.

Blaje led the way, riding at the head of their makeshift caravan. Soren, as almost always, rode at the rear, constantly checking behind for anyone greedy and daring enough to attempt another attack. But that day—he saw none.

As they rode to the city, Davin cloaked them in their disguises as the gems around their necks glowed and faded, concealing them in the same disguises.

"Why don't we change disguises?" Kaile asked in the winds, yet loud enough for Soren to hear.

"Can't," Davin said. "One appearance per stone. And those are damn rare stones."

"Why did you pick the one you wear?" Blaje asked bluntly. "It's as far from your true form as fire from water."

"Long story," Davin replied.

"We've got time," Soren said, leaning forward with his elbows on the camel's hump.

"Yeah, Davin," Seph said. "We want to know. You're beautiful, but why pick that form?"

"Long story," Davin insisted, snorting and spitting.

"You're afraid to tell us, aren't you?" Kaile asked. "Brave with an ax, a squeaky mouse with the truth."

Davin's expression soured as he kicked the camel's sides.

"C'mon," Seph said. "We won't judge… we just want to know."

"We could die together today," Kaile said grimly. "What

does it matter? We're all getting out all our secrets together. Not much you don't know about me."

Davin sighed, with slumped shoulders. "It was a bet."

"A bet?" Kaile laughed loudly up to the sky.

"You said you wouldn't judge!" Davin barked.

"What was the bet?" Seph asked. "Why would you bet something as permanent as that?"

Davin grumbled, "You wouldn't understand how seriously us dwarves take our bets."

Soren snickered into his sleeve, and even Blaje turned back with a wide smirk.

"What was the bet?" she asked.

"The bet was… none of your damned business!"

"Ah, c'mon," Seph said. "Now we *need* to know!"

"You *need* to stop asking," Davin said, pushing them away with the aggression in his words. "You said you wouldn't laugh…" His last words were only just audible under his breath.

"Leave him be," Soren said. "He'll warm up to it. Tell us when he's got a belly full of wine, I'd bet."

"I'm not telling none of you nothin' from here on out," Davin said, whipping his camel's reins and riding ahead.

"Did we hurt his feelings?" Seph asked Kaile and Soren.

Kaile laughed again into his sleeve. "He's sensitive."

"I plan on hearing that bet, if it's the last quest of my life," Soren laughed.

As they rode to the gate of the city, a high arch with a sharp point at its epicenter, there were so many eyes upon him, Soren's skin crawled and he felt the heavy unease as if the entire city was ready to be unleashed upon them.

Over a hundred soldiers flooded out of the city, each carrying an array of weapons, from curved swords to maces and clubs, to long spears with golden tips. Many were on horseback, riding past Soren and the others on both sides. The two rows of riders met behind Soren. The dust from the horses' hooves floated into the air, as if the desert itself had come alive at their arrival at the Brink.

A figure came through the gate. Her dark-skinned arms and legs were bare, with thick black tattoos covering nearly every inch of skin. Her head was shaved on both sides and thick dreads were tied behind. The tattoos ran all the way up her neck and covered the sides of her cleanly shaved head. She was far older than Blaje as she approached, with no weapon visible.

Blaje stood before them, not moving. Her hood was down and whipping at her shoulder as a wind gusted past. The old woman stopped a dozen feet in front of Blaje. So many bracelets were on her forearms that they filled up to her elbow. Jewels and fine metals of so many shades sparkled in the sunlight that they glowed like rainbows.

Blaje bowed to the woman, who didn't return the bow. The old woman said something in their language. It was only a few words, but they were stern—commanding even. Blaje bowed again, not responding.

Seph stepped next to Soren carefully, holding the reins of her camel delicately—not that the camel could run off through the ring of soldiers that surrounded them. She gripped Soren's hand as his other hand rested on Firelight's grip.

They were covered in the spell of disguise, but Soren wouldn't separate from Firelight or Seph, no matter what command the old woman with the sparkling jewelry gave.

Suddenly, the old woman walked forward, her soft white clothes flowing behind her, showing the true contour of her curves in the wind. Blaje then spoke to her with few words as the old woman stopped only two feet from her, peering deeply at her. Blaje didn't bow, and they didn't shake hands, but instead, Blaje sidestepped as the old woman walked past. She was walking straight at Soren and Seph.

Soren readied to slide Firelight free, but a tone filled the air, and Soren's hand froze. He tried quickly to draw the dagger, but his arm was stuck where it was. Seph pulled her staff from her side and prepared to strike it, but Blaje raised her hand in a motion to slow Seph.

The note was coming from the old woman. And in the common language, she said, "No violence. Not yet."

Soren didn't know what to make of the old woman's words, but the word "Wait," slid between his lips to Seph.

The old woman stood before Soren, proudly, with her shoulders back and her chin raised. Kaile and Davin both watched anxiously, with their fingers eager to draw their weapons.

"No violence?" Soren said, his body still frozen except for his head.

The woman shook her head. Seph pulled in toward Soren, dropping her camel's reins. As the old woman circled Soren and Seph, her gaze held an old, almost ancient, wisdom. In her deep brown eyes, Soren saw a glimmer of what he thought might be... rage.

"Appearances can often be deceiving, can they not?" she asked, still circling like a shark around its bloody prey.

"They can," Soren said. "And they must, sometimes."

"You come to my realm, already covered in lies," she said. "You bring hunters after you. And from half a world away, the fiery gaze of the king follows you."

Soren grumbled but didn't respond.

"We are not Silver Sparrows here," she said. "You bring with you calamity, ruin, and fire."

"We'll stop him," Seph said. Her throat was choked with uncertainty, but the words squeezed through.

"You certain of that?"

"I am," Seph said. "So, you're Lady Sargonenth? And you wield the Ellydian?"

The wise woman bowed her head subtly. "You come to my city, Taverras, in search of something—though I doubt you know what that is. I hope you find it, because the path you walk is long and treacherous."

Soren was growing frustrated. Even though his friends were free, he didn't like or understand why she had him frozen in her spell, other than to prove a point, perhaps. Or did she think he was the animal he was known as in parts of the world?

"Soren Stormrose," Lady Sargonenth said, raising her arm to him and sliding her long fingernail down the side of his stubbly face. "It's been a long time since you've been to the sands... they remember you..."

As she said that, her dark eyes sparked alive, the ancient being within stirring. Her words strained, deepening, to reveal something powerful at her core. She revealed her true self in that moment, he thought.

"Let me free," he growled.

She stepped in closer to him, as Seph pulled back in unease. Lady Sargonenth put both her hands on the sides of his face, scanning his features as the front of her body was nearly pressed into his. "I don't like you without your scars. You don't feel as wild, as ruthless without them."

"They're still there," he said. "Always will be."

"Yes, your curse," she said. She stood taller, raising her heels so her face was square with his. She was so close he could feel her breath, smell the incense soaked in her hair and the floral oils on her skin. Her lips grazed his. Blaje lowered her gaze to the sand floor. "The Knight Wolf has marked you, and in a way... I will admit, I'm envious. To have a foe waiting for you to release them from their worldly suffering, it seems... delicious."

Soren didn't respond, but felt uneasy with how close the lady of Taverras was. He felt vulnerable... and angry.

She suddenly pulled away, scraping her fingernails across

his stubble as she turned away. Soren was released from the spell, and the note faded away. She turned as her white robes spun behind her, and the jewelry on her forearms clacked together.

"Your false appearances will only work so much while you are here," she warned. "The king knows you are here. Your show of force at the border showed all of Aladran where you are, and although they may not know why, they will come. Even the desert cannot deter greed and revenge forever."

The lady's gaze hit Kaile with such a sharp, intense fire that he lurched back in surprise, taking a long step back.

"You bring with you interesting comrades," the lady said. "The last of the Whistlewillows, the fallen apprentice of the archmage, and an outcast, exiled dwarf from Mythren."

Outcast? He was forced from his homeland? He never said anything about that... why would he hide that?

Davin didn't seem to acknowledge her words, but seemed more intent on making sure Kaile stood back up, tall and proud.

"Yes," Soren said, moving his hand free from Firelight. "We all have the same goals, and we are bound by our fates. We walk our path together. You may not be a sparrow. But will you help us?"

She turned her back to Soren, but moved her head to the side as the sun glowed on her dark skin, and she suddenly looked years younger under its golden rays. "Yes. We will speak later. Until then, enjoy my city. Blaje Severaas will escort you. Whatever you need, just ask. For your enemy is my enemy, so therefore, we are also comrades."

Lady Sargonenth walked back toward the city. Blaje bowed low. As the lady disappeared back into the Brink's gate, the soldiers that surrounded them didn't budge. Soren knew even though the lady had said they were allies, he thought they might be partly prisoners, until the lady had what she needed from him.

Blaje motioned for them to enter the city, and they did so, pulling the camels in with them.

Soren felt the gazes of the many soldiers on him, and Seph reached out and held his hand as they entered the city of Taverras, together.

Chapter Twenty-One

"I thought you said we were gonna blend in," Davin said, entering across the shadow the towering gate cast upon them. Dozens of soldiers in copper-colored armor with dusty tan linens draping across patrolled the backside of the gate—and all gazes were upon Soren.

"We will," Blaje said. "But unless you want to sneak into the lady's city, and creep into her bed chambers to speak with her, then we're going to have to be a part of this, ceremony, of sorts."

"I don't like it," Soren said.

"Same here," Seph said, fidgeting with her fingers as the soldiers glowered down from on high atop the gate. Many had arrows nocked into longbows, others had swords and spears of a style unique to the desert. The swords were broad and curved, and the spears were adorned with long blue feathers of birds that lived nowhere else in Aladran.

"Zatan is unlike your world out there," Blaje said. "There are customs you won't understand, but if want to get out on the open sands to find your answers, then Lady Drake asked you to come here, to speak with Lady Sargonenth."

"So, we're emissaries?" Kaile asked, rustling the sand from his hair.

"Perhaps," Blaje said. "I'm actually quite curious what the lady will say to you. This, in itself, is an act of open war with Celestra. Harboring you is a treason that would only infuriate the king."

"But she's a wielder of the Ellydian," Kaile said. "She's sworn allegiance to King Amón. She'd be breaking her vow, if the king knew it was us under our disguises."

"The king's no fool," Blaje said. "And there's no lack of spies in his employ. Make no mistake, after that battle back in Londindam, the king has his firm sights upon us."

Soren felt his mouth twist. He absolutely didn't like every eye in the city upon them. They needed to get out into the desert, and soon. *But why does Lady Drake want me to talk with the lady of the Brink? She's forcing me into her war, whether I want to, or not…*

I don't enjoy being a political pawn…

As they walked into the city, the sharp-peeked, spiraling spires spiked up toward the heavens. Taverras opened up wide as they walked all the way through the gate out into the roads. Finely polished, flat stones wove through the city, laid in a striped pattern of light tans, tree-trunk browns, and glassy obsidians. The buildings, at least out on the outskirts, were built of a light-colored creamy stone with a mud-colored clay.

The richly colored banners flapped overhead, snapping in the winds. Emerald greens, sunshine oranges, and pearly whites decorated the brown city, while the robust smells of coffee and tobacco smoke rolled out of bakeries and taverns. Something sweet and delicious smelling made Soren's mouth water.

"For being so old," Davin said. "It's clean here. Far superior to Grayhaven."

"Far," Kaile said.

As they made their way forward, toward a wide market with hundreds of vendors lining the long horizontal road on both sides, a soldier approached from before them. He had a box of lacquered wood, held out, as if to present something to them.

Blaje halted, and the others did the same.

The soldier stood before them, his fiery eyes intense, and Soren could see the hard-worn years of experienced fighting in them. It was enough to make Soren want to fight the soldier, only to test their aptitude in the city.

He opened the box to reveal five braided ropes of a deep red with golden pins at either end.

"Lady Sargonenth provides her protection while you are in her city. Wear them at all times."

Blaje reached in and grabbed one, pinning it to her shirt above her left breast. She nodded for the others to do the same, which they did.

"I will take your camels now," the soldier said in the common tongue, which surprised Soren.

The soldier gently closed the box after they that taken all five out, and pinned them on. Another two soldiers came up behind them and led the camels down the road.

"Protection?" Davin asked.

"We are marked," Blaje said. "No harm will come to us here while we are under the lady's protection. We are free to roam unhindered."

"Good, because I'm starving!" Seph said.

"You will quite enjoy the rich dishes of Taverras," Blaje said.

"Lead the way," Seph said, smacking her lips.

Soren glared all around, with seemingly thousands of people watching them. He'd have to trust, not only in Lady Drake and Mihelik, but now a foreign royal Synth to the king and the Desert Shadow. He felt great unease, and felt a powerful urge to melt into the shadow with the Twilight Veil, but he had to stay with the others. He'd have to see where this road led them, and his grumbling stomach had its own motivations as well.

As they moved through the market, the crowds shifted with them. Everyone seemed to want to get a glimpse of the one who had scarred the king's face and had defeated the Black Fog. And even hidden in their disguises, they garnered far more attention than any of them desired.

Seph ran to a vendor with pastries in lines upon a multicolored, dyed tablecloth. There were some with a golden brown crust from butter, some dusted so thick with sugar they were hardly visible underneath, but her eyes and fingers found the chocolate ones first. She offered the coins from her purse, but the merchant, who didn't speak the common tongue, waved her away with his hands, pointing to the red braided rope clipped to her chest.

Kaile and Davin stood at the table next to the array of pastries. Cured hams were being freshly cut from a spit, and nutty, white cheeses were cut served with fresh, crusty bread. Kaile, Davin, and Soren all held their hands out and thick cuts of the bread were placed in them, and then heaped with the oily meat and sharp cheese.

They couldn't devour the food fast enough.

"Where's the wine?" Davin said, with his mouth almost completely full of food, crumbs falling down his chin.

"Let's get somewhere more... private," Blaje said.

Davin nodded, swallowing heaps of the food, and shoveling in more.

After they'd had their fill, or at least enough to satiate the deep hunger pangs in their stomachs from the long desert ride, they made their way up the road. Blaje led them down the main road that led to the tallest of the spires at the city center.

Back when they were in the desert, looking out at Taverras,

the spires looked like they were placed there by the goddess herself. They were unworldly in their ancient-looking design, twisting up toward the sky. Now, from the ground, they looked like monuments as old as time. There was no way man could construct such a structure, Soren thought. They were the tallest structures he'd ever seen, except the mountains themselves. Even the highest peaks of Skylark didn't compare to the towers at the center of the city.

As they walked through the desert city, sunlight flickered as the banners and walkways above broke the sunbeams, strobing its warmth as the winter winds calmed around the city streets.

Blaje led them all the way down halfway to the city center, eventually leading them to a building beside a tavern, that Soren longingly glanced at a little too hard. As she led them to the building, Soren noticed all that was left of the mob that had been following them was a pack of children. Around twenty of them, with no adults. They playfully fought for the best view of Soren and the others.

"Come," Blaje said, unlocking the door and leading them in. "The room should have what we need, but an attendant will be just outside if you desire anything else."

They walked into the building, with stairs leading up to the right side, and tables, chairs, and soft couches on the other. Thick drapes blocked out the sunlight, and Seph went and flopped onto a purple-upholstered couch quickly.

However, Blaje didn't enter the room.

"Where are you going?" Soren asked, taking his boots off by the door.

"I have things I need to attend to," Blaje said, her expression stern.

"Keeping secrets, are we?" Davin asked, plopping into a chair, letting the disguise spell fade, and taking his boots off.

"I'm the Desert Shadow," she said. "Secrets are my trade. But I have people I must meet with."

"Let me come with," Kaile asked. "There's much I want to learn about this place, and about this world."

"Save your curiosity, child," she replied. "The lady will summon you shortly, save your questions for her. But keep in mind, keep them respectful. This is Zatan. Respect is as coveted as water." Blaje left then, closing the door behind her.

Soren walked over to the table to start lighting candles in the dark, as Sable meowed and leaped up onto the tabletop, making circles around the candles. He lit the candles, and the room glowed a soft, trance-like hew. Davin rummaged through the room, pulling two bottles from the cabinets and setting them onto the table.

"One dark and one light," he said.

"Don't get drunk," Seph said, laying on her back with her hand over her eyes. "It's too early in the day. And the lady might summon us any minute."

"Well, lass, how about I *do* get drunk, and let you do all the talking...?"

"Can't find a fault in that plan," Kaile laughed, and sat at the table with the wine and the candles.

"Blaje told you to ask the lady questions," Seph said with irritation thick in her words.

"We made it here," Kaile said. "Isn't that worth celebrating?"

"In a city surrounded by people who know who we are?" Seph said, her words forced and sharp. "Sure. Sounds like the perfect time to get drunk. Ugh. Boys..."

Sable jumped down from the table and onto the couch at Seph's feet.

Davin uncorked the bottles and poured glasses for each of them. He offered Soren one, but after a scowl was sent his way from Seph—he declined with a wave.

Soren thought long and hard about their upcoming meeting with the lady of Taverras. And he wondered when that would happen—and he didn't have to wait long to find out.

There was a knock at the door. It was a soft two taps before the door handle twisted open.

Davin's hand swung to the grip of his ax, Kaile dropped his wine glass and grabbed his staff from the floor. Soren had heard her footsteps long before she knocked, already knowing it was Blaje before she entered the room. Seph was the last to notice, squinting from the couch as the sunlight filled the room. She stirred from her deep sleep and sat up as the cat stretched mightily.

"You're back," Kaile said, lowering his staff back to the ground.

"Lady Sargonenth will see us this evening," Blaje said, closing the door behind her, joining the two men at the table. Soren sat in a chair in the room's corner, closest to the door, facing it.

Soren's first thought was, *Why does she want to wait to meet with us in the evening? Does she have other pressing things to tend to first? Or does she have things to figure out about us before we meet?* Regardless, the time was arranged, so there was little to do but wait.

"What're we gonna do until then?" Kaile asked.

"Now, I could show you the city, if you wish," Blaje said, pushing an empty glass across the table, which Davin filled with a floral red wine.

"I'd appreciate that," Kaile said. "I've read so much about these lands. I'm curious to see with my own eyes the things I've read."

"We'll go after this glass," she said. "Anyone else care to join?"

Soren soured at the thought of separating, but the spell of disguise didn't do as much as he would hope after the spectacle of an entrance they were forced to make.

"I'll go," Seph said. "I'm hungry again."

"Well, I'm not sitting here by myself in the dark, drinking alone," Davin said.

"Perhaps while we're out," Soren said, "You can fill us in on why you were exiled from your homeland, since you forgot to mention that before…"

"Hmph," Davin said. "Or we could never speak about that, if you don't mind…"

"Have it your way," Soren said. "But now that's two secrets to squeeze out of you."

Kaile grabbed the bottle of wine and tipped it upside down fully, filling Davin's glass to the rim.

"Funny," Davin said, folding his muscular arms over his round, firm belly. "But I am going to finish that before we go…"

Chapter Twenty-Two

※

The city of Taverras was unlike any other in Aladran.
As they walked down the curving roads, which almost no roads in the city were straight, they all curved in the spiral pattern of the city, they were bombarded with the strangest mix of otherworldly sensations. There were stewing cauldrons in the vendors' shops, sending wafting aromas of perfumes of all varieties; woody, piney, citrusy, and creamy sweet. Spices roasted in ovens, rubbed on meats and root vegetables of all shapes and colors. Horned, scaly beasts roasted on spits, turning end over end as their succulent juices basted themselves, causing Soren's mouth to water.

And as they strolled down the main roads of the city, unaccompanied by the lady's soldiers, there was no lack of attention paid to them. Their disguises were up, the red braids pinned to their shoulders, and strangely enough, for all the gazes, Soren didn't feel one bit of tension or hostility around.

There was a strange feeling in the city, a surreal safety, or rather lack of desperation. Did they all revere the lady so much that her word resembled that of a goddess? She had the Ellydian in her, at least Doren level, and Soren assumed that didn't hurt in her control of the city.

Strolling casually through the ancient city was pleasing, and Soren appreciated the rare ability. Not having to hide in sewers was quite the welcome change. They stopped at the merchants they wanted, and Blaje seemed not in a hurry, as Seph, Kaile, and Davin perused and ate what looked most appetizing, and even some things not so much so.

Soren glimpsed Blaje as she spoke to one merchant, an aged woman with a curved spine and many years of pain in her eyes and in the many wrinkles on her face. They spoke in a language Soren didn't know, their Sarin language, but caught bits he thought he recognized. At the end of their conversation, Blaje gave the woman far more coin than what the cost was of the goods Seph ate.

Looking at Blaje, the aura of sunlight glowed around her, glistening on her smooth skin, her perfect nose, and her pouty lips. The loose hairs on her head that unraveled from her dreadlocks swayed in the gentle breeze. There was something about the way she carried herself that was completely foreign to Soren. There was no fear in her. She was completely relaxed and at ease in the city. There was no tension in her shoulders, and her hands were in her pockets as they walked back out into the road.

Soren didn't know if he'd ever met any woman so confident, so utterly in control, and so deadly in all his life.

He felt himself feeling something, something he fought hard to push away. Cirella crept into his mind, and then Alicen. Cirella was long dead, and Alicen had betrayed him in the most gut-wrenching way. He was reminded of his curse, and the scars on his face, thinking that curse went all the way into him, seeping into every part of his being. He shoved any feelings he might have deep inside him.

"Where to next?" Seph asked, crumbs falling down her chin from a pastry half-chewed.

"I want to see the oldest parts of the city," Kaile said. "The Durgath District? Is that what it's called?"

"Why, yes," Blaje said. "You have studied well, haven't you, apprentice?"

"I enjoy reading," he said. "Especially about history."

"Follow me," she said. "It's just up around the bend."

They followed her as she strode up the hill, curving around the sweeping roads as grains of sand washed across the stone roads, nestling in between them.

Only a quarter mile in, they turned a corner to reveal a vast courtyard, where the city reverted to an ancient world. It was an immense square of structures shorter than the surrounding city, except for one building—a cathedral of sorts with a huge bell hanging at the tip of its highest tower.

The surrounding buildings were only one or two stories, and made of a dark gray stone with veins of sparkly white that glowed under the sun's rays. But the cathedral was a marvel like Soren hadn't seen in a very long time. As they walked toward it, past the many rows of men and women in long robes with beads in their hands, Soren had the feeling he was looking at something from the old world. This was a place the Sundar built and worshipped in, not to Shirava, but the old gods.

He'd seen the old world built by the Polonians to the east much more than that which was built by the Sundar to the west, and he almost felt as if he was walking into the old world, but something that was more likely to be erected in the Under Realm. The way the cathedral grew to sharp spires but its defined edges had been melted away from centuries of wind, rain, and blowing sand, whittling it down, yet sanding it to smooth sides.

"Zalzobad Ari Cathedral," Kaile muttered with eager,

quick footsteps towards the center of the courtyard, and its lofty towers.

The bell chimed above, marking the end of an hour and the beginning of another. The bell's toll was sharp at first, but rung low as it echoed throughout the square.

"When was all this built?" Seph asked in awe as she looked up at the cathedral, as the white veins of the rock glimmered in waves, like veins of starlight embedded deep within the dark stone.

Blaje sighed and gave a glassy stare. "Thousands of years ago," she said. "It was built over the span of a hundred years, with the earliest dates within going back before even the Great Divine Flood that washed away the Sundar. It dates back to 2200 before the Great Divine Flood."

"This is four-thousand years old?" Seph said in a voice full of awe and wonder. She brimmed with excitement, surely pleased to be seeing the world outside of Guillead and Mormond Orphanage in her new life.

"It is," Soren said, after noticing Blaje wasn't going to respond to Seph's question. "This is one of the oldest parts of our world, back when dragons still roamed the skies."

As they walked around what should be ruins, but were wonderfully preserved and maintained, Kaile marveled at the ancient construction, muttering to himself about the Sundar and the Polonians of the past. Soren, too, couldn't help but wonder about what times like those must have been like. He tried to imagine the cathedral and the other buildings constructed by hand all those thousands of years ago, in the middle of nowhere, but seen by everywhere in the surrounding desert.

The past, to Soren, was a vibrant, bitter reminder of better times, but he couldn't help but be fascinated by it as well. So much triumph in such a wondrous creation of man—these buildings—but how many souls had witnessed their wonder, nearly every one of those souls had gone to the Halls of Everice. And now he there he stood, witnessing some of the oldest standing structures in all of Aladran—unbroken by winds, time, and floods.

It gave him an unwanted moment of reflection for himself.

All his failures, overshadowing his triumphs. Even those most recent victories—surviving the king and the Knight Wolf, hurting one of the Black Fog, and having Persephone back in his life—were all diminished by all those lost that he could have saved. Those who would still be alive if he would've been better… but he wasn't. And they were all dead now.

"Come 'ere," Seph said, waving for Soren to follow her around a corner, which he did. She was pointing at a stone statue at one corner of the cathedral. It was carved of marble, and although time had weathered it, it still stood. The nose on the woman's face was chipped off. A hand was broken and lost at the wrist, but her features were clearly visible. Her mouth was open, as if singing, her cheeks and jaw soft and elegant, and her hair wavy as it fell down the sides of her face and back. "She kinda looks like me, eh?"

It took a moment for the resemblance to kick in, but yes, even her stature was similar. Soren folded his arms, marveling at such a wonderful creation. Sable purred as she rubbed herself against the robes at the bottom of the statue, eventually leaping up onto the statue's back and shoulders, perched up like a sort of predator, scanning the horizon for her next meal.

Kaile, whose attention was diverted, noticed the statue finally and took his hood down and scratched his hair. "The resemblance is uncanny."

"Doesn't talk as much," Davin laughed. "I like it. Maybe we should swap out."

Seph elbowed him in the belly. He shrugged his shoulders, backing away.

Blaje seemed to not notice, her attention up at the towers that loomed high at the city center.

Soren noticed the afternoon sun was fading, and the shadows growing.

"Should we be off to get a meal and rest before we meet with the lady?"

The others nodded, and began to follow, but Soren noticed Seph's attention was still fixed upon the statue, as she stood before it, not noticing the others walking off. Sable was still upon the statue's shoulders, ready to doze off in quite the uncomfortable-looking spot.

"Seph," Soren said. Again, she didn't seem to hear or notice.

He went to her side and touched her on the shoulder blade.

"She... she looks like my mother now," Seph said, tears welling in her eyes. "I... I forget what she looks like sometimes..."

Soren pulled her into him. "I know the feeling. What an awful habit of time."

Seph sobbed softly as Soren held his arm over her, and she wrapped an arm around his back. Soren, too, saw the features of Violetta Whistlewillow, his friend, and Cirella's sister.

The others noticed and waited.

"It resembles your lost mother?" Blaje asked unexpectedly from behind.

Seph nodded, whimpering.

"I lost my mother too, when I was young," the Desert Shadow said. Soren noticed her motion for someone nearby, a woman in brown robes. The older woman hustled over and Blaje said something to her in their language. The hooded woman nodded and went off.

"What was that about?" Davin asked.

"I will have someone create a likeness of your mother, so

that you may take it with you. So you have a visual representation to remember her by."

Seph wiped her tears and turned to look back at Blaje. Her cheeks were wet as she used her sleeves to dry her tears. She ran over and embraced Blaje, wrapping her arms around her and squeezing. "Thank you," she said.

Blaje stood with the much shorter girl wrapped around her midsection, and Blaje's elbows poked out high, and her mouth twisted. "I only do it because I know the feeling of forgetting the most important person in your life's face. And I wish for you to remember it."

"Thank you." Seph squeezed.

"You should eat," Blaje said. "You'll feel better."

Seph pulled away, and Blaje quickly backed off, striding through the courtyard.

"That's nice of her," Kaile said. "Wish I would have thought of it."

"I know she doesn't like me," Seph said. "But I'm not used to people doing nice things like that for me."

That made Soren's heart skip a beat. He was the one who put her in that orphanage. He wanted her to be safe from the world, safe from the ones who would turn her, harm her, hurt her. But he knew the truth—she was hidden, she was safe there —but her life wasn't easy. Seph was hardened, tough from living there, but now that she was free of that place, the world was changing her.

It swelled Soren's heart to see her growing into a young woman, but also chipped at his core to see her hurt. He'd protect her at all costs from all harm, as long as he still drew breath.

Chapter Twenty-Three

❦

The sunlight waned as they sat at the table inside the tavern. It filled the room with an amber haze that lit the floating dust like tiny, lazy snowflakes. Plumes of smoke hung heavy in the air as Davin puffed his pipe between mouthfuls of food. Crumbs clung to the corners of his mouth and chin—unbecoming for such a beautiful woman. Soren laughed to himself.

Kaile sat across from Blaje, watching her as if examining a rare bird in the wild. The boy's knack for curiosity showed more evidence of why the archmage had picked him. And in Zatan, there was so much more insight into the strange western lands of Aladran than books alone could provide.

Seph sat quietly in her chair between Soren and Kaile. Blaje had a weird effect upon her—Seph was both inspired by the powerful woman, and afraid.

Soren tapped his fingers on the stem of the wineglass in his hand, swirling its cool, fruity contents as he watched Davin take turns eating and puffing. Blaje sat with her long, dark arms folded, with the faded tattoos on her sleek muscles illuminated like glossy drawings in a book, lit by candlelight. The copper and gold bracelets on her wrists sparkled. Her turquoise eyes beamed like sapphires.

They'd be off to meet with Lady Sargonenth shortly, once the sun finally crept off to its slumber. She'd hopefully have insight and supplies to share with them before they made their way out onto the frozen tundra. There was one thing that hung heavily on Soren about the lady of Taverras, though. She was a Synth for the king, for all who wielded the Ellydian and felt the connection of all things must be sworn to him, otherwise they were re-enlightened, or killed.

So, has she flipped, and stands in open defiance of the king? Putting her entire city at risk, or is she scheming something else with Lady Drake? If the king knows we are here, then he knows she is harboring us, and his passion for fire and its destruction could come.

Would she put her entire city at risk for the sake of rebellion?

They would find out soon enough.

During the meal, they talked little. Mostly, they let the air between the four walls fill with the sounds of the surrounding tables. Within those walls and the musty tavern, most all around didn't glare at Soren and the others. They seemed caught up in their own lives, a rare treat for Soren. None stared, and Soren wondered if it was the Desert Shadow with them and the red ropes pinned to their chests.

They filled their bellies with a lamb stew, crusty bread, and hearty roasted turnips. After, the innkeeper placed on the table chocolates and a strange type of fuzzy berry Soren had never seen. It was sour enough to pucker his lips, but sweet enough to make him crave another.

Soren assumed no one was talking because they all were thinking about what the meeting with the lady would end up like. And the thought prevailed in Soren's mind—that they needed to be back on their way further into the desert. If the Archmage Alcarond was indeed on his way to Kaile, then hiding deep in the desert might be their best chance to avoid that conflict. And fighting the most powerful Synth in all the world was something Soren desperately wanted to avoid—at least until Kaile and Seph could become powerful enough to fight him, if it came to that.

Otherwise, Soren knew his only other hope was to rally Syncrons together that were powerful enough to fight the archmage.

Either way, they'd need time.

And time, unfortunately, with the entire world watching them, was not on their side.

After they ate, they decided to slowly make their way toward the tallest tower at the center of the city—where Lady Sargonenth awaited. They walked back toward the Durgath District, as they wanted to marvel at the old walls of the oldest part of the city on their way.

They walked with Davin's spell of disguise, masking their true presence to the world. Soren's hand rested a little easier within the walls of the city. With the reassuring marking of the protection of the lady pinned to their chests, Soren's fingers hung from his belt, and not hovering close to Firelight.

His stomach was filled with the perfect amount of food and wine, enough to cause that all-too-familiar daze of the grasp of sleep reaching deep into him. The many nights of lack of slumber crashed into him in waves occasionally, and as they walked back into the ancient courtyard, his eyelids weighed infinitely heavy.

Seph skipped along beside him, humming a tune that sounded vaguely familiar. It was perhaps from their past together, or something she picked up in her years at the orphanage. Whatever it was, was a soothing melody that caught his ear, and he appreciated her pitch-perfect tone as she hummed and whistled.

Many eyes from under hoods watched them as they strode toward the Zalzobad Ari Cathedral at the center of the square.

The statues that were on its highest walls overlooked the square like vigilant spirits, watching the new world unfold with their eyes carved into raw stone thousands of years prior. Soren looked up at them with a sort of awe in their fine design, and he imagined the men who carved them, painstakingly paying attention to the finest details in lines of their facial expressions and the folds in the creased robes that wound scantily down their bodies.

Lightning strobed in the cloudy sky far overhead, and moments later thunder boomed down from the heavens. A thick drop of rain plopped onto Soren's boot, and another onto the sandy stone beside it.

"At least it's not snow," Kaile said, coughing into his hand and raising his hood.

The sun was still out, yet hidden behind the walls of the city, and thick clouds rolled in from the east. A calm wind rushed through the myriad of walls within the courtyard, howling dully as it flapped Soren's cloak. The breeze then faded to nothing, causing a lack of air that seemed unsettling as the dark clouds blew in overhead.

The men and women around stirred. Those that were sitting stood, dusting off the sand from their clothes before strolling back to wherever they called home. The winter storm that was blowing in was chilly, but not freezing, like it most likely would soon be.

"C'mon," Davin said, pulling his hood over as the winds reappeared. "Let's get out of the open. Bound to get bitter cold tonight."

They turned a corner around the massive cathedral at the center of the courtyard as the winds intensified, carving around each corner like a strong sea breeze blowing in with the tide. Raindrops fell thickly onto them, plopping onto their heads and shoulders. Seph reached down and picked Sable up into her arms, covering her with the sides of her cloak.

"Strange weather," Kaile said. "Wouldn't expect rain this time of year, this far out into the desert." His words were directed at all of them, but he looked at Blaje as he said them, as she walked beside him, with her attention focused up at the sky and the ever-darkening clouds overhead.

"Yes, strange," Blaje muttered.

"Let's get out of the open," Seph said, cradling Sable. "I—"

Suddenly a wind blew in that caused each of them to sidestep, to keep upright. It gusted around the cathedral, hitting them briefly, but faded away quickly.

Each of them halted in their tracks, looking at one another, and back toward the wind. Even though that rogue wind had retreated, Soren felt something wasn't right. He looked down at the red rope pinned to his chest, but suddenly felt that Lady Sargonenth wasn't in control, like she proclaimed she was.

Before he could speak, another wind erupted from around the cathedral, hurtling into them like a hurricane. Soren dropped to his knees and, with a firm grasp of Seph's sleeve, pulled her down as well. As the winds blew past and over, knocking Soren's hood back and causing his black hair to whip at his face and neck, Soren heard a disturbing sound.

It wasn't far off, and he couldn't see it. But as time slowed to a crawl for that brief moment, he thought he heard the sound of a whip crashing through the air, and once he heard the *crack*, he knew his instinct was right, and that they were now in a world of danger.

"Get down!" he yelled in the gusting winds.

The crack came from the other side of the cathedral wall, followed immediately by a terrifying explosion. The boom was so loud it sounded as if lightning had crashed into the earth right beside them.

Soren, pulling Firelight free, looked up just in time to see the wall they were hiding behind teeter.

"Move!" he yelled, his voice barely able to combat the sound of the hurricane winds.

They scrambled. Blaje tugged hard at Kaile's arm, pulling him back as the wall fell, its shadow stretching long over them. They ran, struggling to see through the harsh, biting winds laced with gritty sand. Soren shoved Seph forward, forcing her to run harder, as the entire wall fell with immense weight.

It crashed behind them, causing the ground to tremble and shake. The plume of dust that flew into the air from its collision with the ground blinded Soren. He could barely see Firelight in his own hand, her blade dull from the sunlight stripped away from the dust in the air.

"It's Gideon!" Davin yelled from somewhere nearby.

Soren heard the strike of Kaile's staff, beaming out a C note in the swirling storm. But he didn't hear Seph.

Soren gritted his teeth, reaching out for where Seph should be. He took lumbering steps through the chaos to where he'd shoved her. "Seph?"

"Soren!" He heard her muffled voice cry out. It was so much further away than it should be. "Soren!"

He ran in the direction he thought she was, but in the storm's madness, her voice seemed to come from everywhere.

"It's the bounty hunter and the elemental," Davin said. "This was a trap!"

Soren couldn't see Davin, or anyone, for that matter.

"Stay close," Davin said, "follow my voice."

"I'm going after Seph," Soren growled.

"They're using her as bait," Blaje yelled out in the storm. "Trying to separate us."

"I don't care," Soren said, squeezing Firelight tight in his hand.

"I'm coming," Kaile shouted. "Yell, so I can follow your voice!"

Soren didn't answer, but instead strode low in the storm in the direction he thought her voice had last came from.

Using her for bait? That is one foul fucking plan. I'm going to rip your little head off your little shoulders for this. And if you hurt a hair on her head, even the goddess herself won't save you.

"Soren!" Kaile yelled.

"Soren, don't go," Davin said. "Wait for us. We'll go together."

"There's no time," Soren muttered to himself. "I can't wait one second. Now I just need to find her."

Keep moving, Soren, even though you can't see. Use your instincts. There's no tracks because of the storm, but there's got to be a sign. There's got to be something...

And as if the goddess Shirava was listening, something black appeared at Soren's feet.

"Sable..."

The cat meowed forcefully. She was glaring up at Soren with feline green eyes staring angrily up at him. Sable spun and scampered in the direction Soren was heading, but to the left. She was quick and light in her movement, moving beneath the winds. She stopped and turned back to look at him once more, far enough that she was only just visible to him.

Soren held his hood up to protect himself from the intense sandstorm and followed the black cat.

"Lead me, Sable. Show me where Seph is..."

Chapter Twenty-Four

Sable's black tail slunk through the swirling sandstorm. Soren followed closely behind, watching the cat bound through the blinding storm. All signs of footsteps were washed away from the sands, but Seph's cries for help had vanished, so Sable was Soren's best chance of finding her.

I have to find her.

I have to.

The bounty isn't for her, it's for me...

It's definitely a trap. But I don't care. She's all I have left, tying me to this world.

I have to find Persephone...

Soren was still somewhere in the courtyard. He could tell by the ancient statues he and the cat rushed by, but how far from his friends, he couldn't tell.

The cat stopped suddenly, pawing at a grate in the ground... a grate that led into the sewers.

Soren didn't hesitate. The grate lid was already half-open, laying haphazardly askew. He dug his fingers in and pried it away. Sable leaped down into the darkness, and Soren did the same—Firelight sharp as death clutched in his hand.

Below, the world was dark. The rushing sands above were deafening. They howled and moaned as if it were their last gasping breaths. Below, though, the world was still. A chill took him, and his breath misted before his face. He had no torch, nor light from any source, but the cat's keen eyes beamed a shimmering green as she looked up at him before scampering off into the darkness, further down the long tunnel.

He followed.

His eyesight adjusted, and the storm continued to wreak havoc above. Sable led the way, sniffing and bounding around the thin stream of water through the round-ceiling tunnel. Ahead, a shimmer of light glowed. It was at the far end of the tunnel.

"Seph!" he called down, the word echoing as if in a deep, dark cave.

There was no response, but he ran. He ran past Sable, who noticed and sped up to run at his side.

As he ran, the light intensified, and he yelled again, but no answer. Once he got to the end of the tunnel, he stopped. He swallowed hard. His eyes narrowed as he glared into the room at the tunnel's end. It was a junction between more tunnels in the city's underbelly, with a single torch on the ground, gasping for air.

Above the torch was the familiar face of the bounty hunter Gideon Shaw. His wrinkled face tightened as he sneered, the scar on the side of his face folding along the wrinkles. Beads of sweat sparkled on his brow as the black braid of his thinning hair fell before the maroon armor on his chest.

Seph was beneath him, on her knees, both her hands clutched to his forearm, that wrapped around her throat like a snake, squeezing. Her pale face was flushed pink as she struggled for the air to speak.

"Soren," she mouthed, with his name only just audible. Her face was already showing the signs of bruising from what seemed like punches to her face. Her staff was nowhere to be seen, but Gideon had his whip lying behind him on the stone floor, ready to send flying.

"Can never be too careful with these Synths," Gideon said, his voice rotten as sewage. "I'm sure you'd agree with me there." His arm tightened around her neck and she gasped, air squeezing out of her mouth as her eyes widened and wetted.

"She's no Synth, you fool," Soren said. His fingers tightened around the leather grip of Firelight. He considered throwing it at Gideon's head, but the bounty hunter was a notorious killer. Soren knew that if he missed, he'd be weaponless.

"Synth, Syncron," Gideon said playfully. "What's the real difference? What does good versus bad really mean? He who wins in the end, history proclaims the good. King Amón is going to win this war. Make no mistake about that. His armies will crush the Silver Sparrows, and you'll all die like your sweetheart did back in Tourmielle. That much is certain…"

Seph tried to say Soren's name again, but nothing left her lips.

As the blood filled her head, her face flushed further, and Soren noticed a drop of blood seep out of her ear.

A rage welled in Soren that was so visceral, so primal. His heart pounded blood hotly in his shoulders and tightened fists.

"Let her go." His words were mean with a festering thirst for fresh blood.

"No," Gideon said, flicking his wrist and sending his ferocious whip slithering like a gigantic serpent in the darkness. "Throw down your dagger. Let's settle this like men."

"You want to fight me?"

"It's all I want," the bounty hunter said.

"Then let her go," Soren said.

"Oh, I will, but make no mistake. I want the meanest part

of you. I've hunted all over this world, and you, Soren Storm-rose, are going to be my most prized trophy."

"Then bring it on you little mother fucker," Soren growled.

"Toss away that magical dagger, and I let her go," Gideon hissed.

"You with your whip, versus me with nothing?"

"Yes," Gideon said.

"That's how you prefer to hunt?"

"No," Gideon said. "But you pissed me off by killing my friend Gorgon. Manans are a rare breed now."

"Getting rarer by the day," Soren said, gritting his teeth.

Gideon's mouth widened, full of yellow teeth.

He suddenly let Seph free, and she ran from his grasp. She ran straight for Soren, who reached his hand out for her. Her eyes were full of panic as she extended her fingers, eager to grab Soren. She ran as quickly as her legs could carry her. She was halfway to him.

With a terrifying flash from behind her, the whip careened through the air. Soren gasped, and his heart sunk into his stomach as the whip's tip crashed into her back, cracking like hot lightning cutting into a tree.

Seph screamed in pain as she flew forward into Soren's arms. He embraced her tightly as she moaned in pain. As he cradled her, he looked down to see his hands already soaked in fresh blood from her back, seeping through her torn clothing.

"Keep your dagger, Knight of Tourmielle. I want you to know that I beat you at your best."

Seph looked up into Soren's eyes. Pain stung deep in her lime-green eyes darkened with agony.

"Help me," she muttered, wincing in pain.

Soren looked all around, eager for something, anything, to help. He needed to get her to safety. She needed to be tended to. Her wounds weren't life-threatening, but they were deep.

The gashes in her back poured blood and would surely leave scars.

Before him, the bounty hunter stood with both arms out wide, one hand holding the whip as it slithered along the ground. He tugged it gently, causing it to move unnaturally, almost as if it moved backwards through time. His other hand drew a short sword from his hip. His maroon and black armor shimmered in the faint torchlight.

"You shouldn't have done that," Soren groaned. He took off his cloak and wrapped it around Seph's back. Tears fell down her face from the pain, lying on the cold ground on her side.

"She'll get hers," Gideon said, the wrinkles on his brow deepening as he scowled. "Let the king have his fun with her in Celestra. I don't give a shit what he plans for her. She could be his concubine for all I care. As long as I get mine when I deliver your head to him, that's all that matters to me. And then the world won't be whispering your name in the shadows, they'll be yelling my name in the sunlight! All of Aladran will know my name, because I'm going to be the one to rid the world, finally, of you."

"That's not going to happen," Soren said. He thought about warning the bounty hunter. Telling him something about he was going to die if he fought him, or this was his last chance—but he hurt Seph. He *really* hurt her. Soren didn't want him to run. Soren wanted him to die.

"Lay on your back, Persephone," Soren said, sidestepping away from her. "This won't take long."

She moaned as she lay on her back, a guttural groan escaping her lips.

"Let's see who the better hunter is," Gideon said, bending at the knees, flicking his wrist, and sending the whip slithering to the side.

Soren dug his boots into the ground, rushing forward. He

expected the whip to come in first, which it did—the thick sound of rope whipping through the air—as it whooshed over his head, narrowly grazing his scalp. He knew that if the whip's tip of black metal struck right, it could cause a violent explosion.

When it hit Seph, it didn't explode as he'd seen before.

Gideon has some sort of control over that whip, as if it's enchanted. I can't let it get near me. Best to get in close, make this dirty, make this my kind of fight.

Again, the whip rushed in, Soren deflecting its tip away with a strike of the Vellice dagger. In the same motion, he spun, attempting to slice the tip from the rest of the whip. The infinitely sharp blade Firelight just slid across the black material of Gideon's whip, not cutting a single strand.

Gideon pulled the whip back, snarling with his yellow teeth. The short sword in his other hand was held between them, waving in the torchlight, beckoning for Soren.

Soren rushed in, Firelight flashing through the air, attacking in a crisscrossing pattern. He slashed at the gaps in Gideon's armor, but to Soren's amazement, Gideon shot into the air above him in a monstrous leap. And in the blur of motion, Soren saw the whip moving through the air to the side, directly at him.

Soren didn't have time to react, he let instinct take over.

The animal inside was stirring. He could feel it. He heaved breaths. He could feel the fire burning within. Gideon hurt Seph. He hurt her bad. The beast in Soren was alive, and it wanted blood.

The whip's tip rammed into the ground, and as Soren rolled to the side, the explosion erupted under the city in the thunderous blow that filled the tunnel with a deafening boom, and then echoed down the long corridors. Soren felt the heat on his side as he rolled.

Soren felt the rest of the attack coming before he could

even open his eyes. He slashed Firelight above him, catching Gideon's short sword as it swung mightily down upon him. Soren was impressed by the swiftness and strength of the smaller man, and decided not to underestimate him again.

"That all you got?" Soren asked, the two blades shoved together as Soren was still on a knee.

"I've got all I need to kill you," Gideon growled, spit dribbling down his chin.

Their blades were pressed together so hard, Gideon's sword chipped, and Firelight twisted into the chip, causing the blade to form a crack. Gideon's red eyes widened.

The bounty hunter pulled away, swiping his blade away, nearly slicing Soren's forearm. He leaped in a large arc, flipping and landing with only a soft kiss on the cold ground.

Soren spun to check on Seph. She lay on her side, crawling away with weak fingers, the back of her torn shirt covered in dark blood.

"Hang in there, Seph. I'm coming. Just hold on…"

The whip flew in again, Soren ducking and bashing the tip away with Firelight.

Soren clenched his teeth so hard he felt his jaw pop. His vision blurred in rage at the corners of his sight, but Gideon was as clear as anything he'd ever seen. Soren felt he could sense his moves before Gideon made them, and time began to slow.

Gideon's wrist flicked forward, lunging the whip in again. Soren's legs, bulging with burning hot blood, rushed him forward. The bounty hunter's eyes widened at Soren's speed, as his giant strides put him directly in front of Gideon before his whip even fully straightened behind Soren.

Gideon brought up his short sword, and with all the strength in his arm, Soren hit Firelight as hard as he could onto Gideon's finely crafted blade. Firelight, made of Vellice steel, cut completely through the other sword, its tip falling to the ground.

The bounty hunter pulled back in shock, his mouth turned down in disgust, sucking in air in seething spite.

Soren saw the broken blade grasped in Gideon's hand, as its tip struck the ground, dinging coldly, and bouncing off.

He was thinking about Seph behind him, in grueling agony, and the thought of Gideon using her to bait him into a fight erupted a fire in him. It was deep in his core, down in the same depths he stored the feeling of being helpless when Tourmielle was burned, and his lover taken from him.

Now Seph lay helpless and hurt, by the hand of the man before him, and any sliver of restraint was gone.

Soren knew he couldn't cut the whip—and in that split second, Gideon was distraught by the broken blade, trying to pull away and use the whip again—so Soren devised a different tactic…

He swiped Firelight through the air, sending the enchanted blade slicing through Gideon's wrist that held the whip, easily severing his hand from his forearm.

Gideon cried in pain and anger, pulling his hand back, blood spewing from the wound. His hand hit the ground beside the broken blade. Soren's anger coursed deeper, though. He saw the man before as just a monster as the Shades, as the Black Fog, and this evil needed to be eradicated.

"You hurt her," he muttered in guttural rage, "I hurt you."

Soren threw Firelight away, it tumbling through the air to his side. He sent his elbow into Gideon's nose, bashing it and breaking it into a bloody mess. Gideon squealed again in agony. Soren curled his leg behind the bounty hunter's, and head-butted him, sending the smaller man falling onto his back.

Soren fell on top of him, driving his knee into his stomach, forcing the air out. Gideon's hideous eyes were wide and streaked with red. A scared fury was deep in them.

Soren pinned Gideon's arm down, still clutching the broken blade, as if that was his one chance of surviving the fight.

"You are as good as the tales have said," Gideon said with a bloody cough, wheezing.

Soren didn't respond, he didn't even know if he could speak. All he saw before him was the man that hurt Seph, and every fiber of his being wanted to make Seph's pain go away. He wanted to hurt Gideon, he wanted to hurt him badly.

He beat Gideon with his fist. He hit him so hard the words the bounty hunter tried to utter came out as gibberish. Gideon fought to free his pinned hand, but that fight faded as Soren slammed his fist over and over into the bounty hunter's face.

Gideon's nose crumbled, his jaw broke and twisted to the side. The side of his skull caved under the power in Soren's fists.

All Soren could see was the smile on the face of the man who hurt his only family. He kept seeing flashes of his crooked smile as he hurt her, beckoning Soren to fight him.

And once Soren's fists were done pounding Gideon's face, he raised them to see the broken skull fragments and bits of brain on the back of his knuckles. He wiped them on Gideon's chest as if from instinct. He was hovering over Gideon's lifeless body. Soren was straddling his stomach. He put his hands on both sides of Gideon's unrecognizable face, heaving huge breaths. He felt the adrenaline coursing through his veins. He felt his heartbeat thumping in his brain, and he felt the strain in his eyeballs.

"Soren…" He heard the whisper behind him.

He turned, teeth still clenched, his vision still blurred in rage. He didn't feel like a man. He felt like a wild beast, ready to consume his prey.

But when he turned, what he saw made him gasp.

Seph was standing, arms loosely crossed, her hands shaking. Her green eyes were filled with tears, and she was staring down at Soren and then at the bashed-in face beneath him.

Guilt swarmed Soren. He knew what he did was right. Killing Gideon was necessary, but he looked back down at the brutality he had inflicted on him—and Soren didn't feel like a beast anymore—he felt like a monster.

"Soren…" she muttered again. Her arms were covered in blood and her face was pale.

"Seph…" he murmured. "I…"

Suddenly, she took slow steps toward him, and knelt on both knees by his side.

Soren was so ashamed he just wanted to run. He wanted to run far, far away from there. He craved the forest, he craved loneliness. Just him and Ursa again in isolation, in hiding, becoming nothing in the world again.

But Seph wrapped her arms around him, sobbing into his shoulder.

Soren was frozen in place.

He looked down at the pieces of Gideon's face still embedded on his knuckles and he just wanted to melt away to anywhere else, but what Seph said next caused a sensation Soren didn't expect.

She said, "Thank you, uncle. I love you."

He didn't know what to say, but all of a sudden, he didn't feel embarrassed.

"You saved me, again."

"You… you don't hate me for what I've done?"

"I could never hate you." She pulled her arms off him and placed both her hands flush on his cheeks, forcing him to face her. "I accept you for all that you are, for all that you've done, and for all that you'll have to do."

He didn't have the words, instead a tear fell from the corner of his eye.

"I love you too, Seph. I did this to protect you." He didn't feel they were the right words, but they were all he could muster.

"I know, I know, uncle… This part of you, don't hide it. The world needs it. When all this war is over, then you can let it die. But not until the war is over… do you hear me?" Her green eyes were mesmerizing, like sparkling emeralds from a distant world.

He nodded. "Okay."

She embraced him again, squeezing tightly as another tear dropped from Soren's eye.

"We've got to get you help," Soren said. "You're still bleeding…"

PART IV
ONE WORD TO CHANGE THE WORLD

Chapter Twenty-Five

The Winter Desert

BARREN, waterless, and as icy as the tips of the world, the sands of Zatan are among the harshest places in Aladran.

Few call the sands their home, and for good reason. For when the warm sun of the summer retreats to its warm den, the animals hunker down in dark caves. The insects burrow deep to escape the plague of endless cold. For us, though, it is death. Wintery, grueling death.

The cities of Zatan were erected to build shelter from the open sands. Go there and wait. Wait for warmth, wait for the plants and water to return.

But, dear seeker of knowledge, if you find yourself in the cutting grip of the desert, alert your senses! Sharpen your skills! Become the animal that will fight to the death to survive!

For there are those that live in the desert. But those are not folk you want to meet, those are the folk you want to become, but only temporarily, for a return to civilization requires it.

If you wander out onto the sands, be warned. If you survive, then you may never be the same when you leave as when you entered. It changes you, hardens you, and stays deep within you.

Do not go, but if you must, then may the gods watch over you.

-TRANSLATED *from the language of the Sundar. The Scriptures of the Ancients, Book III, Chapter III.*

As SOREN HELPED Seph back up into the city above, the air was still, and there was a commotion stirring. Men shouted to the north. Soren pulled Seph from the sewers, the blood on her back already scabbing, her torn shirt stuck to it. She moaned as he helped her free. He put her arm over his neck and led her towards the shouts. Sable walked just ahead, meowing behind, as if to tell Soren he wasn't moving Seph fast enough.

Soren turned a corner and saw the source of the shouting. He furrowed his brow and glared at the enormous man who was the source of the hurricane winds, and the distraction for Gideon to steal Seph. The mountain of a man was on his knees, with his hands behind his back and his stony eyes glaring directly at Soren and Seph—as if in defeat.

In the air hung a smooth C note vibrating from Kaile's staff. The mercenary wasn't moving, stuck to the ground by Kaile's spell, but Soren pulled Firelight free anyway as they approached.

The shouting was from a ring of soldiers of Taverras. They yelled in their language of Sarin, which was thick and throaty. Davin and Blaje stood beside Kaile, his staff pointed down at the mercenary elemental. Davin's eyes widened at the sight of Seph, and he and Blaje both ran to her.

Many of the soldiers around ceased their bickering and

looked at Seph and Soren. At that distance from Davin's spell, the scars on Soren's face were vivid, and Seph's short stature and frazzled black hair was a distinctly different sight from their disguises. As Davin ran to them, their disguises faded back to life, but Soren cared not for hiding then. He was only worried about Seph.

Blaje yelled back into the ranks of soldiers, and two of them scampered off quickly. Another set of men approached the elemental from behind, tying his hands and putting a blindfold over his eyes.

"Seph," Kaile said with his mouth left agape.

She winced in pain as Soren sat her on a bench in the courtyard, with statues blown over and cracked all around. Thatched roofing was strewn all about and sand piled up against walls high from the winds.

"We should kill him," Soren said, glowering at the elemental as he was bound, unable to fight them from doing so.

"That's for Lady Sargonenth to decide," Blaje said, inspecting Seph's gashed back.

"I'd ask about the bounty hunter," Davin said, "but your fists seem to explain that well and good."

Soren looked down at the darkened crimson blood and tiny bits of bone on his knuckles.

"It was a trap," Blaje said, scratching her brow. "Why they would choose to attack us in the city is alarming. They'd fare much better in the desert."

"They almost got us," Soren said. "He could've killed Seph with that whip if he wanted. But he wanted me. He didn't need her dead. The king wants her alive, I think."

"Well, you handled him," Blaje said.

Seph cocked her sunken head and peered up at Soren. Her eyes told him thank you.

"We need to get her to a healer," Blaje said, still eyeing the deep, bloody gashes on her back.

"Oh, Seph," Davin said in a gruff voice. "What did that bastard do to you?

"I—I'm all right," Seph said. "It's just a scratch."

"You're one tough girl, I tell ya," Davin said, scratching his chin. "Wouldn't have thought I'd say that before, but you've grown, lass."

The two soldiers who'd run off both returned, but with a woman between them. She wore white linens and had a golden threaded headdress on. Blaje sidestepped, letting the woman through. She first looked into Seph's eyes and then went to her back.

The woman and Blaje exchanged words.

"She's going to take her," Blaje said.

"I'm going with," Soren said.

"I figured," Blaje said. "It's just down the road." Blaje lifted Seph, putting an arm over her shoulder, and Soren took Seph's other side. The woman with the golden threaded headdress waved for them to follow her, and they did. As they walked off, up north, another man ran into the area with the elemental, and Soren heard the strike of a tuning fork and an A note. The Syncron held the mercenary in place, waving for Kaile to drop his spell and go with his friends, which he gratefully did, panting as he dropped his spell, and ran after Seph.

Minutes later, they led Seph into a room off the road with many cabinets and four empty beds. The woman with the headdress patted one bed, and Seph crawled into it on her stomach. Soren, Blaje, Davin, and Kaile all watched the woman opening cabinets and pulling down things from their packed insides. A vial from one, bandaging from another.

A knock came from behind, and the door creaked open. Another woman in the same headdress entered, but this woman was older, at least twice the age of the other. She shoved herself between Soren and Blaje to get to Seph.

"We should go," Blaje said. Her words shocked Soren.

He was about to say his rebuttal, but to his surprise, instead of uttering the words, Blaje had pressed two of her fingers to his lips.

"She is safe here and being cared for by some of Taverras' best. There will be soldiers all around this place. The Manan is bound and in captivity. And the lady will be waiting."

"I'm coming," Seph said with weak words as the woman cut the shirt from her back and began washing the wounds.

"You're staying here," Kaile said, his boot tapping nervously on the floorboards.

"I..." she tried to say something but her words trailed off into tired gibberish.

"Come," Blaje said. "We will return after to see her."

"I can't leave her," Soren said, scratching his forearm.

"Soren," Blaje said, looking deeply into his eyes. "She's all right. You saved her already. Now let her get fixed while we do what we need to."

He sighed deep, and nodded. "Very well. I'll be back soon, Persephone."

She moaned something, but her closed eyes and dangling arm from the bed showed she was indeed right where she needed to be.

"Lead the way," Soren said.

Blaje turned and opened the door behind, ushering for them to leave. They all left the room, with a pack of eight soldiers stationed at the front of the building. Each of them nodded to Soren. He wasn't exactly sure what for.

Soren left Seph back in the room with the healers. He left her without the protection of her disguise. He left her with complete strangers while she was at her weakest. Why? Soren shook his head as he looked down at his boots as they crossed the sandy stones of the road that led to the palace of Taverras.

Firelight was safely tucked away in her scabbard, and he brushed the last bits of bone off his knuckles, dried blood caked between the wrinkles in his skin.

He couldn't figure out why he was so quick to let Seph go, or leave her, rather. Beside him walked the Desert Shadow, the First Blade of the Calica Clan. Her demeanor was as cold as deep ocean ice, stoic as a statue, and deadly as an asp. But for some reason, Soren couldn't figure out why did he trust her so?

He didn't remember the last time he trusted someone so quickly, the way he did with her. He just left Seph alone in a room with people he'd never met, and would possibly never meet again. All because Blaje said it was fine.

His fingers stroked his chin as he eyed her curiously, almost as if he suspected her casting a spell over him, but he knew that wasn't the case. It was trust, or respect, or something somewhere in between. They'd been at the Brink only a short time, and they'd already been attacked, so why in the Under Realm was he trusting her the way he was?

Soren caught the flicker of the whites of eyes beside him. Both Davin and Kaile were looking at him, looking at Blaje. He flashed away his gaze at her. But it was too late, as Davin and Kaile both snickered.

Blaje glanced back at both the two, who straightened out, and their laughter faded promptly.

The four made their way up the winding road that curved right, uphill. Hundreds of citizens stood outside of their homes, outside of taverns and shops, all gathered to watch the Scarred make his way to meet with their lady. As the minutes rolled by, and the road continued to wind around in a giant spiral, the homes turned to three-story and four-story structures, eventually leading to towers that grazed the lowest rungs of the sky.

Eventually, they took a last bend around a corner to reveal their destination, the central tower of Taverras, and the palace of Lady Sargonenth. Siracco Tower harnessed the throne within and stood as tall as any structure Soren had ever seen. He wondered how men of the old world could create such a feat of craftsmanship. Its thin, domed windows twirled up to its sharp spires in waves. The hundreds of smaller spires rippled up the top parts of the tower until the five main spires pointed to the heavens like spidery fingers reaching into the clouds.

Out of dozens of the windows flew banners of all shades, whipping in the high, intense winter winds above.

As they made their way to the front gate, swarming with soldiers, their bustling and commotion quickly halted, and they all stood watching the four of them approach. Soren was sure each of them already knew about the attack back in the ancient Durgath District, and probably knew the fate of the bounty hunter back in the sewers.

The soldiers parted, making a clear path to the front gate of the tower, and as they strode through, some of the soldiers even patted Soren on the back. His fingers flicked toward Fire-light at the first pat, but Blaje moved her hand to cover his, pulling it away from the Vellice dagger.

She didn't look at him once as they made their way through what felt like a sea of soldiers. The gate was already wide open, its barred iron gate hanging above them as they walked through. Within was a warm-feeling, large round room with a huge hearth just ahead. A pair of royals sat in fine silks smoking pipes at a long table. Several other torches hung on the round walls, adding to the glowing hum of light, as well as many candles scattered on tables and shelves around the room.

Blaje led them all the way up the tower, taking a vast amount of stairs that wound around the tower. Looking out the many windows along the route, Soren wondered if everything built in Taverras was built in these spiral patterns, and for what purpose. Many, many steps later, she opened a door on their right, stepping in, and the others followed.

"Now remember," she said. "Respect is the law of these lands. Be respectful to the lady at all times, or you may find the dungeons of Taverras to be your home for the foreseeable future. Are you ready?"

Soren nodded. "Let's get this over with."

Chapter Twenty-Six

The throne room in the palace of Siracco Tower was unlike anything Soren had ever seen—and from his brief experience in the ancient city of Taverras—felt perfectly appropriate. The wide, high-ceilinged room was filled with a myriad of stalagmites which were painted in gold, decorated with candles, and wrapped in the dyed cloths that looked older than Soren.

The windows that swooped around the room reflected the amber candlelight back in, hiding the moonlight beyond, and any stars that might cause Firelight to glow that blood red she loved to show. At the back center of the room, cradled between windows, was the lady of Taverras, seated, whispering to a man who stood beside her.

She saw Soren and the others approach, walking on a violet carpet, which the golden stalagmites straddled. Her legs crossed to the other side under her gown of sunrise-orange silk. Dried desert roses were sown into the sides of the dress, rising from toe to both sides of her chest. Her dark-skinned arms were bare, decorated with black-ink tattoos covering nearly every inch.

The man at her side slunk away after a final whisper from her. He pulled a hood over his head and disappeared into a back corner of the room, just visible past the eye level protruding stalagmites.

Lady Sargonenth's hand lifted from the armrest of her throne, a wooden chair of white wood and a deep blue cloth draped down from its high back. With a flick of her fingers, she ushered them to approach, which they did, and Blaje dropped to a knee ten feet before the lady of Taverras.

"I heard you ran into trouble on your way here," the lady said, her wise, elder eyes glaring heavily at Soren. "I apologize for the attack. That should not have happened within my walls."

Blaje rose. "The Manan is in custody, and the bounty hunter for the king was slain."

"Good riddance to Gideon Shaw," the lady said, leaning back in her throne and turning her head to the side, as if looking out the window beside her. "A nuisance, and a hound for the king. But a Manan, it has been an age since I've seen one. There is hopefully much to learn from the man."

"He may be grieving," Kaile interjected suddenly, causing Blaje to scoff. "Not from Gideon's death. He lost his brother."

"By your hand," Lady Sargonenth added.

Kaile nodded. "We killed him when he attacked us first, when we were with the caravan that was heading here."

The lady seemed deep in thought. Davin cracked Kaile in the side with his elbow. Davin, in his disguise, was as tall as Kaile, so it was just a quick bend of the arm to send the message to him.

"Lower the spell," the lady said. "I want to speak with you as you truly are."

Davin lifted the necklace out from beneath his shirt, and the eldrite stone glowed briefly. But as its light faded, so did the spell that hid them. Davin shrunk and widened to his normal form. Kaile's short black hair grew to its reddish-brown hue, fell down past his jaw. Soren felt the scars on his face return and tighten.

A corner of the lady's mouth crept up.

"There," Soren said. "You see us for who we are. There's no hiding in your kingdom now. The king surely knows exactly where we are. I do have a question for you: knowing that, are you prepared to face the wrath of King Amón?"

Blaje's face twisted at the way he asked the lady what he did.

"Soren," Davin said in a hushed voice.

"You are a Dor," Soren said. "You're powerful, so you've sworn allegiance to the king. With aiding us, have you officially switched allegiances? You know the king's scorn, as well as anyone."

Lady Sargonenth glowered at Soren, her eyebrows shoved down and her dark eyes narrowed.

"Yes, I know the king," she said, with words laced with hatred. "I know what that man does to those that bend away from his will. He will want answers, but we are far from the reach of Lynthyn. This is Zatan. This realm was once its own. We had our own laws, our own values, and we will return to that glory once again."

"You are planning to rebel?" Kaile asked, his mouth hung agape after the last word, as if in disbelief any kingdom would openly fight the capital.

"Even those in the Silver Sparrows wish to remain in the shadows," Davin said. "You wish for open war with the king?"

"War is already upon us." The lady stood abruptly, her words shuddering the room. A low A note hung in the air from her throne. "The Chimaera runs rampant. Killed five in my city again today. The monster, the Knight Wolf, captures and tortures his prey all over Aladran. And the king burns to the ground any city he deems too dangerous to his right to the throne. You, Soren Stormrose, know more than anyone of how the tragedy of the ongoing war within our realm. You know this will build until it envelops anyone and everyone in its wrath. The only way through to clear skies is with that monster dead and buried."

"I agree," Soren said. "But at what cost? You will forfeit the lives of so many in your kingdom, should you help us. It may even cost you the city itself. The king may not make this far of a journey in this time of year, and after the burning of Erhil, but he will come, and his fire will spread."

"Then let him try it!" Her words caused the ground to tremble beneath their feet and the walls to shake in the high tower. "Call me a heretic, label me a Silver Sparrow, but I will not sit by and watch another long-standing city burn! If I must be the first to defy that bastard's word, then so be it. I proclaim the city of Taverras as free and independent. Should the Calica Clan decide to join our liberation, then all of Zatan would be free. All Syncrons would be free to use their magic, free of the bent will of King Amón. We could use our magic to improve this world, not just control it."

Kaile's fingers spread wide, and he took an unintentional stagger forward. He was hanging on her every word like a moth floating toward a flame.

Blaje played with the tips of her thick dreads that hung down her chest. Her gaze was distant, busy, thinking.

"We will need Syncrons to fight the war," Soren said. "Blades cut flesh, but they cannot touch the Ellydian."

"You keep powerful company." The lady sat back on her throne, crossing her legs again, her thighs gliding under the soft silk of her long dress. She was staring at Kaile with a raised eyebrow and a tugged corner of her mouth. "The apprentice has fallen from grace, but his power only grows. Can you feel it, fallen apprentice?"

"With all due respect, my lady, I don't like being called that," Kaile said. "I left. I wasn't disgraced."

"Regardless," the lady responded. "You are an outcast now. You are cut off from the scriptures of the ancients and their knowledge. You are labeled a Synth now by the capital. You are evil to them, but make no mistake, your power is rumored throughout these lands. Many believe you will attempt the Black Sacrament. If you do, and pass, you may rival the archmage's power."

Kaile's face dropped, gazing down to his feet. His long hair fell to the sides of his face, and he rubbed his cheek with the flat of his palm.

"You may not like it," she said, "but the world is going to need you to be as powerful as you can imagine if someone is to dethrone the archmage and the archpriest. Soren has the ability to kill the king if he had the chance, but no one in this world could defeat Alcarond, including myself—except you, and the former Archmage Mihelik. Even Lady Drake would fall to Alcarond's power."

"Seph, er—Persephone Whistlewillow—" Davin said. "She proves stronger every day, as well."

"She is untrained," Lady Sargonenth said. "And very much lucky to be alive still after all these years. Her only saving grace was being hidden by her uncle. I hear she's lucky to be alive from the attack by the bounty hunter today."

Soren's stomach sunk at the thought of the gashes in her back, and that bastard Gideon using her as bait.

"But you saved her," the lady said. "Remember that Soren. You have every ability to do heroic things. You are not defined or cursed by the few failures of your life. Your destiny is unwritten. You have the power to change the course of your life. You will be remembered by the things you accomplish in the coming weeks."

Soren swallowed down his self-contempt and bitterness of the way her words tasted.

"Is Seph going to be all right?" Kaile asked, fidgeting with his fingers.

The lady nodded. The candlelight glistened off the glossy tattoos on her neck as she did so.

"How did they get into your city?" Kaile asked.

"We shall soon know the answer to that question," the lady said. "My people are looking into the bounty hunter's route into the city. Now... shall we get to what you've come here for? Lord Belzaar?"

"Yes," Soren said eagerly. "I need to find him."

"Why?"

Soren slid Firelight halfway from her sheath. The candlelight sparkled off the infinitely sharp steel.

"He sent this to me through a lord named Garland Messemire. I very much need to know why it was sent to me."

"I agree with your curiosity," the lady said, playing with her hair that fell before her chest. "That is the blade with which you slayed Shades and defeated the Black Fog, correct?"

He nodded.

"Then these answers you have, beckon for urgent answers," she said.

"He's at or near Golbizarath, far into the desert, Mihelik said." Soren tucked Firelight back into her home with a soft click.

"I agree with this assessment," the lady said, "and I dare say I would argue with any of the old archmage's assessments. He's the most knowledgeable man in all of Aladran, as far as I'm concerned."

"So, you'll help us get there?" Davin asked.

"If the Calica Clan hadn't sent you their Desert Shadow, I dare say you wouldn't make it to the western lands. But... with her at your side, you should make it, even in these winter winds."

"We are grateful for her presence," Kaile said. "And I personally hope to learn much of your lands, if she's willing to teach me."

The lady sighed unexpectedly, catching Soren off guard. She stood, her silk robes falling down the curves of her body as she walked over to the window beside her throne. She gazed out the window at the heavens beyond.

"Things could be so different in these lands. If there were no evil king, no rotten dogs of his, no Demons of Dusk, and no plague, this world could know peace, and you could be a fine archmage one day. But... the history of our world isn't written by us, it's written by them."

"For now," Soren added.

"Yes, for now," the lady said. "Unless we can kill the king and rid our world of the Demons of Dusk, I fear for our future as a people. The dragons of the north may be the only thing capable of purging our lands of evil, should we fail. Fire and floods are ultimate, powerful destroyers, but they ironically bring about rebirth. The king knows this, in his own twisted, deranged way."

"You're saying the dragons could kill the king, the Shades, and the Black Fog?" Kaile asked, his eyes dazzled as they reflected the warm glow of the many flickering candles all around. His words were laced with curiosity.

"What I am saying, fallen apprentice, is that if we fail, then nothing will be left to save these lands."

Davin folded his muscly, short arms. "She's saying only dragon fire is strong enough to burn everything away, if the king doesn't do it first."

"He wields the Storm Dragon Blade," the lady said. "It's the finest Vellice sword in all the world. The Knight Wolf carries the Ember Edge, second only in craftsmanship to the king's blade. You carry your Vellice dagger…" She raised an eyebrow and sauntered toward Soren. "These three blades are the only weapons in creation that can hurt the Demons of Dusk. We need more. We need so many more to save our world."

"We could go to Vellice…" Kaile said, tapping his fingers on his staff as the lady approached Soren.

Lady Sargonenth was taller than Soren by six inches. She gazed down at him, and him up at her as she stood before him.

"Let me see it," she breathed.

He pulled Firelight free with a high-pitched ring of steel ringing from her tip. In both hands, he held it up for her to inspect.

"Marvelous," she said with awe thick in her breath. "I admit that in my dreams I fear what could become of my city, should the Black Fog enter like that monstrous one did in Greyhaven. A city that has stood for tens of thousands of years would fall, and me and my people would be powerless to stop it. If a horde of Shades invaded, no steel or even the magic of my Ellydian could stop a single one of them. Up until now, they've stayed to the shadows, stayed to the desolation of the night sky, and now I stand here, beholding the beauty of the most magnificent dagger I've ever seen, and it is my only tool to defend my city and its people—and I'm about to let you walk out my gate and out into the open Dyadric."

Soren pulled back, clenching his fingers around the grip tightly and placing it back into its sheath.

The lady closed her eyes and sighed deeply. "But you have a mission, and that mission is not only of great importance to you, but to all those that live here. I too am curious why this blade was sent to you, and only you. Someone knew it would have the ability to defeat the Demons of Dusk, and they sent it to you specifically. There's something happening in our world. A tide is shifting, and I know it will never be the same after.

There's an evil growing. Something is unleashing these monsters into our world, and their army is growing. Make no mistake when I tell you this, Soren Stormrose, the enemy is gathering for something, and by the time we know what it is, I fear it will be too late. Every day counts now, so make them count. I know you've experienced great loss and tragedy in your life, but there's a little girl down in my kingdom who needs you to survive this. She needs you to fight. I need you to fight."

"I will do what I can," Soren said.

"That will be enough," she said, peering deep into him with her wise, old eyes like an owl's. "It has to be."

Chapter Twenty-Seven

"Then you will let us leave your city?" Soren rubbed his chin, thinking about what Lady Sargonenth had planned next.

She'd revealed she was openly defying the king, and even Taverras being, geographically, one of the furthest cities from his kingdom, Soren knew that meant bad things for the city—and the lady.

"I will allow you to continue your quest for answers and revenge…" she said, returning to her throne.

All around Soren and his friends, the golden stalagmites glimmered in the room's candlelight, making him feel like he was in a strange dream.

"However," she added, which Soren expected was some sort of hidden agenda finally leaking through her woven basket of help.

"Yes?" Davin asked, and even Blaje seemed immensely interested in the lady's next words by her tense, leaned-in posture.

"I have a favor I wish to ask. There's something I ask of you, and in return, I will give you the supplies and whatever else you require for your journey to Golbizarath."

"What is it?" Soren asked, having vivid memories of the task Lady Drake had for Soren—finding and retrieving the Twilight Veil. Also finding the body of Ravelle, slain by trolls.

"There's a station in the Dyadric," she said. "I've lost contact with them. It should be on your way, and I dearly wish to know why."

"Lost contact, my lady?" Blaje asked. "With whom?"

"It has been two months since I've heard from Katamon." The lady clenched her jaw slightly.

"Katamon?" Blaje asked, seemingly surprised by the name of the place. Her voice showed she recognized it, but her finger itching her stomach showed curiosity.

Soren folded his arms. "What is this place, and why do you worry about contact with it? In the middle of the desert, and in the winter?"

"Katamon is a small outpost," the lady said. "But there, they are a lookout for the things that happen in the desert—day and night. There is nothing terribly distinct about this outpost... except that I've lost contact, and that is not something that is allowed... or normal."

"Do you believe something happened there?" Blaje asked.

"Yes."

"Do you have a what?" Davin asked.

"Yes."

Davin and Kaile looked at one another, giving curious glances, presumably about why the lady wasn't more forthcoming about her answer. Blaje didn't press either, so Soren decided he must be the one.

"You think they were attacked," he said. "By Shades or bandits?"

"Yes, I believe they were attacked."

"By who?" Soren asked. "Why not just send a scout?"

The lady leaned forward, pressing her elbow to her thigh, and in a quite uncharacteristic manner, rubbed her face with a deep sigh.

Blaje saw this and gave Soren a strange look, pinching the skin at her throat.

"This outpost differs from the others in two ways," she said, scratching her cheek with her long fingernails. "First, there is a man stationed there who is... important... to Taverras. Second, he is important to me... personally."

There was a stern silence after she said that. It filled the room, forcing the quiet hard upon them.

Soren knew respect was of utmost importance in these lands, and he was choosing his next words carefully, as it didn't seem as if the lady would be forthcoming with the specifics of what she alluded to. But before he spoke, he saw Blaje shifting uneasily in her stance. Her gaze was fixed down at her feet, and her hips swayed nervously. It was quite an unusual sight for the normally stoic woman that he had only known a short time.

"Who is this man, and why is he important to you?" he finally asked.

The lady cleared her throat hard, and Blaje quickly looked up at her, eager for her answer.

"The man that is stationed there... is my son. One of five, but he is my youngest. Please check on him. I am worried, as not only protector of this city, but as a mother."

"When was the last time you received contact?" Blaje asked in a voice too loud for the room, as if pushing the words past her shaky throat.

Kaile scratched his scalp as Blaje asked her question. There was something going on with her, Soren knew, but he couldn't tell what yet.

"It has been two weeks," the lady said. "They are to report on the first of every week, and every Friedan. There have been four unreported days. No ravens, and no other sign from the outpost."

"We will check it out," Soren said. "And I hope we find good news for you, but I do worry that..."

"Just look into it before making assumptions," the lady shouted, covering her mouth with her shaky hand quickly after uttering the words. "Please, find my baby boy."

Soren nodded.

The lady cleared her throat hard again. "We are at war against King Amón now. Aladran is officially at war now, but with Edward Glasse summoning the Black Fog into Grayhaven, we have inertia behind us. The winds have shifted, and the sails of change are at full, pushing us forward. Others will join us, but for now, Zatan is in full rebellion against the king."

"He'll send every Synth he has against you," Kaile said. "I know him. He won't let one city harbor the Silver Sparrows for fear of rebellion. Let alone an entire kingdom."

"The king is spiteful, but he's no fool," Lady Sargonenth said. "He'll wait until spring to attack. He knows the dangers of the desert in winter. But hunters, however, the price on your head is too great now, Soren. They will come. I've directed every outpost and city under my reign to alert me to any sighting of strangers in my lands. I hope the Calica Clan will join me in this."

Blaje waited a moment, and then nodded. "The Calica Clan stands with the Silver Sparrows and Soren Stormrose. While in these lands, we will protect from the shadows, and we go to war against Celestra. The Synth, Glasse, has caused a wave of fear in all of Aladran, and whether the king knew of the dark magic of the Synth remains to be seen, but needs to be answered."

"He's going to die either way." Soren clenched his fists tightly, still stained in dark blood.

"Ride quickly by day and under the safety of the sunlight,"

the lady said. "Always find shelter before twilight, for it is far sparser in the desert than in Cascadia and Londindam. For even with the Vellice dagger you carry, you would not survive all that lingers in the dark here. Their numbers are growing with every passing night."

Soren cupped his hands and brought them to his chin, deep in thought.

How will we ever be able to decrease their numbers? The Black Fog is constantly feeding and creating more Shades. I've killed three, but there are thousands of them out there in the world.

But someone knew that Firelight would kill them and sent it to me. I have to know who. There are people out there that know far more about the Demons of Dusk than I thought.

There's got to be a way to defeat them. There's got to be a way to exterminate them all...

"We will ride for your outpost, and then to Golbizarath to find Lord Belzaar," said Soren. "We will get answers for you, and hopefully mine get answered too. And thank you for your support. I have traveled your desert, but I dare say it is far from home for me. And thank you..." He bowed to Blaje, who dipped her head back to him. "We need all the help we can get, but trust is... difficult for me."

"Yes," the lady said. "Your friend was the one who alerted the capital to the presence of the Silver Sparrows in Erhil. She was the one who caused the king to ride down with *fire* on his mind."

Soren didn't respond, but fought hard to hold in the powerful emotions buried deep in his core at Alicen's actions. Even though she claimed she did it for her daughters, and didn't know what the ramifications were for her betrayal, Soren held a seething hatred in his heart for the pain and destruction she caused. He bit his lip and let his hair fall before the scars on his face.

"You can trust me," Blaje said. "I will guide you in our

lands, and fight beside you. My sword is yours as long as our goals align."

"We could sure use it, lass," Davin said with a sneer. "I dare say I look forward to seeing what kind of surprises you have up your sleeve."

"I will fight by your side," the Desert Shadow said. Her voice was gritty and low. "Until the king is dead, or I draw my last breath."

Soren couldn't help but smile widely. "Our party grows. So, we have your blessing to leave the city?"

"You do," the lady said, standing as her silken robes slid down her long legs, draping from her hips to the floor. Her wise, elderly eyes sparkled in the candlelight, like dark marbles shimmering in a dark cavern. "Your niece should be healed soon. You may leave when you deem appropriate, and Zatan will have its eyes and ears out there. But be warned, Soren Stormrose of Tourmielle, Davin Mosser of Mythren, and Kaile Thorne of Ikarus—the Archmage Alcarond rides swiftly in this direction. His sights are upon his apprentice, and the dagger you carry." Her powerful eyes narrowed. "He rides alone, but I fear... nothing in this world can stop the Lyre archmage. No army could withstand his magic. Even I, as powerful as I've become, couldn't withstand his power. Nothing in this world could stop him. The Demons of Dusk, impervious to the might of the Ellydian, would be the only things that could hurt him, and he may be more educated than anyone else on them and their ways. Alcarond is the most powerful Synth in existence."

"You're wrong," Kaile interrupted suddenly, causing gasps in the corners of the throne room from the attendants. Even Blaje, irked with tensed muscles at the apparent insolence against the lady. "Archmage Mihelik Starshadow knows more about the Demons of Dusk than Alcarond. And he may be old and frail, but he's also a Lyre, as long as he still draws breath."

"You are correct, former apprentice." The lady walked toward Kaile, meeting him only inches from his face, inspecting him hard. She looked deeply into him for a long moment. "There may be another way to defeat the archmage…"

Kaile swallowed hard, as her face was mere inches from his. "A way to beat… Alcarond?"

"Yes… You, Kaile Thorne, fallen apprentice to Alcarond Riberia. You… the most trained of his disciples… you could perform the Black Sacrament."

"No," Soren said, his harsh words forcing out hard from his lungs and throat. "Absolutely not."

Lady Sargonenth took an elegant step back, and Kaile staggered back two.

"You know my words are true, whether you want to hear them or not. To defeat a Lyre, you must become a Lyre."

"He's only a boy," Soren said, vividly remembering Glasse's body exploded all over the streets of Greyhaven from his failed attempt at the sacrament.

"I—I," Kaile muttered, looking down at his shaking hands.

"You're stronger than you feel," the lady said. "I'm in my later years, and still but a Dor—an extremely skilled Dor—but Ayl has eluded me in my years. You, you and Persephone, are both already Ayls. She is a Whistlewillow. Greatness is in her blood. But you, you come from nothing, and you're already proving to be one of the strongest Syncrons in all of Aladran. It is not only your only shot at surviving the archmage, but it is your destiny. Do you deny you yearn for such power? Are your dreams not soaked in it?"

Kaile's head shook from side to side, but when the lady asked him about his thirst for becoming a great Lyre, his hands stopped shaking. He folded them calmly before himself and took a deep breath.

"It's true I wish this," he whispered.

Soren rubbed his chin, covering his mouth, waiting to hear the boy's next words.

"It's true that that was Alcarond's plan. He was training me to pass the Black Sacrament, but not for years. I was going to become a Lyre and be placed in one of the capital cities, as its protector, in the name of the king, of course, but... that's all gone now. I—I don't think I could pass it."

"You could," the lady said quickly.

"No child has ever passed the sacrament at his age," Soren said, waving his hand through the air, as if to cut the conversation. "There's got to be another way."

"You know there is not," she said. "Unless you can learn to control the Demons of Dusk to kill the archmage, I'm afraid this is the only way. It's either him, or..."

"No," Davin grumbled. "Hell no. Don't you even suggest that."

"Persephone Whistlewillow may even have a greater chance of passing the test..." the lady said. "It's in her blood."

"If Alcarond comes," Soren said, "then we'll defeat him together. I'm not going to let these two throw their lives away for it, though. And I'm not letting Seph take that risk. She's just learned to use the Ellydian from a book, and a short time with Kaile in training. She's not ready, and far too young."

"With all respect, Soren," the lady said. "Your niece isn't the best at what you ask her to, is she?"

"Ain't that the truth?" Davin laughed.

"Think about what I said," the lady said, turning with one last glance at Kaile, before returning to her throne. "For when the time comes, and all hope seems lost, it may be the only way to survive. The king also surrounds himself with many strong Synths and the deadliest fighters in all the world. If you hope to kill him, his drakoons and untold legions of soldiers, you're going to need to become something... magnificent."

Kaile was stuck in thought, not even moving a muscle. His

head was down, his reddish-auburn hair hanging in front of his eyes. Soren watched him carefully, trying to decipher what was going through the apprentice's mind.

I have faith that one day Kaile will become a Lyre, pass the Black Sacrament, and become more powerful than Alcarond and Mihelik, but that wouldn't be for many, many years. He's still so young, so naïve, and so lost...

"Is that all you wish of us?" Blaje asked, crossing her arms behind her back, standing up straight like the fine soldier she was.

"That is all," the lady said. "I will send a raven if anything should come up that you need to be informed of. May the goddess Shirava watch over and protect you with her light."

Soren nodded. "Thank you for healing Seph."

The lady nodded, and Soren left back for the door. He walked, and Davin followed. Kaile didn't seem to notice, and stood silently like a statue, so Davin grabbed him by the wrist and tugged on their way out. Kaile followed, and Blaje was the last one out.

But before they left, the lady beckoned for the Desert Shadow. Blaje went and lent the lady her ear, as the lady of Taverras whispered to her. Soren watched out of the corner of his eye as he left the throne room.

Soren didn't like that one, damn, bit.

Chapter Twenty-Eight

Twilight had taken the city.

The ancient towers that rose to the heavens, spiked with magnificent and otherworldly spires, faded as the darkness enveloped them overhead. Soren and the others were back out onto the roads of Taverras, leaving the lady and their final conversation behind.

She'd given them the blessing to head for Golbizarath when they desired, and Soren knew that meant at first light.

He'd grown tired of having faith in cities, no matter how safe some lord or lady said they'd be. Over the last decade he'd longed for the forests, the trees, the stars… and he missed his horse, Ursa. He deeply hoped she was still drawing breath somewhere, perhaps in an open glade, running to her heart's content. But he mostly feared her dead, and grieved for his favorite horse, his one true friend.

Winds gusted and howled overhead, pouring through the city, whipping the thousands of flags with great gusts that made them snap and clap against hard stone walls.

They walked back south toward Seph, and they remained mostly silent, with Blaje and Davin muttering to one another as they walked behind Kaile and Soren. Kaile, completely shut down and lost in his own thoughts, walked beside Soren. Soren thought to ask if he was all right, but the boy had lots of thinking to do after their conversation, so he left him to it.

They'd have many nights over the campfire to talk about things like the Black Sacrament.

Soren's heart pounded hard in his chest at the sobering thought of what approached. It was only a matter of time until the archmage came for what he thought was his. The winter storms and harsh desert would only hold a man like that back for so long.

Alcarond was coming, and Soren knew this would be no fight like the one with Edward Glasse. Alcarond was the most powerful Synth in all the world. He defeated and blinded his master Mihelik with the Wraithfire spell, casting him out from the capital.

When the time came, Soren would have to be at his best. Firelight would have to prove her might against the Synth. He couldn't allow Kaile, or Seph, to risk their lives attempting the Black Sacrament until every other last vestige of hope failed.

They were in the middle of a war, but their lives were still all they had. Soren would much rather be protecting his only family, than becoming a martyr for a war that was about so much more than the revenge he truly desired.

Alcarond, for all the evil he'd wrought in the king's name, was *not* the one Soren held his pure hatred for. That was reserved for the king and the Knight Wolf. They were the ones Soren wanted to watch suffer, and he wanted to watch the light slowly drain from their eyes as he twisted his dagger deep into their hearts. But they weren't coming, and Soren wouldn't get that chance while the archmage was standing between them.

Soren would have to figure out a way to defeat him, or at least get him out of his way. But he knew enough about Alcarond to know that he wouldn't give up his beloved apprentice so easily. He'd drag him back to Celestra and "Re-Enlighten" him, meaning torture, and twist his mind until he receded back into his docile, eager pupil.

Soren knew he was going to have to find a way to kill Alcarond.

Once they got back to the building Seph was at, they were quickly shushed by the woman that sat in the chair around the room.

Seph lay on her side in the bed, her back bandaged with fresh white linens. Soren could hear her heavy breath as she slept. But staring at the bandages that covered her entire back, with her bloody shirt cut, shredded, and strewn on the floor—Soren wanted to kill Gideon all over again.

They decided to all head to the building next door and rest for the night, and leave at dawn. Soren, however, decided to sleep in the room with Seph to watch over her. So he sat in a chair in the room's corner, taking his heavy boots off and putting his bare feet by the fire in the fireplace.

Soren didn't sleep but a couple of hours, intermittently, but that was enough. It always had to be enough.

∽

THE FOLLOWING MORNING, Soren could feel the bitter cold creeping in from under the front door. His eyelids felt weighted, his hands ached; they were bruised and swollen. They felt full of stagnant blood and the bruises on his knuckles were darkening. Seph moaned as she shifted in bed, moving onto her back for only a moment, before wincing and swinging her feet to the side—onto the floor.

Her gaze immediately met his from across the room; the dim light of the embers of the fire cast the only light in the room. An old woman was sound asleep on a couch in the room's far corner.

"Did I miss it?" Seph asked with a wide-mouthed yawn.

"What?" he replied.

"The lady. Did I miss meeting her?"

Soren nodded.

"Shit…" Seph slammed the back of her fists onto the mattress.

"Well, you weren't in any condition—"

"What did I tell you about keeping me out of things…" She sat up like a crossbow string snapping tight. Her face twisted in anger.

"Seph… You were being healed. I couldn't drag you up there while they mended your back…"

Her hand moved to her back, and she winced again, pulling her hand back. The old woman in the room's corner stirred awake, standing up quickly to go to Seph, inspecting the bandages.

"See?" Soren said with a tired smirk.

"Well?" She prodded him by poking the bed with her finger. "What did I miss?" Her brow furrowed.

"Plenty of time to catch you up on that while we're out on the sands," he said with both hands up and palms facing her.

"We're allowed to leave?" Her tone calmed.

He nodded. "We leave today."

"Good," she said, beginning to mess with the bandages that wrapped around her torso.

The old woman muttered something in their language and used her hands to try to calm Seph from removing the bandages.

"Better listen to her," Soren said, smiling, watching the two battle the bandages.

"I get so tired of people telling me what to do," Seph said. "It's fine. I don't need them anymore. Really. I'm fine!"

The old woman threw her hands up in the air and left out the front door. An enormous gust of freezing air rushed in from the open door. Tiny snowflakes danced in, quickly fizzling away to nothing from the warmth of the fire. The old woman closed the door behind her, and Soren stood, pouring a glass of water for Seph—handing it to her.

Seph put the glass to her dry, cracked lips and drank in satisfying gulps, letting out a deep sigh after she swallowed.

"I want to leave this place," she said. "I feel like the longer we stay here, the more we're just waiting for something bad to happen..."

"I don't think anything good is going to happen *out there*, either..."

"As long as we're together," she said, "everything is gonna be okay. I feel it."

Soren forced a smile, but was unsure about her statement. He'd narrowly saved her from Gideon, and feared not for his own safety, but for hers. The world knew about the last Whistlewillow now, and the Synths of Aladran would either fear her power, or want to turn it to their side. He truly felt that the world was at war with them.

Wherever they went now, there would be pain.

But there was a blessing in the icy wasteland of a desert. The lady had said her people were watching for hunters. Anyone that would wish to cause Seph harm from the outside world would be spotted by those who protected the desert. That would surely be a great gift.

Soren helped Seph remove her bandages, as per her wishes. Another old woman entered the room. She was a different one from before and came in halfway through and helped. To Soren's amazement, when they pulled the last of the pink, blood-soaked bandages back, all that remained of the huge gashes in her back were scars. There were no open wounds, blood, scabs, or puss. There were no stitches or sticky injuries of any kind, just healed, long scars.

Soren nodded to the old woman in appreciation.

"Well?" Seph asked. "What's goin' on back there?"

He placed the palm of his hand on her back, sliding it down her skin.

It was smooth, with only the small ridges of the scars, causing his hand to skip.

"I—I don't feel much pain," she muttered.

He clapped his hand suddenly on the skin of her back. "How about now?"

"Ow!" she yelled. "Not funny. Not funny at all! That stung!"

An hour later, after Seph was all dressed in a fresh shirt with her winter gear ready on the chair by the door, a knock came. The door creaked open, letting in the winds and bitter cold. Soren instantly saw his own breath from his lips as Kaile entered the room, followed by Davin and Blaje.

"You're all right," Kaile said in an exasperated, elated tone. His eyebrows were cocked high at the sight of Seph, seemingly normal at the edge of her bed.

"I'm fine," Seph said. "Thanks to these women here. I feel like the luckiest girl in the world. I was worried I was going to die back there, down in the sewers."

"Soren saved you, again," Davin said. "It appears he's your good luck charm."

"I don't see it that way," Soren said, scratching his stubbly chin.

"Oh, stop with your mopey self-loathing," Davin said forcefully. "Just cut it out. She's alive because of you."

"Almost died because of me," Soren muttered.

"Well then, maybe you'd just better get used to it," Davin said, strutting through the room with his short legs and plopping down in a chair by the fire, stoking it with an iron bar. "Looks like this is just gonna be how it is from now on. But you don't have to go on moping around like a little boy who lost his marbles. We're all gonna have to fight. That's just how it is."

Soren didn't respond. He agreed.

I should've just kept my mouth shut.

"We should get going soon," Blaje said. "It'll be hours until our first rest of the night."

"I'm ready," Seph said, standing up, causing Sable to stir awake, leaping to the ground by Seph's boots.

"Well, there is one more thing before we leave the city," Blaje said, causing Soren to raise one eyebrow and slide the other down. Blaje was looking at Seph as Blaje reached into the bag that was slung over her shoulder.

Seph looked uneasy, rubbing her forearm. Blaje hadn't addressed Seph directly often, and her gaze threw Seph into a nervous spiral. She crossed her legs and tapped her foot, vibrating the floorboards.

"Here," Blaje said, handing a rolled piece of parchment that seemed to have a clear sheen to it.

Seph walked up and grabbed it delicately from Blaje, averting her gaze up at the much larger woman. "What is it?"

"I had it commissioned," Blaje said. "I had them coat it in wax too, so hopefully it'll withstand some rain."

Seph unrolled the piece of parchment until it was a full twelve inches tall and eight wide. Her lime eyes sparked alive at what she saw painted on the scroll. Her jaw slacked, and she had to brush her wild, frayed black hair back to fully see the painting.

Soren stood and angled himself over to see what the gift was. Over Seph's shoulder, he saw an incredibly detailed painting of a woman's portrait. It was a woman that Soren dearly recognized and missed, Seph's mother... Violetta.

"Oh my," Seph said, covering her mouth with her shaking hand.

"You said the statue back by Zalzobad Ari Cathedral looked like her, so I thought an artist could capture it so you could take her with you. I know how important a mother's love is to her…"

Suddenly, Blaje found her midsection wrapped by thin arms, and a young girl squeezing her tight.

"…Daughter," Blaje finally got the last word out.

"Thank you, thank you…" Seph said with shaky breath.

Blaje patted her back awkwardly, giving Soren a look of not knowing what to do.

"Say you're welcome," Soren said with a laugh.

"You're welcome," Blaje said flatly.

"I'll cherish it," Seph said. She pulled away and stared at the painting, showing it to Kaile and Davin. "I'll never forget her face now."

"It's watercolor," Kaile said. "Soaked into the paper. Smart. Won't bleed that way. The wax is a nice touch, too."

"A true beauty," Davin said. "I can see where you got your looks from."

Seph smiled with her lips quivering.

"It does look like her," Soren said. "I know…" Seph ran over and hugged him, sobbing. "I miss her too."

Chapter Twenty-Nine

The world was bleak beyond the walls of the city of Taverras. Sharp, biting winds gusted head-on, making Seph and Kaile stand with their backs to it. In the early morning light, with its dull, fuzzy light hinting from the east, Soren glared north at the barren wasteland that was the Dyadric Desert.

Behind, the city of Taverras stood like an ancient beacon in the dry, desolate sea of sand. As the attendants readied the camels in warm, protective gear, Soren looked back at the city, clenching his teeth as he did so. He didn't want to stay at the city known as the Brink, but he had a bitter taste in his mouth that was difficult to spit out.

The lady and Blaje assured him they would be safe in the city, that the people there would protect them. He assumed Lady Sargonenth was telling the truth, but it certainly turned out the stark opposite. Gideon had gotten into the heart of the city, hatching a failed plan to get Soren and collect the bounty on his head.

Gideon failed. And in Soren's eyes, the lady of the city did as well.

The red braided decorations pinned to their breasts did little more than cause those in the city to spot them immediately, giving him more attention than he wanted, which was zero.

And if this is the case with a city that pledged its support to us, then there's no place we're going to be safe. We were safe in the underbelly of Skylark, but we were completely hidden then. Everyone is looking for us now…

I'm going to have to trust even less than I already do… but I'm going to have to trust myself, which I find hard after all these years of being wrong…

He watched Seph as she shivered heartily under the thick wools given to her for the journey.

You've got to trust your instinct, Soren. Just like you used to. Back before you were cursed. You have to rely on something, anything, after all. Things are only going to get worse from here…

Kaile stood beside Seph, rubbing her arms. He towered over her, a full three heads taller it felt. Soren had to trust him, the fallen apprentice, he'd been labeled by the lady, and perhaps by all in Aladran. It was too late to hesitate with the boy, Soren knew. He'd already proved his loyalty to not only Soren, but to Persephone. Soren could tell he cared for her, although he tried hard not to think about how much he did.

Davin, Soren trusted, certainly more than he should with all the secrets the dwarf appeared to keep. Soren wanted to know why he was exiled from his homeland. That seemed like an important detail to keep hidden from them. But Mihelik vouched for him, and that was enough to let the dwarf into Soren's pack. He was a mighty warrior, and a comrade. Soren was glad he was with them. What irked him less than the hidden story of why Davin was exiled, was the mystery of what bet he lost to keep the disguise of the young, beautiful woman. That was more a story to be told once Davin had indulged too much after a triumphant battle. But Soren *needed* to figure that one out, too.

Blaje Severaas, the legendary Desert Shadow, was trickier to figure out. Tall, exotic, and breathtaking—Soren was enamored with not only her beauty, but her prowess. He had questions about her. Those in the Calica Clan were already famous for being hardened, devious, and outright some of the best fighters in modern Aladran. Soren wandered what her true intentions were, though. Were they simply to save the world from the ruthless King Amón? He knew better than that. Nothing, and nobody of her caliber was as simple as that. But she would prove to be invaluable on the journey to find Lord Belzaar at Golbizarath. It still bothered Soren why she was so cold to Seph, but the gift of the painting she gave her was quite the olive branch, he thought.

In the early morning light, the buzzards already circled dizzyingly high in the sky. A hazy orange glowed from the east, with the sun covered by thick clouds. The sky cascaded from the soft orange to an aqua blue to a deep blue on the western horizon. And still, the winds raged in hard. The camels grunted and moaned as they were strapped with the protective gear to cover their sides and even strapped to their legs. There were seven camels this time, which made Soren wonder why they needed *two* extra this time. Were the odds of one failing so great that they needed a backup for their backup?

Fucking winter. Seems like it's never going to end this year.

"All right, everyone ready?" Blaje asked in a commanding voice in the winds.

"Ready as a pyn-less whore," Davin said, driving his boot into a stirrup.

"Davin..." Seph said with a scowl his direction, causing him to pause his ascent up onto the tall camel. "Sorry, poor taste. But don't mean it's not true. A prostitute who doesn't have any money needs to..."

"I think she understands the joke," Soren said. "It was more the context."

Davin gave himself a great hoist up from the straps on the saddle's side, and a mean grunt to get his legs up onto the camel. "All right, how about this one... ready as a hard-cocked prince?"

"Ew," Seph groaned.

"What?" Davin shrugged.

"Just ew," she replied.

"Maybe just stop there," Kaile said, helping Seph up onto her camel.

Soren barked a laugh, which Blaje caught, and returned a rare sliver of a smile.

They were quickly off, riding in a single line out into the open desert. Blaje at the lead, and Soren at the rear. Seph was tucked neatly, and safely, in the middle.

As they rode further away from the Brink, and the sun finally peaked over the clouds, Soren took one last look back at the city. There were many outside the city walls, watching them ride off. Soren wondered what they thought as they watched them leave their city. Was it hope that they might find a way to save the city from the king's wrath, or save them from the Demons of Dusk? Or were some just glad to see them leave?

Soren didn't know how to save anything. But he sure wanted answers, and the closer he got to those answers, the better he'd be equipped to hunt down those who deserved their reckoning—their brutal, bloody, painful reckoning.

As they rode on for hours under the hazy sunlight, the warmth of the sun did little to touch the freezing cold that swept through the open desert.

There were a few different types of cold in Soren's eyes, but the bitter, windy one that hit the inside of your bones and made your eyes constantly glass over was perhaps the worst. The gusts of icy winds sucked the heat right out of you. The winds howled, blowing up vast swaths of sand, whirling it in circles at the camels' feet.

Soren eventually rode beside Seph to break the wind from blowing straight into her. Kaile noticed and did the same at her side.

The winds were so loud that hardly anyone spoke, but if they did, they'd have to ride side by side. It was almost more worth it to just put your head down, lower your hood and let the camel do the work. Blaje had told them it would be a hard ride the entire day to reach their first destination for the journey. And in this world, shelter was life at dusk.

More hours passed, and the sun made its huge arc across the sky. The insides of Soren's thighs chafed, and his body was sore from fending off the cold. He felt terrible for Seph, as he knew she had bared more pain from riding through the wintery desert. Kaile, too, without griping, was surely feeling the sting.

Up at the lead of the new caravan, just as the sun was beginning its final descent of the day, Blaje shouted, pointing up ahead. Soren's gaze trailed from where the tip of her finger pointed, and a couple of miles off ahead, he saw the rocky outcrop that rose from the desert floor. It was no mountain or forest, but it certainly was a welcome sight.

It didn't take long to reach the rocks, as even the instincts in the camels seemed to kick alive at the approaching dusk. Shelter or death. All manner of creatures knew the new law of the land.

They rode up to the hill of tan-colored rock with patches of tawny grass and sparse, thin, leafless trees. The hill was perhaps thirty feet high at its tallest peak, with rectangular rocks jutting up from the earth as if giants have shoved them up from deep in the Under Realm.

Soren didn't immediately feel that this would be an appropriate haven from the Demons of Dusk, but Blaje knew the desert better than any. She rode halfway up the hill and dismounted. She attempted to help Davin down, but he waved her away with a harsh chop of his hand and a firm grunt. He leaped down, causing a plume of dust to erupt from his boots.

"I'll get a fire going," Davin said, searching around for kindling and wood to burn.

"No. Get the camels fed and watered," Blaje said, removing her gloves, putting them under her belt. "I will get the fire."

Davin shrugged and went to readying the camels to hunker in for the night.

"Miss Blaje," Kaile said, with a voice attempting to not crack. "Are you sure this is a place safe for the night?"

"Yes," she said coldly, rummaging through the pack on her camel.

Kaile seemed content with the short answer and got down from his camel's back. Soren got down and helped Seph down.

"If she says we're safe, then we're safe," Davin said, walking over to the other camels and feeding them a bucketful of dried grass. He walked next to Soren. "But I'd keep that dagger awful close."

Soren clapped Davin on the back as he went to the next camel.

"How are you feeling?" Kaile asked Seph.

"Not frozen to death, yet. But damned close. Can't feel my toes, and my nose felt like it was going to break off." Sable poked her head out from under Seph's collar, watching Blaje curiously.

"We'll have a fire going soon," Soren said. "Blow into your hands and move your legs."

"We barely made it," Kaile said, watching the sun slip past the mountains to the far west.

"It's going to be a cold one this night," Blaje said. "And I fear it will fair similar tomorrow. Eat, drink, and rest. We will leave at first light."

"How far are we from the outpost?" Soren asked her.

"We will arrive there on our third night," she said. "That will be where we also rest for the night, unless something keeps us from there. Golbizarath will be our destination on the seventh night, if the weather holds."

"Holds?" Kaile asked with his fingers spread and a great shiver through his body.

Chapter Thirty

That night, overlooking the empty desert, most slept hard, or forced themselves to try. Soren, again, sat on the outskirts, watching the Demons of Dusk prowl the night. The Black Fog crawled in every direction; stalking, hunting.

Soren's eyelids drooped heavily, as if weighted, and the icy winds made his eyes water. Thick drops streaked down his cheeks from certain blinks. His hood was pulled down low, and he huddled into himself with his camel at his back, to not only break the wind but supply him with warmth.

The sky was so overcast there was no moon, and no light with which to see the desert well. He couldn't count how many of the Black Fog he saw, but it was at least dozens. Slowly crawling, concealing their true speed and ferocity, they lurked, trying to build the army of Shades that remained hidden in the dark night.

Davin came several times to offer to watch while Soren slept, but Soren kept refusing, wishing for Davin to rest. Soren finally gave in as the first signs of light appeared, so he finally slept for close to an hour.

Once the sun's light finally crept through the slivers of clouds in the east, they packed, ate, and made their way back out into the desert. The Black Fog were gone, disappearing like a bad dream. Blaje had given them a safe place to rest, one that Soren wouldn't have spotted and trusted had she not been there to reassure him. That gave Soren great insight and respect into her knowledge of the desert, and survival in it.

As the day rolled on, they rode north. Again, the winds were unrelenting, sucking the energy and heat from their bodies. It gusted so forcefully that even talking became too much work, so they rode mostly without speaking. Soren rode beside Seph to break the wind. The cold bit at Soren's fingers, toes, and nose.

He felt as if the winter cold would never abate. Out in the desert, there was no escape from the onslaught of freezing winds, biting sands blowing through the air, and dryness that caused his lips to dry and crack.

Soren missed the forests, the mountains, and his horse, Ursa. He longed for the nights of sleeping with Bael beneath the stars, telling jokes and reminiscing about old times. But Bael was dead, murdered by the Knight Wolf, and Ursa was most likely dead—left back in the burning of Erhil.

The day was grueling.

Hours and hours of the camels taking them further into the barren wasteland of the desert. But as the sun finally began to recede back into the horizon, their next resting place appeared.

To the north, a walled encampment appeared on a bluff, looking much more like an appropriate shelter than the night prior. As they rode the last few miles to reach the bluff, Seph and Kaile's faces paled, showing the utter discomfort of riding in the turbulent wintry weather. They both needed rest.

Blaje and Davin, however, both held hardened, seasoned looks. This was Blaje's home, after all, and Davin was just as tough as iron.

They rode up a steep hill at the bluff as the sunlight dimmed. Blaje dismounted and heaved open the high wooden gate made of split tree trunks. Soren wondered where such pieces of wood came from, and how long ago it was. As they entered into the walled outpost, the immediate break from the winds was a relief to all.

They tied up the camels, unloaded the gear from their backs, and fed and watered them. Blaje went to making the fire.

"You two all right?" Davin asked Kaile and Seph, who both looked as if they'd just been through another battle.

"That was rough," Kaile said. "I think I'm going to cringe before sitting on that thing again. I've never felt my body hurt like this."

"I'm fine," Seph said softly. "Just glad we're here, finally."

"And only one more day," Kaile said. "Blaje said we'll be there tomorrow night."

"I hope we find good news," Seph said. "I don't know how well I'll be able to use magic if I have to after another day like today."

"It'll be there when you need it," Kaile said. "I'll teach you some things tonight about how to summon it even when your focus or energy is low. There are a few tricks that work really well."

She nodded eagerly.

They all ate dinner over the fire together that night, eating dried meat, nuts, and a starchy desert fruit Blaje called *palla*. It was only slightly sweet but was hearty and helped fill the stomach.

Seph and Kaile went off to talk about the Ellydian, and perhaps other topics while they laid under the stars. Later, they went and rested on cots with old mattresses. There were three buildings within the walled encampment. Each had wooden ceilings and beds raised off the rocky floor. Soren made them sleep in separate buildings.

As they slept, Davin, Blaje, and Soren remained by the fire, with nothing extra to eat or drink. They instead smoked tobacco that Davin had gotten from the Brink.

There was so much to talk about, but they did little talking as they listened to the blank canvas of sounds from beyond the walls. There wasn't a single insect sound or night bird chirping. The Demons of Dusk were patrolling, devouring everything that piqued their senses. Only the constant winds were there, and Soren was quite content to be out of them, leaving them out in the desert.

They smoked their pipes, gazing up at the infinite spectrum of stars that dotted the sky, thick like ribbons, smooth like stretched taffy, and as wise as the goddess herself.

Suddenly, Blaje broke the long silence. "It's the end of the year."

"Come again?" Davin asked, after blowing a great plume of smoke from his dry lips up towards the star-filled sky.

Soren thought about it, and he didn't know the exact day, but yes, he assumed she was correct.

"Tomorrow is the start of the new year," she said, holding her curved wooden pipe between her crossed legs. Looking down at the wisps of smoke that rose from it.

"A new year," Davin muttered. "Not to be grim, but I suppose there's a good likelihood it will be our last."

Soren didn't reply. That was more something that he would've said anyway, not Davin.

"1293," Davin said. "Time is certainly a quick beast."

"Agreed," Blaje said, lifting her pipe, sparking it with a flaming stick from the fire.

"Blaje," Soren said. "There's something I've been wanting to know, but I don't know that you'll give me an answer…"

She looked at him as she puffed her pipe. She didn't acknowledge his statement, but didn't pull away either.

"When we were with Lady Sargonenth, as we were leaving, I saw she whispered something to you…"

Davin's ears perked up then. It appeared the dwarf hadn't noticed, but was curious what her response would be.

"I'll make you a deal," she said, putting the pipe down, leaning forward with a rare smirk on her face. "I'll tell you, if you tell me why you were exiled from your homeland."

Davin withdrew. He recoiled with a scowl, looking away to the side.

"Seems fair," Soren said, trying to keep his cool. He desperately wanted to know the answer to both questions, and would gladly take them both in the same night.

There was a long silence between the three. Soren just watched, waiting for one of them to give in, even just a little.

It was finally Blaje that spoke. "To be clear, I don't want to say what the lady told me. There's a reason it was only said to me at the end of her meeting with you. I'm just so curious what you could've done to have been forced from your home, but you still have the blessing of Mihelik Shadowstar. You're an interesting fellow, Davin Mosser."

"And I've no intention of telling you, either," Davin huffed. He suddenly stood and walked off to the same wooden building Kaile was asleep in.

"Touched a nerve," Soren said. "Perhaps you were a little too forceful. But selfishly, I'm just hoping it pays off. Even if it's a tragic story, I like to think there's a way we can help him return to his home someday. If this war ever ends. I have this feeling that he's going to go with me to the end of this journey, however it ends."

"So, you're bonded as blood brothers?"

Soren thought about that. "We had our differences at first, or rather, I didn't know how much I could trust him. But yes, I suppose we are a sort of brothers now. I'd trust him with my life, and I'm guessing he'd say the same by now."

"A new year, and how long have you two known each other now? And are already planning on fighting to the end together?"

Time had blurred to Soren, and the last couple of months had both felt like one week and one year. So much had happened, yet even the burning of Erhil felt so far in the past.

"We met around Decimbre 9th, so we've only known each other since then. But war does make for strong bonds."

"That is very true," she replied.

"So, you're not going to tell me, are ya?" he asked.

"Nope," she said, with the subtlest of a twinkle in her eye.

"You know," he said without waiting. "We could die tomorrow. If it proves to be a trap. We could die…"

"And…?" She raised an eyebrow.

"Nothing," Soren said. "Just a reminder about the stakes."

She nodded, lifting her pipe and ashing the old contents between her legs. "Same could be said for walking down the wrong street at the wrong time, or running out of the woods at night."

He paused, the fire before him blurring from his drowsiness. He needed to sleep, but knew that it was fleeting. And in that fog in his mind, only one thought filled it.

"Why are you here?" he asked, leaned over, hunched with his forearms on his thighs, angling his head to look at her over the fire.

She sparked the pipe and drew the smoke in deeply. She stared up at the night sky as she blew the smoke above. "The mission."

"Oh yeah?" he asked, extending his hand out, his gaze on her pipe. Blaje handed it to him. A few of her dreads fell down her chest as she leaned in. He took the pipe. "Which one?"

"To assassinate the king."

"Oh, the big one," Soren said, putting the pipe between his lips and drawing in a puff. He could taste her lips on the wooden pipe. It tasted like sweet lavender. He tried desperately to not look at her lips.

"Isn't that the mission?" she asked with a playful gaze, brushing her hair back over her shoulders.

"Yes it is. But there are so many others to get there."

"I'm in Soren. I know what this quest is. I know the odds. I've lived this life as long as I can remember. I know tomorrow could be the end. It could be the eternal darkness. I'm not afraid, though. And I see you aren't either. You are only scared of one thing, and it's not the one who cut you, is it?"

Soren blew out the smoke and rubbed his forehead.

"And she's laying in that room right over there…"

"I—"

"Don't fear for her. She's in charge of her own destiny now. She's reached the age. She could bear children. She's made her decision. Seph chose to fight. She chose the mission as well."

"I didn't want any of this for her."

"Well, too bad. We can't really make each other do anything, can we?"

"She's all I've got left…" He fiddled with the pipe in his strong fingers.

"Look at me, Soren," Blaje said, drawing his gaze to her. "I'm not going to lie to you. She is in danger, and keeping her alive is going to be nearly impossible. But we can accomplish that, but we're going to have our work cut out for us. The lady may have her eyes watching out in the desert, but the archmage can't get to her. Alcarond will not leave with her still alive. The Whistlewillow name is too legendary."

The fog in Soren's head rushed away, and his vision snapped crystal clear. Alcarond's face grew in his mind. He saw his cold gray eyes glaring. He saw elaborate robes of emerald and black silk, with wide-cuffed sleeves. His staff,

Diamond Dust, was clenched in his firm hand. He was the perfect successor to Mihelik Shadowstar, and where the old archmage was in his seventies, Alcarond Riberia was in his prime.

"We won't let him get to her," Soren growled. "I'll cut his throat before he can mutter a note."

"He doesn't need his mouth to cast," Blaje said, souring Soren's rage. "There's any manner we can imagine that he could call on the power of the Connection of all things."

"Kaile is our only hope," Soren said, feeling reality creep in hard.

"Let's hope the archmage trained him well," the Desert Shadow said. Soren watched her draw from her pipe. Her rosy lips wrapped around the pipe's stem. Soren felt a different kind of adrenaline rush through him.

She's gorgeous. I've never seen anyone like her. So deadly, and so beautiful.

"What?" she asked in a playful tone, throwing one leg over the other, pointing the tip of her foot at him.

"Nothing," he said. "Just thinking about things."

"Which things?" she asked.

"The mission," he said.

"Which one?"

"To stay alive," Soren said.

"Oh yes, the big mission," she said. They both laughed.

"Can I ask you a question, Soren?"

He nodded.

"Would you die for me?"

Her question shook him, causing him to recoil slightly. He'd heard the question before, but never quite like that.

"Yes," he said, recollecting himself. "I believe you are true-hearted, even bearing your reputation as cold."

She stood suddenly, walked over, and sat right next to Soren on the bench. Her thigh touched his, and even through the blankets wrapped over themselves, he could feel her heat on his.

"I don't know how many times I've been here," she said, glaring in to the fire as it danced under the moonlight. "Going to battle, heading into the desert, facing death."

He didn't answer, but he couldn't take his eyes off her.

"I feel a connection between us. Do you feel it?"

He did, but didn't say it immediately.

She didn't wait for an answer. "I feel great sorrow in you. Resentment. Pain. I know those things. I know them well. They've haunted me for as long as I can remember. I believe we share that. That stench in our souls. It's the same."

"Yes, I feel it. Although I would've never thought of it described like that. You've had loss in your life, too."

She nodded, turning her head slowly. He stared deep into her turquoise eyes that reminded him of a magical lake.

He leaned in, his lips gliding toward hers.

Blaje leaned in, and her smell was intoxicating. Their lips met, and he felt the goose pimples run up his neck. Her soft lips pressed against his, and all the chaos of the world calmed. As they kissed, he felt light, yet overwhelmed. A strong bond like rope was tying itself between them.

He suddenly felt stronger, safer, relaxed.

As they pulled away, she put her arm around his and lay her head on his shoulder.

"I don't fear death," she said, as if speaking to herself. "Fight for what you believe in, or whither away in silence."

He liked the line and repeated it. "Fight for what you believe in, or wither away in silence."

"And by the way," she said. "You don't have to ask. I'd die fighting by your side, too."

"Oh," he muttered as she squeezed his arm. "Yes, I forgot to ask that."

"I'm off to bed now," she said, standing, sliding her arm

out from around his. "We'll reach the outpost tomorrow, so you should try to get some sleep, too."

She walked off to the lone structure with no one sleeping inside.

He watched her walk away, and he remembered Cirella.

God damned to hell, he thought. Their connection with their trauma wouldn't break through his own. The pain of his past overwhelmed his current moment of happiness. *Fuck, Soren. Enjoy one fucking kiss.*

Chapter Thirty-One

This is miserable. Absolutely miserable.

The winds, somehow, had picked up even more than the day prior. And as their camels trudged through the onslaught of whipping winds, there was no sort of rest upon the animals' humped backs. Riding in such aching, biting cold sucked the warmth from everything.

Even when they found rocky outcrops that broke the winds finally, they didn't have time to rest. They needed to make it to the outpost before dark, and in this barren wasteland, seemingly devoid of all life, there seemed to be no escape from the misery.

Many of the times during their ride, Soren saw Seph's teeth chattering, and he did all he could to break the bitter winds. Even Sable was completely hidden beneath the blankets on Seph's lap.

A haze filled the desert air, causing the world to feel as if they were in some cloudy, foreign world. There was no sun, no sky, and no reprieve from the cold. If it wasn't for Blaje's instincts, and her steadfast journey into the abyss, Soren would surely have gotten them lost and without shelter for the night.

As the light from the distant, unseen sun faded, Soren got nervous. The world around them darkened, but Blaje didn't even look back once. She only continued riding at the lead.

"See anything?" Davin asked after riding to Soren's side.

"No."

They both looked eagerly for anything out of the ordinary bleak desert. Soren kicked the camel's sides to ride up to Blaje, but suddenly heard Seph blurt out, "Look!" Her arm rose and pointed up into the air before them. It was hard to make out at first, but the structure came into view more as they rode towards it.

There was no mistaking it. It was a tower. Manmade, and beautiful after the painstaking riding of the day, it might as well have been a castle. Soren dropped down from his camel, inspecting the vast surrounding desert. After seeing nothing out of the ordinary, he dug his hand into the sand, lifting a handful before him, letting the grains tumble between his fingers. He sniffed the sand deeply, taking in the musty aroma of the tiny grains that had been shaped by hundreds of thousands of years of wind, water, and friction. It smelled so different than the irony dirt he had grown around, he indeed felt he was so far, far away from whatever his home was.

Blaje didn't call out for anyone who might be in the tower, which somewhat surprised Soren. He assumed it was to keep some semblance of secrecy if something else was within. Davin enacted the spell of disguise upon them. Soren readied the Twilight Veil, putting on the ring near the bracelet, if he needed to disappear into the shadows.

They were soon at the front gate of the outpost, with the colored banners whipping in the winds above. It was an old stone structure, circular and wide at its base, rising up in five tiers, each shrinking in diameter. It had sharp spires on each of its round tiers, each tied with a dyed ribbon. They were all sun faded, tattered and torn, making the outpost feel as if it had been long abandoned and neglected.

As they dropped down from the camels and Blaje approached the huge wooden doors that rose to one single angle at their top, Soren heard nothing from within. Blaje pulled a skeleton key from her pocket and slid it into the lock at the center of the doors. A thick lock popped from within, and she shoved the doors with her shoulder. The doors opened inward, and Sable's head popped up from under the blankets. She keenly stared into the structure with her feline eyes.

As the doors opened, and Soren finally got a look into the interior of the tower, he saw motion on the sand-dusted stone floor. Rats. Rats were scurrying off into whatever holes they could.

"Ew!" Seph screeched. "They're everywhere!"

"Come on," Soren said, leading his camel in behind Blaje.

"I am *not* going in there," she said, shaking her head.

"C'mon," Kaile said, slapping her camel on the rear. "It's just a few rats. They'll leave us alone."

"No, no, no," Seph repeated, shaking her head, holding her ground.

"Persephone," Soren said. "Get in here."

"Ugh," she sighed. "I hate everything about this. The awful desert, the creepy tower, and now those nasty things."

"Well, we're not staying out there," Davin said as the last light of the hidden sun faded.

"I'd rather chance it with Shades than sleep with those monsters biting my toes."

Soren imagined her nights in the orphanage may not have been as easy as he'd hoped, but at least she was safe there. That's what he told himself, at least.

"Come," Blaje said. "Hurry. Get the camels in, so we can find Zefa."

"Zefa?" Kaile asked. "The lady's son, correct?"

"Hurry," she said, not answering his question.

Davin lit a torch with a spark of flint, lighting others around the room, handing them to the others. Soren pulled Firelight free, its layered steel glowing waves of amber in the torchlight.

It was a round room with dingy, stone exterior walls and wooden posts scattered throughout. The camels moved to the stables at the far end of the room.

"Up," Blaje said, and each of them followed.

Kaile and Seph both held their staffs up, Blaje with her curved shamshir blade, and Davin walked at the lead with his double-sided ax. It was a curved staircase along the outer wall that led upward. Soren was right behind Davin, with Seph tucked into the middle of their group.

"Stay together," Soren said. He listened intently for what lay above, but only heard the creaking of the wooden stairs under their boots.

They made their way up to the second floor, to which they found the door unlatched and open. Davin opened it fully with a painful squeal of the hinges.

Once they were all in the room, smaller than the room below, but more put together—less sand on the floorboards, paintings on the walls, six empty tables and cupboards along the walls—they saw no one.

"Nothing," Davin muttered.

"Up," Blaje said.

They went to the far end of the room, to which Davin found the door closed. So, he opened it with another squeal, and they made their way up the dim stairwell. Halfway up the curving stair, with their torchlight warming the darkness, Seph spoke. "Look."

Soren looked beside her, to where her fingers were skimming the wall at her side. A long gash was cut into the stone wall—recently. It was three-quarters of an inch deep and stretched almost a foot long.

"No dagger did that," Soren said.

"What is that?" Kaile asked.

"Weapons up," Blaje said. "Be ready for anything."

Davin led them up the stairs, entering the next floor, another round room with their armory. Swords, bows, spears, and armor hung along the walls and racks around the room. It was enough to arm thirty or more men, Soren thought.

"Nothing," Davin muttered, moving to the next staircase.

Soren's instincts were alive, so much so that he could sense Seph and Kaile's hearts pounding and could feel the tenseness in their bodies.

Good, he thought. *Let them feel that adrenaline pumping.*

It wasn't until they were on the next floor that they saw what Soren expected they might find.

Davin was straddling a huge, dark red smudge on the floorboards. It scraped all the way across the room to the next stairwell.

"Blood?" Seph asked. "Is that all blood?"

None answered.

"Move," Blaje said. "Staffs ready."

"No body," Davin growled. "Whatever was here was pulled higher up into the tower."

"What would do that?" Kaile asked. "Trolls?"

"Maybe," Soren said, squeezing Firelight tightly.

"There are no trolls this far into the desert," Blaje said.

"What, then?" Kaile asked.

"We will know soon," she replied.

Davin led them up the next stair, with Soren behind him, then Seph, Kaile, and Blaje at the rear.

Davin opened the door to one of the upper levels of the tower. It was dark, with all drapes hanging over the windows. Davin held his torch out, dimly lighting the room, and once

Soren stepped into the room, it was immediately clear what happened at the outpost.

"Oh goddess," Seph gasped.

Around the round room were men's bodies, covered in dried blood, with flies buzzing all around the room. They covered their mouths with their shirts. The smell was grotesque.

Soren knew the stench of death all too well, as did Davin and Blaje, by their reaction to the scene. Over a dozen men, with deep gashes in their limbs and necks.

"No armor," Davin said. "They were ambushed."

"This was a massacre," Soren said. "They didn't have a chance. Probably thought they were safe up here."

"The cuts, Soren," Blaje said, inspecting the severed arm beside them.

"I see…" he replied.

"They were here," Blaje said. "Inside."

Soren didn't want to admit it to himself, but he knew Blaje was right in what she alluded to. He didn't want to think it was true, and wouldn't have, had he not seen the Black Fog enter the city of Grayhaven.

"It's not… Shades?" Seph asked in a muffled voice from under her shirt.

Suddenly, Soren caught a glimmer of something in the room. The torchlight didn't reveal the room's far corners, but somewhere in that shadow, Soren saw a sleek reflection that resembled the sheen of sunlight on obsidian stone.

He gripped Firelight tighter, holding it out before him, shoving Davin behind him with his free hand.

Davin resisted at first, but as whatever was in the shadow crept along the ceiling, two eyes of deep, glossy black reflected the torchlight like that of a demon from the Under Realm.

"Get behind me," Soren said, walking out into the center of the room.

The creature slunk toward them, hanging from the ceiling. A long, muscular, coal-black tail slithered down like a thick vine in the shadows. The creature's claws sunk into the wooden ceiling silently as it crawled slowly, like a cat of prey stalking its next meal.

"Seph, vanish now," Soren growled quietly.

Seph seemed as though she wanted to rebel against his wishes, but her words were caught in her throat as the Shade finally came into the torchlight, hissing low with its serpent tongue peeking through its long, sharp yellow teeth.

"Soren..." Blaje muttered.

"I know," he said. "I've got it. I killed three of these bastards. I can kill one more."

"It's huge," Seph said.

Soren scowled at the beast as it suddenly released its front claws from the wooden beams above, hanging upside down like an enormous bat. Its hungry eyes were fixed upon Soren, unwavering, solid as iron. Even as Soren waved the Vellice dagger between them, the Shade's gaze drilled into Soren.

"Seph, disappear I said! Use the spell and get out of here!"

Soren heard the E note strike from her staff, and he felt a sense of relief that she actually listened to his order, but that was until he heard Kaile's voice.

"Seph, no!" Kaile said abruptly.

Soren, unwilling to take his eyes from the Shade, heard the commotion behind him, and quickly—the heat.

A swath of fire burst into the air above Soren, blasting into the Shade. Soren ducked from the heat, pulling his hood over his brow as the flames poured into the beast, who hung motionlessly.

"Seph, stop," Kaile pleaded. "You're wasting your energy!"

The flames receded back overhead, pulling back into Seph's staff. Her eyes were wide and her mouth agape as the Shade dropped down to the floor finally, its muscular legs swinging down to land flat on the ground and its long tail slithering behind.

This monster is far larger than the other three I fought. I need to stay far from its claws and teeth.

Soren remembered the pain of the claws cutting into his skin, and the lack of feeling in them after. The venom from those incapacitated, and there was nowhere to get healed if they found their mark in him.

"Get her out of here," Soren said. "And get to safety downstairs."

"Downstairs ain't gonna be safer if you fall," Davin said in a grave voice.

"I won't," Soren said, widening his stance, tightening his grip on the dagger, and staring right back into the dark eyes of the damned beast that stood over six feet tall on its hind legs.

The Shade before him had a thin head with four horns that curled forward, two larger ones on the crown of its head, and two smaller ones that jutted out from its temples. Like the other Shades he encountered, its long body had a thick skeletal frame, with sinewy, leathery muscles on its sharp bones.

A terrifying hiss erupted from the Shade's mouth, growling low like the demon it was.

Soren wanted to tell them to leave again, but he knew Davin's words were correct. With the Shade in the tower, no locked door would keep the Demon of Dusk from hunting them down and killing them—should Soren fall. Their only chance would be to use the dagger to kill it, should Soren be killed.

But that isn't going to happen. Not tonight. Not when I'm so close to getting the answers I want...

The Shade dropped to all fours, hunching its horned back, whipping its tail behind. It caused similar sounds to the cracking of Gideon's whip, making Soren's instincts flare even more.

He stood his ground, between the Shade and his friends, ready to counterattack should the Shade pounce, but also ready to send the first attack in, should the opportunity arise.

The Shade lowered its head, its obsidian eyes glowing in torchlight, still fixed upon Soren.

"What are you waiting for, you devil?" Soren said. "Don't you want revenge for those three I killed? Didn't the fog tell you about this dagger? If you want a taste, then come get it!"

The Shade let out a demonic growl from its maw, hissing through its sharp teeth, and its eyes narrowed.

Does it understand me?

"You heard me. I killed your kind. They died like dogs out in the winter plains. And here I am—still standing. I'm the one human who can fight back. So… are you scared?"

What happened next curdled Soren's blood.

From its growling mouth, a sound followed that caused all behind Soren to gasp.

It was unmistakable, even in the devilish voice.

A single word came from the Shade's mouth. It growled, "No…"

Chapter Thirty-Two

"Did... did that thing just... speak?" Seph asked through her fingers that covered her mouth.

"By the goddess," Kaile muttered, his words full of awe.

"Soren, you must kill it," Blaje said.

This thing does understand. At least a bit. The Shades can speak? That changes everything we know about them.

They aren't mindless beasts. They have intelligence.

Somehow that made Soren consider them, the most feared thing in all of Aladran, even more dangerous.

I need to keep Firelight between it and me. It knows. It understands what Firelight can do. I've got to put this thing down, and quickly.

"Get her outta here!" he yelled, flashing the dagger at the Shade, who took a menacing stride forward.

Davin grabbed Seph by the arm and pulled her out the door with him. "C'mon lad, nothing we can do here for him." Kaile reluctantly followed, scratching his hair, glaring back as Davin led them away.

"Go," Soren said to Blaje, who he still sensed behind him.

"I'm staying."

Beside her, Sable hissed at the Shade.

"But you can't do anything against it," Soren said. "It's up to me, and I won't fail. Not when we're this close."

"I'm staying," the Desert Shadow said. "Just in case."

Soren wasn't going to argue. There was a fight before him that was more pressing.

"So, you understand, huh?" he said, somewhat hoping for more words, also hoping that was the extent of the monster's vocabulary. For the thought of the Shade knowing more, was terrifying.

The Shade took another powerful, yet silent stride forward, its nails cutting into the wooden floorboards. Its head dropped and its tail slithered slowly.

This time, Soren decided to make the first move. Adrenaline rushed through him, causing him to feel alive, and time to slow. He sensed every move the Shade made, anticipating its next moves before they occurred.

Soren breathed deeply through his nostrils, navigating his surroundings into a quick map in his head. Where every table was, every chair, everything that could be used as a weapon or a shield. His eyes never left the Shade's, and as Soren rushed forward, Firelight's infinitely sharp tip leading the way, the fight began.

The Shade swiped hard with its front foot, sharp claws streaking through the air. Soren swiped at the beast with two quick flashes of the Vellice steel. The first slice cut into the side of the Shade's arm, the second missing as the Shade drew back, hissing and growling.

A thin streak of dark blood ran down Firelight's edge.

The Shade made a movement that made Soren sense it was going to leap back up onto the ceiling, so he planned his next move in his head.

Grab the chair beside me and hurl it up to...

But Soren's guess was wrong, and instead of jumping, the

Shade spun with impossible speed, doing a full rotation with its sleek body before Soren could react, and the creature's tail flew. It whooshed thickly as it collided into Soren's upper arm. The force was so intense it knocked Soren to the side. He stumbled to keep his balance and considered himself lucky the force didn't break the bone.

Sable hissed again from behind.

Soren lunged forward with Firelight again, taking two huge strides forward, cutting with Firelight in a dazzling array of strikes. But the Shade was fast; far faster than something its size should be able to. It moved like a large cat, a menacing panther, as it dodged Soren's blows, even swiping back at him. None of the blows found their mark, as the Shade seemed to sense the danger the dagger put it in. So it cautiously evaded Soren's attacks, growling back at him.

It then went on the offensive, snapping its jaws and swiping with its vicious claws. Soren deflected two of them with Firelight, but was forced back by its strength and ferocity. Suddenly the Shade stood up on its hind legs, transforming from the dark animal it was to a human-like entity, glaring at Soren as they were both at eye level.

It burst forward in a series of attacks, sending its claws at Soren, who evaded by pulling back and knocking away the Shade's claws with Firelight. Suddenly something flew in from behind Soren, a bottle that tumbled end over end at the Shade's head, who quickly tucked its head down as the bottle flew over harmlessly. It hissed in a devilish tone. As if it held the scourge of the Under Realm within it.

The Shade sent its long tail flying, skidding along the floor as it was about to crash into Soren's shins, but he leaped quickly, back and away. The tail glided under him as he jumped back, landing softly.

"I can't get close enough," he said.

"I'll try to distract it," Blaje said.

He wanted to tell her no, but he knew a frontal attack was dangerous against a Shade. Its teeth and claws were too sharp and swift, and it would only take one nick to start shutting down his body. So he didn't try to change her mind. Instead, Soren moved sideways slowly, taking large sidesteps, attempting to get the Shade between Blaje and him.

The Shade never took its demonic hunter's eyes off Soren, though. It knew Firelight was the one real threat in the room.

Blaje threw a chair at the Shade, hurtling through the air. It struck the monster with a thud, but cracked upon impact and fell to the floor. The Shade didn't flinch. Sable hissed again, drawing the Shade's gaze for a split second, before snapping it back at Soren.

The Shade swiped at Soren, narrowly missing his thigh. It lunged at a ferocious speed, heightening Soren's senses. He heard Sable hiss again behind the monster.

The hulking Shade between them was huge, weighing over six hundred pounds, Soren guessed. It swiped again, growling low as it lowered its head, the growl grumbling low into waves that crept out the backsides of its maw.

Aim for the throat. Target its eyes. Its skin is thick, but Firelight pierces it easily. I just need to get close.

Suddenly, the Shade lunged at Soren, all four of its feet leaving the floorboards. It flew at Soren, its devilish claws and teeth leading the way.

Soren ducked and angled Firelight upward. He dove forward, rolling underneath the attacking monster. He rolled quick enough that he was looking up at the belly of the Shade, sliding the Vellice dagger's tip straight down it.

The Shade landed just past Soren. It was confused and angry. Evidently, Soren moved faster than it expected, and drops of black blood were oozing from its belly onto the floor. It spun to face Soren, growling ferociously. Soren heard Sable hiss again, but he couldn't place where Blaje was, and he sincerely hoped she'd fled with the others.

Soren took the moment of his attacker's confusion and sent Firelight in. Its tip was coated in the dark blood as it streaked through the air, swiping in tight, concise attacks at the creature.

The flurry was so fast, the Shade took a lumbering step backward, growling, never taking its gaze off the attacking dagger and the man wielding it.

Sable hissed to the side of the beast, drawing its gaze momentarily. It was just long enough for Soren to slash hard against the Shade's hand, cutting deep into the flesh, hitting the thick bone underneath.

The Shade roared in anger, and in a great burst, it ignored the cut in its hand, pressing forward, causing Soren to withdraw.

The Shade swiped with its claws, growling low, moving back on the attack. Soren pulled back, evading swipes and deflecting others. The Shade stalked him, and Soren knew he couldn't move back much further as the wild beast attacked.

He had to hold his ground, because the other end of the room was only feet behind him. But that decision was taken from him as the Shade suddenly jumped, and Soren tried to scramble out of the way, but it was too late.

The Shade crashed onto him. Soren fell onto his back with the Shade straddling him. Soren only had enough time to stop the killing blows. He drove one hand into the top of its throat and cut Firelight straight through one of its hands. The strength of the beast was like that of a great bear, and Soren pushed with all his might, pressing the back of his shoulder hard into the floorboards, trying to keep the Shade's snapping jaws at bay.

Firelight cut clear through its hand, coating the layered steel in dark blood. The Shade growled again, pulling its hand free, but Soren was quick, sending Firelight slicing through the air, finding the spot between the Shade's forearm and hand, severing the tendon, and sending the Shade's clawed hand flailing to the floor with a thud.

It roared in anger and pain, snapping its jaws at him, only inches from his face. Its bloody stump of a hand quickly pinned Soren's arm to the ground, and under its immense weight, he fought to break free. But even with the slippery blood flowing from the open wound, Soren's arm couldn't budge.

The snapping jaws inched closer and closer to Soren's face. Its hot breath overwhelmed him, smelling of sulfur and smoke. He felt it clog his nostrils and mouth. He suddenly couldn't breathe, and his hand clutched the monster's throat as tightly as he could. He squeezed with all his might, holding the Shade's teeth back from his face, but they were snapping only inches from the tip of his nose.

C'mon Soren, push! Get the monster off of you. You can't stay here, it's too strong. It's too...

Suddenly, there was a flash of steel as something behind the Shade fell from the rafters of the ceiling. Soren was so preoccupied with the fight, he hadn't noticed Blaje had moved above the beast, and was falling quickly onto it. The light steel of her thin, curved shamshir slid underneath the Shade's neck, and she fell onto it with a thud.

Her sword slid under the top of the throat and bottom of the jaw, and she grasped the sharp end of the sword with her other hand, covered in a canvas cloth. She yanked back as if pulling on the reins of a runaway steer. It roared in anger, but the shamshir blade pulled tightly against its neck, turning the roar into a gasp.

Soren hoped the shamshir would cut, but it only scraped against the Shade's charcoal skin. It was impervious to all weapons, except the one in Soren's hand.

With all his might, Soren grunted, fighting to free his hand from the bloody stump that crushed it. Suddenly, Sable appeared, biting and clawing at the Shade's wrist with a feral, wild intensity. It was just enough to lighten the pressure, and Soren was able to pull his hand, and Firelight, free.

He didn't hesitate.

Soren sent Firelight's tip straight into the Shade's eye, driving it in all the way to the guard. The Shade's other eye squinted shut in pain, and it leaped back, as if not even feeling the weight of Blaje on its back. Its eye socket freed itself from the Vellice dagger.

Soren got his feet under him quickly, jumping after the beast, not fearing its teeth and claws. He was more worried about Blaje being stuck, clutching to both sides of the sword under its neck.

The Shade attempted to spin, to put Blaje underneath him, but Soren was too quick.

Soren landed onto the Shade's side, cutting Firelight into the Shade's temple, all the way into its brain.

The Shade seethed in anger, flailing as it pulled back from the two. Blaje released her grasp of her sword and the Shade scuttled to the other side of the room; dark blood dripping out of the wound on the side of its head.

It tried to roar, but instead a hollow, painful moan came from its maw instead.

Soren knew it was dying. Firelight had gone too deep, inflicted too much damage inside. But he couldn't let it die yet...

"What are you, Shade?"

The Shade's one eye glared at him in a hateful rage, yet the monster's gaze was unfocused—hazy.

"You understand me, don't you? At least a little?"

The Shade's head cocked as it huddled into the room's corner, suddenly glancing around the room for an escape.

"Where did you come from? Why are you here? Why?"

Blaje stood beside Soren, both of them pointing their weapons at the Shade, who appeared much smaller and less menacing.

"Tell me, what do you want here?"

The Shade gave a look at Soren that surprised him. All the rage and fury vanished in the dark demon, and it stared at Soren with a sort of... bewilderment. The Shade transformed its demeanor from a lethal, invincible killing monstrosity to an intelligent, curious animal with a soul.

"You used to be human," Soren said. "And I think you can understand me, so tell me... what do you want here? Why are the fog and Shades here?"

The Shade opened its mouth, letting its jaw sink, and Soren's heart beat wildly. He felt his stomach tighten as the Shade's mouth opened, and Soren waited with bated breath for it to answer.

But, instead, the Shade's jaw slacked, its eye rolled back, and its huge body slumped to the floor, motionless. Firelight's infinite black pommel that never reflected any light began to glow. From deep within, an oceanic white rippling glow emitted. But Soren was too distracted with the Shade to pay much attention.

"No," Soren yelled. "Don't die yet. Tell me. Answer me."

But there was no answer from the Demon of Dusk. It lay on its side, its long tail curling into its body, a pool of blood growing underneath.

"Come, Soren," Blaje said. "Let's go find the others."

Chapter Thirty-Three

Soren and Blaje were nearly halfway out the door that led downstairs, before Seph ran up into Soren's arms. She squeezed him tightly around his waist, and he hugged her right back.

Kaile rose on his tiptoes to peer at the dead Shade in the room past Soren.

"Go ahead," Soren said to the curious, young Syncron. "You've never seen one dead before."

Kaile nodded and went past Soren and Seph, sliding with his back against the wall and the doorjamb.

Soren, Seph, and Blaje came back up into the room; an eerie calm hanging in the stagnant air.

"Fine job, Soren, fine job." Davin clapped Soren on the forearm.

"It spoke," Seph said with wide eyes. "You heard it too, right? The Shade spoke."

Kaile knelt beside the fallen Shade, analyzing it with his head swaying back and forth, and he prodded it with his staff.

"Soren attempted to get the Shade to speak again," Blaje

said, standing tall with her arms crossed, watching Kaile. "But it said nothing before it crossed into the Nine Hells."

Davin scratched his beard, and Seph itched her cheek.

"I don't really know what to think about it," Soren said. "If they're intelligent enough to speak, and are entering manmade structures now." His head swiveled back toward Blaje. "I don't know how anyone is going to survive what is coming."

"We need more Vellice blades, and we need to know why Firelight was sent to you," Seph said.

"There are only two other Vellice weapons in Aladran," Blaje said. "And those are in the hands of two of the most powerful, well-guarded men in all the continent. The Knight Wolf carries the Ember Edge, and the king wields Storm Dragon."

"We need them," Soren said.

"Or we need them to know those weapons kill the Demons of Dusk," Davin said. There was a hint of resistance in his voice. "Then at least they could start killing the beasts. Dwindle their numbers."

"But there are so many…" Seph said. "Would those two swords be able to kill the Black Fog? We've seen how many there are out there at night. There are thousands, more even…"

They seemed deep in thought as they all slowly approached the dead Shade in the middle of the room, high in the desert tower. Dark blood pooled beneath.

"Amazing," Kaile muttered. "Its skin is impervious to any weapon, yet it's malleable, smooth to the touch. Alcarond would be…" Kaile's gaze snapped back toward them. "Oh… Sorry…"

"No, what were you going to say?" Soren asked. His voice was firm, pushing past his irritation about hearing Kaile speak about the archmage in such a curious voice.

"The archmage would be delighted to have this sample to

dissect and analyze. The Shades don't appear to die of natural causes, and have no predators capable of killing them, it appears. Except you, of course..."

Seph suddenly became acutely aware of the room, and the windows, only covered by thin wooden shutters.

Soren understood her fright, but didn't know the answer to the question she was surely asking herself.

"Are we safe here?" she finally asked.

"I don't know if we're safe anywhere, lass," Davin said, wrapping his muscly fingers around the grip of his ax. "Don't know if anyone is safe anywhere."

Suddenly, there was a tapping on the window shutter. Like branches blowing into it, scraping it, knocking on it.

Each of them drew their weapons. *It isn't fierce enough to be a Shade*, Soren thought. *A Shade would just rip the paneling off.*

"There are no trees up this high," Blaje said.

Soren approached slowly, Firelight at the ready, coated in drying blood.

"Soren, no," Seph said.

He calmed her nervousness with a wave of his hand behind him. He was soon at the window, where the tapping continued, even growing in intensity. The taps were harder and more frequent. Soren's stomach tightened, and his heart thumped in his chest.

He reached up for the latch, undoing it, and slowly he pressed the shutter open. Soren saw nothing through the open slit except the night sky and the vast desert beyond.

Suddenly, something flew into the room, over Soren's shoulder, zipping past a swipe of Firelight, flying into the far corner of the room. Soren closed the shutter and latched it back tight.

The black bird perched on a bookshelf in the room's corner, its dark eyes scanning each of them.

"A raven…" Seph said. "There's a scroll. It carried a scroll to us."

"Must be the lady," Blaje said. "But what immaculate timing."

Soren went over and untied the scroll from the raven's leg as it let out a series of caws.

He pulled the scroll up before him, unrolling it as the others loomed behind him.

"It's not from the lady," Soren said. His brain tingled, and he felt goose pimples roll up the back of his neck as he saw the signature at its bottom. "It's from Archmage Mihelik!"

"What's it say?" Kaile blurted.

Soren read, '*May this raven find you swift and true.*

I write this in the hopes that this reaches you in time, for time is not on your side. The archmage is traveling swiftly to you. His gaze is set upon you, Soren, your dagger, Persephone, and his apprentice.

I know not what his exact plans are as of yet, but I fear the worst. Soren, I presume your death is his desire, and he wishes to take the Vellice dagger for his own. For it is the only weapon capable of defeating the enemy—the Demons of Dusk.

For Persephone, last heir of the Whistlewillows, he will surely wish to turn her through their fiendish devices in the capital.

Hear me when I say this, and I plead that you heed my words.

Do not confront Alcarond.

He is too dangerous.

Kaile Thorne is capable, and apt, but he stands little chance against the overwhelming Ellydian of the archmage himself. For I, myself, was unable to defeat my own apprentice.

Flee. Hide. Dig in deep to wherever you are, but do not attempt to fight him, for I fear this war will be over before it even begins.

I wish I had more to offer you than these words, but time is running out. He was spotted crossing the Driftmire River in the northern borderlands of Zatan. He rides without the drakoons, without the king or the Knight wolf or the archpriest at his side. We have had our difference aplenty, but I've always admired the feared Alcarond's strongest trait—his wild, blinding passion.

I hope to come up with a weapon that is capable of defeating the archmage, but save for the Demons of Dusk, I know not of a being powerful enough to defeat my former apprentice.

Hide Soren, dig in, until I can conceive something, short of the Black Fog killing him, or Kaile performing the Black Sacrament successfully. Even though Kaile is promising in his craft, I fear he is too young to succeed, and fear for his life. We need him, and we need you.

Survive. We need you. Stay alive to fight what you need to, run from what you cannot.

Mihelik Stormshadow.'

"Well... we're fucked," Davin said, with his head lowered, scratching his beard.

"No, we're not," Soren said, releasing the bottom of the scroll with his fingers. It snapped back up.

Blaje reached out for it, and Soren handed it to her. She unrolled it and read it silently.

"*The* Archmage Mihelik," she muttered after reading it.

"I—I could try the Black Sacrament," Kaile said, trying desperately to hide the shaking in his voice.

"Out of the question," Soren said. "We need you."

"I—" Seph started to say.

"Don't even think about it, lass," Davin cut her short.

"What are you thinking, Soren?" Blaje handed the scroll back.

"We know he is coming," Soren said. "And I presume it's without the king's blessing."

"Why?" Blaje asked.

"He may have pledged his allegiance to the king," Soren said. "But his real ambition lies in the power of the Ellydian to save the world. Everything I've heard about Alcarond points to him being methodical, obsessive even. He needs to figure out how to drive the Demons of Dusk away from our lands. The king burning towns in the name of the Chimaera has nothing to do with the archmage's true aspirations. I believe he will listen to logic. We will reason with him."

"Reason with Alcarond?" Davin said with his veiny arms out wide. "I respect your opinion. But I'm worried you're stark raving mad!"

"What other option do we have?" Soren asked. "Give into the fleeting chance Kaile could ascend to a Lyre? Even if you did become only the third one in these lands, you wouldn't be able to defeat him."

Kaile's shoulders slumped and his head rocked to one side, his hair dropping in front of his eyes.

"Can we hide?" Davin asked Blaje.

"He seems to know quite well where we are," Blaje said. "I don't know if it's spies or magic, but I'm not sure hiding in a cave in the Dyadric would keep him from finding his lost prize."

"Well… shit…" Seph said. "What do you think?" Her gaze fell on Kaile. "Do you think he could be reasoned with?"

"I… I don't know," Kaile said with half his face still hidden. "I think he's furious at me, so he would never listen. He'd probably kill me before giving me the chance to escape again."

"Wait," Seph said suddenly. "What about that spell that Mihelik used?"

"The portal spell? Pfft…" Kaile said with a chuckle. "What about it?"

"You could use it! We could fool him into thinking we're in the Dyadric, when we could be all the way in Ikarus, or somewhere deep in Arkakus, even."

"I can't do that spell!" Kaile said, his head sinking further down, folding his arms over his stomach. "I could hardly fight Edward Glasse. How could I use a spell like that? I'm an Ayl, and a lower one at that… I could never conjure enough magic to cast that spell. The complexity of a spell like that takes years of focus and training on the hardest types of notes; combining, accentuating... the reverberations from such sounds could do worse things to me than the burns on my arms."

Soren knew Kaile's words were true. Hardly anyone had been able to conjure portals in history.

There was the legend of the great Syncron Jeziah, said to have invented the spell, but he was the first known Syncron, and the legends of the great wizard still last to this day.

"I hate to change the subject to something more pressing..." Seph said, rubbing her arms anxiously. "But... are we safe here?" She was staring at the huge, dead Shade corpse in the room.

None of them seemed to know the answer to the question.

Soren finally looked at Sable, who was licking her paw on a table beside Seph. "I suppose that's a good sign."

"Not like we could go anywhere anyway," Davin said. "We're stuck here for the night."

"Soren," Kaile said, brushing his hair back from his brow. "May I... may I borrow your..." Kaile's hand was creeping up, pointing at Firelight in her sheath on Soren's hip.

Soren cocked an eyebrow.

"I'd like to..." Kaile cleared his throat. "Take some parts for... research..."

Soren slid Firelight free with a sharp ring of steel, flipped her over in his hand, catching the blade with his fingers on the outside of the layered steel, handing it over to Kaile, who wrapped his fingers around the Vellice dagger's grip, marveling at the deep black jewel as its pommel.

"Marvelous," Kaile murmured. He turned and walked over to the Shade with Firelight's tip leading the way.

Each of them followed, watching carefully as Kaile slid the dagger into the Shade's flesh. It punctured easily and cut as if it wasn't impenetrable charcoal-colored skin, but a piece of old leather. He cut a square four inches wide from the beast, holding it up in the torchlight, inspected all sides.

"Huh," Davin groaned. "It's just blood and muscle and bone underneath. Just like any other animal."

"They used to be human," Blaje added.

"Aye, that too," Davin said.

"May I?" Kaile asked Soren, holding up the dagger. "I'd like to do a full dissection. I'm not sure we'll ever get this chance again."

Soren nodded.

"Seph, you mind taking notes while I tell you what to write?"

Seph nodded, walking around the room, rummaging for paper and quill and ink, which she found in a drawer near the Shade.

"Then let's begin," Kaile said. "I presume we're leaving at dawn."

"There's a shrine we must reach tomorrow," Blaje said. "We are nearing Golbizarath, and Lord Belzaar."

PART V
THE LAST LYRIAN

Chapter Thirty-Four

Sorcerers

THERE ARE *few in the world that can control the magic that emanates from the heart of our world. And those that do live in a separate world all their own.*

They can do things that we could merely dream of. The sorcerers of Aladran, mystical and deadly, through their magic, define, change, and write our history.

Those that wield the Ellydian can change the path of ancient rivers, create new ones, and some have been said to even cover the sky in clouds, blocking out our divine sun.

But those in that world are subject to their own laws.

There are echelons of power similar to our world, but also to the animal kingdom. The most powerful become gods in their own right, and the youngest and lowest in their ranks must fight to survive against those that could kill with a single musical note cast into the air.

In their world, as in our own, the powerful almost always gain the riches, the beauty, and the spoils of life.

The most powerful sorcerers always become important figures in our history, while the meek fight for scraps. Those most powerful are also written as our greatest saviors and most terrifying oppressors. From the beginning of time, kings and queens have flocked to the power of the Ellydian those sorcerers wield. For he who wields the Ellydian, wields the future.

-TRANSLATED *from the language of the Sundar. The Scriptures of the Ancients, Book I, Chapter XXV.*

-THE TRANSLATION *of the word from the text of the Sundar, Sorcenn, had recently been changed. Originally it was translated to 'sorcerer', but Archmage Mihelik Starshadow has since changed it to 'Syncron' or 'Synth' based on the heart of the wielder, and to fit with the modern names for those who wield the Ellydian.*

AN EERIE CHILL took the morning air as it swept across the desert tundra.

Soren couldn't place what made it so unnerving. Perhaps it was the bitter cold that rushed into their faces and bit at their ankles, or the death in the tower they left behind. Normally they would have taken the time to bury the dead, including Lady Sargonenth's son Zefa, but there was no time to dig six feet down. Instead, a smoldering blaze sent a plume of smoke into the early morning sky.

The pillar of smoke faded as it hit the crimson ribbons of clouds that streaked across the sky like tearing claw marks. They stripped the dozens of men of their jewelry and valuables and hid them in the tower for later retrieval, to be returned to Taverras and their families.

They decided to leave the dead Shade where it lay. Patches of skin and vials of blood were taken by Kaile. The skin hung from straps on his camel to dry in the sunlight, and the vials were wrapped lightly in linens, to hopefully freeze but not break.

Soren had noticed Blaje's demeanor had changed since the discovery of the slaughter that had taken place at the outpost. She, in the short time he'd known her, was stoic, but there was the sense that she was sad, grieving even. They'd bonded through battle, and their kiss. He had a thirst to know more about her, to connect deeper even. And with their deaths looming around any dune ahead of them, the urge was intense. He felt it deep in his stomach when he looked at her, remembering the taste of her lips, and the rich aroma of the oils in her hair.

Something in the tower had affected her as she rode at the lead, her posture ever so slightly slumped, but he noticed.

She'd said there was a shrine they'd rest at that night, so he'd ask her there what was bothering her.

Kaile yawned loudly as they rode away from the tower, and Seph rested her head on the camel's front hump, also hiding her little nose from the rushing winds. They'd both been up into the late hours of the night working on dismembering the Shade, investigating organs, and awing over the never-before-seen structure of the creatures that were invading their lands. Kaile cut and described what he found as Seph scribed furiously, trying not to miss anything.

She drew anatomical maps of the blood vessels, bone structure, muscular build, and even close-up renderings of the face and eyes.

Soren watched them throughout the night as he smoked his pipe. Kaile's hands were covered in blood as he cut deeper and deeper into the beast. Soren sat behind Seph so he could watch her sketch in charcoal, do fine detail work with ink, all the while making notes on the same pages of drawings, and writing a long list of notes to be worked through later.

They finally got to sleep just a few hours before the break of dawn, but Soren got less than that. That night, Davin slept heavily, and Blaje stared off with a distant look in her eyes. She wasn't there with them in the tower. Her mind was elsewhere, and Soren couldn't help but wonder where it was.

That day's ride was as rough as the others. It didn't seem as though Zatan wanted them to move forward, get out of the biting sands that bit at their exposed skin. It felt as if Aladran itself was trying to slow their progress, as if it didn't want to be saved.

Blaje had warned Soren that morning that they'd need to ride hard, no matter the weather, for the shrine was a hard ride over deep sand dunes. The desert had transformed from a flat wasteland to a vast, endless desert of rolling sand dunes in all directions. If not for Blaje's guidance, Soren would be hard pressed to find safety for them without the sun's protection.

So they rode all day, leaving a long trail of camel prints behind them in the sand. The winds would surely cover their tracks over the following hours, and Soren was grateful for that. They didn't need the annoyance of more bounty hunters after them. And as for Alcarond, Soren wasn't planning on hiding, as was Mihelik's wish. They needed to get to Golbizarath, and then they would get as far away from danger as possible—wherever that meant.

But with how close they were to the answers Lord Belzaar held, that was Soren's only focus. The winter desert itself would have to be enough to shield them from the hunters that were after them.

The air thinned as the extreme cold of night approached. The sun sunk into the distant dunes as the long ride's end was in sight. In the distance, straight ahead, peaking over the dune before them, was the top of a tall tower. It had a metal top that looked flat from the direction they rode, but as they ascended the dune, the full spectacle of the solitary monument came into view.

"That's it," Davin shouted through the whooshing winds that blew in from the side. "That's the shrine. And not a moment too soon."

They didn't stay at the crest of the dune to marvel at the shrine below, as the fading light was cutting it too close for comfort. They needed to get down into the safety of the shrine immediately, as the night's gloom grew thick around them.

They rode hard down the backside of the dune, the camels' feet sunk into the deep sand, sliding down it with each step. As they were halfway down the dune, with only a few hundred yards to get to the base of the tower—Soren marveled at it.

He'd seen many things and places in the desert that felt like they belonged in a separate world, but the monument before them may have been the most bizarre he'd seen.

First, the construction of such an odd, yet inspiring shrine in the absolute middle of nowhere, was quite the sight to behold. At its base, and along the spires were spiky fanning structures of sleek, black iron that resembled a sort of angular cobweb decorating the ivory pillars that grew to pointed spires. Five spires surrounding one great white tower that rose a hundred feet straight up. The contrast of the ivory stone and shining black metal made it appear freshly built, and not hundreds or thousands of years old, like he assumed it would be.

"Socrún Ür," Blaje said. "One of the divine shrines of goddess Shirava. A marvel of time, erected upon the holy site, said to be where the goddess dove her hand into the sand, pulling forth a magical well that flourishes with pure water. It saved our people during a great drought that threatened thousands."

"It's magnificent," Kaile muttered. "I've never seen anything like it."

"There is nothing like it," Blaje replied.

"Get inside," Soren said, glowering at the horizon in all directions. "We don't have time to be admiring old stones."

The camels knew the danger of dusk, running to the front gate.

Soren thought he saw movement out of the corner of his eye east, to the darkest horizon. He squinted to see through the haze. Upon the hill he saw the black smoke-like top of the body he'd seen too many times to count.

"Ride!" he yelled.

They kicked the camels' sides hard. They all knew the urgency in his voice.

Just as he yelled, the monstrous Black Fog shot down the dune, its centipede-like legs carrying it as swiftly and as devilishly as anything a nightmare could imagine. It was a half mile off, but it shot toward them as if it hadn't eaten in years. Behind it, another darted over the backside of the dune, hurtling behind and right toward Soren and his friends.

The camels ran as quickly as their sturdy legs could carry them, cries of fear squeezed between grunts as they ran hard, after an already exhausting day. The camels heaved breaths as they ran to the front gate. Blaje leaped from her camel before it had the time to stop its sprint.

She ran to the door, shoving a key into the lock with a fluid movement, twisting it and opening it inward quickly.

Soren watched the two Black Fog run down the dune, already crossing half the distance they'd been. Soren shoved the camels hard inside, which they didn't fight. They hurried inside, shutting the two huge black iron doors closed behind them. Blaje locked them quickly and said a quick prayer in her native tongue. Soren caught her saying the goddess's name in there.

"Whoa," Seph gasped, spinning, marveling at the interior of the shrine.

Again, it was unlike anything Soren had ever seen, and he'd seen some fine throne rooms by architectural masters in his years.

"There's…" Kaile said. "There's not a grain of sand in here."

"Look," Seph said, pointing back at the door behind them.

Along the floor, the sand was running down off the camels' fur, off their packs, and even pulling out from the inside of Soren's boots strapped to his feet. The sand was being pulled under the doors, as if being drained down through an hourglass, except whatever was causing this was draining every single grain of sand from their possession and back out into the desert.

Soren scratched the stubble on his chin, pondering.

Is this the Ellydian? Or is this another form of magic?

Soren had gone through phases of believing and being a non-believer in the goddess, often triggered by the tragic events in his life.

But, is this a spell by Shirava to keep her shrine eternally clean? Or is this a spell by some old Syncron sorcerer?

"What's doing that?" Seph asked, looking at Blaje.

"You don't believe in the goddess?" Blaje asked, one eyebrow raised, the other sunk down.

"Not like that," Seph said. "Not until now, I guess."

"We will be safe here the night," Blaje said. "Even the Black Fog dare not enter this place."

Soren walked over to the iron doors shut tight. The sands pulled themselves out under the door still, washing over and around his boots like flowing water. He placed his ear flat on the door. He could hear the sand scraping under the metal, and he could hear the howling winds outside. But there was something else. Something far darker than the night.

The Black Fog moved silently, its sharp black legs touching the earth with less than a whisper. But he heard them. Not their legs, or their immense bodies scooting the sands beneath them, but a sort of huffing frustration. It was like a bear growling, pacing, stalking its prey, but unable to reach it. It was an audible hunger and hatred that came in the form of a faint roar like a distant crashing of an ocean.

He moved back.

"They're just outside."

"We're safe here," Blaje said. "The goddess will protect us. Rest easy, for if there is anywhere that is still safe from the Demons of Dusk, it is this place."

Chapter Thirty-Five

That was all any of them really needed to hear.

The sight of the sand being sent from every fiber of their clothes out back into the desert was enough to soothe their minds. Even the Black Fog outside the gate didn't bother Soren that much. After all, it was only recent events that had shown the Demons of Dusk entered human dwellings at all. An enchanted mystical shrine by the goddess herself allowed him to let out a deep sigh of relief—at least for the night.

The shrine's interior was dim at first, only faint sunlight creeping in from the tall windows, but once Davin got a fire going in the hearth at the center of the vast main room, Soren once again was taken aback by its splendor.

It was a round room, with the camels fitting into the interior stables on the left side, gulping down water from troughs already filled.

"This is a magical place," Kaile said, letting his fingers glide on the mantel top. They traced around the intricately carved white stone above the fire. "I've never felt anything like it."

"Is it the Ellydian?" Seph asked with wide eyes, marveling at the room.

"I—I don't know," he responded, admiring the vaulted ceiling high above. "The Ellydian can enchant things, but a whole building? For this long? That would have to have been a very powerful Syncron. And I don't remember reading about any stories like that. I dare say, if it is magic, I would believe it to be more the work of Shirava than of a Syncron."

"Never seen the actual work of a god," Davin said, sitting in a rocking chair by the fire, taking his boots off and wiggling his hairy toes before the crackling flames. "I mean, besides us."

Soren strolled around the room, while noticing Blaje was deep in thought, sitting in a cushioned chair of dark leather. She was staring at the wall, deep in a daze.

He decided to give her the moment while he admired the surrounding craftsmanship. It was as finely crafted as the more elaborate cathedrals he'd seen, and that included Lūminine Grand Cathedral in Celestra. What this Socrún Ŭr Shrine lacked in size, it made up in ornate statues of ancient figures carved directly into the stone walls, ceiling, and even the handrail spindles that curved up the staircase. Everything was a perfect white stone, including the floor beneath the marvelous rugs of deep blues and golds. The only noticeable addition to the interior, not of white stone, was the elaborate shiny black iron above that formed the buttresses. Each converging at the center of the ceiling like a spiderweb with thousands of crisscrossing strands of webbing.

The room warmed as the fire grew in the hearth, popping and sizzling. The smell caused Soren's eyes to water from fatigue. It had been a brutal, icy day of harsh winds, and the heat of the fire soothed his weariness.

"Let's go look around," Seph said, tugging her uncle by the sleeve.

Normally he'd hesitate, but he indeed felt they were safe in this magical place.

"Sure," he said. A smirk tugged at the corner of his mouth. Seph, who'd surely had an excruciating day out on the camel's back in the freezing temperatures, looked as lively as if it were a warm spring day.

She ran to the stairs and was already halfway up the curving stairs before he set foot on the first one. Seph was quickly out of sight, and Soren slowly followed.

He turned the corner to the second level. The door was already open. It was dimly lit, yet as large as the vast room below. With the sun completely down for the night, the only light that illuminated the room was from the stairwell behind, and that was behind the doorway behind him.

Soren couldn't see Seph, but he could feel she was tense. She didn't say a word, but she was in the darkly lit room. He could see, though, the starlight and dim clouds through the glass windows, which were wide at their bases and rose to sharp peaks at their tops.

"Seph?" he said, the dark room finally coming into focus slowly. He finally found her standing at the far side of the room. Her back was to him, and her fingers were touching something before her. As what was beyond her finally came into view, his heart fluttered. He saw the bench before her as her knee rested on it. He saw her fingers gliding upon the wooden cover. And finally, he marveled at the silver pipes that flowed up from its back, reflecting the warm glow from the fire below softly. Others held the faint glimmer of starlight. His palms sweated as he watched Seph slowly turn to look at him. A huge smile lit her face.

She waved him over.

"I would have never imagined..." he gasped.

"Isn't she gorgeous?"

Soren walked over and gently touched the key cover. It was

as smooth as any wood he'd ever seen. It was lacquered in dark oil, and it was constructed of a type of wood nowhere near. He guessed it was a mahogany or sapele, possibly even cherry.

But it's so old. For it to be in this condition, seems… impossible.
But so is sand flowing back out under a door.

"Shall we?" Seph asked. "I'll go get some candles." Before she waited for an answer, she was halfway across the room and quickly down the stairs.

Soren sat on the bench, which didn't let out even a whimper of a crack. He put his fingers under the key cover and lifted it gently. It slid back behind the keys like a dream. He let out another sigh as the ivory keys were revealed. They held a luster that made them look wet, damp from a thin layer of water. He didn't press any. No, he'd wait for Persephone.

His head dropped, his hair fell before his eyes, and he couldn't hold back his grin.

How has the goddess brought me this gift? In the eye of the storm, after all we've been through, and stuck in the middle of the desert… is this a dream?

Many footsteps hit the stairs as Seph ran up first with candles in candelabras, already lit. Behind came Davin, Blaje, and Kaile. The light from the candles filled the room, basking the organ in the magnetic rays of candlelight. The pipes gleamed like pure, polished silver, and Seph plopped herself beside him eagerly.

Her arm was flat against his, and memories of her as a child flooded his mind. He saw her, a seven-year-old girl, eager to learn to play, her tiny fingers ready to dance over the keys, filling the room with orchestral, magical sound.

He laughed as the others sat behind, scattered around the room. None said a word. They were waiting, patiently.

"So, what do you want to play, uncle?"

"You pick."

"I haven't played since back there in Guillead, where Kaile

and I first met, and you snooped on me." She gave him a wise, snarky glare. "No, you pick. I don't even know if I remember how to play those old things."

"You don't remember any?"

"I was just playing coy. Of course, I remember some of them."

"Which is your favorite?"

Her smile widened. "Promette de Triumph."

A warm sensation filled him, soothing his stomach, giving brimming energy to his chest and hands. "Good girl. You remembered."

"Ready?" she asked.

"Absolutely."

This was where Soren always started, as he sat on the left side, so his finger hit the A note that started the ballad. His foot hit a pedal, and the note rang so clearly throughout the room, he felt as if he was in a world-famous cathedral, or a concert hall, perhaps the one he saw the master Piphenette play at back in Arnor.

He shifted the A note to a C, letting it ring out with as crisp a note as he'd ever heard. And as soon as her fingers lit the keys, Soren was instantly whirled back into a different world, a different life, and a better time.

As they played together, he became what he was. Sitting beside her, he felt he remembered the man he was.

Persephone shifted back to the child he knew. She was a brimming young girl, full of talent and a sponge for knowledge. Her whole bright future was ahead of her, and Soren was simply happy that she was in his life.

They played together; a cacophony of brilliant notes struck in absolute perfection. The music filled the room, reverberating off the ancient walls as if the room had been designed to make every inch of the room a perfect listening spot. Every spectator was overwhelmed with the low, grabbing bass, the fluid mid tones, and the treble notes that filled the listener with feelings of elation, triumph, and sorrow.

As they played Promette de Triumph, a ballad written by an old master, and one of the ones that was Persephone's favorites to play with her mentor, all sadness washed away from Soren's soul, and he felt waves of glee.

He was the savior again; the protector. There was no tarnish in his soul, no deep, unrelenting regret. He was still the legendary Blade of Tourmielle. Nothing could withstand his skill, his prowess, his heart.

Behind closed eyes, he felt every note fill his ears and his head with the perfect music. It was as if Persephone had gotten better after these terrible ten years. She'd practiced, even being stuck in isolation and loneliness in that orphanage. But somehow, she'd refined, she'd grown, and now—she rivaled Soren himself.

That was, without a doubt, one of the proudest moments of his life. His pupil had become the master.

And as dark as it felt and sounded in his head, he felt he could die a happy man at that moment. All life could leave his bones, muscles, and skin, and he could be at ease. His broken heart could mend, and he could return to his lost love, Cirella.

You'd be so proud of her right now... the young woman our little Persephone has become.

Cirella, if you are watching, I hope you can hear this...

With the spectacle of the perfect organ in the middle of this godforsaken wasteland, Soren thought there might be a goddess, and if there was in fact a goddess watching over them, then perhaps there was an afterlife. Perhaps there was a place Cirella could be sitting on the bench with them. Her fingers could caress Soren's skin, giving him the goose pimples that rose on the back of his arms and the sides of his neck.

Do you see her? You'd be so proud of her...

The song lasted for what felt like the length of a stream, the breath of the wind, and the majesty of the snow-peaked mountain. The sound that came from the magical organ, as all four of their hands pressed the keys in masterful fashion, must have bathed the surrounding desert in an aura of perfect bliss.

Soren felt every fiber of his body on fire with radiant, soothing, overwhelming bliss. He opened his eyes and watched the young woman beside him with her eyelids pressed shut, feeling the music as her fingers fluttered over the keys, transporting everyone in the room to Soren and Seph's special place.

He wished this moment could live on forever, and that's partly how he wished his soul could leave his body, and he could float away in that perfection. There'd be no war, no more struggle, no more being hunted. He wouldn't have to be a symbol; a hero.

But he knew, as the last notes escaped the silver pipes, letting their melancholy notes vibrate from the ancient organ's sturdy pipes, his path wasn't over.

It wasn't even close to being over.

There was too much blood that needed to be spilled.

Too many people had wronged him.

Too many innocent people suffer.

Persephone had lost just as much as Soren. More even.

There needed to be justice.

There needed to be retribution.

And his only solace, would be payment... in blood.

"Bravo," Davin shouted, clapping his thick hands after the final note faded away to the still, empty air.

"Au Saluda!" Kaile raised his glass, clapping his thigh with his free hand.

Blaje didn't clap or say anything. Instead, she hung her head, and tears streamed down her cheeks. They were so plentiful; they dripped down to her chin and fell onto her chest, soaking her shirt in the tears.

Soren knew the feeling, and didn't interrupt her emotions. He'd been there. He knew that sometimes you had to let the feelings happen, let the music take control… so he pressed another set of notes, an A Minor chord, moving to a G.

Seph's eyes widened immediately, full of recognition and welcoming joy. She grinned widely, laughing as her fingers pressed down.

They'd finished Promette du Triumph, and moved to the Grand Ballad of the Dragon.

The ballad began in rolling low notes, bellowing through the pipes like deep winds in a wide, old cave. Seph took her time hitting the high notes that sparkled like rolling water gleaming in moonlight. The song was a testament to the spectacle and power of the dragons that used to scour the lands.

In the middle of the song, the notes melded together like a wild jungle of brimming life, or a chaotic battle of clashing swords and fiery explosions. The room rocked under the weight of the ballad. It filled Soren completely. He didn't even feel like himself. He didn't worry about the present or the future. The ballad protected him from the world. He felt safe and felt as powerful as the sea itself. Nothing could hurt him. He was home again.

The song eventually ended, as they always do.

He grabbed Seph by the hand.

"You're incredible," he said.

She couldn't hold her happiness in. She gave him a great toothy grin, and her eyes sparkled with life. Her youth had returned, pulling away with welcome the shadow of a hardened life that ten years of pain and sorrow had created.

Soren saw out of the corner of his gaze, Blaje was sobbing, her face tucked down into her lap. She was heaving breaths as she cried. Tears streaked down Kaile's face as Davin sat back with his arms folded over his chest in contemplation.

Sable jumped onto the top of the organ and fell asleep on

the reverberating organ's top. That made both Soren and Seph laugh together.

They continued playing songs late into the night, never missing a single note. It was as if they'd both been practicing separately, waiting desperately to be reunited for this one moment. This was the concert of their lives.

And Soren didn't want to think about it, so he drove the thought far from his mind, but he knew this may very well be the last time they played together. So he enjoyed it. He was present, and loved every single second of the gorgeous music.

He had everything.

He had his family.

He had his friends.

He had victory in his life again.

He had control.

Nothing could hurt him. He was invincible. A great dragon's fire couldn't burn him. A twisted Synth's spells couldn't stop his fingers from finishing what he'd started. There was nothing.

Nothing except him, Persephone, and the music.

They played deep into the night, each playing tunes that the other joined in on.

It was a magical night, and one that Soren knew he would remember the rest of his life—no matter how long or short that may be.

Chapter Thirty-Six

※

It was the sort of exhaustion that was all-consuming. Not so different from the kind after a hard-fought battle won. His soul felt cleansed, and all regret had dissolved away. His ears subtly rang, leaving a trace of the music lingering, reminding him of the beauty of the divine organ.

Seph slept feet away in a soft bed, sand free, with impossibly clean and soft sheets. They were in one of the highest rooms of the tower, where Blaje sat in a chair by the entrance, standing watch, or perhaps just deep in thought.

Soren wanted to go talk to her, check in with her emotions back down there by the organ, but his eyelids were overwhelmingly heavy. Long nights of restless sleep, or no sleep at all, had seemingly caught up with him. Sable seemed to notice and slunk off from between Seph's legs to in between his. She purred softly, quickly dozing back off into sleep.

Soren fell into a deep, warm, welcoming slumber.

For what was hours, but only felt like minutes of shut-eye, Soren stirred away from a hand prodding his shoulder. His eyes barely peeked open, letting in the light of the golden-reddish sunlight that pierced the drapes from the windows.

"You gonna sleep all day?" Davin asked, while Soren looked to see Blaje was the one gently nudging him awake. "I suppose we could stay here another day. I've never seen a place so spotless. We could stay here a week even, as long as no archmages or archpriests or Knight Wolfs come looking to disturb our peace and quiet."

"That is not an option," Blaje said, her fingers leaving Soren's shoulder. "We need to get back out on the sands."

"Is our next destination going to arrive just in the nick of time again?" Davin asked. "The last couple of nights have been a little too close for comfort."

"No," she replied. "Today is different. The next couple of days will be."

"Different?" Kaile yawned. "Different how?"

"We will be entering into the Ashgrove around midday."

"The Ashgrove?" Soren asked, reminding himself about what his old master Landran had told him about when they were last in these lands.

"You'll see," Blaje said. "Better to see than have me explain it to you. Now, let's get the camels loaded back up and be on our way."

"Golbizarath is close?" Seph asked.

Blaje half-ignored Seph, but nodded, looking out the window beside her.

"Should be just a couple days away now," Kaile said. "Lady Sargonenth said it was seven days from The Brink. So... maybe four?"

Blaje, again, nodded. "Perhaps three. It depends."

"Depends?" Seph asked.

"You will all see, at the grove," the Desert Shadow said, keeping her mystery.

By the waning hours of midday, Soren got his first glimpse at the mysterious place Blaje referred to as the Ashgrove. The vast dunes had calmed, transforming from great, sharp-peaked, shifting dunes to rolling hills of hard sand. Before them, appearing as either a break in the desert, or the beginning of something new—something strange.

Once they made their way to the Ashgrove, a new wasteland where wildlife once grew, once thrived. It was like a dead, decrepit oasis that once existed—now just looking like a haunted jungle devoid of all joy or life.

A canopy sprawled overhead, with dry, cracked branches scraping each other in the biting, freezing winds. Blaje led them in, with the camels resisting setting foot into the Ashgrove. There was still sand on the forest floor, but it was much rockier. The camels did walk in. They entered through a wide break in the dangling, dead vines and ancient tree trunks.

None said anything about the place as they entered, each of them deep in thought about such a desolate, decrepit forest.

Once they were fully enveloped in the shadow cast down through the thick branches, Soren felt the relief of being safe in a place where the Demons of Dusk should not enter. But such a place usually brought its own sorts of monsters. Back in the Myngorn, it was the two colossal bears that nearly killed him and Ursa, before what was later revealed to be Mihelik, called them off.

In the Ashgrove, Soren knew he'd have to be on his guard. He'd have to let instinct permeate through his relaxed feeling of being safe from the Black Fog here.

Blaje led them down a trail that led deep into the Ashgrove. It was well traveled, beaten down by boots and camels' feet over the millennia, but that gave Soren little reprieve from his thoughts. Blaje rode without hesitation, deeper and deeper into the heart of the dead forest. They rode for the better part of an hour before she pulled back the camel's reins and got down from the saddle. The others did the same, each of them scanning the dim, hazy forest all around.

They were completely surrounded by the Ashgrove then, with little signs they were still in the Dyadric Desert.

Even the smell was different. It smelled like a dingy attic, or a stagnant cellar basement—full of woody smells, and the subtle aroma of something burning far off. It was musty and dank. Even the breeze that got through the maze of trees and vines smelled old and smoky.

"How long do we have to be here?" Seph finally asked, the first words uttered since they'd entered.

"We'll make camp here tonight," Blaje said, grabbing kindling off the ground.

"It's still early," Soren said. "We could keep going a few more hours."

"We rest here," Blaje said, not meeting his gaze, but continuing to add to the bundle in her arms. "We would not want to get lost. The light fades quickly the deeper we get in. Best to be cautious in the Ashgrove."

"You didn't answer Seph's question," Davin said. "How long are we going to be in this place?"

"Golbizarath is at the end of Ashgrove," she replied, dumping the sticks at the center of the clearing, by a divot in the earth where fires had been made, but not for what looked like years. "It's protected by it. Like a moat around a castle. The fortress of Golbizarath is secluded beyond what a normal fortress in Zatan would be. There are things that happen there that are meant to be hidden. And the Ashgrove itself is notorious for keeping travelers that venture in. Even I, the Desert Shadow, tread carefully here."

Soren wasn't sure what to think about that. He trusted her, and he welcomed the safety from the Demons of Dusk for the days it would take to reach their destination. "I feel like there's something you're not telling us."

"Just stay close to each other, and all will be fine," she said. "But don't stray. Especially at night."

"Why?" Kaile asked.

"Just do as I say here," she said. Her tone grew stark. "We shouldn't run into any problems, but keep our fire stoked bright."

"Blaje…" Soren said.

"Just do as I say…" she said. "There are things about this place that are as old as time, it feels. This was once an oasis, but it was long ago cursed. So do as I say, and we'll get through without issue."

"Cursed?" Kaile muttered.

"I'm guessing that's just a figure of speech," Seph said. "Like calling a mountain unclimbable."

"I'd do as she says," Davin said. "If the Desert Shadow says to be wary here, then wary we should be."

They got the fire going up to Kaile's height and burning so hot Soren could feel the heat from ten feet away. The camels rested nearby, and Soren couldn't help but watch Blaje as she stared deeply into the flames.

They'd eaten, drank and were enjoying the shelter of the Ashgrove as each of them waited for slumber to take them. Kaile, Seph, and Davin stared with glossy eyes at the fire, each deep in their own thoughts. But it was Blaje who Soren was most curious about. She wept while they played the organ. She seemed to change once they entered the shrine and found those within hacked to pieces by that Shade.

He stood, stretched wide, yawned, and went to sit beside her. The others noticed, but paid little mind. The darkness in the trees all around deepened to deep shadow, and the starlight was hidden beyond above.

"Nice night," he said. "Peaceful."

She didn't reply. In fact, she didn't take her gaze from the fire. Soren didn't know if she heard him, or even noticed he was beside her.

He nudged her shoulder. "Hey."

She startled back to life, turning her head sharply to see him. "Oh, Soren..."

"Everything all right?" he asked.

She groaned subtly, pinching the bridge of her nose. "Yes."

"Out with it," Soren said. "There's been something weighing on you ever since we got to the shrine. Before even..."

She reached into her pocket and pulled out a tight roll of parchment, one made for tying to a raven's leg. Also within her palm was a small pipe, one used for calling a raven. "I need to write Lady Sargonenth, but don't know what to say."

"What do you mean? Tell her what happened there. She's a mature woman. She will be able to handle it."

"I—I don't think I can write the words."

Suddenly, something clicked. Soren knew it was more than the lady of Taverras losing her son. Blaje lost something, too.

"You were... close with someone there?" he asked softly, all too familiar with the fresh, bitter taste of losing one close to you.

She nodded, biting her lip. She suddenly cleared her throat and wiped her eyes. "It doesn't matter. It was all a long time ago, anyway. A distant memory."

"It may be distant, but that doesn't make it hurt less."

She sighed. "I guess you know just as well as anyone."

He brushed a strand of her hair back behind her ear. "You can grieve. It takes time."

She glared down at the dirt between her feet.

"It was her son, wasn't it?" Soren asked, suddenly feeling the others finally listen in. "Zefa was his name?"

Blaje cocked her head up at him, an eyebrow raised, and her eyes narrowed. "How'd you know that?"

"I didn't. Not 'til now. But it makes sense now. You acted different after the lady mentioned his name back at the Brink. But now it makes sense. I'm so sorry, Blaje..."

"It was a long time ago."

Seph seemed more interested than any in the moment. She was stroking Sable's back, her eyes unblinking, reflecting the firelight.

"How long ago?" Seph asked.

Blaje cleared her throat, ignoring the question.

Soren wanted to press her to answer Seph, but there was obviously some sort of forced distance she wanted to keep up between them. Blaje looked up at the swaying branches above, but then let out a deep sigh and replied to Seph's question. "I was a bit younger than you are. He was a soldier, and I was an apprentice of the Calica Clan. It was forbidden. It was secret. I was young. And it was so hot…"

Seph was leaning in, lapping up each word Blaje had decided to share with her. Soren could tell it was special to Seph.

"How'd it end?" Seph asked. "If you don't mind my asking."

"We knew there was no future there," Blaje said. "As much as we dreamed of a life together, no lord of Zatan could wed a daughter of the Calica. He would have his throne, and I, mine in my own right. His mother found out about us, and forced us apart. I hated her for years, but deep down, I knew she was right. Now he's got no throne, and I'm alone all the way out here."

Seph stood and went to her side, sitting next to her. "You're not alone."

Blaje nodded at Seph, grabbing both her and Soren's hand and squeezing. "I know." She turned to look at Soren and looked deeply into his eyes. He could see the anguish, the hard years of loneliness, and the hardened warrior inside. "We walk the same road."

He heard her words. But they sunk deep into him. He knew exactly what she meant. They weren't only going to

Golbizarath together. They may be going to their ends together. This was no errand. This was the mission. The stakes were too high. The war was too engulfing. There would be no end except victory or defeat, with all the elation and heartbreak in between.

"We walk the same road," he said. "And I'll walk it with you, until the bitter end…"

Chapter Thirty-Seven

There was no rest for Soren that night. There were only the howling winds, the scraping of dead trees, and the chirping of insects in the Ashgrove. That, to Soren, was a wondrous, welcome sound. It reminded him of his favorite place—the deep forest. No Black Fog or Shades hunted where wildlife still flourished. Bats flapped their wings in frenzied patterns above the stoked fire's smoke.

Each of the others slept, and Soren hoped for them to stay that way. With each passing day, they were closer to his destination. And after that... perhaps deeper into the desert, and as far away from the encroaching archmage as physically possible. Against any other foe, the five of them had a great chance of victory. Even against the Knight Wolf, there'd be a chance.

Soren may be completely vulnerable to the curse the Knight Wolf and his Synth Zertaan put on him, but the others were untouched by his inability to even lift a finger against his greatest foe. Against Alcarond, however, none would confront his overwhelming magic.

Soren spun Firelight in his fingers, the reflection of the flames dancing along the layered steel, but shedding no light onto the infinitely black pommel. On his wrist, the Twilight Veil sparkled. The three-inch-wide gold band on his wrist wove with a decorative floral pattern, interlaced with the same blue stones that adorned the ring. The ring was a thin golden ring with three of the gemstones inlaid on one side.

This may be my best shot against him, when the time comes. Stealth, surprise, and one sharp dagger straight through the heart or deep into the neck.

He eyed Firelight's pommel, remembering how it glowed and sparkled with the death of the Shades, and the fight with the Black Fog.

There's still a chance I can reason with him. Against the Demons of Dusk, we are all on the same side. If I can just convince him that the king is only doing harm, and that we need to unite against him and the Demons of Dusk, then we could have a new powerful ally if he sees reason! The most powerful being in existence! We could win... but that is a gigantic if...

Soren thought that if he could get the archmage to understand what he knew, then the war tides could shift in their direction.

He thought about the Shade uttering the human word, "No." That moment changed everything. A part of their brains from when they were men and women still remained. Either that or the Shades were far more intelligent than anyone, including Alcarond and Mihelik, knew... if only there was a way to reach him... if only there was...

Soren noticed his focus was shifting. His eyelids drooped, he sheathed Firelight, as it had suddenly grown heavy in his hands. He leaned back and let out a soothing sigh and yawn.

I'm getting tired. I guess one night of sleep made me...

But suddenly he realized he wasn't just tired. There was something happening, but whether it was in his mind, or in the Ashgrove, he couldn't tell. All he knew was that he heard it... singing...

It was a sweet, clear woman's voice. It was distant, yet familiar. He couldn't make out the words. It was more a humming and singing of long drawn out words that he didn't recognize. But it was exquisite, pristine, perfect.

The glow of the fire dimmed, and the world darkened around him. He stood, his legs achy and slow. He took lumbering steps forward. Soren didn't know where the woman singing the song was, but his strides propelled him forward, and before he knew it, he was walking into the dense forest, dead twigs and branches scratching his skin and breaking as he walked straight through.

Soren didn't have a care in the world, as the curiosity of who was singing such a majestic, perfect song, took over his mind and body.

Entering deeper and deeper in the Ashgrove, the light of the fire faded far behind, and all he had left to see was the dim light of the moon that made its way through the dense branches above, giving him only just enough to thread through the trees.

The trees opened up to a wide clearing, where at its center a woman in dark robes sat; a hood covering her head and sitting with her back to him. The song was intoxicating and all-encompassing. It was all he could think of, the blending of notes and the delicate pitches and harmonies. It flowed through him like a dream, and all he wanted to do was to plunge head-first into it. The song was so perfect, but there was something painstakingly familiar about it. But he couldn't put his finger on it, until…

The figure turned slowly, shifting on the log she sat upon. Her robes twisted and their folds deepened as she spun to face him, and suddenly everything came together. The song, the voice, the face—it all came crashing down in a second that made Soren's heart beat like a drum, and all the words he wanted to say caught in his throat.

All that was able to squeeze its way out of his mouth was, "Baby? Is that you?"

He took a step toward the seated woman. From under her thick, dark hood, her oceanic blue eyes piercing into him. The tips of her golden hair flowed onto her chest, but no smile lit her lips.

"Sor," she replied. Her voice held a deep, somber gravity. She didn't rise.

"Cir—Cirella, baby... how? Why? I—"

He ran to embrace her.

But only mere feet from her, and the chance to get that one last hug goodbye he never got. She halted him with her hand raised; her pale palm hovering between them.

"We can't," she said, her voice hollow like speaking through a wide, empty tree trunk.

He stood frozen, withheld from wrapping his arms around her and pressing his lips to hers. His fingers spread at both sides, his mouth was agape, and his mind raced through the fog to understand what was happening.

I'm dreaming. This is surely a dream. But why can't I run to her? Why won't she let me say goodbye?

"Baby, what is this?" he said, forcing the words past the overwhelming emotions that gathered in his chest and throat. "How are you here?"

She whimpered, letting out a hint of a cry. Her hand lowered, and she spun back, facing away from him. Her head slunk, and the air chilled briskly.

"I don't know," she said. "I don't know where I am, what I'm doing here, and how you are here with me. But I'm grateful for it."

He took cautious steps forward, walking around her backside, gently sitting beside her without touching. Soren noticed he wasn't breathing, unintentionally, he was holding his breath. He forced himself to breathe.

"Cirella... whatever this is. I'm grateful for it. There's so many things I've wanted to say to you. I—I wanted to say how sorry I was, am, for what happened. I—I should have stopped it. I should have saved you."

"You saved her, Sor." She faced him with a hint of a smile curving on her lips. "That's enough. You don't have to be sorry for the way things happened. That's all in the past now. You need to focus on what's important now. You need to be ready for what's to come."

"What's to come?" he asked softly, unsure of the answer.

"Hurt, pain. More of what already curses you."

The air in his lungs depleted, and he felt all his power fade. All his strength he built up to fight the world vanished. He was suddenly just a boy who wanted to be held by the one thing he loved more than anything in this world—and he couldn't.

"It's all right," she said, lifting her arm and placing her pale hand on his. All the life of her tan skin had faded, and a chill hit the back of his hand where her normally warm touch would be. "You're stronger than you realize. That's one of the reasons I fell in love with you."

He choked back his tears, or at least tried his hardest.

"I—I love you so much. I don't know how to live without you. It's not fair. I wasn't meant to go through this world alone. Everything's gone. Our life, our future."

"It's your life now. Your future. And you're not alone, Sor..."

"Seph..." He wiped his tears away.

Cirella nodded.

"She's going to need you. Now, and for what's coming."

"What do you mean? What's coming?"

"I—I don't know. But I feel it." She pulled her hand back and her face winced. "Pain. Anguish. Confusion."

He gave a deep sigh.

"Your road isn't over," she said. "This is all too important. You're too important to fall. There's more at stake than your resentment and sadness. You need to grow into what you were born to be. The last ten years have set you back, caused you to crawl into yourself; hide. But those days are over. You had your time to grieve and loathe. Now is the time to spread your wings."

"I—I'm trying..."

"I know you are." She scooted closer, so they were nearly touching. "Listen, Sor, we don't have much time. I can feel myself slipping away, like sand through our fingers. I don't know why we're here together. But it isn't only you who didn't get to say goodbye. You need to shut up and listen to me, too." A smile finally spread wide on her face as the teardrops fell. "I'm sorry for the way things ended, too. I also wanted to spend my life with you. I wanted to have your children. I could've done things differently. I could've saved you."

"No, baby. Don't say that..." He wiped his tears away, the rest dripped down his cheeks, landing on his shirt. "You didn't do anything wrong..."

"It doesn't matter now," she said. "All that matters is this. This moment. This love. This goodbye..."

"No, Cirella, don't... please..."

"This is our moment," she said. "The thing we've both prayed for the most. The one impossible thing that's here, now. You have to be strong, Sor. The world needs you. That little girl, who I loved more than life itself, needs you..."

"I need her too," he said. "I don't think I would've made it this far without her. I'd probably be alone in some forest, waiting to die."

She lifted her pale hand and touched the side of his face. Her frosty touch caused more tears to stream down his face as he choked on his sadness.

"I love you. Always have. Always will," she whispered,

resting her head on his shoulder. "I wish I could live in this moment forever."

He didn't answer, only cried as hard as any other moment he could remember.

"I want you to move on. You hear me, Sor? I want you to find love again. I want you to be that young handsome man who was so full of life and energy that I fell in love with. There's still time. You still have a whole life to live."

"It doesn't feel that way…"

"Listen, Sor. I feel like there's a reason I'm here, and we get this moment, and I have this feeling deep down, that something terrible is going to happen, and you're going to hurt. You're going to hurt again, but you've got to push through it. Everything depends on it. Everything depends on you being the strong leader that you were. Persephone is strong-willed, but she's vulnerable. She's young, untrained, and she's got the world coming against her because of her blood. But she's got that raw grit in her to survive. Believe in her. Believe in her ability to survive."

"I'll do what I must. For you…"

She smiled and leaned over with her lips puckered.

"I love you, baby," he whispered. "I'll love you forever."

"I love you more," she whispered back.

Their lips touched, he closed his eyes, and felt… nothing…

He opened his eyes, only to see the dim forest, with nary any light but that of the moon that trickled through the trees.

"No," he muttered to himself. Then anger welled hard in him. "No! Not again!"

He balled his hands into fists and drove one down onto the log where he sat. He felt the wood buckle and splinter under his fist. He hit it again, harder. And again. "No! No! Don't leave me again! Don't leave!"

Blood pooled under his fist and he collapsed onto the log as he heaved harsh breaths and the tears flowed easily down his face.

He cried onto the log, wrapping his arms around it, hoping for any sign of her. Her scent, a golden hair... anything. But there was nothing, and he felt completely empty and alone again.

While he cried into his arms, he felt a rustle of soft fur on his forearm. He looked up slowly to see the black cat purring as she rubbed her sides against him.

"Sable..."

She meowed, looking him in the eyes, and licked his arm with her scratchy tongue.

He choked down his tears and wiped them off his cheeks.

"Was that real? It felt so real?" He rubbed Sable's back, and he could feel the fur under his fingers. *This is real. So, was that real?*

I guess it doesn't matter. That's as close as I'll ever get to saying goodbye. He cleared his throat. *Don't tell the others. It's not worth talking about. They have more important things to focus on.*

"Now, how do we get back?"

Sable jumped down from the log, and wandered off out of the clearing, her tail raised high, proudly.

"I suppose you know the way. Good cat..."

Chapter Thirty-Eight

A talk with a fallen lover—ten years dead—was something Soren decided not to speak of. Instead, he'd returned to the camp, watched the ring of dead trees all night, eagerly waiting until the break of day. And when it finally came, the sunlight that washed over the lands, filling the sky with its golden light, Soren felt a small sense of his wounded soul sewn back together.

He couldn't explain it, perhaps never would be able to, but he got what he got. He got his goodbye.

"Didn't sleep again?" Davin asked with a wide-mouthed yawn.

Soren laughed to himself. "No. Not last night."

"Good. You fight better without it anyway," Davin muttered, scratching his armpit.

Seph rustled awake; Sable stretched out her long body, sinking her claws into Seph's blanket. They slowly got up from their ring around the campfire, and the camels watched. Over a half hour's time, they ate dried meat, stale bread, and packed the camels back up.

Once back on the trail that led deep into the Ashgrove, Seph seemed to catch a growing smile on Soren's face.

"What's wrong with ya?" she asked, riding beside him.

"What do you mean?" he replied.

"You could give two fucks about anything right now. You look as if you had lighthearted dreams last night, but I doubt you slept a wink."

"You're right," Soren said. "You sure are insightful and intuitive. Keep those traits with you. They'll serve you well."

She cocked an eyebrow. "Why are you acting so weird? You're not usually this bubbly in the morning. In fact, you're usually a wet cloth that needs to be wrung out a dozen times before midday, to even get a smile outta ya."

He leaned forward on his camel's hump. "Listen, Seph... I'm glad you're here. I'm glad you left the orphanage and found me. Whatever happens—know that I love you very much, trust yourself and your instincts, and I'm proud of you for the woman you're becoming. Whatever happens, believe in yourself. You're stronger than you know."

Her raised eyebrow turned to two flattened ones.

"Did you stash a bottle of something somewhere you're not sharing?"

"You heard me," he said, flicking the reins to ride up at Blaje's side, while Seph fell back to ride beside Kaile.

Soren looked over his shoulder. Davin was at the tail of the pack, riding with the spare camels, with Seph and Kaile talking in the middle.

"Are we making good time?" Soren asked.

She didn't respond immediately. For the clear-headed moment of bliss Soren held, Blaje seemed to be submersed in the opposite. A dark cloud had fallen upon her. And as they rode through the underbrush of the dead Ashgrove, the pillars of light that sparkled down through the swaying branches above cast a majestic radiance upon her, piercing her sadness.

"Soren… I want to apologize for my mindset of late. I don't do emotion well, and it's rarely the case I let them show. I'm a soldier still. They won't interfere with the mission."

He reached over and touched her hand. Her eyes widened as she glared at him with her intoxicating turquoise eyes. But she didn't pull away.

"You don't have to apologize for anything. I know your pain. At least I have my own, so I can imagine. It doesn't really ever go away. But the pain dims over time. It's a part of you now. Use it. Harness it. That may be your last bit of strength when the odds aren't in our favor. That shit… that's what makes us different. That's what makes us dangerous."

She nodded, and he pulled his hand back and they continued riding deeper and deeper into the mysterious Ashgrove in the middle of the desert.

"Soren Stormrose… you are quite the remarkable man. You seem to live up to the legend about you, yet also you're nothing like that man I've heard tales of most of my life. I'm pleased to ride to war with you."

"Thanks, Blaje. Yes. I'm glad we walk this path together. I feel we will need each other's strength for what's coming…"

˜

THEY RODE through the Ashgrove that day. The ancient trees grew denser as they rode deeper into the dead forest. Branches were more twisted and gnarled as the tree trunks grew wider, their roots deeper. Insects chirped louder and fell into a dizzying haze of ambient noise around them.

As night fell, they made camp again, each of them eagerly finding sleep after another grueling day's ride in the frigid cold.

Soren, however—as much as the fingers of sleep scratched at him, inviting him in, beckoning for him—didn't sleep a wink. All he could think of was her. The memories they shared. Even the small moments one tends to forget about until that lover is gone. The long walks along a river, sitting for a meal under a spectacular sunset, long nights lying in bed after sex, staring into each other's eyes, running each other's fingers along the other's skin.

All those fine memories finally won against the darker ones, and he wanted to enjoy every second of them.

~

On the encroaching eve of the seventh day, a red sun dipped down into the western clouds, causing the streaking, wispy clouds to cut through the sky like raking, bloody claw marks.

The Ashgrove thinned, its thick, deep forest left behind. The camels' feet trampled upon the thin twigs below as they approached the last reaches of the dead forest. As they took their last steps out of the forest, no one spoke as they left the safety of the Ashgrove behind; they beheld a new sight, leaving them all breathless.

They emerged from the forest into a vast valley that swept across the desert. The winds howled as the sun only gave them a couple of hours before the Demons of Dusk would creep out from their hiding holes. The Ashgrove was an immense semi-circle behind, that ran on for miles, cradling the valley like the forest itself was afraid to get too close to what rose from the desert floor like an ominous beacon before them.

At the center of the valley, erected upon the hill that rose like a mountain in the middle of the bleak emptiness, was a huge, single tower. It looked as if Shirava had pulled up a stretch of earth with her fingers from the heavens, leaving a monolith that looked like nothing else in the Dyadric. Beyond the tower was the seemingly endless desert that stretched on forever. It was a hopeless, miserable sight, and the dark tower did little to inspire hope.

"That's it?" Seph finally broke the silence of many long moments of each of them glaring at the tower, only two miles out in the valley's center.

None answered, even Blaje, who looked as stoic as Soren had ever seen her. A chill wind whipped through, tussling her dreads over her lean shoulders.

Soren had mixed emotions about the fortress below, in the middle of the desert.

Golbizarath. Lord Belzaar's home, and the place I'll finally find the answer to how this dagger came to me—intentionally. The only weapon that can kill these monsters, and has saved my life more than a few times.

He's down there, but there won't be time to escape into the night after. Not all of us. With the Twilight Veil I could sneak out, back out into the night, back into the Ashgrove, but there's no way they're not going to sit here while I go in alone. We're all going in for whatever happens—together.

Blaje led them down the valley, leaving behind the safety of the trees. The winds gushed hard, sending biting sand into their legs, and caused them to have to hold their hoods up. The sky looked as if the goddess had set it alight, crimson streaks crossing the sky in huge swaths. The earliest hints of starlight sparkled to the east, causing the camels to pick up their pace.

They didn't even have a discussion about camping one last night before heading to the fortress, and that caused a grin to snap on the side of Soren's mouth.

These are true warriors I ride with.

Even with the certain doom of twilight approaching, they rode for answers; they'd come too far not to.

They rode those two miles, glaring up at the lofty tower of the fortress. At its base were cliffs that resembled the bottom part of a mountain. But the higher the rock rose, it transformed into stone walls with archaic windows, cliffs with battlements with arrow slits, a final spire at its tip with a golden dome that rose impossibly high from such a single tower. Nothing was even close to its eerie majesty in the surrounding desert.

The sun hung low in the sky to their left, sinking under the fiery clouds. As they made their way before the fortress, they moved from a single file line of camels to a wide-spread arc, one hundred yards before the front gate to Golbizarath.

Soren never planned to sneak in and take the lord by surprise—after all, Belzaar had done nothing to prove he was an evil man, so Soren would give him the chance to live, and get the answers he held. There didn't need to be blood spilled that night.

And with Lady Sargonenth and the Calica Clan's support of Soren and the Silver Sparrows, perhaps Soren didn't need to unsheathe Firelight.

But as the front gate opened outward and the soldiers of Golbizarath flooded out, Soren kept his hand close to the mysterious Vellice dagger. Kaile and Seph held their staffs low, ready.

The fifty soldiers that emerged from the huge iron gate reminded Soren more of the drakoons than warriors of Zatan. The drakoons, King Amón's imperial guard, were soldiers trained in the northern continent of Eldra, also where Archpriest Roane was born. The soldiers of Golbizarath wore dark, matte armor of steel covering a dark tan leather. Their helmets had sharp spikes shooting out their backs, and in many of their gauntlets were held long spears of black metal with long tips of silver steel.

They were dressed and ready for combat. They knew Soren was coming. But the fact that they left the safety of the fortress perhaps meant they meant not to fight, Soren thought.

After the fifty soldiers stood between Soren and the fortress, a man walked through the risen iron gate with two females at his sides. As the man walked out of his fortress, his distant gaze inspected Soren and his comrades carefully. There was a hint of fear in his eyes, even standing behind the rows of soldiers.

He came and stood at the center of his soldiers, with the two females slightly behind. One appeared in her early thirties and the other, much younger—ten or so. The man, presumably the man Soren had sought ever since Garland spoke his name, naming him as the man that gave him the Vellice dagger to be delivered specifically to Soren, folded his arms while inspecting the men and women that had traveled through the Ashgrove to his home.

"Soren Stormrose, the Blade of Tourmielle, rides through the desert to see me, a lord in his lonely tower, seeking only peace," the man said, pulling his purple hood down to reveal his dark-skinned bald head and a short black beard with strands of gray streaking through. His clothes draped heavily over his body, thick with folds and creases at the tops of his sleeves. His robes caressed the sandy desert floor as the freezing winds rushed past. The young girl behind him fought the cold air by rubbing her skinny arms, but her frosty breath vibrated as she shivered.

Soren, who still sat atop the camel, replied, "I have traveled far, yes, to find you. I hope we can speak without violence. I too, come in peace."

The lord of Golbizarath seemed to be deep in thought. Not touching his face or neck, but breathing heavily through his large, round nostrils.

"Approach," the lord said, with the two females behind him huddling together.

The five of them rode down the valley, with all their weapons still sheathed, except Kaile and Seph still holding their short staffs, visibly, but low.

When they came twenty feet from the lord, Soren dismounted, and the others did the same. There were no disguises. They were in full view of the assembly of soldiers—the scars on Soren's face grabbing most of their attention.

"I bid you welcome to my home. I am Marcus Belzaar. This is my wife and daughter. We are the stewards of these lands. I invite you into my home so that we may speak, and find shelter before the darkness falls."

"I want to trust you," Soren said. "But forgive me, I require some form of assurance."

"All due respect to you and your companions," the lord said. "But what would you do if I didn't give that? Stay out here? Slaughter us without answers and invade my home?"

Soren knew the lord was true in his remark. He'd have to trust him, somewhat, if he was to get the voluntary answers he needed.

"I am no Syncron, and none of my men are wielders of the Ellydian. If the apprentice of the archmage or the Whistlewillow with you decided to use their magic, then I regret to acknowledge that we would fall under their might. So, please, let us have words and not violence in my home."

"What do you think?" Soren asked quietly to Blaje.

"No choice," she replied quickly. "We need in that tower one way or the other. He's right. Trust him or kill them all here and force him to tell you what you wish to know."

"Very well," Soren said. "We accept your invitation. But know, Lord Belzaar, if this is some form of trick or trap, we will be forced to defend ourselves."

Lord Belzaar nodded. His wise, old, dark eyes glared into Soren's. He walked toward Soren, all of his soldiers eyeing the approach uneasily. Extending his hand, Soren took it and they shook. Both uneasily studying the other.

"Please, follow me," the lord said. "We will have food and drink this night while we speak. It has been a long time since the Desert Shadow has been in my part of the desert. I welcome you Blaje Severaas."

"Lord Belzaar," she said with a dip of her brow and chin.

"Now, come," he said, turning sideways and inviting them through the front gate of Golbizarath. "We have much to discuss."

Chapter Thirty-Nine

Walking into the interior of the ancient fortress of Golbizarath, Soren kept Firelight close to his fingertips. Seph walked so close to him, their arms swiped against each other as they entered. The camels were led in and tended to by a couple of young boys.

After they were inside, the iron gate was lowered into place with a low thud, and huge wooden doors were swung closed and barricaded from the inside. That reminded Soren of the Shade that had killed all at the Katamon Outpost. He wondered if they knew the new happenings of the Demons of Dusk this far into the secluded desert.

They followed Lord Belzaar and his family straight ahead in the main entrance to the fortress. It was a gigantic cave of smooth, carved stone on the interior of the mountain. There were several wooden buildings on the inside of the cave. One was apparently a barracks as the soldiers were moving in and out of it. There were two others that were stables with dozens of camels within, and a couple others that Soren assumed were storehouses.

Lord Belzaar led them to a staircase at the back of the

cave. It was a stone stairway on the back wall that led to a wooden stair. It led them to the cavern's ceiling.

Once they entered the upper parts of the tower, they left the dusty, sandy floor below to new wooden planks under his boots. The second floor was a windowless set of rooms with bathing stalls, wash racks with hundreds of clothes drying on racks and many new sets of eyes on them from women and children who sat silently around the vast room.

They were led up several more floors, mostly hidden behind wooden walls, until they reached a grand hall with fine, plush carpet, fine oil paintings, and a hearth with a roaring fire. At the room's center were long tables; one set with silverware and glasses already filled with water and wine.

The lord motioned for them to sit. His wife and daughter sat at another table to the side.

Soren knew if there was a secret plot to end Soren's journey, it may well be in the food and drink that might be served. Kaile and Seph's powers would be useless with bellies full of poison.

"We brought our own food," Soren said as politely as he could muster. "We wish to share words, not a table, and we will be out on our way first thing in the morning again."

Lord Belzaar seemed not to care at the dismissal of his invitation. "Very well, then let us go on up to my office, if that is all you wish."

Soren nodded, following the lord back to the stairwell. Lord Belzaar waved for his family to remain in the dining hall, which Soren didn't like, but they were deep in the wolf's den now, and there was no turning back.

They followed him three floors up into the tower. They were led into a room with another hearth of black stone, which the lord quickly walked over to and placed fresh logs on. There were already burning candles around the room, melting onto the candelabras. Around the circular room were old paintings of lords past, and landscapes of magical sunsets and divine sunrises. Soren wondered how many lords and ladies had resided over the ancient fortress over the generations.

Lord Belzaar sat behind his desk of fine wood. Aside from the burning candles, its top was only filled with a short stack of papers, a quill, and a bottle of ink. Soren and the others sat in chairs of soft leather before the lord.

"So," the lord said, tugging the front of his vest down. "Where do you want to begin? I have many questions, and you have at least your *one*."

"You know what information I seek?" Soren asked, somewhat surprised. He sat with his back straight, not settling too much into the over-comfortable chair.

"Why else would you come all the way to me, in the middle of Zatan in winter? I'm certain Lord Garland Messemire told you I gave him that Vellice dagger you carry. I see no other reason you aren't hiding from those that hunt you for the… *immense bounty* on your head from the king."

Soren scratched his forearm, not loving how insightful the lord seemed.

"Who do you hold allegiance to?" Blaje suddenly asked, crossing her long legs and glaring at the lord.

Lord Belzaar let out a laugh, opening a drawer to his right and pulling out a pipe and box of tobacco. "That certainly is the question most appropriate for this conversation to start, isn't it?" He stuffed the tobacco into the pipe and lit it with a candle. "Where do you think it lies, Desert Shadow? If it resided with the king, do you think I would have freely invited you into my home?"

"Like you said," Kaile replied quickly, leaning forward with his elbows on his thighs. "You knew you couldn't defend yourself against the Ellydian, so what choice did you have?"

"There's always a choice," the lord replied, his brow

furrowed as he let out a great plume of smoke from his dry lips.

Davin pulled out his pipe and stuffed it. Lord Belzaar slid a candle along the desktop toward him.

"My devotion is and always has been to the desert, and the people I'm sworn to protect," Lord Belzaar said.

"That doesn't answer the question," Seph said.

"Persephone Whistlewillow," he said, putting both his elbows on the desk as he puffed his pipe, eyeing her with his elder eyes. "Alive after all this time… I must say, I'm surprised to see Blaje riding with you, protecting you, after the pain your family inflicted on hers. But these days, the world is full of surprises and miraculous alliances, aren't they?"

"Blaje?" Seph asked with raised eyebrows and a hint of sorrow in her voice. "What is he talking about?"

Blaje sighed and lowered her gaze.

"Yes," Lord Belzaar said, stroking his beard as the candle-light glistened on his dark skin. "I support Lady Sargonenth and the Calica. For I support Zatan."

"Blaje?" Seph pressed. "What's he talking about? Did my family do something to you?"

"Not now," Blaje said out of the corner of her mouth.

"So, Lord Belzaar," Davin said in a low voice, holding his smoldering pipe before his lips. "We're here, and you know why we've come all the way into the middle of nowhere, so… are you gonna tell us what we came all this way for?"

"Davin Mosser," he replied. "You are a long way from home, aren't you? I haven't seen a dwarf in ages. Especially one as battle hardened as you. Helped these outlaws all the way here, fighting goddess knows what along the way."

"Outlaws?" Davin asked. "That scoundrel of a king should be the outlaw. Not us!"

"I'll tell you what you wish to know," Lord Belzaar said, running his fingers over his bald head. "But I have questions first. This is my home, so I have the right to do so. I get word of things that happen in Aladran, but not all. You have insight, I must admit, I deeply desire to know. I receive word from the king's men, but I wish to hear from the Silver Sparrows."

Soren felt his mouth tighten.

All the others waited for him. Soren noticed Kaile's knee bouncing, and it seemed more than normal—which he thought was odd.

Is he nervous? Is he nervous about the lord asking about the Silver Sparrows? He should know I won't reveal anything.

Kaile itched his shoulder, looking over it.

"You all right?" Seph whispered to Kaile with a light touch on his shoulder.

"Yeah," he muttered back.

"I will tell you what I can," Soren said. "If you're against the king."

"I am," Lord Belzaar said. "Even those in Zatan have suffered under his rule. It is time for a new age. I dare them to come to my lands. Those in their castles in Celestra wouldn't last a week in our world. To think they can just sit there and rule us has always been an illusion. We are the strong. We are the resilient. Zatan is ruled by no one but our own. Let him know that we stand alone. And against his fire, we will create our own new, bright future."

I want to trust him. And I admire his vigor, but I need to be cautious. We are far from safety, and these lands are not my own.

"Do you trust him?" Soren asked Blaje, bluntly. There was no reason to hide it.

"Enough," she replied.

"So, what do you want to know?" Soren asked.

Lord Belzaar leaned back and crossed his legs under his robes. "Where did Archmage Mihelik transport you to at the burning of Erhil?"

"I can't answer that."

"You were in Cascadia. I know that much. Very well... Is Mihelik alive still? Did he survive the spell? The old archmage is well past his finest years."

Soren looked at the others. "Why do you want to know that?"

"I need to know because we aren't only going to war with the king, but all his army. Alcarond, the Knight Wolf, the archpriest, all of them. There aren't many who have a chance of defeating the archmage, so yes, I dearly wish to know if he is alive. Alcarond's apprentice here may have a chance once he's grown his skills, and grown into a man, quite frankly."

Kaile's leg continued to bounce as he scowled back at the lord.

"Yes," Soren said. "The old archmage lives."

"Excellent," Lord Belzaar said. "Now, I'd like to know..."

Kaile suddenly stood, his fingers spread wide and his face instantly flushed of all color. His eyes were impossibly wide and red. His panicked gaze shot around the room.

"Kaile? What's wrong?" Seph asked, getting to her feet, unable to calm him.

Soren's instinct kicked him to his feet.

Something is wrong. Something is terribly wrong.

He remembered Cirella's warning to him.

Something terrible is going to happen.

"Seph!" Soren roared, waving for her to join him.

Lord Belzaar stood. "What is this? What is wrong with the boy? Guards!"

"I—" Kaile muttered, as if under a spell or in a trance. "I —there's something... here..."

Seph ran to Soren's side as he yanked Firelight free, her edge gleaming in red light from the starlight that beamed through the windows.

"Guards! Guards!"

Two soldiers ran into the vast room at the top of the tower, rushing to their lord.

Seph stood behind Soren, holding her staff.

"Cast a spell," Soren whispered. "He's here…"

Davin heaved his double-sided ax up, and Blaje pulled her shamshir blade free. Kaile remained panicked, holding both sides of his head as he glared all around the room.

"He?" Lord Belzaar asked, pulling his own sword free. "Who is?"

"Him…" Soren said in a low voice from the back of his throat.

A fiery explosion burst into the stairwell. The blast rocked the entire tower, sending magical flames rushing into the room. Soren dove, covering Seph's body from the flames that roared overhead, roaring and catching the beams overhead alight.

Soren fell onto Seph, an A note ringing from her tuning fork in her hand, and the spell Skin of the Fae covered her skin in a cool, blue glow. Soren knelt quickly, glaring back at the stairwell, blazing in white ivory flames. A shadowy figure stood there, hood over his head, his cloak impervious to the fire—and a mix of minor notes ringing out.

He's here. He's come to take Kaile back… I can't let him do that… I've got to stop him somehow… But… I don't know how…

"That's far enough," the shadowy figure said. His hands were raised, glowing in pure white light. His wide sleeves draped to his waist and his long robes whipped at his ankles from the flames behind.

"Alcarond…" Soren said.

"Soren…" Alcarond replied. "You took something of mine… and I want it back…"

Chapter Forty

The archmage looked like a demon had appeared in the room with them. And Soren had a terrible feeling deep in his stomach. He squeezed Seph's wrist, holding up Firelight in his other hand at Alcarond. Firelight glowed in divine red light as the archmage's hands were engulfed in white.

Alcarond pulled his hood down, and Soren heard gasps around the room. Kaile held his staff, which shook in his trembling hands.

The tones that rang out from the archmage were terrifying. Soren knew the Ellydian well enough to know that those kinds of sounds together usually spelled absolute authority over every other power in the world. Usually, whatever came next was absolute havoc and mayhem.

Alcarond's dim gray eyes darkened as the flames behind him slowed. Tiny specs of white gleamed at the center of his eyes. His focus was completely on Soren and the Vellice blade in his hand. From Alcarond's glowing hand, a staff of magical white energy grew. It beamed in moonlight, glowing brighter and brighter until the light faded to reveal a sleek black staff of metal with white jewels embedded in its top—resembling a dragon's head with a toothy maw and spikes running down its back.

The archmage's long black hair whipped over his shoulders, strands of silver streaking through. His fine robes of royal blue rippled and folded over his powerful frame and shoulders.

Kaile withdrew into fear, staggering back as panic overtook him.

Davin and Blaje stood with wide stances, glaring at the archmage. The sounds of footsteps came from the fiery stairs behind.

"Alcarond," Lord Belzaar said in a voice, trying to push the words through the fear in his throat. "What are you doing here… why are you?"

Alcarond's mouth moved, and the word "Traitor," crept out. He pointed his staff at Belzaar, and white flames erupted from the dragon's head at the lord. The flames engulfed the desk as one soldier shoved their lord away. The flames rocked into the soldier, incinerated him as he screamed in agony. Lord Belzaar fell to the floor, the magical flames flowing just over him.

"No!" Soren yelled.

I need answers from him. You can't die, Belzaar, not until I know what you know!

"Alcarond, stop!" Soren yelled. "We need to talk."

"Talk?" Alcarond said, halting his attack on Belzaar. "The fires of infinity will judge this lord's soul. The fires of the king will judge yours."

"That's what we need to talk about," Soren said, standing fully and holding Firelight out to the side. "The world has changed. Everything has changed. We need to talk. It's bigger than the king. There's something stirring in the darkness. Glasse called the Black Fog into Grayhaven. There's more than just this war going on in Aladran. Something dark is growing."

Alcarond let out a deep sigh unexpectedly. "Yes. I know."

"Then you know we need to figure that out. We need to join forces and fight this new evil."

Alcarond's teeth showed—gritting. "That evil is for me to decipher, drive out, and destroy. And that weapon in your hand is a piece to this puzzle. You, however, are not needed to save this world from what lurks and plots. King Amón has grown obsessed with your end. That scar you left on his face will not go unpunished. Your fate has been sealed, Soren Stormrose. That fate is not for me to decide. You chose your end already."

"That's not true," Kaile said, shrinking off his fear, mustering as much courage in his voice as he could. "We don't have to do the king's bidding. You saw what he did to all those innocent people in Erhil. You were there. We don't have to let him do that to anyone else. There's a new future coming, master. I've seen it now. I've seen the hope that…"

Alcarond sent a wave in Kaile's direction. Kaile moved his staff between them, but the invisible spell Alcarond cast sent Kaile falling mercilessly to the floor, shoving his face into the floorboards as he yelled in pain.

"I will deal with you later." Alcarond's words seethed with anger, the sounds hissing through his clenched teeth.

"Leave him alone!" Seph said, pushing Soren to the side, and sending a glowing plume of fire from the tip of her staff.

"Seph, no!" Soren yelled, pulling her back.

The spell fizzled away in the air, not even halfway to Alcarond. It disappeared as if it had never been cast. All light drained from her staff. The blue light faded from her skin.

"Pathetic," Alcarond scoffed. "Your lack of training shows in every aspect of your casting. You may technically be an Aeol, but you are weak, unguided, and lost." He cleared his throat, lifting his chin as the flames brimmed with fresh life behind him, creeping up the walls and pouring up onto the ceiling, causing the room to grow hot, and Soren's head beaded with sweat. "But we will correct you. You *will* become strong. Because I'm going to teach you."

Soren jumped in front of Seph, shoving her back behind him.

"Soren," Davin said. "We've got to do something, quick…"

"The only way you're going to train her is if you see reason," Soren said. "There's no way I'm going to let you take her, or him…" Soren pointed to Kaile, whimpering as he was completely flattened on his face and stomach.

"What would you do to stop me?" Alcarond asked, his hair tussling on his chest from the magical flames behind. "Throw your dagger at me like you did the king? You may think you hurt him, but all you did was solidify your end. The king will win this war, and he will kill you after he's taken everything from you. The king has even grown angry at his finest soldier for keeping you alive like he did." A wry, menacing smirk lit the corner of his mouth. "The Knight Wolf's game with you has sparked a feud with the king."

"I'll kill them both," Soren growled.

"You were right about one thing, Soren. This war you wage isn't the real war. There's something else that's feeding the Demons of Dusk. Edward Glasse's concealed ability to summon the Black Fog has changed everything. I need to know what he did, how he did it, and who else was with him in that dark magic."

"Then let's find out together!" Soren said. "We would make a formidable force! Seph needs training, and you or Mihelik are the ones who could make her more powerful than we could imagine… but we need—"

"Do not say his name before me!" Alcarond shouted, the fires behind intensifying. "He had his chance. He ruined everything. We could have saved this world together. Instead, he burned the only answers we had. Those scriptures were what could have saved these lands from the Demons of Dusk, and instead, now, they're entering our cities. Soon, there will be nowhere safe from them. The Black Fog will turn every last soul in this world into Shades, until there is nothing left but their darkness. All life will fade… all because of his foolishness."

"It's not too late," Soren said. "This dagger was sent to me. And that man over there was the one who made sure Garland Messemire gave it to me. Someone knew it could kill the Demons of Dusk. When I killed the Shades and injured the Black Fog, the black pommel glows from within. Someone out there knew that, and sent it to me. There's more going on than you know. That's why we need to work together. We can solve the mystery of who sent them here, and why they're here. And we can rid all of Aladran from King Amón's madness. There can be peace again. But I can't do it alone, and neither can you, while you're under his thumb."

Alcarond's face twisted, and he scowled. "I'm under no thumb." He raised his staff toward Soren. The mixed tones that reverberated from his staff resonated louder, and white flames sparked from the dragon's head. "And you will not speak to me so…"

Soren could sense the archmage was focused on his rage, and not logic. Something came to mind suddenly, and the words poured from his mouth. "The Shade spoke."

The flames on Alcarond's staff faded. "What did you say?"

"I fought a Shade in Zatan. It was in a tower. It spoke to me before I killed it."

"What did it say?" Alcarond's anger faded, but his question was forced. "Answer me!"

"It said, 'no.' It responded to what I'd said to it."

"You're certain? You're sure?"

"Yes. I tried to get it to say more, but it died before it could, if it even would have."

Alcarond was deep in thought as the sounds of soldiers shouting on the floor beneath them intensified.

"Up here," Lord Belzaar cried in pain. "Hurry!"

"This changes things," Alcarond said. "If the Shades have some form of intelligence, showing in the use of our language. That either means they're learning from us, or a glimmer of their old humanity remained under their impenetrable skin. I need to know more."

"Put your staff down, and let's talk," Soren said, lowering Firelight. "You're a reasonable man. We used to trust each other. We can have that trust again. I want to make this world right. But I can't do it alone, and neither can you."

Alcarond lowered his staff's tip a couple of inches. His gaze dropped as he thought. Soren's hopes flared.

There is a chance he will listen to reason. There's a chance he can come to the good side.

But that hope didn't last long.

Alcarond's staff rose, pointing straight at Soren.

"No," he said, the word seething in anger. "I need them, those two, and I need that weapon you carry. But I don't need you. I will not ally myself with a failure. You had your chance, and everyone who trusted you died because of your failures. The Knight Wolf and the king will come for you. I just need what I came for."

"I'll never go with you," Seph shouted. "You fight for that madman who kills women and children for his sick, demented pleasure? You're okay with that? You know that makes you evil too, right? You stood there while he burned Erhil. You did nothing. You allowed it. You're supposed to protect this world, not help destroy it."

"You know not what you speak of, young Whistlewillow."

"Then show us that you're good," she replied. "Show me this legendary archmage who's supposed to be the most powerful Syncron in our world, not this evil Synth before me."

"Synth?" he spat, hating the word. "I train the brightest Syncron in existence. We are reforming our order, and we will need to grow strong to weed out this new evil that is forming in our ranks. You will become powerful like me, in time, but first you must see the error in your current ways. You will come to the capital, and I will show you the way."

"Over my dead body, you will," Soren said.

"Mine too," Davin said, hefting his huge ax before him.

"Me too," Blaje said, waving her curved sword threateningly.

Alcarond began to laugh. It was a low laugh from deep within. "You know the folly in your words," he said. "Your life is not for me to take, Soren. But if your friends proclaim that I must shed their blood and take their lives for me to take these young Syncrons, then so be it."

Soren held Firelight before him, ready to throw, should that be his only chance.

I don't know how to defend against the archmage, but I'm sure as hell going to try everything to save Seph. That's what Cirella would have me do. That's what her parents would wish of me. I can't fail her like I did everyone else. Fight, Soren, fight!

The archmage lifted his arms and flames erupted from his staff as he gripped it in both hands. "Then so be it. If you won't give me what is mine freely, then I will take it by force. I won't be deprived of what is…"

Suddenly, from above, the ceiling quaked, the rafters shook and the surrounding windows shattered as freezing air rushed into the room. Alcarond's eyes widened, showing it wasn't him that was causing the room to shake.

Soren looked at Kaile, who was still stuck to the floor from his master's spell. Seph was still behind Soren, unable to cast.

"Soren?" Davin said, uneasily.

Before Soren could speak, the stone walls erupted with a deafening roar, splintering and crumbling all around them.

The ground beneath their feet convulsed violently, throwing them off balance and causing chunks of rock to rain down from the ceiling. Each of them struggled desperately to stay upright amidst the chaos. As the stones separated, a howling wind swept through the tower, extinguishing the candles in an instant and plunging the room into darkness.

With a thunderous crack, the top of the tower began to break away, the ancient stones groaning under the immense strain. Slowly, inexorably, the uppermost section of Golbizarath was wrenched free from its base and lifted twenty feet into the air, as if plucked by an unseen giant. The moon and the night sky burst into view through the gaping wound in the tower, casting an eerie light over the scene.

Time seemed to stretch and slow as the top of the tower hung in the air for a heartbeat, teetering at a precarious angle. Then, with a final, ominous creak, it tilted to one side and began its descent. The massive stone structure plummeted towards the desert floor, gaining speed until it crashed down with a cataclysmic explosion. The impact sent a shockwave rippling through the ground, the sound echoing for miles across the barren landscape.

And above them, in the air, a swirling portal of magical light of all colors cast down its wondrous light.

Soren's mouth widened in a brilliant grin, and hope had returned.

Alcarond's staff burst into white flame.

"Stop this madness at once," a powerful elderly voice came from deep within the swirling portal.

And as the old Syncron emerged from the portal, Davin shouted, "Yes! He's come!"

The old archmage leaped out of the portal, atop an enormous silver bear's back. He floated out of the portal's center and onto the wooden floor of the room, now the top of the tower. A second, hulking bear followed—snarling and digging its huge claws into the floorboards, which creaked under the immense weight of the two. The old archmage held his staff high at Alcarond, his white beard whipping in the freezing winds.

"This has gone far enough, Alcarond!" the old archmage said, his words booming like thunder.

"Mihelik Starshadow," Alcarond growled. "You've finally emerged from whatever rock you were hiding under."

"This madness ends now," Mihelik said. "I should have prevented your decay sooner, but I'm here now to fix what I should have stopped long ago…"

Chapter Forty-One

There, in a moment of pure, raw power, the two archmages of the last fifty years faced each other yet again. The old master and his former apprentice, each with staff in hand, each glaring down the other with wicked thoughts. Although the old man was blinded in their last battle, he still had his pale eyes set on Alcarond. This wasn't a standoff to quash an old grudge, Soren thought. These two were here to settle a score—one last time.

The two bears roared, spit flinging from their huge yellow teeth. Seph covered her ears, and Davin and Blaje both huddled to her sides. Kaile remained chest to the floor, unable to move, but he was able to turn his head to see Mihelik.

"Archmage!" he said. "How did you…?"

"I came because there was no other way," Mihelik said, pointing his staff at his former apprentice, a symphony of notes ringing from it like one singular, heavenly pitch. "Alcarond would never leave you be. You're his prize. But I can't let him take you and continue pushing you down his dark path. The Synths must die, along with their rotten king. Glasse was the final straw. You and your ilk were never made for this world, Alcarond. This world was meant for so much more than the pain you sew."

"You cannot defeat me, master," Alcarond said. "Even with those monsters, you're weakened. I can feel it. The portal spell depleted you. You couldn't beat me at your best in Celestra. And you cannot defeat me now... I never wanted to have to kill you, but what you did to the old scriptures. All that knowledge, incinerated forever. But that's you... always looking inward, always wanting everything for yourself."

"You became obsessed, Alcarond. We cannot let that darkness return that the scriptures spoke of. That is not the Ellydian. It's something else. Something evil."

"Evil is here! Don't you see it, you old fool? Glasse summoned the Black Fog. He called it, and it heard his call. The Demons of Dusk grow in strength and number with every passing night! And now, Soren has told me that the Shades can speak... they're smarter than I imagined. They're not wild beasts, they're intelligent predators. And now every town and village and city is at risk from here to Cascadia to Arkakus. They are all going to die, and you're okay with that? We have the opportunity to embrace a power even greater than the magic of the Ellydian. The single most powerful weapon in existence, and it's as useless as a twig against the Demons of Dusk. We had the knowledge at our disposal, but it burned away through our fingertips. We had the ultimate weapon, and you fucking burned it!"

"No one should wield that evil," Mihelik said, his voice booming in the cold air, which whipped up as dark clouds rolled in fast. Snow fell idly down, and the ground grew slick as they melted on the floorboards. "We are getting closer to deciphering the way to fight back against them. After all these years, Soren has discovered there's something about the steel crafted by the masters of Vellice that can kill them. We need to find more. The king's sword Storm Dragon, and the Knight Wolf's Ember Edge could be used against them!"

"You've forgotten the wrath of our king," Alcarond said, his face strained with wild rage. "He thinks so little of the Demons of Dusk. They are but an inconvenience in his war against the Silver Sparrows. He dreams not of ways to defeat them, but instead, dreams of fires consuming all that defy him, threatening his claim to the throne. He dreams of Soren's head decorating a corner of his room. It's up to me to save this world." His gaze turned to Kaile. "But I can't do it alone. I need Kaile to come home. His powers someday will grow so that he may fight by my side against our great enemy." Then his dark gaze with reddened eyes turned to Seph. "And her... she'll become my second apprentice, pledge herself to the throne, or... the long line of the Whistlewillows will be naught but history."

"You touch her," Soren roared, anger burning his throat. "There will be nothing left of you for history to remember!"

"You," Alcarond said back. "You, the loser who has become perhaps the greatest failure of all knights of Aladran, have absolutely no worth in this world, except for that piece of metal in your hand. Your life has been claimed by the Wolf, but I will enjoy taking what joy you have left in this world. And know this Soren *Smythe*... if she does not join willingly, your niece will endure torment unimaginable, until her will bends, her spirit breaks, and she becomes my protégé."

"You will do no such thing," Mihelik said. "I failed you, Alcarond, but I will not fail them! They are the next generation of great Syncrons. And they are far too powerful to be under the tutelage of a madman like you..."

"Do you honestly think you have a chance?" Alcarond said. "By the goddess, you do! You think a couple of forest bears, a few swords, and two young Ayls can defeat me? The archmage of Aladran? I have become so much more powerful since we last met, and here you are, barely able to balance yourself atop that monster?"

"You used the Wraithfire spell," Mihelik said with deep spite in his voice, as the snow fell hard, lightening the sky in the reflecting moonlight, quickly coating the ground. "And you used my feelings for Sophia to distract me." Deep pain laced his words. "You knew how to hurt me, and you did—I'll give you that, but even with these old bones and useless eyes, you will not be leaving this place with these two young Syncrons. I swear by the goddess, if you try, I will end you."

A wide smile crossed Alcarond's face. "You know what, old man? I think I may enjoy this…"

There was an intense silence that fell over the tower. The injured Lord Belzaar lay in a growing pool of blood. The shouts from the stairs vanished, and all watched the two most powerful wielders of the Ellydian squaring off. It was a clashing of giants that rarely appeared in this world, Soren thought. It had been ages since Syncrons as powerful as these two had faced each other. And as they watched the two as their staffs lit in dazzling light, they could feel the immense power growing from both of them—the only two living Lyres in all of Aladran.

"I would give you one last warning, Alcarond," Mihelik shouted in the falling snow, thunder roaring in the distance. "But I know you. You're too hardheaded to see your folly. For my sins in failing you, I will not right what I have wronged in this world."

Curling strands of pure, golden light surged in Mihelik's wooden staff of dark wood, causing the white jewels embedded in its tip to glow bright.

Alcarond's staff shimmered in blinding white, with the

white jewels of the dragon's eyes emitting the same divine glow. He hefted his sleek black staff of shimmering metal into one hand, pulling his sword free with the other. The ring of its steel sliding from the sheath mixed with the smooth tones ringing from his staff.

"This is where it ends... master..."

Alcarond's gaze was sinister, maddening, and full of burning hatred.

Mihelik leaned forward upon the huge silver bear's back as it let out a thundering roar at Alcarond. Winds blew in hard, and Soren dug his heels into the slick floor, Firelight eager for a chance to end the archmage's dark legacy.

"You've chosen a path to darkness," Mihelik said in a booming, wise voice. "So be it, my apprentice... may the goddess have mercy on your soul!"

Golden magic surged forward in a powerful beam at Alcarond. The air sizzled under the weight of such powerful magic. The spell collided with Alcarond's—a pillar of white flame erupted from the dragon's head staff. As the two spells kissed, a terrifying explosion burst outward, breaking the wooden floorboards under their feet, and sent the surrounding stones of the tower blasting outward, down onto the desert floor far below.

Soren dropped to a knee under the buckling floorboards. The floor beneath both bears snapped under such weight. Seph let out a scream as the other bear tried to escape from the collapsing floor, but fell through, tumbling down, scraping and clawing.

"Mihelik!" Davin yelled. "The tower, it's collapsing!"

Mihelik either didn't hear, or was too wrapped in the battle to care. The golden magic poured out of his staff like light flooding in through thick, opened drapes. Alcarond's spell, too, grew to an inferno, catching all that it touched in white flame.

The floor, strewn chairs and tables, all caught alight in the intense, magical fires.

The floor buckled on the far end of the tower, behind Mihelik, and Soren began sliding down. Seph grabbed his hand as they all slid together. One of the bear's paws burst into the floorboards before lifting it up and stepping back.

"The tower's coming down," Blaje said. Her stare into Soren showed deep worry. "We can't stay here."

"Mihelik, we need to get out of here!" Soren yelled in the air filled with the two ringing, sharp tones of the staffs, the crackling of the magic spells, and the booming thunder growing ever closer.

Mihelik's ear wiggled as Soren said that, but he didn't relent in his attack upon Alcarond.

"This is war," Mihelik spoke, only loud enough for Soren to just barely hear it over the chaos surrounding them. "And in war, there can only be one victor…"

"What's he doing?" Seph asked, with her back against the rear wall of the tower. Belzaar lay unconscious beside her, with his dead soldiers broken next to him. Kaile still lay on his stomach near the archmage, now elevated above them.

"By the goddess," Mihelik roared, his words rippling through the storm, "I will not let you take them! Obliterous Noctum!"

Soren watched as tendrils of blue light slithered down from the sky like tentacles, wrapping around the staff like glowing sea vines. The old archmage let out a shout as the staff surged in a burning golden light interlaced with sea blue. The magic grew so bright Soren had to cover his eyes, and the snow melted high above, sending raindrops plopping heavily down.

"I will not let you take them, even if it means neither of us leave this tower!"

Past the intense battling magics, Soren saw Alcarond's

glower shift. His eyes widened and there was the subtlest look of fear in his eyes.

"Ribbons of the Moon!" Kaile said. "He's casting Ribbons of the Moon! Get down!"

The blue and golden magic blended to a dazzling mix of the two, doubling in size, then tripling—growing until the beam had turned as tall as Mihelik upon the bear's back. It was as bright as the sun, as hot as molten iron, and as terrifying as death.

Mihelik roared, coupled by the bear, and the magical beam shot forth, erupting into Alcarond's spell, shooting through it like a razor-sharp arrowhead splitting wood. It burst through, flying into Alcarond with an explosion that rocked the far side of the tower, knocking a deep section behind him free, sending the stairs crumbling over a hundred feet down to the desert floor. Alcarond yelled in rage as the magic tore into him, lighting his robes in the unworldly magical heat.

An orb of blood-red light glowed before Alcarond, pushing the flames back. Alcarond fell to a knee, holding himself up by his staff. Behind the red orb, Alcarond pushed himself up by digging the tip of his sword into the floor. He stood with both legs spread wide, his singed robes blowing in the freezing winds, blistered burns covering both his arms.

From the floor beside Alcarond, the spell that held Kaile down had lifted, and he was getting to his feet, his staff in his hand, and that same blood-red magical glow flooding off its tip.

"Kaile!" Seph shouted. "No! What are you doing?"

"I—I can't let him die, Seph. Not like this…" Kaile's face was twisted, uncertainty and struggle evident in his reddened eyes.

"Kaile! Put down your staff!" Soren yelled. "You don't know what you're doing."

"I—I can't stop myself," Kaile said, his gaze darting

around between his hands, the glowing staff, and Alcarond, whose face grinned widely past his pain.

"Kaile…" Mihelik muttered, pulling his spell back to his staff, defeat heavy in his throat. "What are you doing?"

"I can't let you kill him. I'm sorry, Archmage Mihelik, but I can't let you kill my master…"

No… Kaile… No…

Chapter Forty-Two

"Put down your staff, Kaile," Soren shouted as fierce lightning tore the sky, roaring thunder erupting above. "This is between them. Alcarond is not your friend. We are! Put down the staff!"

Kaile rose, standing tall as the tower teetered. A dark cloud seemed to grow over him, making Soren's heart pound in his chest. Kaile's staff moved from Alcarond, to pointing directly at Mihelik. Tears welled in Kaile's eyes under his whipping, wet hair. "I don't want to hurt you, archmage. But I can't let you kill my master. I need him."

From behind Soren, he could feel a hand on the side of his arm, using him to pull herself up the slanting tower. He looked over to see Seph glaring with mean spite and determination deep in her face. Her staff glowed in her hand, and an A note rang clear. Blue light coursed through the staff of Brayburry gray with steaming silver Elfvein through the grains. The black jewels at its tip glowed that deep blue, and the golden dragoneye jewel burned in ravishing white light.

"Kaile, don't do this…" she growled. "You have a choice. Just like you did in Erhil. You chose good. You chose to escape from their evil. You came to us because you needed help. You're my friend, and I'm going to need you. Please, please, don't do this."

"He's made his choice," Alcarond said. "He's an obedient little dog, following his master because he's lost his way." He laughed.

Kaile's eye twitched as the archmage said that.

"You're going to have to defeat them both," Blaje said to the old blind archmage. "He's got his hooks deep in the boy. You've got to kill them both!"

No... This can't be happening... Kaile promised. I believed him... How could he do this to Seph? Didn't he hear Alcarond's words? He wants to hurt Seph, he wants to hurt my Persephone...

That is not going to happen...

Seph stood beside Soren, magic pouring from her staff, ready to fight. Davin heaved his double-sided ax before him, and Blaje came to Soren's other side, waving her shimmering blade before her.

Snow came down hard, enveloping the tower in slick sheets.

Soren squeezed Firelight tight, digging his boots into the snow.

I've got to get to Alcarond, then maybe I can save Kaile from his grasp. Once Mihelik attacks, then I go for it. One chance to kill the archmage. I'm only going to get one chance...

The bear's foot fell through the breaking floorboards again, lifting it and finding fresh footing on the growing snow.

Mihelik looked uneasily at the two on the far side of the crumbling tower. He shifted in his seat and sighed, not wanting to hurt the young apprentice, but knowing his archnemesis needed to be stopped.

"Show no mercy," Blaje said. "They've made their decision. They've allied with King Amón. They're Synths."

Mihelik sighed again, struggling to muster his strength to

hurt Kaile, the lead of his promising new generation of Syncrons.

"He's not," Mihelik said. "I can save the boy. There's still time."

Seph stepped forward, her frayed black hair whipping at her shoulder in the bitter, high winds. "The king killed my parents. I lost everything that night that they burned my home and my family. They died, and I have nothing now..." Tears streamed down her face and she gritted her teeth to stop the quivering in her lips. "That man you call master, that evil man who stands beside you, did nothing to stop the king from killing all those people. Everyone I ever loved. Everything I ever cared for died that day with them, and I'd be dead now too if Soren hadn't had hidden me away and saved my life that day. And now you defend him?"

"I—I can't help myself," Kaile said, his voice shaking and his hand trembling, but his staff's tip slowly glided to aim at Seph. A small glow lit the bottom side of his neck. "But I can't let you kill him. I just can't. I wish I could explain it to you, but I don't know how. I care for you, Seph. You mean more to me than you possibly know. But I can't let you kill Alcarond. I need him. And he needs me..."

"Enough of this!" Alcarond said, with fresh waves of white magic convulsing on his staff. "By my side, Kaile Thorne. Before you is the man that single-handedly betrayed our brotherhood. He destroyed our most prized possession! Ancient truths gone forever to his greed. There were secrets in there that could have saved countless lives from the monsters that ravage us in the night. But instead he abandoned all reason, and that power is gone forever now. There's only one way this ends, former master... for all you gave me, I am grateful, but I cannot forgive..." a dark, toothy smile grew on his face, "...nor would I want to. Killing you is going to be the greatest accomplishment of my life."

"You want my life?" Mihelik asked in the freezing storm as the silver bear roared viciously. "Then come and take it, you failure of a pupil! Your atrocities are beyond forgiveness, and you deserve nothing but the great reckoning. For your betrayal to not only me, but all the people of Aladran… may your soul rest in peace."

White flames poured from Alcarond's staff toward Mihelik, who fired back a huge inferno of flames from his. They collided at their center, with the silver bear taking lumbering strides forward, digging its enormous claws through the snow, climbing up the teetering tower. It was an enormous mix of colliding, fiery magic that rocked the tower in pure, violent destruction.

Both archmages' faces were strained, gritting their teeth, letting their hatred of the other show. The blisters from the burns on Alcarond's arms showed in the light of his magic.

"Don't do this!" Seph shouted, and as she did, magical flames erupted from the dragoneye stone on her staff, flying at Alcarond. Kaile ran between her and Alcarond, holding up his staff. A spherical spell of a warm blue glowed around him and Alcarond as her spell blasted onto the magical sphere protecting them.

"Seph…" Kaile said slowly. "Don't do this. You can't beat either of us. It's not going to end well if you attack him."

"I'd rather die than go with him… and you…"

Soren's heart ached as he heard her say those words, and violence was brimming inside of him. He wanted to throw his dagger at Alcarond. He knew he could split him between the eyes at that distance, if Alcarond gave him the chance. But something inside was telling him to refrain. If he threw Firelight away, it may fall over the backside of the tower, and he desperately needed it.

"Soren?" Davin asked, his ax swaying in his hands.

"Wait," Soren said.

"What?" Blaje asked, eager to lunge forward, but Alcarond was thirty feet away, up the tower.

"Something is happening," Soren said. "But I don't know what. Just wait a second…"

Blaje sighed deeply. "All right, but we're going to need to do something Soren… soon…"

Seph did something that surprised everyone then. She flicked another tuning fork with a flash of her fingers, switching from her easy A note, to the more difficult to use, E. "Infernous!" The magical flames from her staff quadrupled in size, sending a wave of incinerating flames at Kaile.

Kaile slammed his staff's bottom tip to the ground. He shouted in frustration as his sphere thickened. Her flames coursed onto the sphere, pulsating under the weight of her spell.

"Stop it, Seph!" he yelled. "This isn't a game anymore."

"Impressive," Alcarond sneered at her aptitude in switching pitches to use a more powerful spell against Kaile. "She's far more learned in the Song of the Ellydian than I realized. She will become a powerful Syncron someday, under my tutelage."

"Never!" Mihelik shouted, pulling down Ribbons of the Moon again, slithering their way down from the stars into his staff.

"Soren," Blaje said. "We've got to do something. Now!"

"Hold another moment," Soren said.

"I hope you're right about this…" Davin murmured.

I do too…

The spell Ribbons of the Moon erupted from Mihelik's staff, plummeting through Alcarond's white magical fire, pressing it back with staggering power until it too collided into Kaile's sphere. Both Alcarond and Kaile winced under the weight of the ultra powerful spell of the old Lyre archmage. Seph pressed her attack further, striding forward as the hellish spell poured out of her staff onto them.

Mihelik and Seph had them on the defensive, and Soren sensed it was time to act.

"Now!" Soren said, rushing forward, Firelight leading the way. Blaje and Davin ran to attack too, without hesitation. "Don't kill Kaile, unless there's no other way…"

The three ran up the tower, Soren ready to drive his dagger through Alcarond's skull.

Mihelik bombarded the two with one of his most powerful spells, and Seph showed her true strength as she resembled a powerful sorceress, so much older and deadlier than the seventeen-year-old orphan.

As the three of them ran at Alcarond, staggered from the Ribbons of the Moon spell, the second bear emerged from the stairwell behind Alcarond and Kaile. It towered above them as they spun to face it. Standing on its back legs, it sent its huge claw down at Kaile, cutting into his back and knocking him to the ground. He kept his staff in hand, and the sphere that protected them somehow remained, protecting them from Mihelik's spell.

Kaile cried in pain as the bear roared; its long yellow teeth showing, its huge maw opened at the fallen apprentice as it towered over him.

Alcarond, still fighting off Mihelik's spell, waved his free hand at the bear. "Propulis Avantis!" The wind shook as a wave of air exploded from his hand, sending the bear careening back up the tower. It clawed at the slick ground, but its claws only slid through the snow as the spell sent it to the back wall, and in a moment that caused Soren to gasp, the bear flew up over the wall, fighting and clawing, but flying over the backside of the tower, plummeting down.

"No!" Mihelik shouted, true rage lining the word as it erupted from his throat. More strands came down from the heavens into his staff, as the sounds of all the notes in the battle mixed to a deafening roar.

Soren and the others were almost to Alcarond and Kaile, weapons ready, and revenge yearning deep in their hearts.

But then, something happened within Alcarond that caused Soren's pulse to quicken, his blood to pound in his shoulders and the follicles of the hairs on his neck to straighten.

Alcarond grabbed his staff with both hands, placing the bottom tip to the ground. Magic still poured from its dragon head tip at Mihelik's spell, but Alcarond closed his eyes, tucked his chin to his chest and began to chant.

"What's he doin'?" Davin huffed.

"He's casting," Blaje said.

I need to kill him, now. This is my shot. He can't cast that spell... he just can't!

Soren flipped Firelight over in his hand, gripping the tip with his fingers, aiming true—he sent it flinging from his fingertips, end over end, squarely aimed at the center of the archmage's eyes.

Just as Firelight was inches from Alcarond's face, still lowered in deep concentration, a flash of dark wood came between Firelight and its target. Firelight stabbed into the knobby wood to the crossguard. Soren's jaw dropped as Kaile stood between him and the archmage, Firelight's handle sticking from his short staff.

"I—I can't let you kill him..." Kaile muttered, audibly in great pain from the bear's attack, struggling to keep the spherical spell around them both.

"Traitor! Liar!" Seph screamed as she poured more magical flames onto them.

Soren only had his fists, but he didn't care. That betrayal was enough to tell himself that if Kaile was going to get in his way of his revenge, then he was no friend, but an enemy.

"Kaile, no," Davin said under his breath as he ran.

Blaje was the closest to Alcarond, running with her long

legs. She held her shamshir blade over her shoulder, ready to strike.

But... Soren's greatest fear of the confrontation blossomed, as Alcarond's eyes opened suddenly, engulfed in white flames, beaming out like pure moonlight splitting through dark clouds.

"By the power of the goddess Shirava," Alcarond said in words booming through the lightning storm, "and the ancient gods before her. I call upon the strength of the great Ellydian, truest power of life. Give me the strength. Bless me one more time. I call forth the flames of antiquity! Give me strength, and let my fires burn true! Wraithfire! Heed my call!"

No! It can't be! Not again! He's going to use the spell against Mihelik again!

"Blaje!" Soren yelled. "Kill him! Kill him now!"

Blaje jumped, flying through the air, her curved sword leading the way. Kaile moved between them, but she plowed through him, far stronger than the thin boy.

Just as she was about to cut Alcarond's head free from his neck, a bright light erupted from the center of his chest; blinding, brilliant, and terrifying.

The light from his chest grew into pulsating flames outward, like waves from a meteor hitting the center of a great lake. It blew her back, Kaile too... extinguishing his magic. Blaje grunted as she hit the floor hard on her side.

Alcarond roared as his feet left the ground. His gaze was up to the heavens, all snow melting from the heat of his spell before it touched him. His arms were out wide, his staff in one hand. Mihelik's Ribbons of the Moon collided into the light at the center of Alcarond's chest.

Alcarond rose ten feet into the air, with the waves from his chest turning from a pure, white light, to an incinerating, hot, fiery sunrise orange. Everything around him erupted in flames. The stone below him, the sky above, everything burned.

Kaile quickly put up his sphere spell around him and Blaje

as he cried in agony. The pulsating spell from Alcarond shoved Kaile and Blaje back in blasts, with the orange flames devouring everything around the protective sphere.

Soren and Davin were held at bay from the heat, with Seph far behind, still sending her futile flames as the floating archmage.

Mihelik unleashed the full extent of his spell at Alcarond, the silver bear beneath him slowing its progress forward, and eventually staggering back from the encroaching flames.

"Mihelik," Soren yelled. "Stop him! He's going to bring the whole tower down! Seph, you're going to have to figure out a way to get us out of here."

"What?" she asked, still fully fixated on her spell.

"Stop your spell!" he said, sliding down the snowy tower back toward her. "It's useless against him. You're going to have to get us off this tower, before…"

Soren couldn't finish his sentence. The explosion from Alcarond's Wraithfire spell was unlike anything Soren had ever seen. As the white and orange flames exploded from the archmage's chest, Soren thought that may be it, that may be the end of all their journeys. It crossed his mind that may be what legendary dragon fire felt like, tearing flesh from bone, rendering nothing left but ash.

The explosion was so violent, Soren felt the stones beneath his boots break apart and crumble down. He fell through, plummeting down into the darkness. And all he thought in that single moment, was… *I didn't do enough. I should've been better for her, for my Persephone…*

Chapter Forty-Three

✿

There's a certain feeling you get when engulfed in the magic of the Ellydian. It's warm, yet terrifying, and exhilarating—like touching true divinity.

Soren felt it all around him. His skin oozed with it. It felt like being soaked in wet oil, yet drifting through pillowy clouds. He felt no ground, no air, no cold, no worry nor fear.

He thought he may be dead, but he knew the feeling too well of magic. He'd been around it his whole life in one form or another, whether it was from friend or foe. Soren knew it was magic, and as soon as he felt hard ground under his boots again, and the crunch of deep snow, he knew he was alive—but he didn't know for how much longer.

The world reappeared before him, vast and open, the horizon lit in moonlight scattered all around. The tower stood tall to his side, with broken bits of stone rubble and wood crashed down around him. His frantic gaze continued around, quickly finding its primary target.

Seph stood beside him, an E note ringing clearly from her staff, and a gigantic orb of blue light surrounding the area.

"Seph," Soren gasped, nearly out of breath, heaving deep breaths. "You did this? You brought us down?"

"Ugh, what happened?" Davin said from behind. Soren spun to see Davin and Blaje on their backs, both dazed, both without weapons in their hands. Lord Belzaar's body lay motionless beyond them.

"I—I tried to bring us down," Seph said. "I—I think I did it…"

"The archmage," Soren said. "Where's Mihelik?"

Seph's arm raised, and she pointed her small index finger to the other side of a fallen chunk of the tower. Soren ran over to where she pointed. She followed, and so did Davin and Blaje once they got to their feet.

Soren ran around the backside of the tower to a gruesome sight that made his stomach lurch.

"Oh, no… Mihelik… no…" Soren said, the words quiet and full of futility.

Before him, on the ground motionless, was the old archmage. His blind eyes were wide and stricken with panic before his end. His robes were all but burned completely away and his smoldering flesh was blackened. His body was broken from the fall from the tower with his spine twisted and his leg bent behind his arm. Smoke rose from his burned body, and where no farewell words would ever be muttered, instead a single clear note rang from his staff. It was a somber, heart-aching, tragic A Minor. It struck Soren to his core as he felt it fill his ears, vibrating against the tiny hairs within, traveling down his ear canal, into his brain, heart, and eventually scarring his soul further.

Soren slammed his fists down onto the snowy ground as the great silver bear beside the fallen archmage whimpered. The bear sniffed his body, letting out a sullen moan.

"Goodbye, old friend," Davin said with a deep sigh of grief.

"Archmage..." Seph cried. "You can't leave us like this... we need you..."

"Yes, you did," Alcarond's voice boomed from above.

They all looked above to see the archmage floating down like a god. A perfect orb of orange and white light circling him and Kaile as they floated down. While Alcarond glowed with powerful magic and the full strength of the Ellydian, Kaile appeared sullen and injured.

Soren was weaponless, in fact, they all were, with their swords and axes strewn away from the explosion.

Seph ran over and grabbed Mihelik's staff from the charred bones of his fingers.

Alcarond and Kaile landed twelve feet away, as the fiery orange orb dissolved. Aside from the blistered burns on his arms, Alcarond looked as strong as he ever had.

The silver bear growled fiercely and lunged at him at impossible speed.

With a wave of Alcarond's staff, still ringing in its perfect pitch of a mixture of beautiful, terrifying notes, he sent the bear soaring through the air, colliding into the tower's base, sending the huge beast clear through the thick, stone wall.

Soren panicked. They were all severely vulnerable before the most powerful being in all of Aladran—perhaps the world, who had just defeated his only rival.

What do I do? How can I protect Seph against him? I need to think... I have to be able to do something. This can't be the end. It just can't...

Seph struck Mihelik's staff with an A note, hopefully able to wield it with the simplest note.

Alcarond laughed, and Mihelik's staff was plucked from her fingers easily as it drifted to the archmage's hand. He then held two—his and Mihelik's—causing Soren's stomach to sink further.

"It's over," Alcarond said.

"No!" Soren said, running at Alcarond.

Again, he felt the pull of magic upon his body, as he was lifted into the air helplessly by another of Alcarond's spells. Alcarond smiled wide, showing his teeth, his dark eyes narrowing on Soren.

"Kaile," Alcarond said. "Get Persephone. She's coming with us."

Soren's eyes shot wide and panic ran down all his nerves. His heart pounded and his muscles tensed. His throat tensed, wanting nothing more than to kill the archmage, but he, again, was helpless to stop the evil that plagued every part of his life.

Kaile sighed, still in crippling pain, then began a slow walk toward her.

Seph's eyes welled with tears.

Davin and Blaje both stepped between Seph and the approaching apprentice. Both of them had their fists held up.

"Don't even think about it!" Davin shouted.

With a wave of his staff, Alcarond sent Davin and Blaje flying to separate sides, revealing Seph, with her arms wrapped around herself, quaking in fear and anger.

Kaile reached her, standing arm's length from her.

"Seph... I'm sorry..."

She pounded both the bottoms of her fists into his chest.

"You bastard!" she cried. "You lying, mother fucking bastard! How could you... I trusted you!"

"Don't do this Kaile," Soren pleaded from above. "If you take her, you know what Alcarond and the king will do to her there. You've seen it. You know the nightmare they'll force her to live through. You can't. I know what she means to you. You can't betray her like this. She'll die if you help him take her, and I'll hunt you to the corners of the world if you do!"

Kaile grabbed her by the wrists. She fought to break free from his grasp, crying and gasping through panicked breaths.

"Please don't do this," she cried. "Please. He's all I have.

Soren is all I have left in this world. Please, don't make me go with him. I'm scared Kaile. I'm really, really scared."

"I—I can't..." Kaile muttered, his face flush and his eyes reddened. His brow was littered with beads of sweat, even in the cold winter winds.

"I cared about you," she pleaded. "I really cared about you, and you do this to me?"

A flicker of recognition and courage fluttered through Kaile then. Something she said triggered a vibrant flame from deep within him. He let go of her arms, drawing his staff from his hip. He spun.

"Master," he said, striking a C note quickly. "I'll go with you. I'll do what you wish and face what consequences I must. But I won't let you take her. She belongs here with her uncle. I won't take her back to be tortured in Celestra by the Knight Wolf. I won't let you harm her..."

A maniacal look twisted on Alcarond's face. "I grow tired of your insolence, my apprentice. You will do as I command."

"No!" Kaile roared, magic erupting from his staff. "I won't let you do to her what you did to all the others. I won't let her suffer. For my failures, I will go with you, but you will not make me hurt her."

"You act as if you have a choice, boy..."

Alcarond smirked as a dull white glow glittered from the dragon's eyes on his staff. The same glimmer on Kaile's neck he'd seen moments ago at the top of the tower glowed again. This time larger and brighter, with a symbol like a tattoo glowing brightly.

He's marked like me, Soren thought. *Alcarond has cursed Kaile the way the Knight Wolf and his Synth Zertaan marked me... No...*

Kaile seized, shaking and screaming in agony, clutching the mark on his neck as the sheets of light slipped between his fingers.

"Kaile!" Seph yelled as she wrapped her arms around him as he shook.

"Get back!" Soren yelled, but it was too late.

Kaile grabbed her by the shoulders, a desperate look on his face. "Seph, I'm sorry... I'm so sorry..."

"Don't do this... You don't have to do this. I trusted you... I trusted you..." she cried.

"Whatever happens," Kaile said in a soft voice. "I'll protect you. Or I'll die trying. I want more than anything to just run away with you. We could go somewhere and be happy together, far, far away from all this madness. But... I can't. His grip is too tight on me. I can feel him like fingers squeezing my mind from the inside. He's too powerful. I'm trying to fight it, but I can't... I'm so sorry, Seph. I wish things would've worked out different. Maybe I should've died back there in Erhil. Maybe I shouldn't be alive to do what he's making me do... I'm so sorry..."

"I'm sorry too," she cried. "Maybe you *should have* died back there. Maybe I should have too..."

Soren's heart ached as tears streamed down his cheeks. He again, felt the deep guilt of failure in his soul. This was truly his curse, and another scar that would never leave him.

"Bring her to me," Alcarond said. "It is time..."

Kaile grabbed her hard by the wrist, pulling her back toward his master.

"Let me go! Let me go!"

"Kaile!" Davin shouted. "Don't do it! He's gonna kill her!"

Blaje didn't yell, perhaps she knew the archmage's control over his apprentice was too powerful.

"The king will be delighted to hear of your defeat," Alcarond said with sharp glee to Soren. "I'll tell him every excruciating detail of your failure again, fallen knight of Tourmielle. He'll lavish in having your only family, and last in the line of Whistlewillows in his kingdom. In fact, maybe he'll put a baby in her, keep the line strong with his and their blood."

"You bastard!" Soren cried, his voice cracking through the pain. "I'm going to kill you for this. I'm going to cut that tongue from your wretched mouth and shove it all the way down your throat until you suffocate on it!"

"Not today," Alcarond said as Kaile finished pulling Seph all the way to him. Alcarond smiled wide as she joined them. The fiery orange orb grew around them again from the dragon's head staff. Seph fought and squirmed to break free of Kaile's grasp, but under Alcarond's spell, there was no breaking free. "Perhaps we will meet again, Soren Stormrose. But I believe if we do, you will be in chains, or under the Knight Wolf's Ember Edge hovering over your neck. Your constant failures are a disgrace to your name, and all of Aladran." He spat on the ground in Soren's direction. "You deserve your fate and misery. May the goddess have mercy on all the souls that trusted you."

Soren had no response. He wanted to yell out. He wanted to make Alcarond leave Seph. But deep down, he knew the archmage was right. They were all dead because of him, and there would be no vengeance for him in the end.

Kill me. Was what he wanted to say. He wanted to beg for death. He couldn't take the pain anymore.

But suddenly Cirella's voice pounded in his head, pushing through the pain. "You can't die yet," she said. "She's going to need you. She's going to need her uncle…"

"Come," Alcarond said, and Kaile pulled Seph further into the enveloping orb. Kaile's face was pale again and his eyes were closed, fighting a battle in his head behind his forced actions.

"Soren!" Seph screamed as she fought to break away from them, her free hand reaching toward him with her skinny fingers spread wide.

THE FALLEN APPRENTICE

"I'm... I'm sorry," he replied, still stuck in the air, unable to fight. "I'll come for you. I promise, Persephone... I'll come for you..."

The archmage's orb raised into the air, and with one last look of panic on her face, the orb spun away, launching high into the air, arching like a bolt, soaring far away into the night sky, northeast—toward Lythyn, its capital Celestra, and the king.

All hope drained from Soren's body as he fell to the ground, landing on his feet. But in the air, a shimmer of metal glimmered in moonlight from behind the orb. It was tiny, gleaming white at first, but then a blood red as it hurtled through the air. It arched through the air, before falling directly at Soren, flying end over end.

Soren reached up and grabbed Firelight by the grip, feeling its power in his hand, and he felt great relief as the Vellice steel blade had been returned to him.

"Thank you, Seph," he said. "Thank you. I'm coming for you..."

But suddenly, another stark realization gripped him.

Davin and Blaje huddled to him. Sable ran out from the inside of the tower to them, alongside the silver bear. Lord Belzaar, with very little strength, crawled toward them too.

Soren held Firelight tightly at his side, peering up the surrounding hill at the predatorial black onyx eyes that glared down at them. There were dozens of eyes as the Shades stared motionlessly down the valley at them, eager to seek revenge on their fallen against Soren.

"There's too many of them, Soren," Blaje said. "You can't kill that many by yourself."

"Get into the tower," Soren said.

"It's barely standing and there's holes all over it," Blaje said. "There's no hiding in there, and the night is still young."

Soren knew she was right, but didn't know what else to do, but try to kill every one of those Shades up on the hills.

"Soren…" Lord Belzaar coughed. Soren went over to him, kneeling by his side, still glaring up at the imposing Demons of Dusk. "Don't you want to know what it is you came all this way for? Before we all die?"

"Yes," Soren said, suddenly remembering his mission and gazing down into the dying man's eyes. "Tell me. Who sent me this dagger?"

"You know him. You know him well. It was… it was your old master. He told me to get it to you. He said you'd need it for the war ahead, and he paid me well for it…"

"My master? Landran? He's alive?" Soren's mind reeled at the thought. *Landran is alive? How? He's been dead for years!*

"You lie! He can't be alive. You're lying!"

Lord Marcus Belzaar coughed, spitting up blood on his cheek, wheezing. "I do not lie. Landran Dranne is very much alive, and he's helping you from the shadows."

"Why wouldn't he just come to me?" Soren grabbed the cuff of Lord Belzaar's tattered shirt. The man's eyes closed and his head fell back. He shook the dead man. "Why? Why wouldn't he find me if he's still alive? Why wouldn't he just give it to me himself? Why would he hide from me after all this time? Don't die yet! I need answers!"

"He's gone, Soren," Davin said. "And we're gonna need the beast inside of you to wake up. They're coming…"

The Demons of Dusk began their approach down the hill, slowly at first, sliding down with their sharp black claws and slithering tails.

The huge silver bear growled, but stepped back.

The Shades stalked slowly at first, but as Soren stood before his friends, Firelight their only defense, the Demons of Dusk, all at once, began their attack.

They ran down the hill at frightening speed. A swarm of them, all running down from all sides. Soren's palm sweated as he squeezed the dagger.

"I'm sorry," he said to them all. "For everything. I'm sorry this is how it ends…"

None responded, but tucked into each other. They had no weapons, and all hope had vanished. The ground shook under the weight of so many Shades rushing at them, devilish teeth flashing as they hissed. Their teeth dying to rip Soren apart.

But suddenly, a roar from the sky boomed like thunder. It was like nothing Soren had ever heard in his life. The Shades suddenly halted their approach. They looked up to the sky frantically, all of a sudden not looking like a swarm in unison, but a frenzied lot of scared creatures.

"What was that?" Davin asked. Sable jumped all the way up onto Soren's shoulder, looking north.

Soren squinted to look the direction the cat was focused. At first he thought he may be dreaming, and that this was all one terrifying nightmare, but as the huge wings of the creature in the sky glided toward him, he realized it wasn't a nightmare, but another harsh reality.

There was a new terror in this world.

The dragon flew down at terrifying speed, its enormous body plummeting through the air as its enormous wings spread wide, gliding down directly at them. It let out another roar that shook their earth and air. Smoke smoldered out of the corners of its mouth and the huge horns curving out of its massive head glimmered in moonlight.

It swooped down, roaring as it unleashed unworldly hot, scathing orange flames onto the world before them. The Shades cried in rage and pain as the flames incinerated them. The huge gray dragon tilted its descent in a vast arc as it blasted its flames down onto the ring of encroaching Shades.

Its gray, cracked scales had seen many winters, and the mad, furious eyes of the monster were beaming with deep wisdom of such an ancient creation of the gods. It was one of the most terrifying things Soren had ever seen in his life.

Soren's mouth fell agape at the destruction of such a being. The snow all around them melted under the heat of the distant dragon's flames. In one fell swoop, the enormous dragon, over a hundred feet from maw to tail, had eviscerated the Demons of Dusk, sending those unscathed by dragon fire fleeing away into the desert.

"By the goddess..." Blaje muttered, the words barely slipping between her lips.

The dragon, as quickly as it appeared, flew out deeper into the desert, unleashing fire upon the winter desert as its roar rippled through the air for miles. Soren finally closed his jaw, and past the unreal sight, he remembered that Seph was gone.

He turned to his friends, both hands clenched into fists.

The three of them looked at each other. Mihelik lay dead, as well as Lord Belzaar. The second silver bear limped out from behind the tower and Sable meowed longingly.

"We'll get her back, Soren," Davin said.

Soren didn't reply. Too much anger welled inside him.

"The dragon returned to Aladran from Eldra," Blaje said. "It came to fight the Demons of Dusk. It's a sign. Shirava has intervened! We can win this war!"

"I don't care about the war, or the Demons of Dusk, or the Knight Wolf, or the king.." Soren said, hatred lacing his words. "All I care about is getting her back. I won't lose her to those devils."

"We're with you, Soren," Davin said. "To the ends of the earth."

Blaje nodded. "To the ends of the earth."

"We can't let her suffer and die all alone up there," Soren

said. "As long as I still draw breath, I'll kill whatever gets in my way of her. And I couldn't ask for better warriors to be at my side. Hang on Seph… we're coming…"

The End

Continue Reading C.K. Rieke

Read Book 4,
The Dark Synths

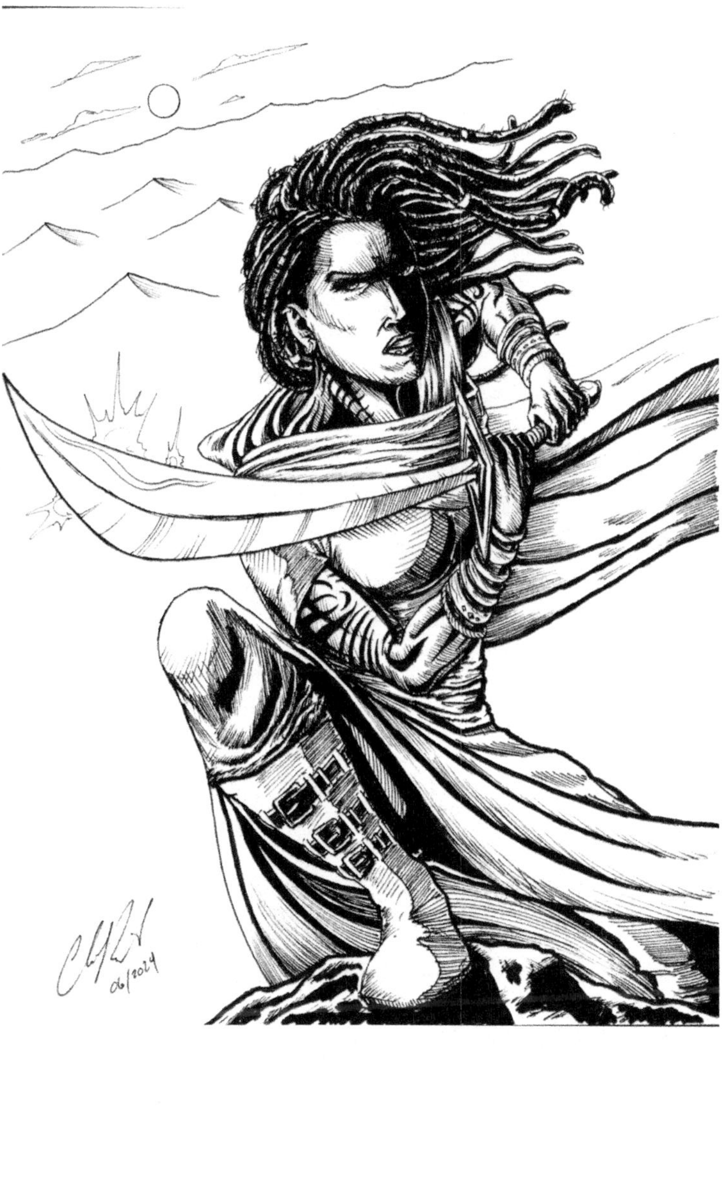
06/2024

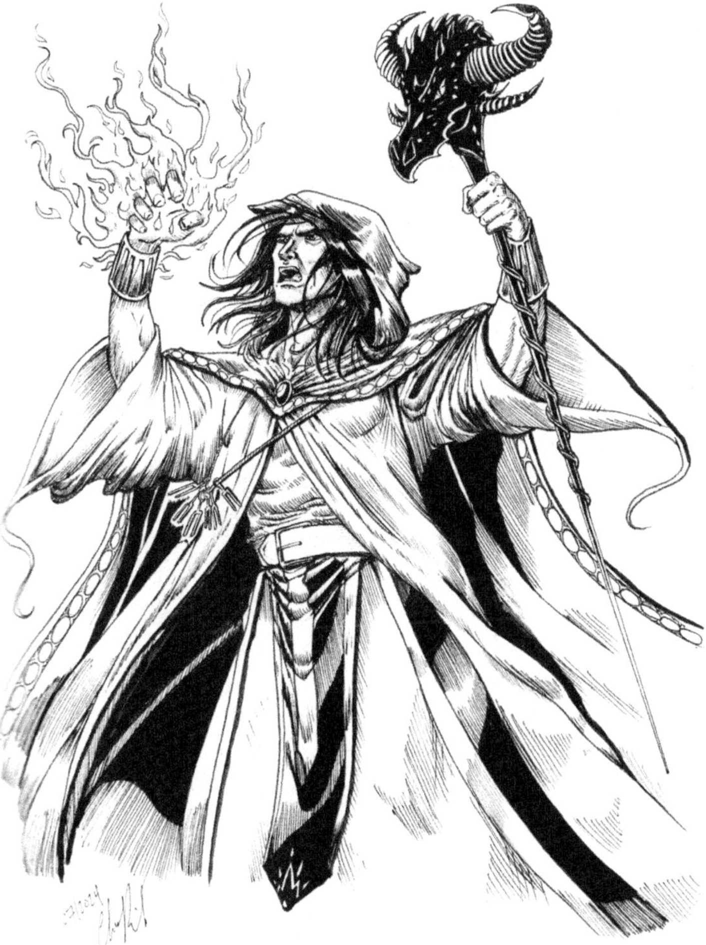

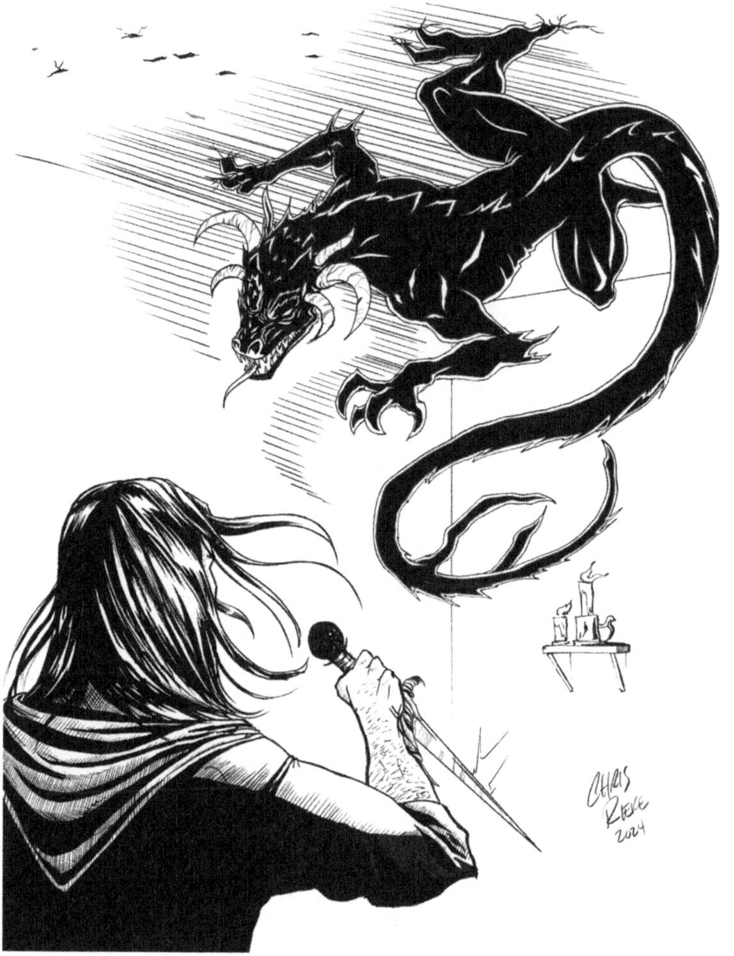
CHRIS
RIEKE
2024

Pronunciation Guide

Aeol – A-ol
    Aladran – Ala-drawn
    Alcarond Riberia – Alka-Rond Rye-beer-ia
    Arkakus – Ar-kackus
    Arnesto Piphenette – Piffin-ette
    Arnor – Are-nore
    Ayl - Ail
    Bael - Bale
    Belzaar – Bell-zar
    Blaje Severaas – Blayge Sever-os
    Cascadia – Cas-cad-ia
    Celestra - Selestra
    Cirella – Si-rella
    Davin Mosser – Davvin Mozer
    Dor - Door
    Doren – Dor-en
    Ellydian – Ellid-ien
    Erhil – Air-hill
    Garland Messemire –Mess-i-mere
    Golbizarath – Golbee-za-wrath

PRONUNCIATION GUIDE

Guillead – Gil-ee-ad
Ikarus – Ick-arus
Katamon – Cot-a-mon
Larghos Sea – Lar-goes
Londindam – Londin-daam
Lynthyn – Lin-thin
Lyre - Leer
Lyrian – Leer-ien
Malera Amón – Mal-er-ra A-maan
Manan – Maw-nin
Mihelik – Mi-hay-lick
Myngorn Forest – Men-gorn
Roland Carvaise – Roland Car-Vase
Shirava - Sheerava
Siracco Tower – Seer-a-co
Solomn Roane – Solum Rone
Song of the Ellydian Pronunciation Guide
Sundar – Sun-dar
Syncron – Sin-chron
Synth - Sinth
Taverras – Tav-er-ass
Tourmielle – Tour-me-el
Vellice - Vellis
Yancor Brothers – Yank-or
Zatan – Za-tan
Zefa – Zeffa
Zertaan – Zer-taan

Magic of the Ellydian

The Ellydian Magic System

Lyrian/ Lyre– Highest Level – Must successfully go through the Black Sacrament. Unknown power limits.

Aeol/ Ayl/Aeolian – Mid Level - Can manipulate their own bodies as well as outside objects.

Doren/ Dor/Dorien – Lowest Level - Can move/manipulate objects outside of their body.

Syncron – A wielder of the Ellydian who uses their magic for good.

Synth – A wielder of the Ellydian who uses their magic for evil.

Singular notes and tunes (Such as A) are the easiest to cast with. More complex variations (Such as G Minor or C Sharp Minor) cause much more powerful and different spells, but require more focus and training. The Lyres may use melodies of varying different notes to cast superior spells.

MAGIC OF THE ELLYDIAN

The sounds produced must remain constant for the spell to stay intact.

The Black Sacrament – A spell, that when cast, will either kill the wielder, or elevate them to the supreme level of Lyrian.

Author's Notes

Well, here we are again. This will be the end of the first trilogy in this series. If you've been reading this far or on the readers' group email list, then you know I'm roughly planning to do this series as two trilogies and then one final big master ender. This book will be my 18th book finished.

What I'm really hoping for is to have my 20th book finished by the end of the year. If you've been following my journey, I'm part of the Facebook group that's gotten huge now, but I was in the first thousand members. It's called 20Booksto50K, and it's all about indie publishing. The name doesn't mean much nowadays, but it was initially about having 20 books published. That's the conference I go to every November. And let me tell you, I am fucking excited for November! So yeah, the 20th book in my backlist will be a big deal for me, a milestone, and I personally hope it launches me to a new level.

I was really excited to bring the character Blaje into the series. Not only is she a new love interest in Soren's fucked-up relationship past, but just writing an ultra-badass desert assassin is always enjoyable. She brings her own fun to explore. Plus, I thought her name was pretty cool.

So Kaile—from the beginning, I envisioned his treachery at this point. That boy certainly carries a lot of trauma with him, and his betrayal is going to add a lot of layers of complexity and depth to the trio of main characters, which I really enjoyed building and hope you enjoyed reading. I imagine he's going to get pretty powerful spells back in the capital with Alcarond. That's going to be a whole mess, isn't it?

Speaking of Alcarond, who doesn't love an epic wizard battle? Yes, Mihelik was planned to fall at the end of this book tragically, and that leaves only one Lyrian sorcerer in the world. I'm gonna miss writing Mihelik, though. His relationship with Alcarond was special to me, and I hope to get to delve into it even more, post-mortem. Also, I loved Ribbons of the Moon spell.

We are definitely going to get some more inside looks at Celestra, the capital, in the next book. I imagine there's going to be some dark inner workings going on there.

And finally—dragons!

This was by design to add more conflict of the war, and that one massive old dragon is going to be a player in the war at hand. So Soren's not alone, but he's certainly going to feel alone with Persephone gone. If you thought he was messed up before, wait till the next book; he is going to be one hot freaking mess.

Yeah, the first trilogy here was really meant to build their relationship to pretty much tear it all apart at the end of this book. I'm really excited to be moving forward, and I hope you are too. This book took me a little over five months to write, which is fairly on course for me at my most productive. I feel good about it, although I would like to be faster. But it's just hard and time-consuming to write whole books! But I love it.

So here it is, June 9, 2024. Things to look forward to this

AUTHOR'S NOTES

year: I'm going to continue my—although I hate the word—routine, for lack of a better term, routine of writing in the morning, going to work, drinking way too much coffee, working out, and then working on office hours a couple of nights a week responding to emails and whatnot.

I'm sitting here thinking about all the notes I have to go through to get ready to write the next four books in the series. I'm getting really excited to plot and scheme and get ready to twist daggers into hearts. Maniacal laugh, maniacal laugh.

So, thanks for joining me on this journey. I think I'm around the 10-year mark of when I first started writing and eight years of publishing is coming up, so I'm just going to keep putting fingers on the keyboard, getting my dark fantasy thoughts out on the page for you.

Cheers, and I'll see you in the next one.

C.K.

About the Author

C.K. Rieke, though he constantly dreams of oceans and mountains, was born and lives in Kansas. Art and storytelling were his passions, beginning with "Where the Wild Things Are" and Shel Silverstein. That grew into a love of comic books and fantasy novels. He always dreamed of creating his own worlds through the brush and keyboard.

Throughout his college years, Rieke ventured into the realm of indie comics, illustrating and co-plotting stories that hinted at the epic narratives to come. But it wasn't until his early thirties, inspired by the works of fantasy luminaries, that he turned his hand to writing his own tales. The labor of love that was "The Road to Light," painstakingly crafted over two years, marked his debut into the literary world under the guidance of a revered editor.

Within the pages of his novels, Rieke spins tales of daring adventure and intricate character arcs that ensnare the heart. Yet, be warned, dear reader, for his pen is not without its blade—occasionally, beloved characters meet their untimely demise, prompting fans to pen letters of both torment and anguish.

C.K. Rieke is pronounced C.K. 'Ricky'.

Go to CKRieke.com and sign-up to join the Reader's Group for some free stuff and to get updated on new books!

www.CKRieke.com

Printed in Dunstable, United Kingdom